MÉTIS BEACH

MÉTIS BEACH

CLAUDINE BOURBONNAIS

TRANSLATED BY JACOB HOMEL

DUNDURN

TORONTO

This edition copyright © Dundurn Press, 2016. Originally published in French under the title *Métis Beach*. Copyright © Les Éditions du Boréal, 2014.

Cover Image by Esther Bubley
Printer: Webcom

Library and Archives Canada Cataloguing in Publication

Bourbonnais, Claudine
[Métis Beach. English]
    Métis Beach / Claudine Bourbonnais ; Jacob Homel, translator.

Translation of: Métis Beach.
Issued in print and electronic formats.
ISBN 978-1-4597-3351-0 (paperback).--ISBN 978-1-4597-3352-7 (pdf).--
ISBN 978-1-4597-3353-4 (epub)

    I. Homel, Jacob, 1987-, translator II. Title. III. Title: Métis Beach.
English.

PS8603.O94426M4713 2016   C843'.6   C2016-902733-3
                                            C2016-902734-1

1 2 3 4 5   20 19 18 17 16

We acknowledge the support of the **Canada Council for the Arts** and the **Ontario Arts Council** for our publishing program. We also acknowledge the financial support of the **Government of Ontario**, through the **Ontario Book Publishing Tax Credit** and the **Ontario Media Development Corporation**, and the **Government of Canada**.

We acknowledge the financial support of the Government of Canada through the **National Translation Program for Book Publishing**, an initiative of the **Roadmap for Canada's Official Languages 2013-2018: Education, Immigration, Communities**, for our translation activities.

Care has been taken to trace the ownership of copyright material used in this book. The author and the publisher welcome any information enabling them to rectify any references or credits in subsequent editions.

—*J. Kirk Howard, President*

Printed and bound in Canada.

VISIT US AT

 dundurn.com | @dundurnpress | dundurnpress |  dundurnpress

Dundurn
3 Church Street, Suite 500
Toronto, Ontario, Canada
M5E 1M2

For G.

॰

Let us cease being presumptuous, cease believing that the fights we lead are definitive. History is a series of cycles, marked by struggle and victory, victory and struggle.

— Dana Feldman, *The Next War*

All the characters in this book are the fruit of my imagination and any resemblance to real people, living or dead, is purely coincidental. I took liberties with places and names, beginning with Métis Beach, to which I added an accent for fictional purposes. To my friends in Métis-sur-Mer, who were so helpful as I researched this book — you'll find yourselves nowhere in these pages.

C.B.

1

GAIL

I

The past is like a gun in the hands of our enemies. What we've said, what we've done, whether deliberate or not, the mistakes we've made when we were kids — sooner or later someone will find out about them and point them at your head.

I made a promise to myself I'd never write again; I've paid too high a price already. And if I find myself wandering through this story now, my own story, it's to establish the truth and hope that with it, I might regain those I loved and lost — through my own fault.

On that morning in October 1995, I woke at dawn, still on edge from the previous night's meeting. A grey light filtered through the window. It was too early to take in the hills on the other side of the canyon, along with their great white lettering, still hidden by the thick smog that rose from the city. The sight of that sign was the consecration of my success, a feeling of revenge experienced every time I contemplated it from my office window, in my house all the way up Appian Way.

In the car on the way home, I had unleashed my anger on Ann, who'd been troubled by the intensity of my words. I saw the way she stiffened in her seat, and I regretted it instantly, "If that's success, I want no part of it! What are they trying to do? Silence us? Take away our freedom to write? It's the money, goddamn it, the money that's making us cowards!"

She touched my arm, and with that soft but unyielding voice she used in such moments, when she wished to calm me down, said, "It's okay, Romain, forget what just happened. It won't happen again, you'll see." And I thought, *How can you be so sure?*

It was Chastity's abortions that had provoked the most violent responses. Letters, calls, sometimes threats, not to mention the small groups of demonstrators that had begun parading silently in front of the La Brea studio we called The Bunker, their anger a burning ember, the colour of painted blood splashed on their signs. Gloomy looking pro-life demonstrators would arrive early in the morning, icebox and folding chair under their arms, as if they were going to a baseball game, and leave late in the evening with, or so I imagined, the feeling of having accomplished something. They ignored us, and we ignored them. We did our job, they did theirs. Each of us defending our own understanding of freedom of speech in this country, though always keeping a distance from the other, in a show of feigned but civilized respect. To me it wasn't a problem; to me that's what America was all about.

Chastity was a character in my television series *In Gad We Trust*. I had finally succeeded in selling my first script after years of disillusionment and struggle, at a point when I'd pretty much stopped believing it would ever happen. "When perseverance pays," the newspapers had said. Success at the ripe age of fifty, which wasn't a common story in Los Angeles, made me into a sort of celebrity that was apparently mocked, or at least that was what some large, drunken fellow from ABC had told me at a party, his warm hand on my shoulder, a dumb smile on his lips, "Have you heard what they're saying about you? That they ended up saying yes to you for humanitarian reasons." I had no qualms about it. I'd even learned to laugh at my own expense, speaking with derision of a miracle worked by *Gad* himself, adding sometimes, "Like a pregnant woman who thought she was sterile her whole life."

Don't get me wrong though — the story I'm telling you here isn't a comedy. This scriptwriter hasn't laughed in a long time.

It was a stimulating and exciting time, despite the whining from various quarters. Complaints told us we were on the right track — boldness doesn't always please. At least that's what we told ourselves, until the attacks became more personal and the head office of our network, It's All Comedy!, became preoccupied with remarks made by an influential columnist with the *Los Angeles Daily News*. We were in the middle of filming the second season, surfing on the instant success of the first, which had put wind in our sails and given us enough arrogance to ignore the negative comments. But this, this was different. The criticism had turned into a vicious mess.

"These Hollywood types never go after Jews. But Christians — why not?... Would these eager defenders of freedom of expression have been so eager to defend Julius Streicher's anti-Semitic pamphlets in Nazi Germany? Of course not."

And of course, within "of course not" sits the malicious intent of the author. So much so that after the text was published, the author was interviewed on a popular talk-radio show, and the putrid wind — Jews, money, Hollywood — blew once again through the town's populist media. And Josh Ovitz, president of It's All Comedy!, felt himself the target of these cruel attacks.

I told Josh, "Don't let it distract us. We know what this disgusting propaganda is all about. Another reason not to give a single inch."

The whole affair had shaken the crew and provided the impetus for a series of long discussions among the staff, *How far is too far?* It's around that time that a certain scene, which hadn't been thought of as problematic after a first read, had suddenly become so. And Josh had asked all of us over for a meeting. On a Sunday afternoon.

In production meetings, I had the reputation of being pugnacious when defending my ideas. We'd wanted dark comedy, we had dark comedy. A handful of complaints from saggy sanctimonious nothings in Orange County wouldn't paralyze us.

"Okay, Roman …" Dick, a producer friend, was speaking. "But the stuff on God.…"

Flabbergasted, I stared at Dick. I suddenly wondered if the complaints, which until that point we'd treated with either indifference or amusement (hadn't we popped a bottle of champagne in honour of the first one?) — and now these fallacious newspaper articles — would complicate our task. *Censor myself? No way!* Sure, what we had undertaken was edgy, but it wasn't revolutionary in any sense — the American public was ready for it. *The Simpsons* on Fox had opened the way. Now, new cable outfits had taken the baton and run with it, taking greater and greater risks. To me there was something a hundred times worse than sedition: vulgarity.

And here was Josh Ovitz, an intelligent young man, a bit over thirty and intrepid, a pure product of East Coast education, out of arguments. Without much resistance, he was signing on with Dick and all the others around the table, including Matt, a man whose work I admired, and Ann, who'd participated in the writing of the series. *Ann? You agree with them?* Before my astonished air, she lowered her eyes, while Josh's assistant distributed photocopies of the scene in question, which I was asked to read out loud. I staggered through it without the enthusiasm with which I'd written the thing:

Season 2 / *In Gad We Trust* / episode 4 / scene 14: interior, Paradise Church, day

(After a particularly lucrative religious service — the faithful had once again been generous — Gad Paradise and his son are chatting in the room behind the altar. Gad takes off his preacher's garb.)

GAD PARADISE

You know, God, he's like a Mafia Don. God-Bonanno. God-Al Capone. God-Lansky. God-Father. D'ya get it? God-Father! If you go behind his back, God can have you dead any time, any place. Divine prerogative, right? You following me? (*Gad picks up the collection bags filled to the brim, and begins opening them.*) But if you work hard for him, well, well (*he snaps his fingers*), he'll be generous right back! (*Gad empties the bags on the ground.*) Everything that falls to the ground is ours. If God wanted any of it, he should have reached out from Heaven and held out his hand!

God, what a schmuck!

Around the table, total silence. Dick shook his head. "You can't call God a schmuck, Roman. You know me, I generally don't give a shit. But that, even I can't abide."

"We're not the ones saying it, a character is."

"It won't fly. No one is okay with it. It's just … anti-American."

"Anti-American! Having a laugh at God is *anti-American*?"

No one reacted. I was stupefied. Matt, a tall man with a deep voice, added, "It's a small phrase. It doesn't have an impact on the story." Everyone nodded and Dick added, "Right, a small, blaspheming phrase."

I went on, indignant, "You, Dick? Nagging me about blasphemy? You can't say two words without cussing!"

Dick pressed his lips together, no doubt keeping some choice words to himself at that very moment. Ann was facing me, her back straight, looking at me as if to say, *They're right. The series is explosive enough. They'll never be able to accuse us of deference. Just let it go.…*

"Blasphemy hasn't been a crime in this country since 1971! We've got the Constitution on our side, for crying out loud!"

Josh grabbed a pen and drew a line over the phrase in his copy. He stood up, avoided my eyes, and spoke to the room as if I'd already left, "Good, we're all agreed, then. We're filming the scene tomorrow without the phrase, okay?"

All agreed. "Wait!" I protested. Josh looked sorry now, sincerely sorry. Who was behind this censorial operation? The board? The shareholders? And no one thought to inform me about it before now? Finally, I found my words, rage filling me, "Today, it's just one phrase. And tomorrow, what will it be? What are we going to be shooting for our fifth season? The Waltons?"

Josh rubbed his hand in his hair. "We're wasting our time, Roman. How many of us around the table? Eight? So it's seven against one."

"I'm the writer!"

I glanced over at Ann, and she put on a brave smile. My heart tightened. Josh continued, "Please, Roman, in the future, let's try to avoid easy formulas and simple phrasing, okay? I'm sure you can find something better to write. In fact, I can't see how it affects the scene. Really."

Avoid easy formulas?

If I was being honest, I'd have admitted that Josh was right on this one. The phrase certainly wasn't the best one I'd written in my career. But considering the circumstances ... not saying anything? Because that was the whole point of this improvised — though not so much when I came to think about it — intervention: to shut me up. Ann watched me, imploring me with her eyes to not say anything. She knew how angry I could be, knew that the simple idea of being muzzled sent me back to my childhood, which I didn't like to talk about and which she didn't entirely understand. A childhood made of bitter and unpleasant memories, like a dish you hated as a kid and promised yourself never to eat again when you grew up. I'd spent my entire life fighting for a way to express myself, with total freedom, without concessions or constraints, and I wouldn't, at my age, fifty years old for crying out loud, let myself be told, *you can't say that*! Especially just because a gang of fanatics might feel offended.

"Shit, guys!"

I glared through the window, still annoyed. I'd left the windows without drapes on purpose, so I'd never miss a moment of the view — though there wasn't much to see this morning. I'd been so hostile to them, as if they'd let me down.

They said yes to you for humanitarian reasons.

What idiots, those ABC suits. The way they had of avoiding your eyes, those big network types, incapable of looking at you square and telling you they don't like what you've written. Searching for ready-made formulas as if clutching a handrail. "We regret to inform you we can't purchase your script.... Doesn't correspond to the mandate we've chosen...." Their sorry smiles, fixed in scornful pity. Their empty, hurried words, assuring you of an admiration they don't feel. Almost twenty years of constant refusal.

I smiled. All of it was over. Now I was working with Josh and It's All Comedy!, a young, specialty outfit, audacious and visionary (it would produce *Jungle* and *My Way*, two of the most popular cable shows of the 2000s). They might not have paid as much as the big networks, though I had received four percent in capital actions in addition to the rights and the seventy thousand per episode, including episodes I didn't write myself but supervised. No, I wasn't suffering horrible deprivation....

So, did you make it, then?

I heard Ann upstairs, drying her hair. My watch showed seven-ten. Staff was scheduled to meet at the La Brea studio at eight-thirty. With traffic, it would be a good hour to get there, perhaps more. You could never really tell in this city. A city built for cars, an automotive paradise — though more often than not it was automotive hell. Before going to bed I'd promised Ann: yes, I'd join the majority and accept the amputation of Trevor's dialogue — Trevor, the young actor who played Dylan Paradise, Gad's son. Yes, I'd make sure Trevor heard nothing of the previous night's discussion. I'd put my arm around his shoulder and take him away from the group, two men speaking, two men with important things to take care of, and I'd tell him something like, "You see, Trevor, I've reconsidered.... The phrase isn't exactly the find of the century.... What if instead you answered Gad with a simple: 'Right ...' you know, with a devilish smile, a gangster's smile." And I'd wink at him, maybe give him a slap on the back, friendly, complicit, and Matt and Dick would silently thank me, *you can always count on Roman*. And it was true, you could always count on me. The actors knew it as well — if there were black eyes to be handed out, I was always first in line. It was my problem. Not theirs.

Ann appeared at my door, car keys in hand. Seven-forty, we were already late. Giving me a surprised look, as if I hadn't been the one waiting, she exclaimed "You're not ready? You know Dick, he's going to kill us."

I thought about the word Dick had chosen the night before: *anti-American*. Like others had said *sacrilegious* in a different time. Or *antichrist*. Or *heretic*. A loaded word, calling forth pyres and excommunications. Using the Flag, the Cross, to reduce you to silence. A warning: *You're anti-American ... your scripts are anti-American.... Be careful....*

As if I wasn't American myself. What more did they want from me? What did I still have to prove? I, Romain Carrier, a.k.a. Roman Carr, arrived in 1962, naturalized in 1979 under President Carter, a few years before, "Born in the USA," an anti-Vietnam song I'd come to hate for the way it had been used by Republicans, misinterpreted, becoming a patriotic hymn for aggressive beer-guzzlers, reminding you that if you weren't born here you weren't really American.

"Ready, Romain?"

Romain. The name my parents had given me and that Ann insisted on using. Her sexy way of saying it, the oh-so-slightly exaggerated uvular trill, almost a caress against my skin when she was in a flirtatious mood. She took my buckskin coat off the chair and handed it to me. "Please hurry, okay?" On my work table, the photocopy that Josh's assistant had handed out, the offending sentence crossed out in blue ink. She glanced at it with concern. Then she smiled and the phone rang. She made a small gesture telling me she'd wait in the car.

God, I loved her.

2

"He really told you that? I mean he actually said it was her 'dying wish'?"

In the Pathfinder, Ann examined my face anxiously. "Oh, Romain, it just gives me the creeps. What are you going to do?"

"I don't know."

I was confused, didn't know whether I should be angry or rattled or both. The man on the phone, so distraught it was hard to understand what he was saying at first. "Who?" I asked, impatient. "Jack ... Jack Holmes.... In Montreal." "Listen, I'm in a hurry. I don't know who you are. I'm going to hang up."

I started the motor, pressed my foot on the accelerator, and the Pathfinder began its descent down Appian Way, a mile of winding road bordered by half-million-dollar homes — at the cheapest. It was a road that you couldn't take at high speed. A road that required careful driving, a descent to Laurel Canyon of no more than seven minutes, but exasperating when you were late. Next to me, Ann, nervous, her hand on my thigh like a weak supplication for me to slow down.

"Don't hang up!" the man had said on the telephone. "I'm Gail Egan's husband.... It's Gail.... She's not well, not well at all...."

A jump back in time, like stumbling off a cliff. A sudden shadow over my face had alerted Ann, "Something's wrong?" She thought of the people we knew in L.A. Or perhaps my friend Moïse in New York. "Nothing serious, honey?" *Gail Egan*. Ann had heard of her, of course, and had seen those cards that Gail persisted in sending me on my birthday every year, without exception, on the dot like a reminder from a dentist's office. And yet, any sort of relationship with her had ended long ago, too many terrible memories. Métis Beach, Gaspé, and now this — would this be another of these moments that brought everything back to the surface?

"Honey, tell me what's going on...."

I asked the man on the phone, "Something happened to Gail?"

"She's in hospital."

"What do you mean, she's in the hospital?"

"She ... she...."

He swallowed a sob. Behind him, shards of rusty voices blared out of a speaker.

"Is Gail sick?"

"She doesn't have much time left...."

"What are you saying?"

"Gail ordered the doctors to keep her alive ... until you got here...."

"Until I got there?"

"It's last minute, I know...."

"I ..."

I stopped talking, seized by an avalanche of confused thoughts. Gail *dying*? Followed by such anger that it surprised even me — why did she ask for me, now, *after all these years*? Now that things were finally going well for me. Couldn't she keep from ... from what, exactly?

"Listen, Jack...." Then I heard myself stutter through a series of boring excuses. Yes, I understood his pain. No, I couldn't leave Los Angeles, the shoot, a delicate situation, a controversial series.... The more I heard my justifications, the more ridiculous they sounded.

"It's urgent!" Jack interrupted. He'd spoken loudly, with a seething anger that announced danger. "It's a matter of hours. I know you're far. I'm sorry...." Then in a deep voice, irrevocable. "You're her last wish."

"I can't, Jack."

"Wait!" he shouted.

And I hung up, guilt like fresh skin.

3

Gail would say, "Some people are born in the wrong country, like others are born with the wrong sex."

Very early she'd put her finger on the source of my anguish. I was in the first category; she was in the second. Not that she would have liked to be a man, no, only that she wanted to have been born a few years later, when women were able to choose their lives — have a career or choose to be mothers, marry or not.

Words that were disarmingly sincere coming from the mouth of a young girl, spoken with a mix of lucidity and resignation, as only adults know how to do, when grave crises appear. But we were too young to be that lucid, we were only seventeen (I was four months younger than she), and miserable. It might have been the only two things that united us, really — besides the dream of living a life far from our parents — because in the end, we came from such different worlds.

You should have seen Métis Beach back then. Métis Beach and its satellite, our village, that the English called the *French Village*. A traveller passing through would forget it before the dust had time to settle in his wake. A series of modest wooden structures, covered in asbestos shingles. Tiny lawns dotted with sickly bushes, beaten down by the wind coming off the river that was so wide here it was called the sea. Rue Principale and its few shops. There was Mode pour toute la famille, my mother's store, which we lived above; Quimper's general store, which doubled as the post office; a bakery, Au Bon Pain Frais; and finally Leblond cobblers. The *caisse populaire* had its counter at Joe Rousseau's place, a small white house at 58 Rue Principale, with no sign. (We used to say he'd hit it big, Joe Rousseau, since his rent, electricity, and heat were all paid by the government.) There was the "modern" church and presbytery, built in 1951. And Loiseau's garage that held the limousines for all of the rich English from Métis Beach in the summer. Bentleys, Cadillacs, Lincoln Continental Mark IIs, and Chrysler Imperials. Black and shiny like seal skin, beautiful cars with gleaming chrome like in the movies, with the drivers in their dark suits, their caps raised on their foreheads when they were off-duty, having a drink at Jolly Rogers on Route 6, today called the 132, before returning to their tiny and badly ventilated rooms over Loiseau's garage. They dressed sharply, but weren't of the elegant class that stayed in the grand hotels of Métis Beach.

Métis Beach was to the west, at the very end of Rue Principale. Rue Principale turned into Beach Street — the same street, like an airplane that would bring you from a dull, gloomy country to another place, a shining paradise. You didn't need a border or a gate to know you were moving into a foreign place. The hundred-year-old pines and spruce, the cedar rows, told you that much. Through them you could see verdant lawns decorated with massive rose-bushes, and great summer homes all made of wood with tennis courts beside them. Lives of luxury, sports cars, and endless garden parties. Playing golf till sunset. In Métis Beach, tea time would end well before four o'clock, whisky was poured freely, sometimes as early as noon. We watched them with envy, all the way till Labour Day, when they left in the soft sunlight of early September, with the children and the maids. It would then be my father's job, as well as the other men's in the village, to take care of their homes, shutting off the electricity and the gas, purging water from the pipes, and covering up the windows with wooden boards for the winter to come.

Gail's house, the Egan house, was my father's responsibility.

Strangely, I can't remember ever having envied their wealth. It was their freedom I envied, that arrogant freedom. Art and Geoff Tees were two of them, often seen at the wheel of their convertible MGAs (bottle green for Art, red for Geoff), the radio spitting out wild rock music. You could see them driving full speed on the 132, cigarette at their lips, beer bottle in their hands — they were barely sixteen for God's sake! — accompanied by their girl-friends from Montreal who came to spend their summers in Métis Beach — it was said that they slept with them, in the same bed! The sort of behaviour you'd only see among the English. Among our Protestant neighbours. Where apparently they spoke freely of condoms and tampons, while in the French Village, we didn't even know such things existed.

Their existence was an itch we'd have to scratch our whole lives until it bled. Unless we left.

The last time we saw each other was in December of 1986. Gail knew I was passing through New York. Her husband had an accoun-tant's meeting in Union City, New Jersey, on the other side of the Hudson, and she'd come with him. She'd phoned me in L.A. I was surprised and thought it might be my friend John Kinnear in Métis Beach who'd given her my number, and perhaps John had even told her I'd be in New York that week. I can't remember, but I'd been surprised, very surprised. "Romain, it would be nice, no? For lunch?" And I hesitated before answering. We had left each other on bad terms years before, and I still felt she'd stolen something from me. I had the feeling I'd been betrayed by her, that I'd been unable to help her — to save her. "Lunch?" I thought for a moment, yes, no … perhaps my friend Moïse might join us? It might be more *pleasant*. "Moïse?" Surprise in her voice, perhaps disappointment. "Yes, of course. I haven't seen him in such a long time. It would be great." And so we made plans for Zack's, a deli on the Lower East Side. Moïse had gotten there a good half-hour late, covered in snow, breathless as if he'd run across Manhattan. We laughed, Moïse and I, but not Gail, she barely smiled. She was wearing a dress from another time, her eternal shawl draped across her shoulders as if in a perpetual state of hypothermia, throwing disgusted glances at the salamis that hung from the ceiling like stalactites. She sighed with irritation at the impassioned conversation Moïse and I began about the scandal of the hour, Irangate, which had sullied Reagan's presidency. To distract herself, she began tearing the labels off our bottles of Beck's.

"Are you okay, Gail? Everything's good on your end?" She had little to tell us. Her home in Baie-D'Urfé, the animal rights organizations she was volunteering with. When it came time to order, she dug her heels in, "No vegetarian dishes?" In the end she had a tomato salad, barely ripe, their hearts still white, and mineral water. She pecked at her food, a hand gripping the shawl around her small breasts, throwing haughty looks at our plates full of pastrami.

"You keep going like this, boys, and you'll be dead at fifty."

What had I felt? Pity. Pity and a little anger. I was wondering why she'd come to see me. *What was the point?* After a taxi dropped all three of us at Rockefeller Center, we began walking towards the *New York Times* building where Moïse worked. A fine but abundant snow was falling over the city, its chaos now muted like a mountain in winter. Moïse was playing the fool, catching snowflakes on his tongue, and Gail walked ahead of us, head down, splitting the crowd like a ship racing for port after months of hard sailing. I escorted her to her hotel near Broadway. What could we say to each other? Between us, there was the weight of the separation for which she was ultimately responsible. She had behaved reprehensibly, egotistically. And we both feared our words would wake the monsters of our shared past. The events of summer 1962 had shattered our lives, marking us for the rest of our days, though it had affected Gail even more than me, I would come to discover.

She said, shame-faced, absorbed by the tip of her boot drawing strange shapes on the snowy sidewalk, "Well, see you next time."

"See you next time...."

I remember the small furtive pecks we gave each other on our frozen cheeks, then her hand buried in a large mitten pushing the woollen hat she wore down over her sad eyes. Forty-two years old, lost in a man's coat, successive layers of shawls and scarfs, she looked like one of those students in Washington Square who found their clothes in an Army surplus store on Canal Street.

After that I wouldn't see her again. It had been my choice, my decision. Turn the page for good.

4

"You're not saying anything?" Ann asked in the Pathfinder.

In front of us, Laurel Canyon Boulevard was paralyzed by a long line of stopped vehicles, their brake lights diluted in the fog.

"We can't know about Gail," I said. "It might be another of her tantrums."

She glanced at me out of the corner of her eye, more surprised than indignant. "A tantrum? You don't call people to your death bed for a tantrum. How can you say such a thing?"

She turned the radio on, cycling through the stations. Traffic reports, the same as usual; streets were clogged throughout the city. Then a couple of ads shouting at us. Exasperated, she lowered the volume and continued, "What you just said about Gail is pretty terrible, isn't it?"

Yes and no. Gail wasn't easy to live with. She always thought of herself first and expected everyone to yield to her suddenly changing moods. A woman of fifty-one now, perhaps she'd softened with time. I turned to Ann, "You're right. But things were complicated with Gail. Not like they are with you, honey."

And that was true. With Ann, there never were any real fights. We had a bond that our married friends admired, a fulfilling sex life — just like they talked about on the covers of women's magazines. Of Gail, only a memory of something unsound, a thin crack in a windshield, a misunderstanding, long-winded shouting matches to get her to come to bed with me, one of those women whom despair and anger light like a match, distress a constant in her eyes. I always came away from her unnerved.

Ann measured her smile, not wanting it to be triumphant. I knew her, she wasn't jealous or the type to delight in easy flattery, *not like they are with you, honey*. At least she wouldn't show it.

Ann. Lord, her beauty had cast a spell on me seven years earlier, when we first met at the art gallery on Rodeo Drive, where I worked to help pay the bills. Her mother, a regular customer of the Kyser Gallery, had introduced us. "My daughter studies film at UCLA. I thought you might give her a few tips."

"Tips? You know, I might not be the best one for...."

"Come now! Don't be modest! Sure, there's your talent, but there's also that nice mug of yours, young man...." Followed by a hearty wink. Meanwhile, behind her back, her daughter rolled her eyes.

Laureen Heller was a small skinny woman, moved by the morbid fear of gaining any weight at all, her face worn smooth by too many facelifts. Her taste in art was exuberant — charged, gaudy, garish, like the décor in her large Tudor home in Brentwood. She was a great customer and Ted Kyser, the owner, couldn't afford to lose her. She bought two or three paintings a year, sometimes more, a welcome relief in the summer of 1988, when business was particularly slow because of the seemingly endless writer's strike.

While her mother scampered about the gallery, Ann spoke into my ear, "Can I take you out for a drink?" Stunned by her advance, I burst out laughing, charmed by this young woman, so sure of herself. We ended the night a bit past sober in an Italian restaurant in Venice Beach. I was enchanted by her eyes in the flickering candlelight, her jokes and funny faces, her brown braids, thick and heavy like hemp rope.

Seven years later, Ann no longer looked like that young slip of a girl who had so easily charmed me, but she was still as beautiful, with more sensible hair, her pearl grey suit and her immaculate blouse. She'd gained a warm maturity, acquired a profound sense of responsibility. We were a couple, yes, and also business partners in *In Gad We Trust*. Without Ann, none of it would have happened.

She continued, going through her bag, "We're going to be cannon fodder for Dick. Not sure we'll make it out alive this time. One hour late. And maybe two if we don't start moving soon. Why can't we just have a phone in the car?"

"Because it's the only place I can get a moment's peace."

My tone had been unintentionally dry. Ann hunkered down in her seat, sighed. Yes of course, a phone. It would certainly be safer. And with all the complaints we'd been getting at It's All Comedy! you never knew, there were all sorts of crazies in this country, like the guy who'd shot Lennon in New York, and the other one, something like Hickey? Hinckley? Who'd almost got Reagan in Washington to impress Jodie Foster, like in *Taxi Driver*. There were crazies by the barrelful hearing voices and not seeking help.

I told Ann, "Okay."

"What, okay?"

"For the phone. I'll take care of it. I promise."

That's how it was with Ann. Simple, easy. I drove in silence and thought back to the time Gail had come to live with me in San Francisco. Nineteen seventy-one. All of it seemed so very far away now. The large apartment on Telegraph Hill that cost me an arm and a leg, an aberration so that Gail might live comfortably, so that she wouldn't feel too much out of her element. But she didn't care. In fact, she cared about very little at all. With her, I was constantly navigating some tortured roller coaster. In the dizzying highs, she could disappear for days. Or drag me against my will and with five minutes' notice to some nudism and primal scream expedition somewhere in the Sierra Nevada. Or force me to follow her to a retreat at Shasta Abbey, the Buddhist monastery in northern California where all the hippies loved to go back in those blessed days, in order to "learn how to accept one's sexual impulses without surrendering to them or suppressing them."

When she began writing long condemnatory letters to her father in Montreal, I knew she was entering one of her agitated phases. Or if she began sending him Allen Ginsberg's amphetamine-laced writings and those of his artist friends — "the best minds of my generation starved by madness" — accompanied by a note in her muddled handwriting, "Your daughter's doing incredibly well, she lives a quiet life in San Francisco, as you can tell."

A disturbed young woman, unable to defend herself against her fate.

"Gail is an unstable woman, Ann. She might have decided, just like that, to...." *To what?* I thought. "I can't understand why she's asking for me. Not after all these years."

"She's going to die, Romain! You talk about her like she was a stranger. You loved her, didn't you?"

I didn't answer, I didn't know what to think. Ann continued, "My God, if ever life drives us apart for one reason or another, the idea that you have so little consideration for me would be hard to bear."

The Beatles were playing on the radio, a ballad that sounded ridiculous given the circumstances. "What happened to her, cancer?"

"Leukemia."

"Didn't you tell me she was so careful with everything she ate? Like a sort of religion, I mean? If a woman like her dies of cancer so young, what chance do the rest of us have?"

We were finally out of Laurel Canyon, and inching east on Sunset Boulevard. I couldn't help but think of those cards Gail had continued sending me, best wishes, animal images, drawn and watercoloured by hand. Sometimes she would slip in pamphlets for animal protection groups or pictures of herself, more embarrassing than anything else, like the one showing her tied with old grey-haired hippies to some dam somewhere in Quebec, for some endangered fish.

A flash of guilt. That evening, with Dick and the others — Josh, Matt, and Michael Hausman, the ad director at It's All Comedy!, and their wives. We were having supper and drinks at my place, and we discussed a few problems with *In Gad* and talked once again about the theme of abortion, certainly the most controversial element of the series. Chastity had had two abortions in the first season. Dick and Josh voiced their misgivings. It was an explosive subject, they said; people were killed in this country to prevent women from getting them. "So we censor ourselves?" I answered, annoyed. "Madmen kill doctors, so we'll avoid offending their insane beliefs?" Josh had answered, "No, Roman, that's not what we're saying. But two abortions in thirteen episodes; it seems a bit unlikely, no, a little forced...."

"Forced?" I laughed. "You really want to know? For me, each of Chastity's abortions reaffirms the right of women to do what they please with their bodies." And the women began applauding, their martini glasses still in their hands.

"And men don't have anything to say about it?" This was Dick, already drunk, you could see it in his eyes. The discussion had become more heated, glasses being drunk faster and faster, and we eventually moved to the table, Dick walking towards it unsteadily but single-mindedly. And for whatever reason — I can't remember now — Dick demanded that I share with the assembled guests some of the cards Gail sent me. "You got nice little bunny rabbits this year? Or mean little mice?" Before I could answer, Dick, both his elbows on the table, explained with perverse pleasure that "my first flirt" sent me sweet little cards with Winnie the Pooh on them every year.

"No, you imbecile," I corrected, half-amused, half-annoyed. "They're watercolours, like Beatrix Potter."

"Oh, well, excuse me, good sir!" he laughed, acting offended.

Josh's wife, a tall blonde with silicone breasts, asked, "You've got to be kidding. How old is she?"

"Your age!" Dick shouted.

The entire assembly laughed. Dick turned towards me, his face red. "Come now, Roman! We want to know! Rabbits? Mice?"

Around the table, the guests were becoming impatient. And, like a coward, I'd gotten up and grabbed a card out of my office. I knew for certain that Ann had put herself in Gail's shoes, projecting herself as the potential future ex-wife everyone would one day make fun of. I sought out her eyes to try to reassure her, but she'd turned away from me. All these important people at my place, having a nice evening. At Gail's expense.

Why cards? Why did Gail feel the need to keep a link with me, one I no longer wanted? Was there something I was missing? Or was it a way to force me not to forget?

"You have to go, Romain. You have to go to Montreal. You'll regret it if you don't." In the Pathfinder, Ann had spoken with authority.

"Regret what? I can't save her, she's damned."

"It's not a tantrum. That seems clear."

"The shoot."

"Dick will understand, you'll see."

5

Two hours late, I dropped Ann at the studio in La Brea, an anonymous white stucco building between a Taco Bell and a small shopping centre. Before the demonstrators began marching in front of it — there were only five that morning — no one knew that inside a TV show was being filmed. There were no signs with the It's All Comedy! logo, only doors and mirrored windows to discourage curious passersby. The Bunker would have been inviolable if only the idiots hadn't set their minds to bothering us.

As expected, Dick was raging when we arrived. On the set, a few of the actors — Avril Page, Bill Doran, Kathleen Hart, and Trevor Wheeler — stood at the end of the set, in silence, coffees in hand, while cameramen and technicians busied themselves, pulling cables, adjusting the lighting for the umpteenth time. With an expansive, angry gesture, Dick encompassed them all. "You know how much these delays cost me? I'm not a fucking bank!"

Ann walked towards Dick, trying to calm him. Dick was short, brown, and as impulsive as a southern Italian; he was also practically bald, and his fingers were like sausages. Ann told him about Gail, and he grumbled a few ill-intentioned apologies (for Dick, it was always business first, before family drama and death) and told me, without looking at me, "The scene, you haven't forgotten about it, right? We're going to do as we said we would. Whether you're there or not." And Matt appeared, a New York Knicks cap on his head, a New Yorker with whom I shared a number of affinities. He was six feet at least, no more than an inch taller than me, with brown hair and a quick wit. From time to time we would be mistaken for brothers, though he was younger than me, and larger. The Knicks cap on his head wasn't just for show; he wasn't like those fat sedentary guys who spend their time drinking beer, never far from the ball cap of their favourite team. Matt had actually played basketball, and at a pretty decent level, with the Red Storm of St. John's University, Queens. Each season he'd played with the team, they'd won four times as many games as they'd lost. He had Irish roots and the same Catholic education I did. And with this education came our shared aversion for what the church had tried to stuff down our throats — hell and all the nonsense on masturbation, the usual bullshit. So we felt the same pleasure in making *In Gad*, as if we were taking revenge on the era we were born in, thinking of the shy, inhibited boys we'd been, thankful at having lived through it without too much lasting damage. After all, many of our generation had never had an opportunity to break the shackles of their atavism, the chance to free themselves and laugh about the whole thing — *laugh about the whole thing on TV.*

Matt would take care of Trevor. I regretted not being able to settle the problem myself, even if I had total confidence in Matt. He had tact, he was a team player, like in his days with the Red Storm, and Ann would reinforce the message, "A small modification. No, not censorship, why would you even think that?" And Matt might toss out one of his theories about film direction, one that fitted with his former basketball career — intensity, look, and physical presence often more important than the text itself.

After all, I'd be gone for only a day or so.

I was about to kiss Ann and head for the exit when Dick caught me by the sleeve and said, as if uttering a threat, though his eyes were filled with compassion, "Don't come back depressed, okay?"

Los Angeles International Airport. On a Monday morning. Filled with businessmen and tourists. A group of young nuns caught my eye, Latinas mostly, and I asked myself whether, in their congregation, they ever prayed that *In Gad* might be removed from the airwaves. One of them smiled at me, a mouth full of small white teeth, a kindly smile I tried to return. Why would such young women become nuns in 1995? The newspapers had written, in reference to *In Gad*, that in Hollywood, film and TV people had this idea that Christians were potentially dangerous citizens, fanatics — a misconception created out of a total misunderstanding of the values of a large portion of the population. All part of the culture wars. There might be some truth in that, though who was I to say? I made my way to the American Airlines counter, as usual. The girl there recognized me, "New York?"

"No, Montreal."

She seemed caught off guard, though kept smiling. "First time there?"

"Yes," I lied, to end the conversation.

A ticket to Chicago, then Montreal. Take-off in thirty minutes, no luggage.

Thirty-three thousand feet in the air, flying to another country, mine, I guess, a country I had fled in complicated circumstances in 1962. The question hit me suddenly: had I ever loved Gail Egan? I remember this one time in Métis Beach, after an afternoon spent at the Riddingtons' home with my father, destroying a nest of carpenter ants and replacing a portion of the rotten railing that they had colonized. After, my old man had driven back home in our Chevrolet Bel Air, one hand out the window, letting me pedal back home on the brand new bicycle my mother had given me at the beginning of the summer, making me swear I'd take care of it "just like Dad does with his Chevrolet." I was thirteen and finally tasting newfound freedom on my new bicycle, wandering about as I pleased in Métis Beach, carefully watching the properties with their cars in their large gravel driveways, hoping beyond hope to hear a shout from the other side of that border. *Come on, Romain! Come play with us!* A fool's hope.

The young people of Métis Beach never saw us unless we were with our fathers, repairing something or other in their homes; for them, we were some sort of subspecies, perhaps even untouchables, *Dalits*. They couldn't even imagine spending time with us.

At least that's how I saw things. How I interpreted their cold indifference.

Flying along on my new red bicycle with white mud guards, I saw her walking along Beach Road, tennis racket in hand, looking lithe, self-aware, already conscious of her beauty, in short white shorts, far too short for the French Village, fine thighs, tanned, very tanned. I followed her at a distance, full of pride on my new racer, as proud as those vacationers from Métis Beach who paraded the beautiful cars they had received for their sixteenth birthday. My brand new CCM bicycle! None of those cheap brands that you found in low-cost bike shops, imported from Czechoslovakia, a Communist country as poor as its people, sad like the eyes of children condemned to ride around on terrible bicycles.

Unknown to her, I was riding behind her, zigzagging carefully so as not to put my feet on the ground, carving into my mind every detail of her, my head churning wild thoughts, guilty ones: her sculpted calves, firm thighs, the bulge there, just over the thigh, inside....

"Gail, look who's following you!"

Johnny Picoté Babcock. Came out of nowhere. His redhead face, splashed with rust. Gail had whipped around brusquely, forcing me to brake hard, and I almost flipped over my handlebars. Johnny Picoté burst out laughing, and went on aggressively, "What the hell are you doing, eh?" I mumbled something like, "*Rien ...* Nothing." And he walked towards my bicycle, a malicious grin on his lips, his fist closed around a rock he dragged across my mud guards, a scratch some four inches long that was like a knife in my side, a sharp pain that reached all the way to my heart. Gail said, "Leave him alone, he doesn't speak English." It wasn't entirely true. I understood quite a few words, and could even speak a few of them, including some pretty complicated ones: *lawn mower, rake, shovel, gutter.* Spending so much time with the English, I ended up learning a few of their words. Red with shame and anger, I got back on my CCM and was about to go on my way, when Johnny Picoté Babcock planted himself in front of me. Like the bad guys in a Western, he gave me a long, hard stare, the sort that says, *next time, you won't get off so easy.* I understood then that I would never be able to rival the boys of Métis Beach.

Sure, it was pretty early to be asking the flight attendant for a drink, but I did anyway, a screwdriver in a tiny plastic glass. From the seat next to me, a woman of forty, quite pretty and clearly in shape, threw me an amused grin, *So early? Afraid of flying?* I thought back to that time, long ago now, when Dick had tried his hand at political analysis, pitching the line that the Watergate scandal was not as bad as the media were trying to make it seem. I asked him, surprised, "You've never been to Washington? Or New York?" He avoided the question by mumbling something about Woody Allen, "Allen Stewart Konigsberg, that's his real name, you knew that, didn't you?" I hadn't known it. "That shuts you up, right? Well, there's no need to go to New York to know that." In the end he admitted, defeated, that he had a phobia about air travel. "I envy depressed people. I hear when they take a plane, they don't care whether it crashes or not."

Dear Dick. The prototypical American who'd succeeded, comfortable in his own skin, and totally uncaring about the rest of the world, which he only half-assedly understood. He'd never been farther from California than Las Vegas, though that didn't stop him from loudly proclaiming his opinions on the rest of the planet, and mocking my "Canadian origins." This other time, we thought we'd seen Paul Anka at Spago, a fine dining place in West Hollywood, and I mentioned he was Canadian. He went off on a grotesque tirade, his words tumbling over one another in an almost incoherent mess thanks to the martinis he'd swallowed, "Ah, Canadians! Insipid and immature, just like their national symbols!"

I said, irritated, "You're trying to insult me?"

"Insult you? It's the truth, Canuck! What the hell! Beavers and mounted police about as dangerous as a horde of prepubescent girls? If you wanna be respected in the world, you've got to be feared! Give it up! Now, think about virile and ruthless animals like our eagle! Think about the chiselled chins on our sheriffs and our Marines! Come on, even your soldiers prefer to release doves into the wild than shoot clay pigeons!" His mouth full, his fork aimed at me, "Never forget — trying to be loved at any cost, goddamn it, that's for wimps!" Then, wiping his chin with his napkin, "We should've given you political asylum when you came over, Roman, freaking political asylum."

After a four-hour layover in Chicago and a two-hour flight, I reached Montreal in the middle of the evening, dead tired. Jack's call early that morning, a lost day in flight and here I was in this deserted airport, scattered customs people with their sombre faces, and a certain unexplained tension, as if the world outside was on curfew. I saw the occasional traveller, looking tense, standing around television sets in the rest areas and restaurants, and couldn't quite see what was fascinating them. Nothing had attracted my attention in Los Angeles or Chicago. The Braves had won the World Series two days earlier. Maybe Canadian football? Hockey? It seemed early in the season to be so interested. But perhaps people were bored to death in Montreal.

In the taxi on the way to the hospital, the radio so loud it gave me a headache, I realized to my great shame the extent to which I'd become so witlessly *American*. "Americans, ignorant?" Dick would say. "Why take the time to interest ourselves in what other people are doing, when their single burning ambition is to imitate us?"

At the Montreal General Hospital, crowds gathered around television screens. On every floor, rooms flickering with the bluish lights of screens, from which could be heard rousing music interspersed with cries of *Yes!* and *No!* sung like joyous refrains, filled with optimism. What a strange time Gail had chosen.

"I knew you'd come. Thank you."

I pushed the door open, my heart beating with apprehension, the shock even greater than I anticipated, but before letting myself feel any of it, to postpone the terrible moment, my eyes turned to Jack, a man of fifty or so, his face lined by fatigue, shoulders slumped, salt and pepper hair. Facing the bed, a small television was on, but without sound, only images. Gail was either staring at some blank spot on the wall or sleeping, it was hard to say; she was extremely thin. I searched for signs of flesh beneath the sheets. To avoid crushing her, I passed my hand over the sheet before sitting down next to her.

"Romain...?"

I couldn't speak. I was paralyzed. She continued, her face the colour of chalk, "*Comment ... tu es?*"

How are you, *comment tu es*. Her broken French hadn't changed.

"I should be asking you that question."

She raised her shoulders, a hint of a smile that seemed to say, *Oh, I'm done for, the question is barely worth asking*, followed by another smile, this one courageous; she wouldn't accept me pitying her. "You think this time is the right one, for you, Quebeckers?"

The Quebec referendum on sovereignty, live on television. She was about to die and was thinking about politics. I said, not knowing what to answer, "I don't know, I hear it's tight."

"So, it was a good idea to vote by ... how do you say it in French again?"

"*Par anticipation*," Jack said.

"Right. That way, before dying, I might change the course of things. So that we stay together."

Why did she insist on speaking to me in French in the state she was in? Even I was tongue-tied in French, words coming to me slowly.

My throat tightened. She coughed, a wheeze to break your heart. Jack came nearer to her, and wet her withered lips with a small moist sponge, before she fell into somnolence again, the effect of morphine, no doubt.

Seeing her so fragile, so close to the end, a wave of guilt overcame me, whose origins I couldn't pinpoint. Guilty for what? For having been the one who burned the last bridge. Forgetting, here and now before such sadness, that there had been a reason for it, yes, *a reason*.

"Can you stay ... just a little longer....?" Slowly, she opened her eyes. "Do you know where I wish I could be now? Do you remember....?"

Her unfocused eyes staring off in the distance, perhaps remembering her parents' great wooden house, in Métis Beach, the happy childhood she had before she became a young woman to be married off. The unforgettable summers, from St. Jean Baptiste Day to Labour Day, long days in the sun and the tennis courts and the sea in small dinghies, wind in their sails. Campfires and roasted marshmallows, scary stories the kids told each other while the adults drank inside. The films shown on Thursday evenings at the clubhouse, classics with Marlon Brando, Vivien Leigh, James Dean, and Natalie Wood. Cokes sipped on the deck of Little Miami, the incredible view you had there when the sun set. The long drives on winding roads, hair in the wind, in one of the Tees boys' sports car — though Gail had never had any affection for the "trouble-makers, deadheads, and daddy's boys who thought they could do what they wanted." Carefree days, a summer camp, where the young ones in Métis Beach had nothing to do but have fun, and ignore the responsibilities they would later acquire, when they became lawyers and businessmen, while we, in the French Village, would continue to work hard, bending passively to the whims of our parents, waiting without illusions for the monotonous life that was preordained.

Gail moved slowly, as Jack looked on. She lolled, almost as if nodding, and Jack helped her up in her bed, placing a pillow against her back. Shoulders bent, he left the room and returned immediately with a burly young man, reddish brown hair, my height. A nervous type, briefcase under his arm. Gail's face brightened. Who was this man? A mastodon, really, at least two hundred and fifty pounds. He walked towards me and offered me a moist hand, as Gail introduced us in such a hushed voice we could barely understand, "Romain, this is Len Albiston ... Len, Romain Carrier...." Then Jack took over, and gave an embarrassed, hazy explanation — Len was a reporter, he worked for the *Calgary Herald*; he was in Montreal to cover the Quebec referendum....

All well and good, but what was he doing in this hospital room? Why introduce him to me now?

Gail seemed to have read my thoughts. She spoke, her voice barely audible, "I know, Romain ... It's a strange moment...." Len's face reddened so suddenly that I began thinking unpleasant thoughts.

Suddenly tense, I said, "Gail?"' Then turning towards Jack, "What does all this mean?"

Jack raised his shoulders, helpless. "Be patient. She'll explain."

After, I couldn't remember how it was told to me. Gail had become animated all of a sudden, a sort of miracle, her eyes full of life, her voice energized. Len had stood in the corner of the room, shooting anxious glances at the television, raising the sound a little. He had an article to write for the next morning, and it was late, past ten, in strange and painful circumstances, but he was a professional, a conscientious journalist who was the pride of his ... mother?

"My son, Romain. Our son. Summer of '62."

Len's cheeks burned. This young man who seemed to have no connection to me, *my* son? My heart beating, I was too stunned to speak, too shaken to know whether I should even speak. *Gail? What did you just say?*

She gave Len a relieved look, and her face softened with a glow of serene resignation that the dying have when all of life's files are finally closed. *You see, Len. It's done, it's done.*

What was I supposed to say to that? *Wonderful!* Or, *Come here, my boy!*

Embarrassed, Len looked at his watch, then went through his pockets and pulled his wallet out, from which appeared a card, his business card. He handed it to me, hands shaking. He had to leave and make his way to the Yes camp's headquarters before the speeches, before the results. He went to Gail, took both her hands and kissed her on her forehead, the sort of kiss that people who love each other give. He seemed to know, somehow, that she wouldn't be there anymore when he was done with his article. He was overflowing with emotion, tears in his eyes, the way he took Jack in his arms and, finally, the way he shook my hand, saying that he'd like to see me again, for lunch, maybe, but not now because he was so busy and he had to return to Calgary, but maybe in a few weeks. He'd come to L.A. if I wanted him to. And that was that. He took his raincoat, put his briefcase under his arm, and walked out.

I took my head in my hands. Why had she hidden this from me for all these years? *Yes, why, Gail?*

The strange vitality that had filled her was gone. Sudden pain contorted her face. Worried, Jack pressed a button that alerted a young nurse. Another dose of morphine, and the lines in Gail's face were soothed.

On the television, talking heads babbled away. Then, shouts of joy from one side of the question — the game was over.

Through the window, day would come soon, autumn light would illuminate the city. Montreal, a battleground, its streets filled with election signs like so many abandoned flags.

A weary feeling overtook me — the love of my youth had died, and I was the father of a complete stranger.

6

"I've been thinking about you a lot, Romain. Are you okay?"

"Yes, Ann."

"Are you coming home today?"

"No. Tell Matt and Dick they can do what they want."

"What they want? You're joking, right? Are you sure you're okay? Are you alone?"

"Yes."

"You shouldn't be alone. I know you. Why don't you come back to L.A. this afternoon?"

"I need to … *understand*."

"What?"

"To rest…. Jack and I, well, we kept a vigil for Gail, all night."

"Oh, Romain! It must have been terrible."

"Give me a day or two, okay?"

"A day or two? But … why? I'm worried Romain, worried for you."

"Don't be. It's just shock, is all. I'll call you back, okay?"

She sighed. "Okay, but please, take care of yourself…."

"I love you, Ann."

And, of course, I said nothing about Len.

I was exhausted. After five hours of agitated sleep in a motel just outside of Montreal, I drove some six hundred kilometres, stopping only to get gas, fill up on coffee, and swallow a hamburger — which meant I now had a stomach ache. With nausea in the back of my throat, my hands shaking on the wheel, I scanned the cone of light at the edge of my Jeep's headlights, but I could barely distinguish the various Métis Beach properties, in front of which vegetation had grown even denser over time. I sought the silhouette of the grand hotels that had filled the summers of my childhood; fire had probably got the best of them. After all, they were old wood structures that even then weren't considered particularly safe. And, suddenly, I was overtaken by a clear memory of the Métis Lodge fire of 1957, with flames as a high as towers, panic at the idea it might spread to surrounding buildings, infernal heat that melted the tires of surrounding cars. I was twelve when I'd watched the terrifying spectacle, shuddering at the frightening vulnerability that consumed me for days, the brutal understanding that everything held on to the thinnest of nothings.

Had Gail's house been there? The Egans' shingled home, with its white shutters, right next to Kirk on the Hill, the Presbyterian church of Petit-Métis; it was a true curiosity with its steeple built beside the church itself, right on the ground. No, I couldn't see a thing. The fog was too dense, reflecting my headlights back at me — a fog to split your soul in two.

My thoughts wandered to yesterday morning with Ann, as we inched forward through Laurel Canyon, where you couldn't see past your nose because of the smog. It was as if an eternity had passed since, but fast-forwarded — Jack's phone call, Gail gone, and I, the father of a thirty-two-year-old.

What would Ann say to all this?

In the past two or three years, her hints had become more and more insistent: "A child, Romain. Why not?" And each time, I had to remind her of the promise we'd made before moving in together. "It isn't for me, Ann. Not at my age." I was forty-three then, and she was only twenty-eight, a very young woman who didn't yet think about these things seriously. Jokingly yet with underlying seriousness, her dark braids framing her pretty face, she'd said, "I don't have that narcissistic ambition to reproduce, if that's what you want to know." And I asked her whether she was sincere or making fun of me. "I'm serious, Romain. Too many people have babies for the wrong reasons. And what about the child? He becomes a chain that ties them together for life, and they end up hating each other."

I shuddered when she said that, then understood that her parents' divorce had affected her far more than she let on. But she was thirty-five now, almost thirty-six; she knew that it would soon no longer be a choice, but an actual impossibility, and that impossibility gave her the feeling that she'd be losing something she'd regret forever, something essential. Sometimes I feared that her desire for children would break us apart. I tried not to think about it too much.

As the Jeep cut through the thick fog, the absurdity of the situation became clearer. What was I doing here? What was I looking for, exactly? Unrecognizable places, as full of life as a cemetery, with villas readied for winter, windows shuttered.

There, on the right, wasn't that the house of that old madman, Clifford Wiggs?

In my memories, it was the most impressive mansion in Métis Beach, despite the fact that Clifford Wiggs wasn't the richest among them. William Tees, Art and Geoff's father, was that man, with his Phantom V, the same car as the Queen of England, as shiny as church silver, a car we salivated over, enthralled when its driver had it washed and waxed at Jeff Loiseau's. The Tees' home was on the cliff, immense with its smaller cottages for guests, but far more discreet than Clifford Wiggs' place with its costly artificial pond, home to two swans, and flowerbeds that extended as far as you could see, filled with annuals. That alone cost him a fortune, hundreds of dollars is what was said, and all torn out at the end of the summer, what a waste! And that one summer when, with his gardener — rumours swirled about the two men — he brought over fifty pink flamingos from the Quebec City zoo to celebrate his fiftieth birthday. The news had burned through town within minutes it seemed, and my parents and I, like most everyone else, had driven past his property to look at the strange creatures. There they were, cackling, shitting on the lawn in front of some twenty guests, and my scandalized mother had said from our Chevrolet with its windows down, "That sodomite will burn in hell."

I smiled thinly, my first smile in forty-eight hours.

I'd lost my bearings. No sign of the pretentious wrought iron sentry box that Clifford Wiggs had ordered from an Italian iron-worker in Montreal, which the other vacationers had viewed with disgust. The English of Métis Beach considered ostentation a sin, doubly so if you had a lot of money to spare.

On my left, the Riddingtons' home? The Babcocks'? Everything was black, deserted. This place wasn't speaking to me, for Christ's sake! This place wouldn't speak to me. So what was I hoping to find?

At the hospital, Gail hadn't had time to explain. Jack, his face ashen, had made me understand that I shouldn't tire her out with my questions, "It's hard enough as it is for her." As if I couldn't see death going about its sinister business, slipping into her like water into a car fallen off a bridge.

He's your son, Romain. Len Albiston is your son.

Why hadn't she mentioned it to me in San Francisco, when we lived together? Was this why she'd been so depressed at the time? It *was* that — she had a child and had abandoned him. In secrecy and in shame. A girl-mother, irresponsible. A *slut*.

When we'd sharply debated abortion at my place with the It's All Comedy! gang, Matt's wife, a small brunette with a strident laugh, had asked me, all aflutter at the idea of digging up my secrets, "For a man to speak as you do about women, their rights, their bodies, you must have seen it up close and personal, no? An abortion, I mean." My answer had disappointed her, no, it had never happened to me; none of the girls I'd been with had found herself in that situation, and I was proud of that. I was a responsible man. She snickered, as if she didn't believe me, "Are you certain? I had one once, and the guy never knew."

Matt was suddenly worried, "Are you talking about me?"

"No, honey, of course not. It was a long time ago." I made an effort to search through my memory, trying to find a woman who might have done that, *to me*. Women who got pregnant and said nothing?

I had been so sure of myself. What an idiot.

Had Gail considered getting an abortion? Had she been forced to keep the child? Why, for heaven's sake, hadn't she told me?

Then, suddenly, at the near edge of Beach Street, a sight as comforting as a familiar face in a room filled with strangers: THE FELDMAN-MCPHAIL WELCOME. My heart in my throat, I turned left and entered the driveway. The crackling of gravel under the Jeep's tires sounded like a small happy chortle. All my childhood I'd associated that sound with Métis Beach. It wasn't like in the village, where we were proud of our asphalted driveways, something you never saw among the English.

And there it was, behind the hundred-year-old cedars, enveloped in the milky fog, one of the most beautiful houses in Métis Beach — my home.

7

Cold wind whipped in from the sea. I stepped out of the Jeep with my buckskin vest on my back and no gloves. I was staggering with exhaustion on my stiff legs, and my whole body shook. I turned the rusty key John Kinnear's son kept hidden under the veranda, fearing it might break and I'd be stuck outside.

The house was cold and dark thanks to its covered windows. I immediately felt that mix of apprehension and excitement I used to feel as a boy, when my father left me in the dusty dark of these grand mansions for the time it took him to go outside and stand in front of the windows so that I could push out the protective planks, now freed from their hooks. Light would flow through the rooms, like magic. I so enjoyed accompanying him to Métis Beach in late spring! Visiting the homes of Egan, Bradley, Hayes, Newell, Pounden, Curran, and Riddington — all properties in his care. I followed him, proud and excited, as if we owned the houses ourselves. We had to prepare the homes by St. Jean Baptist Day, inspecting them for winter damage. The sheer number of dead flies! Piles of them on the windowsills, which I was tasked with cleaning up, sometimes grimacing when their wings stuck to my fingers. "I don't want to see a single one, you hear?" My father's authoritarian, paralyzing voice. And so I tracked dead flies with excessive zeal, all the while making sure I didn't touch anything — my father's orders — in the vast and echoing rooms, almost ballrooms, with a slight whiff of a closed-in smell, perfume to my nose.

In the darkness, I fumbled my way to the kitchen, found the main breaker and turned the power on. I remembered doing that too, with my father.

A few burnt bulbs, spider webs, and fly carcasses.

The place hadn't changed much. Simple furniture with pure lines, of the Shaker style that Dana Feldman had liked so much. The appliances were new. Tommy, John's son, who took care of the house for the Americans who rented it in summer, had replaced the oven and refrigerator last year, and also bought a washing machine and a microwave for a total of more than $2,000; the tourists were becoming more and more demanding, Tommy said. Dick never understood my stubbornness in keeping the house, "If you never go there, what's the point?" I rented it out for nine hundred dollars a week, to New Yorkers especially, and gave three hundred to Tommy. The rest served to pay taxes and upkeep; no profit, quite the opposite — I lost money on the house, and yet I couldn't get rid of it. "You're too sentimental," Dick said. Maybe. Even Ann was surprised, she who would have loved to see the place. "Let's go together, just once." But I couldn't, always stopped by fear of dwelling on the past. And now, here I was.

In the living room, the bookshelves that had once been filled with works of all kinds now held only a few paperbacks with garish covers, left behind by renters. The sort of books you tore through in a few days and left behind like empty packages.

"Let's see," Dana had said, cigarette between her lips, her hand drawing a line along the spines. "Steinbeck ... I've got *The Grapes of Wrath*, *Tortilla Flat*, and *East of Eden*. Here, take them. Ah! And here I've got *A Farewell to Arms* by Hemingway, my personal favourite."

And in the evenings, under the beam of my flashlight, I devoured them in my bed, leaving burn marks on the pages of the *Merriam-Webster* Dana had lent me for when I didn't know a word. My English got better by leaps and bounds as I learned more and more complicated words: *ludicrous, gambit, looting.* Reading books at full steam, barely taking in their message, a glutton going through a box of cookies, attacking them with an insatiable appetite. Dana would give me a surprised look when I came to her place to cut the lawn, with three or four books under my shirt, "Already, you've read them all?" And so she pulled out other volumes, books in English with ever more complicated words, and sometimes French books, like Prévert and his spectacular *Paroles:* "Pope Pius' papa's pipe stinks."

The more I read, the further my horizon stretched.

Then, one day, "Here, read this. Better educate you now, before you get into any bad habits."

Simone de Beauvoir, *Le Deuxième Sexe.* A book on the Index.

"What is it?"

"What every man should know."

Man. It had been pronounced with such solemnity that I was flattered. My shaking hands, ready to turn its pages — what wonderful knowledge was hidden within? I was so disappointed when I read its first few lines, some scholarly gibberish — "One is not born, but rather becomes, a woman." An obscure impenetrable jargon in two volumes that I read as a challenge during my convalescence in the winter of 1960, mononucleosis having forced me out of the Rimouski Seminary during the first term of my second year. A winter of boredom spent reading and sleeping, exhausted by the smallest effort, Simone de Beauvoir's words finding their way into my dreams, violent erections that would wake me and that I looked on with consternation, too tired to do anything about them.

And so my education about women's struggles began, associated with exhaustion, during an obstinate battle against a resistant virus. In my mind, I formed a clear impression of having drawn the lucky number in the human lottery — being born a man. *For a man to*

speak as you do about women, their rights, their bodies, you must have
seen it up close and personal, no?

No. Dana Feldman taught me everything.

Oh, the hours I spent in the house with Dana and her sister, Ethel!
Dana, bent over her Underwood, her fingers flying over the keys,
while Ethel stood at her easel applying the colours she prepared
in old Heinz tins, working the canvas with a wide trowel. The
Feldman sisters in the midst of creation, with the whole house in
joyous disorder! Ashtrays overflowing, the jackets of the albums
they listened to constantly (Thelonious Monk, Ray Charles, Count
Basie, Billie Holiday, Kenny Burrell) strewn all over, and the smell
of whisky mixed with the Kools they chain-smoked — the perfume
of sedition. If my parents had known! Their son, his voice squeak-
ing, about to break, spending whole afternoons at Dana Feldman-
McPhail's home, an American widow of thirty-seven, whose husband, John McPhail, a wealthy industrialist from Montreal, had
lost his life in an airplane accident in 1956. Dana and John had
met in New York during the Second World War. After John's death,
she left Montreal, to return to that fabled city, from which she sent
me fantastic postcards — the Empire State Building, the Statue of
Liberty, the giant billboards on Times Square that turned passersby
into vulnerable insects. A real New Yorker, except in summer, which
she loved spending in Métis Beach. She wrote, far from the bustle
of the city, surrounded by silence and untamed nature that could
only support sparse humanity.

Dana the American. Dana the Feminist. Dana the Jew. If
there was anything that our communities shared, it was the mis-
trust we felt towards her

On the living room walls, made of pine, hung a few paintings
that Ethel had created as she sat on the veranda, inspired by the work

of Jasper Johns, whose palette had begun to veer towards grey at the time. Ethel, secretly in love with Jasper Johns, isn't that what Dana told me once? They crossed paths a few times in galleries in New York, perhaps they'd even had an affair, I no longer knew. I should call Ethel. It was a sacrilege to see her paintings now dotted with mildew in the glacial house in Métis Beach.

I climbed the grand staircase, wandered among the rooms, their mattresses bare, and made my way to one of the tower pavilions, where Dana had had her office. The room was small and circular. Stuffy, with boarded-up windows. She used to isolate herself up here for hours when she needed to concentrate. She sometimes forgot to eat, but never to smoke. It would billow out of the room when you opened the door!

I pulled open the drawer and fell upon a copy of *The Next War*, a first edition of her 1963 bestseller. A sober cover, red letters. She had the admiration of an entire generation of women for it. And the hatred of a generation of men.

Laureen Heller, Ann's mother, was so excited when she heard I'd known Dana. "Dana Feldman? *The* Dana Feldman?"

"Who is she?" Ann asked, a hint of annoyance in her voice at feeling out of the loop.

"Oh, my dear, you're far too young to know Dana Feldman." She laughed, and gave me a lecherous smile which I hadn't known how to interpret. "It's thanks to her that I left your father. Don't hate me too much for telling it like it is, sweetheart. All my friends who read her book, *The ... The War ...*, what was it called again?"

"*The Next War*," I said.

"*The Next War*! Right! All my friends who read it left their husbands. And your father knows, my dear. Oh, yes, he does! How many nights did I spend reading it right under his nose while he listened to his trivialities on television. I remember it well...." She barked a hard laugh. "He would chortle at all this 'feminist racket,' as he called it, even if I caught him, one day, with the book in his hands, the lout, sorry dear, I know, I know, he's still your father, but in any case I caught him red-handed and I thought, 'great, he's finally interested in a female perspective.' But no, how foolish I was! He was staring at the back cover, at the picture of Dana Feldman. And he said, 'What a shame such a beautiful woman is spouting such idiotic ideas.' You know what I answered him? 'Well, I'm beautiful, too.' To tell you the truth I was more than beautiful. Did you know, Romain, that I was an extra on *Every Girl Should Be Married*? So I told him, 'I'm beautiful, too, and just watch me have idiotic ideas!' And that's when I asked for a divorce. You should have seen him! But, no, my dear, don't worry, you know it better than I, he's far happier today with Loretta. By God! As fat as she is, and she looks fifteen years older than her age. A real slow-motion car crash, but, hey, if that's what your father was looking for, I respect his tastes, but right there, there's your proof we weren't made to be together...."

Ann had rolled her eyes, like every time she heard her mother bad-mouth her father's wife. Then Laureen turned towards me, suspicious. "Did you know her intimately, Dana Feldman? You seem a bit young...."

Embarrassed, I'd turned red to the ears.

Yes, Dana and I had our secrets.

8

It was almost noon by the time I woke up from a dreamless sleep, only to be greeted by a terrible headache. It was impossible to make out my surroundings in the thick darkness. My hand searched for the flashlight I'd turned off before falling asleep on the living room couch. The embers were still warm in the hearth, but not enough to heat the room. Shivering, my hands and feet icy, I got up, groggy, unsure of my step, *goddamn this headache.* I was about to put on my coat and go out to warm up in the Jeep when, suddenly, I heard pounding on the door and a furious man's voice shouting, "Who's in there?" Even before reaching the vestibule, I heard the door open and slam against the wall. I stopped cold.

"Hey!" I shouted, "Who's there?" No answer. Indistinct grumbling and heavy breathing. "Who is it?" I repeated, my heart racing. Then a powerful white light began dancing along the walls, moving closer, before pointing straight in my face.

"Romain? What are you doing here?"

"Fluke? Harry Fluke? Is that you?"

We faced each other, both of us surprised. Watching each other like two boxers on opposite sides of the ring. An old man, his mouth permanently twisted with scorn, curved like a bishop's staff. God, he was old! In one of his hands, a baseball bat, in the other his flashlight.

"For God's sake, get that light out of my eyes!"

He obeyed, trembling, wobbly on his legs. He murmured something about a wave of thefts in the past few weeks.

That bastard Fluke, still sticking his nose everywhere. Like that time when I was a kid and he accosted me on Beach Street, his head poking out of his Plymouth's window, a derisive smile on his face, "Where are you going, like that?" Of course, Fluke knew. The books under my shirt weren't particularly subtle. But he never told my parents.

Seeing him now, I couldn't help myself, "This is my house. Please get out now!"

But Fluke didn't move. His eyes scanned the living room, as if he was looking for something, something forgotten.

"You came back to vote, right? To vote yes in the referendum?"

"I told you to get out!"

"All the same, you Separanazis!"

"Out!"

Fluke grimaced, then smiled, as if there was an old joke between us. "Or what," he jeered. "Or you'll call the police? Don't you think they'd be happy to pull up an old file?"

Seeing the rage in my eyes, he changed his tone, "Fine, fine. Okay. I'm going."

He turned around, wobbled towards the open door. An old beat-up Lincoln waited for him, with a bumper sticker on its back, proclaiming, "WE'RE RIGHT TO SAY NO."

Get lost, Fluke.

A grey November sky, opaque. I'd been gone from L.A. for two days, and I was thinking about Ann worrying herself sick over me.

My head felt like it was splitting open, and there was no Aspirin in the bathroom. Before shuttering the house for winter, Tommy emptied it of anything that might not tolerate changes in temperature or might be destroyed by rodents, like bedding and towels. He kept all of it at his home in Pointe-Leggatt. He also emptied the kitchen cupboards, taking the sugar, salt, spices, condiments — not even leaving the shadow of a jar of instant coffee. Tommy took care of the house well. Perhaps I didn't pay him enough. I promised myself I'd look into it; I was lucky to have him.

I needed a cup of coffee and some food. I splashed water on my face and walked out into Métis Beach's foggy cold, before deciding that with the welcome I'd received from that idiot Fluke, the anonymity of a snackbar in Mont-Joli would be preferable. I'd come back later to inspect the place.

"The past is a foreign country; they do things differently there," old Leo said in *The Go-Between*, that magnificent film based on the L.P. Hartley novel.

Warming up in the Jeep parked on Beach Street, I watched the Egans' home in the pale light of autumn, a grand cedar-shingled mansion, three stories high, with six bedrooms and a tennis court. I felt like Leo, his memory fading, working to remember the summer of his thirteenth year spent at a classmate's family manor. Called upon to be the messenger between a young lady and a simple farmer, witness to a clandestine and tragic love story, he would be marked for the rest of his days.

Yes, the past is a foreign country.

The Egans' home had lost some of its splendour, with its boarded-up windows, its shingles blackened by the elements, and the driveway and tennis court needing serious work.

I saw myself thirty-five years earlier on that doorstep, perfectly terrorized, a bouquet of carnations in my hands — flowers I hated, but my mother had insisted, "You can't go empty-handed, Romain! You should be grateful to be invited!" I was in my Sunday best like a ridiculous choir boy, hair slicked back, parted on the side. My mother had driven me there in our Chevrolet, and before I got out, she flattened a rebellious lock of hair using two fingers wet with saliva. "You'll be polite, eh? Don't forget — it's an honour."

In the half-moon gravel driveway, Mr. Egan's Bentley, Mrs. Egan's Alfa Romeo, and another car, more ordinary, a white Studebaker I'd never seen — it would end up being Reverend Barnewall's, a man I would meet for the first time that evening.

I had received an invitation for supper at the Egans; I, Romain Carrier, son of a carpenter and handyman for the very same Egan home. I was so terrified I'd vomited my breakfast, though I hadn't told my mother.

Gail flashed a nervous smile when she opened the door, followed immediately by a puppy, shaking with excitement, appearing out of nowhere and jumping on me. "No, Locki, no!" His paws on my clean pants, a moist nose between my legs. Gail, embarrassed, looked up and told me, "He's a Labrador. A great swimmer. My father bought him to take care of us. Just in case there was ever another accident."

That was the only reference to her father's misadventure, without which I would never have been invited there.

"He saved Robert's life," Mrs. Egan, still in shock, had told my mother. "Without your courageous boy — an angel, Mrs. Carrier, a guardian angel — Robert would no longer be with us, you understand? He'd no longer be here...."

My mother hung up the phone, turned towards me, her tone accusatory, "Is that true? And you didn't even tell me?"

July 1960, a Saturday evening, the night Robert Egan humiliated me.

"How about that, Reverend Barnewall? John Winthrop introduced the fork to America more than three hundred years ago. Looks like they still haven't learned to use it correctly."

Of course, the comment was directed at me. Snide, hurtful words, whose only intention could be to injure. It had been said in French, too, so that there could be no confusion. Red with shame, I put down my fork on the tablecloth, staining it with brown sauce. I had learned how to hold a fork from my father. You held it like you grabbed a handful of sand. I saw Mrs. Egan and Gail wince, as if not knowing which was worse — the stain on the white tablecloth or Robert Egan's cruelty. No one had spoken over the course of the meal except for Robert Egan and Ralph Barnewall. They talked about how to fund the Métis Beach church, and golf, and cars, and I don't know what else — two satisfied men not actually listening to one another.

I sat stiff-backed on my chair, my appetite gone. I was praying I might somehow become invisible, and not reappear until the end of the meal. What torture!

In the grand living room, before moving to the table, Mr. Egan, a glass of whisky in his hand, had introduced me to Reverend Barnewall of the Anglican Church, a fat, soft man with a turkey neck. I'd been invited to sit, then promptly forgotten. Impossible not to think of Françoise working in the kitchen. Françoise was my neighbour whom my mother loved dearly. She was always singing her praises. To me, no one could be as boring! Always cackling, or prattling on tediously, speaking of marriage and the house she dreamed of having, how fantastic her choux pastry was, how she was the youngest cook to be hired in Métis Beach. With all the excitement of being invited to such a meal, I hadn't even considered how awkward it would be to see her appear and begin serving the meal, "Does *monsieur* want his roast beef well done? Would *monsieur* desire more potatoes?" I imitated the others and answered her coolly, not looking at her in the eye. She was furious, and hadn't tried to hide it. *This is my place here, not yours. Don't play at being the pretentious little boy, understand?*

She was sixteen, and I was still fifteen. Sometimes her eyes seemed to fill with what I thought was warm concern when she looked at me. Her conversation made strange detours, like when she insisted on how glad she would be to own a business with her future husband, "a business just like the one your mother has."

It was indeed in the order of things that one day I would take over my mother's clothing store, now that I wouldn't be returning to the Rimouski Seminary.

At the table, I wondered whether Robert Egan was replaying the scene of his rescue in his head, the way I was. It had happened the previous Tuesday. Louis and I had been walking on the beach, when we'd seen him suddenly sink into the waters of the St. Lawrence, where he'd been swimming. I threw myself into the water and dragged him out. All I could grab was one of his legs — all covered in hair, I remembered — before hooking my arms under his. I pulled him to the surface. When we got back to the beach he pushed me away violently, humiliated and angry at having shown weakness, which is why I couldn't understand why Mrs. Egan had called my mother to tell her of my exploit and invite me to dinner the following Saturday. After all, I'd seen him *relieving himself* in his bathing suit out of fear. A proud man like him! Constantly comparing himself to others, always challenging those around him. He had the reputation of being a sore loser. A nasty guy, not particularly tall, though muscled, with his downy brown hair beginning to thin on the top of his head, a thick moustache like Burt Reynolds, brown eyes circled in white that watched others with constant animosity. The infamous Robert W. Egan in front of me, shocked, humiliated in his soiled red bathing suit, but still aware enough to go back in the water and wash himself off before pushing me with the flat of his hand down onto the rocky beach, while from the top of the cliff Mrs. Egan, who hadn't seen the whole incident, began to shout, with Gail at her side, "Robert! Robert! Are you all right? What happened?"

Louis had fled. He was far away by then.

It was only when dessert was served that Robert Egan began pretending to be interested in me. Which made me more uncomfortable than the cold shoulder he'd offered so far. He had had quite a few whiskies. At the other end of the table, Mrs. Egan seemed on edge, stiffening every time he poured himself another glass.

Reverend Barnewall was in rapture before the dish Françoise had placed in the middle of the table, a spectacular mountain of profiteroles dipped in chocolate. Robert Egan, meanwhile, smiled stupidly, a bitter twist to his mouth.

He questioned me about my studies, my projects, and my future. I had no idea what to say.

For me, the seminary was in the past tense now, and without the seminary, no chance of going to university.

Robert Egan looked at me, feigning curiosity, "Why?"

I felt myself redden. I wasn't going to mention what I'd come down with the previous winter, and the suspicious looks I'd gotten for it — mononucleosis, *the kissing disease*, transmitted by saliva and poorly washed glasses, contaminated glasses, perhaps from the seminary canteen. I'd been sent back home. Fever, aches and pains, fatigue, loss of appetite, my ganglions as big as golf balls on my neck, under my armpits, around my groin. Three months' rest required as my liver had been affected with jaundice. Furious, my father, who didn't trust clerics, wondered what had been done to his son, and my mother, in a protective mood — even she felt ambivalent towards them — did not insist that I return. No, I shouldn't go back, not after what I'd seen there but had hidden from my parents. Little Gaby Dumont's face, his fingers the colour of ink, his eyes bulging, found hanging in the dormitory bathroom. I'd gotten sick right after.

"So you're done with your studies? What are you going to do, then?"

I'd been hired that fall at McArdle's sawmill. My father had found the job for me. I took no joy from it. It was a hard job — ten, twelve hours a day in the sawmill, the noise of the machines deafening, enough to make you go mad, not to mention the risk of accidents, but it would be money I could set aside, deposit at the caisse populaire at Joe Rousseau's house. And after? Maybe someone in Métis Beach would offer me a job, a position in Montreal, in their company. Hopefully I'd eventually go to Montreal and knock on every door, and find a job in the big city where there were museums, and movie theatres, and places to listen to music, the sort of music the Tees bothers listened to — Ray Charles, Roy Orbison, Johnny and the Hurricanes. Or maybe leave for New York, the incredible city Dana told me about with such enthusiasm. Yes, one day I'd go there, walk in its streets, maybe even live there if I had the money for it, find a new job, why not? Like in *The Buccanneers of the Red Sea*, that Dana had given me, the story of a young pirate seeking justice who, during a terrible storm, tells a young sailor who can't swim and is afraid of falling overboard, *Your courage will come from the choices you can't make.* The impression that the book was talking directly to me, to the fearful boy I was and yet, for God's sake, I was dying here, I would have to push myself one day, and build my own story. No time to waste on girls like Françoise who expected that boys would give them their future; they could take care of their own. And anyway she was too tall — a good head taller than me — and too fat — at her age she already had her mother's chubby ass — and her hair was done up in a bun that smelled like the sour odour of cold oil, like all the women who wore complicated hair and kept it fixed on the top of their heads for days.

But I couldn't say all that, or any of that. And anyway, how could I explain what I meant in English?

My answers disappointed him.

Next to me, I could feel Gail tense up, her fists tightly glued to her thighs.

"There's my mother's store," I ventured. What else could I say? "And I could continue cutting the grass and ... take care of your houses when my father gets old...."

"I see!" Robert Egan exclaimed with poorly hidden sarcasm. "Great projects there, my boy. Let's drink to that!"

"Robert!" Mrs. Egan cried.

He opened another bottle of wine, poured a glass for Reverend Barnewall, who pretended to say no before accepting, his eyes gleaming. Vain protests from Mrs. Egan, a beautiful woman with disappointed eyes, who knew well there was no point anyway, while Gail sat in silence, frozen, only her eyes speaking to the apprehension of what she suspected would come. Robert Egan ignored them, he was among "men." He got up, staggering, caught a wine glass in the oak cabinet behind him, filled it halfway and placed it before me, proud as if he were doing me favour, a favour among men.

"Robert, damn it! He's a boy!"

Perplexed, I looked at the glass in front of me. We didn't drink at home. Alcohol wasn't even allowed in the house. My mother said it turned men into beasts, and my father did *that* at Jeff Loiseau's place or with friends at the Jolly Roger.

"No, sir, no, thank you."

"Oh, how reasonable! And how old are you, young man?"

"Fifteen."

"So what's the problem?"

"We don't drink alcohol at home."

"Catholics," murmured the reverend, his eyes raised skywards.

Robert Egan burst out in a tinkling laugh. "My boy, this isn't alcohol. It's a Bordeaux. A great, a very great Bordeaux."

"I don't know what a bordo is. We don't have any, at home."

At that point, chaos erupted. Mrs. Egan got up from the table and stormed out of the dining room, pushing the swinging door violently. Next came the happy barking of Locki, the young Labrador that appeared in the room and ran around the table, his claws clacking on the wooden floor, looking for scraps. "Come now!" Robert Egan grumbled, "What's with all the noise?" Françoise had disappeared into the kitchen. Ashen, the reverend stared at the dog as if afraid of being bitten. Gail caught him by the collar and dragged him into the living room. Teetering, the reverend got up, but Robert Egan caught him by the wrist. "You wouldn't refuse a good cognac, now, Reverend?"

Half-heartedly, Ralph Barnewall sat back down. Robert Egan was laughing out loud now, as if he was thinking back to one of his favourite jokes. "Catholics! Those damned Catholics!"

Gail, furious with shame at seeing her father so drunk and so impolite, intervened, "Dad!" But Robert Egan continued to chortle with Reverend Barnewall, who'd become rather pale.

"You know what, Reverend? These Catholics ... the ones from around here ... the women ... Well...." He stopped himself, as if suddenly aware he was going too far. But no, in fact it was comedy, a theatrical gesture to increase his effect, "The poor women, Reverend, they've nowhere to get ..." He brought his large, resentful face near the Reverend's, "sanitary tampons!" Ralph Barnewall recoiled and his face burned red.

Gail began to scream, tears of rage in her eyes, in her throat, "Dad, shut up!"

And Robert Egan, as if his daughter was a ghost he couldn't see, repeated, his head lolling back, making sure his joke had been heard, "Sanitary tampons, Reverend! My wife and my daughter have to stock up in Montreal. Don't look for them here, they're impossible to find ... as rare as virtue among the girls of the all-American Bar."

And Gail, again, "Please, shut up!"

Robert Egan leaned towards Ralph Barnewall, something soft and unctuous in the way he moved, like a snail without a shell, "Because they incite women to vice, according to our Catholic friends! Vice, Reverend! Can you imagine all these Catholic women...."

"You disgust me!" Gail shouted. "Come on, Romain, let's get out of here."

9

January 1959, I remember it still. A snowstorm, with heavy, sticky snowflakes falling, a nor'easter blowing. Louis and I had gone to Clifford Wiggs' place, that old nutter, something that had been formally forbidden. But there was no chance of being seen with the weather the way it was, and the snow and wind hid our tracks. Suddenly excited, Louis began making snowballs with pieces of ice inside, and threw one at an uncovered window of the garage, breaking it in a thousand pieces. Suddenly, laughing madly, he threw another, harder still, and a second window exploded. I yelled at him, and he called me a fag. By the time I got close enough to assess the damage, he'd disappeared, leaving not a trace behind. I couldn't see a thing through the heavy curtain of snow that the wind made and unmade. He left me there by myself to deal with the consequences, the same as the day I saved Robert Egan from drowning.

Spending time with Louis was asking for trouble. He hated the English ever since his father's fatal accident at the McArdle sawmill. They refused to compensate his mother, claiming he'd been drunk that day, as was often the case. Louis would never forgive them. His own brand of revenge was to attack their property, anything really, their houses and cars and even animals. I heard he was behind the disappearance of cats, as well as seagulls found broken on the rocky beaches. Killed with a slingshot. Standing before the broken windows, snow blowing in, I could feel anger growing in me, followed by dejection. I was to go back to the seminary in a few days, and return only when summer came. I had had diarrhea that morning, and pain in my stomach all day. Suddenly, from Beach Street, I heard a voice that put ice in my veins: "Hey, you there!"

My heart beating, I turned and saw a young man, a Montreal Canadians tuque on his head.

"You okay, my boy?"

Yes. Why? What do you want from me?

"Seeing you walk in the snowstorm, with your back bent and all, I told myself something was wrong."

He walked towards me, his long black coat covered with snow, and looked over my shoulder, noticing the broken windows. "Who could have done that?" I felt myself weaken. There was no way he wouldn't put two and two together. But instead he came back and stood before me, his face serious, as I shook with fear and cold in my heavy clothes, wet with snow. He said, softly, to my great surprise, "The wind, probably. I'll take care of it tomorrow. Good old Wiggs won't even know about it." I hesitated when he offered me a cup of tea in his small white church barely visible in the snow — was he making fun of me? One of those churches that was visited by the English, most of them living at Pointe-Leggatt, all descendants of the Scottish immigrants whom John MacNider, the founder of Métis Beach, had convinced to come across in the early nineteenth century. They were people of modest station, like us — people who were from a different world, yet close enough for Fluke to hate us.

He introduced himself: John Kinnear, the new pastor of the United Church, barely twenty-three, with a wife and a baby on the way, his eyes free of judgment and full of laughter. He took my wet clothes and hung them near the sizzling heater in his cramped, spare office, which housed only two chairs and a table. He mentioned he should probably try to do something nicer with it, as if apologizing, but he'd just arrived. The Christmas service had been conducted by his predecessor, an old man with a bulbous nose I'd only seen a few times. He was retired now, but had taken everything with him. The young pastor was laughing, saying he needed to organize everything. We started talking about hockey, and he laughed when I told him we no longer ate Campbell's soup at home since the riot at the Forum — "Clarence Campbell, Campbell's soup, my father says the same difference." The incredible laughter of that friendly man! And in the days to come, as I anxiously awaited my departure for the seminary, I sought his reassurance, confiding in him as I had never done with anyone before — my fears, my anxiety. He was the only person in the world who wasn't embarrassed when he said the word *masturbation*. We'd spoken about it one afternoon, for heaven's sake, and the state I was in … stammering with embarrassment, my words all tumbling out together, telling how Father Bérubé at the seminary forced us to look at his damned *Book Without a Title or The Perils of Onanism*, a firm arm around our shoulders; sixteen ugly, old etchings, stained in some places, with a young man whose health declines from one picture to the next, until the last shows him emaciated, his body covered with sores, its caption reading, "At seventeen, he expires in terrible pain."

Once again, that liberating laughter, "It's nothing but rubbish, Romain. These days, we know that isn't true. Medicine mentions it as part of the sexual development of an individual, as long as it isn't done excessively or out of boredom. So, nothing to worry about, right?"

Nothing to worry about? What about those sinister stories repeated over and over by Father Bérubé, with his monkey eyes, his fetid breath, and his damn *Book Without a Title* under his arm, hammering in the lesson that we were risking *eternity*, "Earth is a steel ball in the universe…. This ball, every thousand years, a great black bird comes and grazes it with its wing…. When the grazing of the great black bird wears down the entire ball, well, then, it'll only be the *beginning* of eternity!"

Once again, the young pastor's laughter, his hand on my shoulder taking the sting out of the words, "Rubbish, Romain. That's pure rubbish."

Rubbish?

The anger I had felt then, a jolt of anger, like two hundred twenty volts through me. All these people lying to me — *why?*

And I returned to the seminary in Rimouski, revolted but far too scared to show my indignation. So I said nothing, bitterness in me, all of them liars, liars, and worse than liars, if what was said about Gaby Dumont was true. He was the smallest of us, easy prey, soft skin, milky even, not a single hair, not a pimple, almost a girl, that's what the older kids said. "Hey, girl, show us your cock." And immediately someone would inevitably answer, "Never mind, he's keeping it for Father Johnson and Father Rivard." Everyone laughed, and to my great embarrassment, I laughed a few times as well, though there was nothing funny about it, only tragedy. The luck we had not to be *targeted*, even though I never knew whether it was true or not, and none of us knew really. Little Gaby wet the bed, which was probably the reason behind his nocturnal comings and goings, but we had too much fun imagining something else, something degrading, with sex, and rumours circulated. And aren't rumours more exciting than simply knowing that a thirteen-year-old still pissed his bed?

One night he got up silently, as he often did, and brought his sheets with him, as he often did. He tore them up and made a long rope with them, swinging them over the pipes in the bathroom. We found his body in the morning, his neck broken, his eyes popping out of his skull, his skin blue, tongue sticking out and shit in his pyjamas. The stench of it made our eyes water. Jokes were made, but not many, *a shitter and a pisser to the end*, but they were nervous, really, it was panic; we all had nightmares about it, some of us falling ill — I'd developed the symptoms of mononucleosis right after. His parents were told that their son was psychologically fragile, not made to be happy in a seminary — as if we were — and his parents, devastated, thought they were entirely responsible.

But we'd been the hangmen. With our cruel jokes. I felt so guilty I couldn't return to the seminary, even once I'd gotten better.

I got out of the Jeep, my collar raised against the cold, and knocked on the door of John Kinnear's church, with its white and forest-green sign — THE UNITED CHURCH OF CANADA, SUNDAY SERVICE: 11:00. No answer. Not much of a surprise. The last time we spoke, John had told me about a conference in Scotland at the end of October. He told me he'd be going with his wife and Tommy, and travel Europe a bit while they were at it. Still a shame, though. It would have been nice to talk to him. If he knew that I was here while he was away! So many years of him trying to convince me to change my mind, "Why don't you come and visit us? It's ancient history now. I don't understand, Romain, feels like some sort of mental block to me...."

Back in the Jeep, I put the heater at its highest setting. In my rear-view mirror, I saw Fluke coming towards me in his old Lincoln. He passed me without slowing down, though he did take the time to shoot me a contemptuous look. I thought back to the time I thought he might denounce me. It still made me laugh today, thinking back to those boxes of Tampax I'd found in my mother's store, one night when my parents weren't there. I'd been shocked at first, as if I'd found porno mags in my parents' bedroom, but that was quickly replaced with pride — my mother wasn't one of those Catholics Robert Egan mocked. She sold them, but to whom? Certainly not Dana who, one day, had gone to the store with her sister Ethel. Words had passed between my mother and them, sounds like *axe* or *pax*, and then my mother straightened, "Who told you?"

Dana mentioned Margaret Tees.

My mother sold them to Mrs. Tees, but not Mrs. Egan?

"Don't worry," Dana said, "thank you."

And both women had left, perhaps a bit surprised by my mother's reaction. But they had remained polite.

Their faces when I'd knocked on their door, a bag hidden under my jacket. Their irrepressible laughter, embarrassing me, "You'd think he was a pervert!"

"No, no, he's far too sweet for that."

No, impossible to forget *that*.

I put my foot on the gas, heading towards the clubhouse.

10

Thursday nights at the Métis Beach clubhouse!

They showed *On the Waterfront, Buffalo Bill, Johnny Guitar, Moby Dick*, and everything with Gary Cooper. Free entry. I was off to the movies with Jean and Paul, Françoise's brothers. We were all terribly excited, with the sort of enthusiasm some hoped we'd have when it came time for confession. She'd be joining us later, once she was done in the kitchen at the Egan house, scrubbing pots and pans. Her hands were already calloused, and at her age!

We always sat in the last row, near the door, as if we weren't entirely welcome among the youth of Métis Beach, though we knew we were supposed to be. After all, their parents — whom we worked for — kept telling us to participate in community activities. A way to contribute to our education, a social duty even, if not a type of charity. And so we'd go to the movies, filled with an equal measure of enthusiasm and apprehension. It wasn't always easy to understand the plot of the movies, all shown in English. We'd have one eye on the screen and the other scanning the room, watching their reactions, trying not to embarrass ourselves — laughter, surprise, and fear we feigned with as much expertise as women feigned their pleasure, as I would realize with amazement years later when I watched *When Harry Met Sally*.

Thursday nights at the clubhouse! Cokes and chips bought at the small canteen with its aggressive neon lighting, enjoyed in the electrifying darkness of the room.

Gail would sit in the first row, flanked by Johnny Picoté Babcock, with his idiotic doe eyes, always ready to put his arm around her shoulders.

When she laughed, I roared; when she seemed affected by the plot, I put on a sad face; when she appeared to be scared, I prepared a reassuring smile for her.

She never turned her head in my direction.

I hadn't seen Gail since that terrible night at her parents' house when she'd taken me by the hand and dragged me into the garden, tears of rage in her eyes. She spoke of her father with anger and disgust, "It would have been better if you hadn't been walking by that morning. He could have drowned, and I...." I listened to her in silence, almost afraid. She had burning embers for eyes, promising a roaring fire to come, impossible to control. "I'm sorry, Romain. It was my idea, a stupid idea." So Gail had been the one who insisted on having me over. That's why her mother called, "He saved your life, Robert!" And her father had relented, "Well, fine. But if we need to suffer through a boring evening with a shy boy, let's at least invite that old Barnewall...." Gail spoke rapidly on that cool, moonless night. She was steaming — and not particularly coherent — as if she expected to be interrupted at any moment, "I'll never depend on a man like my father. He's so arrogant! And I'll never live my mother's ridiculous life! I'll be a lawyer. With an office and important clients! I'll be independent! You understand? Do you understand?" All the while, I had an expression of such helpless envy sketched on my face. There was no need for a fancy education at a private Protestant college in Westmount for me to know that a woman who wanted to be a lawyer would never fall for a boy like me.

We hadn't spoken since that fateful dinner. As if nothing at all had happened that evening.

I was so timid, for God's sake! I envied the boys of Métis Beach who approached her with assurance, like Art Tees, always monkeying around to impress her. He whistled and jeered during love scenes on the silver screen, or when two people kissed. The scenes never failed to embarrass us boys from the French Village — but just one of Art's jokes, and we all breathed easier.

Every time, Françoise would join us some three quarters of the way through the movie, knocking down chairs in the dark with her fat behind as she tried to find a seat. Her brother Paul would give up his every time. And every time she smelled like grease and onions. And every time, as soon as the movie was over, she placed a rough hand on my shoulder and whispered, "Tell me what happened from the beginning."

How I hated it! I couldn't care less about her! I only had eyes for Gail. I tried to attract her attention but couldn't do it. I was just too shy. I watched her joke around with the others at the canteen, a Coke in hand, and Johnny Picoté on her like a leech. If I was lucky, she might wave at me from afar, but generally she didn't even look at me before leaving, probably thinking that *Françoise and me....* Jesus!

Then came that evening in July 1962, the summer I turned seventeen. *Rebel Without a Cause* with James Dean and Natalie Wood was showing at the clubhouse. An event, a real one, and we all dressed accordingly. Leather jackets over white t-shirts, with greased hair for the boys, high-waisted pleated skirts, white socks, and cardigans for the girls. A film that most kids in Métis Beach had seen in Montreal already, twice or three times for some of them — *once you've been there, you know you've been someplace* — and they shivered with excitement, electricity in the air.

Gail arrived at the wheel of her mother's Alfa Romeo with a friend of hers, Veronica McKay, whose parents owned the large Norman-style house to the east of the Egan property. They were laughing, elbowing each other in the ribs like partners in crime preparing their next heist. As if they knew something extraordinary was in the works. The clubhouse parking lot was filled with small sports cars, their motors purring; you came to the high Mass led by James Dean in your car, certainly not on foot.

My father had refused to lend me his Chevrolet Bel Air. Voices were raised at home, and I slammed the door as I left. I was heartbroken to see that the Coutus' Rambler was gone, Jean and Paul had left already. They'd been luckier than I with their folks. All I could do was jump on my old CCM that had lost the lustre of its first summer, even if it meant getting there with rings of sweat under my arms. What humiliation.

I spent a long time in my room, anxiously contemplating my sparse wardrobe. A discouraging sight. My mother owned a clothing store, sure, but she didn't sell jeans and leather jackets. They were for people raised in barns, and for thugs you read about in the newspaper, stories about robberies in Montreal or Quebec City.

I chose black pants and a white button-up shirt with short sleeves. The collar was heavy, stiff as cardboard, and chafed my neck. I gave up trying to do something with my too-short hair, and settled for slicking it back with a part down the middle.

The reflection in the mirror over my dresser was a sad sight: a little kid from another decade who'd aged too quickly. I looked like someone had been trying to shelter me from modernity at any cost. My uneducated parents couldn't understand that the future belonged to the young.

Go out and have fun? Life isn't fun and games, son! It's made of duty and responsibilities.

Yet in that summer of 1962, I felt like a man, proud of my six-foot frame, a beard beginning to shade my cheeks, my body, better proportioned now, had begun to grow stronger from the hard hours at the sawmill. It was nothing like the previous summer, when the rest of my body had not yet caught up to my hands and feet, still growing, waking me in the night in painful spurts. I'd been in pain all summer, so much so I spent almost no time at all in Métis Beach, unless it was to honour my contracts. Once I went to the Egan house with my father, where we were supposed to repair the garage's rotten roof. I could barely stand straight on my legs, and lacked any coordination at all, but I was bigger than my old man by a good head already — though that didn't stop him from treating me like a child, "You're useless, good for nothing!" I sought his affection all through my childhood without ever finding it — he was distant, icy, and when we found ourselves alone, he kept a sour look on his face at all times. His eyes, usually lively when he was with other people, became empty. The nail never properly hammered, the paint never applied well, the gutter not clean enough — always something to criticize me for. And if a few dead flies escaped my vigilance, he picked them up with his fat fingers and stuck them under my nose, "And what's this? Are you blind?" That summer, I had lost my balance after stepping on a piece of rotten roof, and my foot had gone right through it. Instead of worrying about me, he began yelling, loud enough to attract Gail's attention. She came over from the garden and stared at us for a moment, perplexed, and my pride had been so hurt that I avoided her for the rest of the summer.

But that summer of 1962, everything had changed. I was a man — I believed I was — and my English was getting much better thanks to two winters working for McArdle.

Inside the clubhouse, Jean and Paul were waiting for me, greased hair, satin jackets and collars popped, simultaneously embarrassed and proud of their get-up. I had a seat reserved next to them, as usual. Françoise freed herself earlier than usual, waved her hand at me when I walked in, all excited like a little fat girl in a candy store.

"Sorry, boys. I want to be closer to the screen tonight."

Jean and Paul looked at me, offended, as I continued on my way and sat in the third row, only a few seats away from Gail and

Veronica McKay, my eager eyes on Gail. A few times, she turned her head towards me, small movements, a question in her eye, as if she felt spied on. I smiled at her, and she frowned. Maybe she didn't recognize me in the darkness. Or she was looking for someone else.

We were all distraught at Plato's death, played brilliantly by Sal Mineo. At the end of the movie, Gail, Veronica, and the other girls were wiping their eyes with tissues, teasing each other. The boys, meanwhile, dreamt of being those rebels with tortured souls, modern heroes far more attractive than their fathers' and uncles' great men of the war.

Nicholas Ray's work filled me with a powerful feeling of failure. I had lost my chance when I abandoned the seminary. Too late now, I couldn't go on to study like the characters in the film, or the kids of Métis Beach who were already in university or would soon be.

On the dew-covered lawn in front of the clubhouse, some of us walked in a veil of our own thoughts. In the gravel parking lot, motors were being revved up, and car headlights cut our silhouettes out of the surrounding night. Gail chatted away with Veronica McKay, her head still on a swivel as if she was looking for someone who hadn't come. She seemed nervous, overexcited. Art Tees came to offer her something, and she spoke to him brusquely. He turned back and walked to his bottle-green MGA, looking vexed. You could see it by the way he jiggled his keys around his finger. After such a night, and such a movie, a boy rejected by a girl could do nothing but feel humiliated.

And yet I was walking towards her, my heart about to beat through my chest, my knees wobbling. As I got to her, I spoke breathlessly, "How's university?"

She seemed insulted, all of a sudden, as if I was making fun of her. "I see you haven't heard the latest news."

Next to her, Veronica was ignoring me with awe-inspiring expertise, "You'll come and get me after? I'll be over there, with Johnny." She pointed towards a group of kids smoking around Mrs. Babcock's Mercedes. She disappeared and Gail straightened her arms before crossing them over her breasts. She clearly was in no mood to continue the conversation. From the corner of my eye, I saw Jean and Paul's Rambler, with Françoise in the passenger seat, staring at me with her cow eyes, boiling over with blame.

I went on, "You're not at school anymore? Why?"

Falsely enthusiastic, she answered, "I'm engaged, didn't you know?" I hesitated, and she laughed, indignant, full of rage. She cursed her parents for forcing marriage on her only a few weeks past her eighteenth birthday, in October, with the heir to Drysdale Insurance, a certain Donald Drysdale. Everything organized already. A large, expensive wedding at the Montreal Ritz-Carlton; everybody would be there — all the richest families in the country, a few cabinet ministers, and even Frank Sinatra himself, who had agreed, for an indecent sum of money, to sing *Love and Marriage*. I felt my heart tearing.

"Great."

"Great?" she said, disgusted. "My life is going to end! Gail Egan will cease to exist! I'll be my husband's wife and my children's mother, like all the rest of these interchangeable women."

"What about being a lawyer?"

She shuddered. "They don't give a shit! A respectable woman stays at home, takes care of dinner parties, children, and the help."

"Don't get married, then. Marriage and children, it's all a trap. Simone de Beauvoir said it herself. Have you read her?"

Her eyes narrowed. Those eyes shining such a strange light that night. She barked a laugh, "Who?"

"Simone de Beauvoir. She's a feminist."

"A what?"

"A feminist."

An insane laugh, wild, as if she were looking at a donkey that had learned how to add and subtract. Hurt, I was about to turn around and leave, when Veronica called out to her, "Gail! I'm here!" She was seated in the sporty Mercedes next to Johnny Picoté, who looked like a grotesque rockabilly caricature with his ridiculous hair. An oily banana. He was taking Veronica home, or so we understood from Veronica's shouts.

"Come on," Gail said.

"Me?"

"Yes, you. Who else?"

And I followed her through the parking lot, my heart tripping over itself in excitement. She told me to get into her mother's convertible Alfa Romeo, started the engine, and accelerated, going through the gears with precision and confidence, as if she had long years of experience. She wasn't a girl anymore, she was a woman now, with a woman's body — I could see her thighs under her skirt that had hiked up a little, by accident or design I couldn't know, and her firm, full breasts under a pale pink cardigan. Burning tension between my legs, an overpowering desire to touch her. She drove at top speed, her brow furrowed, her ponytail with its ends whitened by sun bouncing on the back of her neck. I didn't know where she was taking me, and didn't dare ask. Gail Egan! In a car with Gail Egan! Oh, the faces Jean, Paul, and Françoise made when we passed them on the clubhouse's small gravel road. A flash of childish vanity filled me, the ardent belief that my life was now better than anything I could have dreamed of. I was becoming one of them, one of the kids of Métis Beach. Yes, I, Romain Carrier.

Gail turned left onto Beach Street. We sped past Clifford Wiggs' property, and I thought of those two swans found dead in the pond early in the summer, and wondered what Gail would think if she knew what I knew. "Bang, bang. On the first shot," Louis had told me. With arrows. Some thought it could be wild animals, but a wild animal didn't leave perfectly round holes, and so Louis received a fair share of suspicion. In the end, there wasn't much proof.

"But why?" I asked, shocked.

He lowered his eyes, wiped his nose with dirty fingers. "They treat men like animals and animals like men. They killed my father, I kill their animals."

"And what does Wiggs have to do with your father?"

"He's English. All English are guilty. If they ask you where I was yesterday, I was at your place, okay?" And two days later, when Frank Brodie, Métis Beach's private policeman, came by my place, I lied, not knowing I'd come to regret it.

We passed John Kinnear's church, and Gail yelled in the humid air, a sort of primal scream, filled with despair, that made me shudder. *Insane*, I thought. *She's completely insane.* The speedometer kept climbing, and the car burning into the night vibrated on the slick road.

"Do you know how my mother's selling the marriage, as if it were the most natural thing in the world?" She pinched her nostrils and took Mrs. Egan's shrill tone, the voice of dinner parties and forced compliments, "My girl, you'll see, with time, you'll come to appreciate him. What's more, you'll live a life of even greater luxury than your mother! Can you believe it? You'll be able to buy all the dresses you want, and go and get them in Paris! Oh, my girl, it's wonderful!"

The Alfa Romeo peeled off Beach Street and raced down Highway 132.

"I envy you, Romain. I know you think your world is small and stifling, but you can leave it if you want, and that would be the best thing for you. You can hope for better. I can't."

I said nothing. I didn't believe her. After a few miles she took a sharp right, climbed Lighthouse Road, and drove to the point that plunged down towards the sea, where the Métis Beach lighthouse stood guard. Gail parked the car a little further down — the tide was high that night — and turned the headlights off. Behind us were the homes of the two lighthouse keepers who spelled each other off, day and night, to keep it running.

The din of the waves crashed against the rocks. The stars in the sky looked like a dance floor. Gail took my hand, and we walked along the beach, avoiding tidal pools. My heart beat so hard I felt its tremor to my shoes. Incoherent, breathless, Gail spoke rapidly in a mix of French and English. She spoke of Don Drysdale whom she would marry, the marriage she didn't want to a young man of twenty-four she had no interest in. She talked about the cock he would put in her, it would absolutely revolt her, she knew — and she knew because she'd already done it, or almost, with a boy "as nice as you are," the brother of a friend of hers. It happened in their house in Westmount, her parents weren't there, and the help would remain silent as usual, for fear of being accused of lying and getting fired. "The children are the bosses too, you understand?" That evening, her friend said she'd done it with the other boy who was there. "All … all the way?" Gail asked. Yes, all the way, but not Gail, she was naked in the brother's room, but hadn't been attracted enough to the nice boy to "let him put his … you know." She spoke without modesty, seemingly filled with despair, tears of rage in her eyes mixed with something wild, something insane. She told more stories, unfinished and shocking, that embarrassed me to the point I doubted I'd actually heard her right. I was trying to think of the right way to kiss her when she grabbed me by the nape of the neck, forced my face against hers, her burning breath like a panting dog, and kissed me urgently, with her tongue.

The next day we learned what had happened to Johnny Babcock and Veronica McKay. On the 132, at the intersection of MacNider road, a car turned left, and the driver didn't see the Mercedes coming at full speed. The steering column pierced his chest, and Veronica's neck was broken.

That night, Métis Beach lost its colour as if it had been drained of its blood. Devastated, the Babcocks and McKays returned to Montreal, followed by other families who claimed they simply

couldn't continue enjoying the summer, not after such a tragedy. That night, while the mutilated bodies of Johnny Picoté and
Veronica were being extracted from the wreck, the golden youth
of Métis Beach were fast asleep, dreaming of the tortured heroes
of *Rebel Without a Cause*. One scene in particular was likely running through their minds, the one where the end of the universe
is explained as the anxious young men and women gaze at the
celestial vault of the planetarium: "Earth will not be missed ...
the problems of Man seem trivial and naive indeed.... And Man,
existing alone, seems to be an episode of little consequence...."

The funerals were held ten days later in Montreal. All Métis Beach
was there for a whole week of July which, for us inhabitants of the
place, seemed as empty as the end of September. A few families
returned, but it wasn't the same — tennis courts remained deserted,
boats sat on the shore with their sails lowered like beached whales.
Even Mrs. Tees' garden party was more intimate and sober than
usual that summer.

I prayed — in a manner of speaking — that Gail would return.
She had lit a fire in me, struck a match, and left me to deal with the
consequences alone! A constant, burning heat, a pit in my stomach, and my mother's suspicious glances when she rifled through
my stuff. Once she threw a copy of *National Geographic* in my
face — given to me by Old Man Riddington — because of two
pictures of African women with bare breasts, "That's what you're
really interested in, eh? Don't tell me it isn't."

I'd become a ticking time bomb. An incurable agitation filled
me, a tumult between my thighs, not like the pitiful, terrifying
erections of my time at the seminary, quickly extinguished by guilt.

My prayers were answered. Gail returned a few days later with
her parents, more fragile than before, her eyes strange and absent.

She never spoke of the accident, and when the tennis tournament organized by the clubhouse was cancelled, she said with a small, almost cheerful voice, "Johnny would have won anyway, he wins every year," as if he were still alive and it was all a bad joke, Johnny and Veronica would be back any Thursday now to watch a movie — though those too had been cancelled.

Gail ignored me for days at a time, then, without warning, she came to the store, "Is Romain in?" She dragged me to the beach, pulling at me with an impatient hand, and kissed me passionately, not caring at all if she was seen.

Sometimes she asked me over to the clubhouse to drink a Coke. Other times, if there were friends around, she could ignore me entirely. I simply didn't understand.

Then she would be waiting for me in front of her house on Beach Street until I passed by, returning on my CCM from old Riddington's place where I mowed the lawn under a steely sun, and she threw herself on me, sniffing my collar like a dog, apparently excited by the odour of fermented sweat that clung to me. I told her, "No, Gail, I'm disgusting." But she continued, even if she knew we were being watched. She would kiss me with the same ardour as the first time, in the pressing urgency of someone waiting for her execution.

"She's a fragile girl," Dana warned me, with that air that parents take when they're worried about their children. "The accident really rattled her. More than all of us. And her father is mad. Robert Egan is a vicious man we should all be careful of. Don't forget it."

Many of the kids in Métis Beach stood up to their parents, so why not Gail? Why hadn't she said no to this marriage?

"Some people prefer to suffer than to disappoint others," Dana said. "Advocating for themselves is too painful — it means risking someone's contempt."

But Gail hated her parents; she wanted nothing to do with their acceptance. "Oh, Romain, it's more complicated than that, especially for a woman. Believe me."

One day, in one of her agitated moments, Gail decided we should have a picture of us. She told me, her eyes feverish with a sudden passion that I was careful not to encourage, "When I'm married and bored to death, I'll just look at the picture that I'll hide somewhere he'll never find, and it'll be like a little victory. A victory for independence. Do you understand?"

She said we should ask Françoise to take the picture, and I quickly cut in, "No, Gail. Not Françoise...."

She looked at me with a teasing glimmer in her eye. "It's funny that a boy like you wouldn't have more nerve...." She ran up the stairs as if she had good news to give and made her way to the kitchen where Françoise was preparing supper. Her parents were out for a round of golf, and wouldn't return until late in the afternoon. A few minutes later, she returned, pulling a sullen and stubborn Françoise. Gail would later tell me, "You should have heard her when she said, 'You know what your parents think of you and Romain,' the disgust in her face when she said that!" But Gail insisted, and even shouted, "Just a picture, damn it! Just one!" Françoise threw her apron on the counter and followed Gail into the garden — all the while grumbling — where I was waiting for them, as taut as a bow. Her eyes! As if she were saying, *This will cost you dearly, Romain Carrier! You can count on it.* Gail placed a small camera in her hand, a flat Minolta. "What do you want me to do with that?" In an equally dry tone, Gail answered, "Certainly not pies." I barked a laugh. Furious, Françoise pressed the button, probably imagining it was a trigger. "Happy now?" With a heavy pace, she returned to the house.

By then I was rather nervous, and didn't like what I was seeing from Gail. But I let myself be pulled into the garage anyway, where we began kissing. "If Françoise knew," Gail said, her voice triumphant, "she'd be green with envy." She imitated Françoise, mocking her fat behind. I didn't find it funny. "Don't worry, Romain. Nothing can happen to us here. We're in another world, another galaxy. We could spend our lives here, living off motor oil and paint. She laughed then, and kissed me, her hands in my pants, in the dark and humid garage, among the disorder and the diesel fumes. I was dizzy, my heart beating quickly. Suddenly, I heard gravel spitting from under the Bentley's wheels, "My parents?" Gail wheezed. I put my hand over her mouth, "Hush!"

Through the small windowpane we saw them walk into the house before immediately coming out again, led by Françoise, one hand pointing towards the garage. "There." The hate I felt for her at that moment.... Followed by panic. There was nowhere to go.

"Hide!" Gail said. She pushed me behind a pile of garden chairs. Walking heavily, Robert Egan came down the driveway and pulled open the door with his powerful hand.

"I know you're there. Come out, now!" His face purple with rage, his eyes popping, he held a golf club in his hand. He grabbed his daughter's arm and squeezed hard enough to force a small squeal out of her, before slapping her in the face. He turned towards me and raised his club in the air, threatening to smash it on my head. I backed up, terrified, making a barrier of whatever I could get my hands on, tools and cans of paint, finally banging my elbows and knees against Mrs. Egan's Alfa Romeo.

Gail was shouting, "Don't hurt him! He did nothing!" But Robert Egan wasn't listening. He cornered me between a paint-splashed stepladder and the sharp propeller of a boat engine. "No, Dad! No! Please!" Around us, objects of all kind were raining to the ground.

"My girl will marry, by God! Leave her alone!" His club whipped through the air, scratching Mrs. Egan's car, which I managed to slip around, catching my feet in some empty bottles. I stepped through the broken glass and managed to leave the garage and run off, like a rabbit chased by a fox.

By the time I got home, my father was waiting for me. He already knew. Robert Egan hadn't lost any time. My father jumped at me like a frothing animal. And he hit. His hard fist in my stomach, leaving me panting. "What got into you? You want to bring shame on us, is that it? What do we look like now, you...!" He was about to hit me again when my mother screamed so loudly that my father pushed her against a wall.

Straightening, searching for breath, I said, "Don't touch my mother, you dirty...." but my voice was no more than an inaudible cry among the cacophony of tears and shouts. "You're done for in Métis Beach! I'm going to cancel all your contracts. We don't want to see you back there, understand? You'll keep a low profile for the rest of the summer, and after that we'll see what happens!" They couldn't ask that of me, it was too cruel. What would I do?

"We'll see wha..?" my voice tapered out. "We'll see what?" My father straightened, as if I'd hit him.

"Shut up!" He was about to grab my collar with his calloused hands, but I pushed him off me with my shoulder and got back up, challenging him with my newfound six feet of strength.

"You want to throw me out, is that it?" My mother, hysterical, began throwing dishes to the ground.

I looked at her one last time, then turned and ran down the stairs into the street, and ran as far and as fast as I could.

II

I waited for darkness to fall, my whole body shaking like a leaf. The night was warm, with no wind. Slivers of voices and music burst forth from the Tees' mansion and reached me on the beach. Above, an almost-full moon — a quicksilver disk trimmed away, a small nothing preventing it from perfect roundness, a cotton sphere resting in a hand.

The cream of Métis Beach, at least what was left of them in the summer of 1962, had congregated at the Tees home for the annual garden party, a prestigious event whose secondary purpose was to finance the Protestant churches. Long tables covered in white tablecloths, uniformed servants in black and white, alcohol in indecent volume, a cold buffet — though refined in taste — and a string quartet. In the humid air, notes of Vivaldi, Bach — none of the music that you'd play if you wanted your guests to dance. Margaret Tees had required a certain amount of sombreness that summer as a sign of respect for Johnny Picoté Babcock and Veronica McKay, as well as the mourning families, and all of the parents of Métis Beach, really, who couldn't help fearing the worst each time one of their children borrowed their car or drove on their own. It was known now that the kids weren't as responsible as previously thought: we learned that Johnny Picoté drank at least four beers at the clubhouse that evening, beer Art and Geoff Tees brought by the crate — two? three? — and it had been easy for them, the Tees being the owners of one of the largest breweries in the country. But I'd seen none of that.

My mother and Françoise spent that morning making hundreds of cucumber sandwiches that Mrs. Tees ordered every year and my mother agreed to make, even if it meant she had to close her store on a Saturday. Margaret Tees paid well, and she thanked my mother profusely. Meanwhile, my mother took some pride in the fact that a great lady of the world who counted among her friends the wife of Lester B. Pearson trusted her so much.

They began working in our kitchen at seven in the morning, the pungent, nauseating smell of cucumber floating through the house, all the way to my bed. When I left my room, Françoise looked away from me. She just couldn't look me in the eye since the incident in the garage. My mother, defending her as usual, felt it necessary to add, "You know what your father said, you stay here!" I thought I saw a satisfied smile on Françoise's face, or maybe not, but I didn't care, I had other plans, which I'd put into action when they left in their black dresses and white aprons, heading up to the Tees mansion, the cucumber sandwiches all carefully stacked in boxes on the Chevrolet's backseat.

I stood on the beach in the moonlight, my heart beating with apprehension and excitement. I could feel my penis like a weight in my pants, raw, as if it had been rubbed with sand.

They could all go to hell! My mother, my father, Françoise, Robert Egan … I refused to see the danger as you refuse to accept blame you don't deserve. I was seventeen, for God's sake, I wasn't a child anymore!

"Romain, is that you?"

In the darkness, Gail was waiting for me, huddled in an Adirondack chair taken from her parents' garden, a sidelong smile on her lips. I had expected something else. That she might make an effort, and not just sit there in dirty shorts and an ample, half-buttoned rumpled cotton shirt, almost masculine really. "Gail, are you okay?" She didn't answer.

Suddenly, she laughed like a glass sphere crashing to the floor when she saw Locki jump towards me, his tail whipping through the air, "What a truly stupid dog! If he was actually trained, and he listened to my father, he would have *attacked* you!" My heart tightened — certainly not the sort of joke I wanted to hear.

"Gail, are you sure there's no one around?"

"Do you see anyone? They're all over there, having fun. Perfectly *insensitive* to the tragedy of others."

She spoke as if there were someone around her to be angry at. I was upset and disappointed that she was in this state — she was drunk, I could smell it on her breath, and her clothes were dirty — almost repulsive. This is how she wanted to welcome me? She had planned this moment, and I wasn't sure I wanted any part of it at first; it was too risky, and she knew it, she wasn't stupid. Yet she was insistent, imploring, and seductive, "It's important to me, to you, to both of us. Something special will bind us together, forever. Do you understand?" And of course I believed her, or wanted to believe her, a girl like her who was interested in me, even if a part of me was saying, *You're being had, man, this girl isn't well.* But what's the point of ruminations, if not to torpedo your heart? I much preferred concentrating on my pleasure.

Of course it was mixed in with a certain degree of anxiety; after all, I was a seventeen-year-old boy, assaulted with these sudden urges as strong as the need to piss in the morning, just at the *idea* of doing it for the first time. We knew we would be going all the way that night, a prospect both enticing and frightening, though I was beginning to believe she might be making fun of me, seeing her limply moving her head, her hair tangled and flush against her skull, and that savage light in her eyes, more incandescent than the night we'd seen *Rebel Without a Cause.*

Disappointment in my voice, I said, "You want me to go?"

She straightened. "Why?"

"You don't look so well. Are you sure everything is okay?"

"Of course everything's *okay*, what do you *think*? Everyone is having fun tonight. And so will we."

The sarcastic edge to her voice cut me, but not enough for me to refuse the arm she offered so I might pull her to her feet. She bumped against a chair and held onto me heavily. Staggering, she brought me into the house, bathed in darkness. I hadn't stepped foot in the place since the infamous dinner with Reverend Barnewall, and I couldn't repress a thrill of vengeance thinking of Robert Egan: *This time I'm here to sleep with your daughter.*

"No, Locki! No!" The dog had followed us, barking, scratching us with his claws. We were playing, why not him as well? "I said no!" Incensed, Gail grabbed him by the collar, pulled him towards the great French doors, and tied him outside, on the veranda; we heard a few more barks before he lay down, his nose pointed towards the sea.

"Here, drink this." The bottle of Southern Comfort she'd already gone to work on. I brought it to my mouth, a big mouthful, burning, I felt it going all the way down to my stomach. Gail dropped onto the couch; on the coffee table, a piece of art that looked like an egg fell to the ground and rolled away without breaking, and again her laugh put ice in my veins. I glanced nervously around the room, as if a trap was about to spring. What was that on the chair there, a glimmer of movement when I looked quickly, something left to dry ... *Robert Egan's red swimsuit*? Anxious, I said, "And what if your parents decide to come home early from the party?"

"*Relax*, Romain."

She pushed away a lock of her blond-white hair that kept falling over her eyes, took my hands, and placed them on her breasts. "Kiss me." I obeyed clumsily, my hands motionless on her breasts, as if I might break them, as if I feared I might detonate if I moved. A musk came off her, dried sweat and body odour. Around us, in the living room lit by the moon, the four great windows opened onto the sea made us as vulnerable as thieves in daytime.

"Gail...?"

She pushed me away brusquely. "You're shaking? *Why?* There's nothing to fear, *I told you!*" She swallowed another mouthful of Southern Comfort. She began speaking very quickly, eyes fixed on the floor, as if she'd been offered a reprieve, and had only a few hours left to pour everything out from within — her marriage, her parents.... "Do you know what I am for them? A *commodity*. Merchandise. That's all I am."

Carefully, not wanting to offend her, I risked saying, "Why are you agreeing to it?"

She stiffened, rage in her voice. She'd been promised as a way of closing a deal. She would marry Don Drysdale of Drysdale Insurance, the eldest son of the company's owner. Her father owned shares in it, but they weren't as valuable as the union of their two families. The marriage loomed on the horizon, and her parents were overjoyed. "And what about me? I think I'm going crazy, Romain."

She grabbed the bottle, took another swig, a portion of which ran down the front of her neck. She looked entirely incredulous when I said, "No one can force you to marry a man you don't love."

It was followed by a bitter laugh. "Well, they certainly don't care about that!"

"Do you love him?"

"I don't know."

"You don't know?"

"No, I don't know. Maybe so, maybe not. But it doesn't matter."

She loves him? Why lie to me?

"If you love him, why are you against the marriage?"

She looked at me as if I were an imbecile, "You don't understand anything, Romain. Come on, this is our last chance."

Baffled, I followed her to her room on the second floor, my legs like wet rags. She mentioned the marriage again, always with the same desperate rage — the Tees would be there, and other families from Métis Beach, not witnesses, no, but voyeurs, "You know, the same sort of people who look at a man being put to death from behind a pane of glass." She muttered something about Marilyn Monroe, found dead two weeks before, "I think I'm meant to die young. Even younger than Marilyn...." And with an air of defiance, she pulled the engagement ring off her finger, a ring mounted with a diamond — I noticed it for the first time just then. So it was serious with Don. I glanced up and saw my guilty reflection in the mirror over the dresser.

"Gail, no...."

"No *what*?"

"Let's go back down. It's not a good idea."

"For who? Your vicar? Come on."

I glanced anxiously around the room — a young girl's bed, with a pink and white comforter, matching wallpaper, Beatrix Potter authenticated watercolours that Mrs. Egan had so proudly ferreted out at an antique store in London. A room decorated for a child, it wasn't right for what we were about to do, a sacrilege against childhood.

She shot me a knowing look, mixed with a desire for vengeance. But revenge for what, exactly? *Does she love him or not, this Don Drysdale?* As if reading my thoughts — and seemingly to humiliate me — she pulled a picture of him from one of the dresser's drawers and pushed it towards me with a triumphant air. A flash of jealousy filled me as I saw this young man so sure of himself, athletic body and perfect teeth, as unbearable as a blinding light, and then, as if she wanted to be forgiven, she began kissing me passionately, her lips against mine, famished, pulling her shirt off, my God, those firm breasts, far fuller than I thought, their points like prune pits. "Hush!"

She put her finger against my mouth. She was shaking, removing the rest of her clothes, her eyes filled with light, with the pleasure of seeing me watching her. I was excited, of course, though in the back of my mind I couldn't help feeling I wasn't taking full advantage of the moment. I was too nervous, too clumsy. I couldn't help thinking of Don, handsome like the actors on the screen at the clubhouse. I was afraid to disappoint Gail. I knew I'd disappoint her.

"Come on!"

"No, Gail. I don't think...."

"Please, please! I know you've been dreaming it for a long time. Tomorrow it'll be too late."

"I ... I don't know...."

She stumbled towards me, and I submitted to her with fearful docility. She undid my belt, took my clothes off. I felt blood rushing to the bottom of my stomach. A fog in my brain, I didn't even know where I was anymore. She said, panting, "Help me." I tripped trying to take off my pants and my underwear, my cock hard, aimed at her, her eyes avoiding it entirely. Timidly, I lay down next to her; the tension slowly cleared as our lips touched, her warm body next to mine, her salty, fresh skin, then her suddenly agitated hands finding their way towards my crotch, an electric shock that ran down to my toes, she guided me clumsily into her, moist heat, sublime, my head emptied, my conscience completely gone, and a groan shuddered through me, without warning.

Her disappointed eyes, and the shame that filled me.

She moved away brusquely, no doubt she was thinking of Don, with whom she'd done it, I was sure now. I wanted to die, to flee. I couldn't hold a candle to him. What humiliation. How could I have believed that such a girl was actually interested in me? And what time was it? Late now? How much time had we spent in that room? I was seventeen, for God's sake, and I had just done it for the first time, and that's all there was? That disappointing?

"Romain, please! You're going to ruin everything!"

I jumped out of bed in a panic. I wanted to stammer embarrassed apologies, something like, *It would have been better if we hadn't done it, it was better before.* But you couldn't say something like that. I tried to collect my clothes strewn across the floor, looking for my belt, my shoes, my shirt. I wished I could be far away from this place. I needed to think about what had happened, alone. Gail insisted in a plaintive voice that I come back to bed. I didn't answer. She got up, furious, her hair half-covering her face. "What are you afraid of? It's like that's all there is in you, fear!" The remark should have upset me, but I barely heard it. I still needed to find my socks and one of my damn shoes, which Gail picked out from under the bed, and threw at me maliciously, like a bone to a dog. I must have looked ridiculous, down on all fours like an idiot, half dressed and half shod, blind to the miracle before me, Gail naked, her small round breasts, a shining spot between her legs, but it didn't interest me anymore, my genitals had withered, a hermit crab back in its shell. We heard a noise on the ground floor.

"What's that?"

"Nothing! Just the wind!"

"No, there's someone there!"

Then a terrible cry in the night, a terrifying howl.

Panicking, Gail wrapped herself in a sheet and ran out of the room, a cold shower wouldn't have had sobered her quicker. My heart beating, we ran down the stairs, into the living room, and reached the veranda in which a heavy, strange silence lay. "Locki?" Gail said in a nervous voice. "Locki, is that you?" She saw the blood on the veranda, viscous, steaming. She screamed, desperate shouts that were heard all the way to the Tees mansion. In a panic, I ran until I thought my heart would explode, first to the back garden, then down the cedar staircase that led to the beach, and due east, my ankles turning on the stones. That poor dog, stretched out, its throat slit, not completely dead yet. Light burst from the Riddington place, and then the Hayes'. In front of me, far away, under the nearly full moon, someone was running towards the village, a broad-shouldered silhouette, familiar.

I made my decision. I would denounce him to the police. Louis kept killing animals, the bastard. The next morning, there was a knock on the door. But it wasn't Louis they were looking for. It was me.

12

The wind blew stronger, clearing up the sky over the sea. That cold November wind! My breath forming clouds of steam, shaking in my buckskin jacket, I forced myself to walk as slowly as possible, letting the names of the houses I passed come to me: Joe Rousseau of the *caisse populaire*; Roger Quimper of the general store; Jeff Loiseau the mechanic; Lionel Coutu — Françoise, Jean, and Paul's father … Rue Principale. Its modest wooden homes, all jumbled together on small plots, some still had their asbestos shingles, some of their yards entirely asphalted over. Small houses of one or two stories, scrupulously maintained and freshly painted, just like it had been back in the days. Nothing had changed really, except for doors and windows replaced by newer materials, and the cars in the driveways, more luxurious now.

Loiseau's garage, the bakery, and Leblond's shoe shop had disappeared; Quimper's general store, swallowed by the grocery chain Metro. And Louis' house, which had always been a shambles, was a video rental place.

Only Mode pour toute la famille, my mother's store, remained almost unchanged, except that the front had been painted bright yellow, in stark contrast with the dull white of the houses surrounding it and the melancholy grey of the sky and sea. The same sign with its outdated lettering, the same mannequins in the shop window. On the second floor, our apartment seemed inhabited: lace drapes dressed the windows, and a child's drawing had been taped in one window. My old room.

Troubling, this nostalgia that brings tears to your eyes, even if the memories aren't that great. Places, smells, sounds — the happy jingling of the bell over the store's front door — something you thought had been deactivated from your memory, erased, like toys with their batteries removed, and here you are, throat tight with emotion.

"Can I help you?"

It was her. Françoise. She looked older than fifty-two, her face saggy, her heavy body even more massive, and her short hair almost the colour of eggplant.

She squinted, then her brow furrowed as if she suddenly couldn't see. "Romain?"

I can't say how much time we stood there, watching each other, intimidated and disbelieving. Clearly she wasn't very happy to see me — her tight smile was almost a grimace. I too was shocked to realize I still held a grudge. After a long hesitation, I said, "You look well," a comment I realized she couldn't return when I saw my reflection in one of her large lateral mirrors. She didn't answer, watching me, her mouth dumbly slack, as if she was afraid of me, a man in a wrinkled suit, my face drawn, a three-day beard on my face; it all implied there was something wrong with me.

I turned my head and looked quickly around the shop: impeccably sorted displays, on the left side men's clothing, on the right, women's and children's. Like when my mother ran the shop. I said matter-of-factly, "So you got the store?" An embarrassed look on her face. "You own the place, right?"

"Yes. I...."

"The old man gave you a good price?"

The phone rang, and I saw relief in her eyes.

"Just give me a moment, okay?" She went into the back to grab the phone instead of picking up the receiver right next to us, on the counter.

I began wandering the aisles, forcing myself to look relaxed. Memories were coming back to me, not as unpleasant as I had feared. As if my mother were still alive, and I imagined her working between two displays — a good, nervous woman, with constant aches in her legs that made her suffer. She ran her store with a firm hand, without sentimentality; she was alone at the helm and happy about it, always ready to give us orders, boxes to move or shelves to stock. My father dragooned into building shelves, or repairing a broken floorboard. Her store. Her pride. Her *woman's pride*, since there weren't many women at the time who managed a store unless they were widows. My mother brought home more money than my father, maybe twice as much despite his work as a carpenter and the repairs he did around Métis Beach. But they never spoke about it; it was my father's shame to bear.

I made my way into the men's section, where I looked through the coats. A rather spare selection, outmoded fur-lined jackets and trench coats. Nothing that caught my eye until I moved into the "outdoorsman" section and I noticed a good-looking waxed jacket. I was about to try it on when Françoise reappeared, still with that embarrassed air, "No, that's not what you need. Come, I've got something better."

"I forgot how cold it was here."

She forced a smile, almost mocking, "Yes, it's been a while." A long, uncomfortable silence followed.

She led me to the front of the store, near the windows, and presented a selection of down jackets I'd missed. I tried my hand at continuing the conversation, offering a smile I hoped was friendly, "You must be pretty happy to have the store. You used to say it's what you wanted most in the world."

"I'm fulfilled," she replied dryly, "As you can see." She grabbed a coat and took it off its hanger. "Try it. One hundred percent down. About your size. Black is okay?"

The jacket fit me well, and it was both light and warm. For some reason, I expected a compliment out of her, like *Still so slim? Or Not a trace of grey in your hair yet?* But Françoise said nothing.

She checked the length of the sleeves. Her practised eye looked me over coldly, without desire, thank God. If she'd given me that old flirtatious attitude like back in the day, I wouldn't have had any idea what to do. Those old meaningful, complicit looks she shared with my mother, enough to get me embarrassed or angry — women with their mad ideas about marriage. My mother even kept some worthless objects she won at bingo as marriage gifts for us.

"You haven't asked me why I'm back, Françoise."

No surprise to her, apparently, "You came for the referendum. To vote." I burst out laughing at the thought of that idiot Harry Fluke who scared me that morning. She stiffened.

I said, more seriously, "No, to tell you the truth, I didn't even know about the vote. Pretty embarrassing, right?"

She looked me over suspiciously, then turned her back and walked away. I heard her say, "Gail? Gail Egan?"

Who else?

"She died in the night between Monday and Tuesday. Cancer." I waited a beat, "You're not going to say anything?"

She took refuge behind the counter, seemingly absorbed by a carefully organized pile of papers. "What do you want me to say? That it's sad? Of course it is. I'm not some cold hag, you know."

"Did you hear anything about her? Did she still visit in the summer?"

"No, not Gail. Her father did, though. He's so old. If you could see him. A nurse comes with him. Mrs. Egan died a long time ago. Cancer as well." She came out from behind the counter, went to the display of men's gloves, and picked up what looked like the warmest pair. "Need some of these as well?" The self-confidence of the sales clerk had returned, and I said yes and thanked her. "Did you still see each other? Gail and you, I mean?" she asked me, polite, though clearly not wanting an answer.

"No, it's been years. You know, I have my life in the States now, and…."

She cut me off brusquely, "Yes, everyone knows."

I looked at her, stunned. *Why so much anger? Wasn't I being nice to her?*

"If you want, Françoise, I'd like us to talk."

"About what?"

"About what happened in the summer of 1962. I feel like there are fragments I lost. Can you help me find them?"

I would have thought she'd at least be curious, maybe even teasing, *yes, of course, everyone knew about the baby except you*, but that wasn't the case, she seemed absolutely ashen instead.

"It was too long ago. I can't remember."

"You forgot that summer? With everything that happened?"

"I don't know, Romain ... I don't have the time ... I'm busy."

"Busy?"

Her cheeks reddened. We were alone in the store and not even the shadow of a customer in the deserted streets of the village.

"Invite me over, tonight."

"I don't know ... I'll need to look at what's in the fridge. I...."

"You'll find something. You were an excellent cook, as I remember. I'm sure you still are."

The compliment pleased her, though she didn't smile.

I said, "Six-thirty, okay?"

She mumbled something that could have been agreement, then protested when she saw my credit card, "No! Don't. It's on the house."

Calculating quickly, I realized it came to three hundred dollars.

"No way, Françoise, I can't accept."

"No, I'm telling you, no! It's a gift!"

A gift? With that tone? I didn't insist, thanked her, and left.

13

"After all these years, we should celebrate a little, no?"

She had so much lipstick on, her mouth was like a caricature. Françoise opened the door to her small house on Rue Principale, decorated somewhat garishly — golden picture frames, heavy wall-coverings, and massive furniture — proud to show me the table she had set for us, a large block of foie gras in the middle of the table; she'd been keeping it for just such an occasion. "It isn't every day you get a visitor from so far away." Her tone was exuberant, playful, a troubling contrast with her behaviour a few hours earlier at the store. The wine glass she held in her hand could have contributed to her strangely euphoric attitude. At the sight of five place settings on the table, I froze.

"You expecting others?" I had been hoping we might speak just the two of us.

She gave me a small shrill laugh and shook her head as if it wasn't what we'd agreed on. I was irritated — it wouldn't be possible to have a conversation now that her brothers were coming — who else but Jean and Paul could have been invited? And, of course, the doorbell rang.

Jean and Paul. Barely fifty, but they looked like old men. Paul more than Jean, with his sallow cheeks and waxy skin. Jean was a bit plumper, with the hard belly of a pregnant woman. His hair, however, was greyer, almost white. He held out a firm hand, without warmth, giving me a bitter look, while Paul skimmed the wall and foundered into the living room, avoiding my handshake. Years ago I disappointed their sister's inordinate expectations, and the brothers still held a grudge.

"Come!" Françoise pulled me into the living room. A tray of oysters lay on the coffee table. Her husband Jérôme had picked them up at the grocery store and managed to shuck them in record time. "Without even hurting yourself, right honey?" Jérôme, a delicate man with an embarrassed smile, acquiesced with the same timid nod he'd given me when I arrived and Françoise had said boisterously, scanning me from head to toe, "Look, it's the coat I was talking about, it suits him well, doesn't it?

In the living room, on the burgundy velvet couch, Jean and Paul waited in silence as Jérôme worked the minibar, making them a drink. I had hazy memories of Jérôme, the timid eldest son of Roger Quimper, the owner of the general store. Back then, he had the smooth, fearful face of a sixteen- or seventeen-year-old youth, so quiet you sometimes forgot he existed. "Jérôme? He was with us that night? Are you sure?" That was Jean speaking from behind the wheel of his father's Rambler, one night in Little Miami, as if suddenly waking from a dream, "Hey! Jérôme!" And Jean turned to ask him before noticing he wasn't in the back seat stuck between Françoise and the door, his usual spot. Even Françoise hadn't noticed. How we'd laughed that night! Jérôme? Left behind in the bathroom!

Well, so be it. Françoise had decided on this poor, thin boy, his back bent, head retreating into his shoulders, always glancing at you sideways even when you stood right in front of him, as if he suspected you of something. He looked like his father, who inspected us from behind the store's counter when he'd see us jostling one another in his store, without a dime in our pockets and a strong temptation to grab something.

Jérôme had taken over the family business in 1977 and had recently brought it into "the modern era," Françoise explained, pride in her voice. "With a nice Metro sign, just like in those ads on TV."

She was a businesswoman, Françoise was. My mother's store and a grocery store, not too bad at all.

A rum and Coke for Jean, a beer for me, a glass of white for Françoise, scotch for Jérôme. "And you, Paul, your usual hooch?"

Paul laughed nervously, revealing bad teeth. Jérôme handed him a room-temperature ginger ale in a pint glass, with three maraschino cherries on a toothpick. Paul said, as if apologizing to me, "I quit drinking years ago. No choice. It was that or die."

"Cirrhosis," Jean clarified.

I learned that Paul hadn't worked in years, was living off welfare, and not doing much with his days. As for Jean, with his two children gone from the house, he lived with his wife in Mont-Joli and worked as a civil servant in a local government office, but not for very much longer.

"Retirement at fifty-three. Not bad, eh?"

"And what are you going to do?"

His face lit up, "Nothing! Isn't that great?"

I shivered and Jean noticed it, sure enough. An awkward silence that, after a few moments, Françoise tried to talk her way out of, talking about everything and nothing, pushing oyster after oyster on us. "Come, eat more! We have to eat them all! Have you tried this sauce? You should taste it! It's Jérôme's favourite. There's ketchup in it!" Without much appetite, we downed the oysters, except for Paul. "My liver, I can't," he repeated, holding his stomach every time.

Perked up by a second rum and Coke, Jean began talking about the village and its inhabitants, those who'd died, those who'd left for the old folks' home, the English of Métis Beach who'd panicked at the idea of a second referendum, though not as much as in 1980. It had been traumatizing nonetheless, there was no doubt about it, especially after Parizeau's words — money and the ethnic vote — that wouldn't help, you could be sure about that. Harry Fluke was thinking of selling everything and moving to Ontario.

"Well, better this ending than another," Françoise rejoiced. "This way, it's the status quo."

Jean and Paul's jaws clamped shut, but both kept their disagreement to themselves, happy enough to let their sister steer the conversation. Squirming in her seat, Françoise told me how the English population was getting older and older, and their children were no longer interested in spending their summers here. "They think it's too cold. And they've got houses elsewhere. In Florida, the Caribbean, the South of France." Some had even sold their properties to French people. "Who would have believed it? There's less inequality than before. The English aren't as rich, and we're a little bit more so. It isn't what it used to be, and we're better off for it."

This time Jean and Paul rallied to their sister's opinion and said in unison, almost comically, "Yeah, good for us."

Then the eternal and predictable questions about my job in Hollywood. Françoise seemed excited by the fact that I had worked with Aaron Spelling on *Fantasy Island*. She said, "Oh! Tell me everything!" like a little girl about to get a surprise. "What's the dwarf like? You know, what's his name again?"

"Tattoo."

"Tattoo, right! He seems nice."

"He died."

"Tattoo?"

"The actor. Hervé Villechaize."

"Oh? They do say dwarves don't live very long."

"He killed himself, two years ago."

My answer was ignored. She refused to be distracted and went on excitedly, "And the other one, the tall one? Ricardo ... Ricardo what?"

"Ricardo Montalbán."

"Oh, yes! I'd put my slippers under his bed any day!"

Alcohol was making her exuberant, and Jérôme didn't seem to be enjoying himself, "I'm just kidding around, honey ... you know that."

I told them I only worked on the scripts and, consequently, I'd never actually been on a set or met the actors. Françoise made no attempt to hide her disappointment. I could have won back their attention by telling them all sorts of savoury anecdotes I'd been told by Aaron Spelling himself, like how ABC would have preferred to have the great Orson Welles play Mr. Roarke instead of Ricardo Montalbán (the erstwhile legend hadn't found work in a while, dragging his two hundred thirty-eight pounds to Pink's in Hollywood to order nine hot dogs at a time); but what did Françoise and her brothers know about Orson Welles?

No chance in hell they'd talk to me about *In Gad*. I still remembered a conversation with Josh when we spoke of distribution rights for the first time. The show would be broadcast in Canada, but only out West and in parts of Ontario. Something about cable, antennas, and territories. It wasn't likely they had heard about it, which reassured me. I had no inclination to launch into fastidious explanations and justifications about Chastity's abortions and the complaints we had received. I didn't want to face Françoise's shocked look. She seemed to have kept a sentimental attachment to the God of our childhood. I'd noticed my mother's bleeding crucifix, looking like raw meat, hanging above the marriage bed when I'd gone to the bathroom. There were other things that had been owned by my mother in her house too — the silverware, the d'Arques crystal glasses on the dining room table — but I felt no nostalgia, only a twinge of tenderness. But Françoise quickly explained, "Your father gave them to me after your mother's death. I said no, I couldn't accept it, but he insisted...."

My father. Of course he'd given my mother's things to Françoise. Like the rest of it. Everything was clearer now, Françoise's discomfort that afternoon, her insistence on giving me the coat and the gloves. I said, without a trace of bitterness, "If I understand correctly, he left you the store as well."

The colour drained out of her. "If you want, we can figure something out, Romain."

"Why? He gave it to you. And what do you want me to do with a clothing store?"

"Money. If you sold it."

"Money? I don't need any, Françoise."

"It's not fair. I tried to reason with him...."

I burst out laughing. "Reason with the old man?"

"Romain, I don't want you to think...."

"Think what?"

"I ... well ... never mind."

Perplexed, I watched her turn tragic in her inebriation. What would I do with a store? Jean, protective brother that he was, turned the conversation onto another track and became briefly interested in Gail and her disease, "Cancer?" "Leukemia." "How old?" "Fifty-one." Silence, then.

"And Louis?"

I asked the question with a far dryer tone than I'd anticipated, and Jean gave a half smile, as if we were finally getting to the conversation he'd been waiting for.

"What about Louis?"

"He's probably in prison somewhere, after everything he did."

"Louis is doing time in Orsainville."

"Well, there we go!" I exclaimed. "It's what I was saying, right? And for what? Murder? Did Louis ended up killing someone?"

Jean bit his lip, then swallowed the rest of his rum and Coke — he didn't drink wine, didn't like it. "No, not for murder."

"So for what?"

"Robbery."

I laughed harshly. "After robbery, it'll be murder. He'll get there. Believe me. When you kill animals, that's the next step. All serial killers begin that way. It's well documented."

Françoise became very nervous; her hands trembling. She took our plates, almost knocking over our glasses, but we held onto them. I had the feeling I was the only one around the table to see that something was wrong with her, her moist forehead, visible sweat under her arms, and no one to help her, nobody to say, *Are you okay, Françoise?*

Jean said, "Louis didn't kill the Egan dog, if that's what you think."

Again a nervous laugh broke in my throat.

"Don't laugh," Paul said, "It's true."

"Sure it is," I heard myself say in a voice that was quickly losing its confidence. "The cats, the seagulls, Clifford Wiggs' swans...."

"Louis is innocent."

Françoise stiffened, inexplicable tears in her eyes, and disappeared into the kitchen, leaving a pile of dirty plates on the table. What was happening, good God?

"I was with Louis, that night."

Paul spoke, his face red with the sudden attention.

"You?"

"Tell him," Jean ordered. "Tell him so he stops thinking we're liars."

Were they making fun of me? I was convinced I'd seen Louis' silhouette under the almost full moon, his black clothes, the way he had of running with his fists clenched, head forward....

In a tired voice, Paul began his tale of that evening's events. The Buick Louis had stolen in Baie-des-Sables, which he drove through the village, bottle of whisky — stolen as well — in hand. Louis was drunk, red, glassy eyes, dumb smile drawn on his face. "Hey, Paul! I've got good whisky! Come on, let's go for a ride!" Paul hadn't been able to resist the temptation. "I climbed in," he said. "I shouldn't have, but I did. I liked to drink in those days. We got on the road to Mont-Joli and went to visit one of his friends. We drank the whole bottle, just the three of us. We were too drunk to get back on the road, and the cops found the car easily. They knocked on the door, nearly knocked it off its hinges, but we escaped through a window, hard to believe, we were so drunk we could barely stand. It was past ten o'clock by then, and it was dark. We roamed around part of the night, avoiding cop cars, and ended up finding a shed in the back of a house, where we slept a little until the next morning. You couldn't have seen him that night in Métis Beach."

"I don't believe you."

"No?" Jean was speaking now, anger in his voice. "When Paul came back home the next day, our father was waiting for him. Believe me, he got it good. We didn't forget it."

"Exactly," Paul added, with the tone of someone telling a tale of derring-do. "The old man wasn't big, but he was strong. My eye was like a grapefruit for two weeks. You wouldn't remember it, you disappeared that day."

Jean gave me another of his satisfied smiles. "Exactly. You ran away to the States. Just like a criminal."

I chose to ignore that last comment. "So who killed the dog? One of you?"

Jean laughed unpleasantly. "You really want to know? That's what you want? Well, sit your ass down because you're not going to like what I'm about to tell you."

They thought it was me. It was my turn to laugh, "Me? I would have killed Locki? Why?"

"To make sure Louis would be accused of raping Gail."

I smirked this time. "You know this whole rape thing, it's a lie. It's crazy old Robert Egan's invention."

"That's not what people here thought."

Jean was having fun, that much was clear. He was on his fourth rum and Coke. Jérôme had brought the Bacardi bottle to the table, and Jean was pouring drinks for himself. In an authoritarian voice that clearly annoyed Jérôme, he called out to Françoise in the kitchen. She reappeared, distraught, mascara smudged.

"Françoise, tell him what you heard the next morning at the Egan place. It'll help him remember, maybe."

Françoise protested, "It's ancient history. I don't think it's worth us talking about it...."

"Romain has come all the way from Los Angeles to understand things. He's an important man over there," he declared, with undisguised irony. "A man who probably isn't used to wasting his time. So tell him, tell him what you know."

"I … I don't know, Jean."

"Come now, sis! You know the story by heart. How many times did you spin us that yarn, eh?"

I shuddered. *How many times did you spin us that yarn?* Like a dirty joke you never get tired of repeating.

"Go on, now," Jean insisted, "what are you waiting for?"

Françoise lifted her eyes to mine. Discouraged, she began speaking, stuttering slightly. I could feel Jean's eyes on me, penetrating like the blade of a knife, but I ignored him. Françoise looked tired all of a sudden, weariness dragging her face down.

"The next morning, it was Sunday. I didn't work on Sundays, but Mrs. Egan called me, crying, telling me I should come over immediately. I skipped Mass, just to tell you how much I hurried. I got there, there were suitcases piled in the vestibule. Gail was in the room upstairs, and I could hear her crying. Her father and mother were shouting at each other in the living room. They ordered me to help them pack everything up because they were leaving that evening. I couldn't understand why, it was only August 19, I remember the date, they still had a week left.… I thought a member of the family in Montreal had died, someone that Gail liked a lot because she couldn't stop crying.…"

She turned to Jérôme and asked him to fill her glass. She took a long swallow. "Mr. Egan said something about the police, to make sure someone got arrested. Gail was yelling from her room that it wasn't him."

"Who, me?" I asked.

Françoise didn't answer. Jean encouraged her to continue. "The phone rang. Mrs. Egan picked up. She was on edge. She was talking to someone, I don't know who, but someone close enough to the family for her to tell them everything.…"

She returned to her wine glass.

"Tell them what?"

"That when Mr. Egan and she hurried back from the garden party at the Tees', Gail was in a state of shock. She had shrieked so loudly on the veranda that the neighbours, the Riddingtons, who had gone to bed already, came out of their house in a panic to see what was happening. Mr. Riddington drove to the Tees in his bathrobe to tell Mr. Egan, while Mrs. Riddington tried to calm Gail in the house. Mr. and Mrs. Riddington discovered Gail in tears, half-naked. Mrs. Egan had been a nurse in London during the Second World War. She said she had experience in ... those kinds of situations.... She'd seen cases like Gail's in the hospitals."

Was all of that true? Why did Gail never say anything? The few times I tried talking about it with her.... "What happened after? Your father, your mother, what did they do?" I had asked. She had told me nothing, closing up entirely like a pouting child, a sort of amnesia or incomprehensible stubbornness. She didn't want to talk about it. *Why? Because of Len?*

"Go on," Jean said.

Françoise lowered her eyes, and said in a suddenly reserved voice, "Mrs. Egan was saying how the first thing she did when she got back from the garden party was open her daughter's thighs and stick a cloth well ... you know where ... she pulled it out and sniffed it. She said over the phone, '*My daughter was raped by a French-Canadian bastard.*' And then she said your name."

"And you believed her? Tell me you didn't believe her, Françoise."

Jean came to her sister's rescue, "The Riddingtons saw you running along the beach. The Hayes as well. They were all clear: it was you. And you didn't look like you were out for a jog."

"That doesn't make me a rapist!"

Jean smiled. "Why did you run off to New York if you had nothing to hide?"

"Exactly," Paul added.

"When you have nothing to hide," Jean said, "you don't just flee. Your mother died of a broken heart, and that's on you. And you poisoned your father's life. Seems to me you're pretty much responsible for all of it, don't you think?"

I couldn't believe what I was hearing, "I had to save my skin! That goddamn Robert Egan bought off whoever counted as a judge in those days. They were going to lock me up! I slept with Gail! I didn't rape her! And why the hell am I justifying myself to you people?"

"You're the one who came here looking for the past."

"The dog, who the fuck killed the dog, then? Who?"

"It wasn't Louis."

Jean stared at me, challenging. Knowing he was going to score a few points, he said, "You see, Romain, we don't really care about the dog. In fact, we don't really care about what happened to you. You made it, right? Look at you. Expensive jacket. Rolex on your wrist. I can't even imagine where you live. We, well, we had to take care of your parents when you left. The dog, rape or no rape, it's all the same to us. You ruined your parents' life. You left and you never came back. Oh no, excuse me, once, you came back once, to bury your mother, but it was too late by then. And now, now you come back just like that because you want answers to your questions. What, all of a sudden, after all these years, you're having trouble sleeping? Who cares? It's nothing compared to what you forced your parents to live through. You might not know it, but a few years before dying, your father could barely walk anymore. Stubborn as he was, he refused to move out of the apartment over the store. Françoise ran his errands, prepared his meals, gave him a bath every two days. A bath! Can you imagine what that meant to him? And when he wanted to go out, like on Sundays, for Mass, we would go get him. Took two of us, and we'd pick him up in our arms and carry him down the stairs to put him in the wheelchair we bought for him. He couldn't accept what he'd become. He complained, sure enough, when we helped him, but he always agreed in the end to be rolled up to the church, where we lifted him up a second time to get him up and sit him on his pew, third row, on the right side. You remember that, at least? Probably not...."

Françoise was crying now.

"Tell us. Tell us what you were doing when we were taking care of your old man? Tanning on a beach in California? Probably more interesting than feeding your father and wiping his ass. You see, Romain, Françoise never stopped feeling guilty about the store. She felt guilty towards you, because she inherited what should have been yours. Well, I think she deserved the store."

"It's late, Romain. You need to leave."

This time, Jérôme spoke. His voice was strong, peremptory. It surprised everyone. I got up without saying a word, their hostile eyes on me. On unsteady legs, I made my way to the door. I heard Françoise moaning and her brothers trying to console her.

II

DANA

I

Twenty-one dollars and eighty-five cents. That's all that was left of the thirty-five dollars I'd grabbed in a panic from my dresser drawer. Standing in front of the ticket counter at the Montreal Greyhound station on Drummond Street, I counted and re-counted my money, my hands shaking. How could I survive with this little in New York? In my back pocket, I had a postcard Dana Feldman had sent me. I kept reaching for it, like checking your gun before a robbery, just to make sure it was still there. Her address was on the back:

Harperley Hall
41 Central Park West, Apt. 8E
New York

As fantastic as the city was on glossy paper, it was monstrous once you got there. Buildings gave you vertigo when you stood at their base, enough to make you doubt there was a sun above. The strident cry of cars and the deafening grumble of air conditioning units filled the air.

The smoke that rose from the city! As if it was built on an active volcano, or a cozy plot in hell. Torrents of pedestrians hurtling down large avenues, pushing you out of their way if you didn't walk fast enough. Disgusted looks of harried travellers in Penn Station, where the bus abandoned me to my fate after an endless night on the road where, wracked by nausea, I vomited on the bathroom floor. There were so many people here, I'd never seen so many in my life. The whole thing made me dizzy. All these people on their way to work on a Monday morning — August 20, 1962. I remember making an effort to record that date in my clouded mind, knowing that nothing would be as it had been, a violent break with my past. All the men and women around me were dressed in modern clothes, though at that point I wasn't exactly sure what that meant. They were different down to their physical features, and there were blacks as well, my first time seeing black people outside of Thomas Riddington's *National Geographic* and Sidney Poitier movies at the clubhouse. And there were young people with surprising hairstyles, long fringes on their foreheads, hiding their laughing eyes, idling about, eyeballing me impudently, pushing me out of the way when I came too close. It was unreal, frightening. Less than thirty-six hours ago I'd been in a different country, busy losing my virginity in circumstances I couldn't quite remember, and here I was catapulted by the brutality of fate into this unmeasurable place, alone and terrified, waiting for Dana Feldman to return from Métis Beach — and she never returned to New York before Labour Day. I had two long weeks when I would have to find a way to survive, while hoping that Dana could save me from this nightmare.

What would they say about me in Métis Beach? How would my parents react? Anxiety rose in me as I thought back to Métis Beach's private policeman, Frank Brodie, who had appeared at our door, "Police!" *Police?* The soles of his shoes slapped on the kitchen linoleum, his voice more suspicious than usual, and far more excited. It was barely seven, my father was out already, and my mother had gotten up at dawn to begin preparing Sunday lunch.

"Romain?" she'd said, worried, "What did he do?" From my room, where I hadn't slept a wink, desperately replaying the film of the previous night's events — Gail, the butchered dog — I heard

Frank mention my name in that sombre voice he used only in the direst circumstances, "I want to ask him a few questions." Frank Brodie, asking me questions? Why? The damned dog, it was Louis!

"What do you want with him?" My mother was getting impatient, annoyed.

"Is he here?"

"No."

"Are you sure?" My mother was lying to him, but Brodie insisted. Insisting wasn't Brodie's style. After Clifford Wiggs' swans had been found dead, he had asked me about Louis' whereabouts once, and then left, satisfied.

Frank Brodie wasn't a particularly bright guy. We made fun of him in the French Village, but were forced to respect him. Fifty or so, he had a bald head like a turtle, and a very fat ass. He patrolled in his black Buick looking bored, turning a blind eye to the alcohol smuggling in Pointe-Leggatt, boats coming all the way from Saint-Pierre and Miquelon, dropping off their cargo in the middle of the day. It was hard to believe he was the representative of law and order in Métis Breach. He had no uniform, and no real power besides staying in contact with the provincial police to report whatever crimes he saw.

"What do you want with him?" My mother seemed caught off guard now.

And those words I heard, like a punch straight to the solar plexus, "They say your son raped a young woman in Métis Beach." *What did he say, exactly?* My mother's muffled cry followed by the sound of broken glass in the ceramic sink. Who had sent Brodie? Robert Egan? And why rape? Who had said anything about rape? Brodie went on, ignoring my mother, "I want to talk to him. I know he's here." My heart began pounding. Frank Brodie, not a particularly smart guy, but you needed to take him seriously, especially if he was making such a serious accusation. Panic-stricken, I searched for my clothes in the half-light, bumping against the furniture. Going through my drawers, looking for money, my papers.

"What … What are you saying?" And the soles slapping closer and closer to my room. Without thinking, I jumped through the window into the cold morning, my jacket in a ball and my shoes in my hand.

In the beginning I didn't sleep at all, spending my nights walking up and down the still-busy avenues, despite the late hour, sometimes mixing in with the joyous crowds that poured out of theatres, giving myself the illusion of security. I walked until I was exhausted, staggering like a drunk, my clothes dirty, my ankles full of flea bites, pestered by suspicious cops, their truncheons quickly out and ready to cut through the air, getting shouted at, "Get out of here!" each time I slowed down or stopped to contemplate a shopfront, a place of interest.

I tried resting in the lobbies of apartment buildings, where I was insulted and spat on. Parks were far too dangerous. Subway entrances always had cops too ready to stick their damn nightsticks in your sides. Then, one night, as I followed a guy who seemed as disoriented as I was, I discovered the night theatres of 42nd Street and their sinister fauna. For fifty cents, I could afford a few hours of poor sleep, while insipid double features, cowboy and adventure movies, played in a loop, until a guard pulled you out of your dreams with a smack of his stick and, on the second warning, threw you out without a refund.

For basic hygiene, I bought soap, a toothbrush, and tooth-paste at Duane Reade, and I carried my goodies around with me in a brown paper bag. By day, trying to keep my mind intact, I'd grab a newspaper out of a garbage can and find a restaurant where I'd order a cup of coffee and sit there, drinking it as slowly as possible. A waitress would sometimes take pity on me and slip me a piece of cake or a sandwich wrapped in paper that

I'd devour outside. Their slightly flirty smiles, their maternal benevolence warmed me.

I still remember that waitress who worked at a Broadway deli, a young woman, not particularly pretty, with full cheeks and dark brown hair, doe-eyed, whose face reddened whenever a customer tried to have a conversation with her. There was something attractive about her, perhaps her fragility, which reflected my own. The morning sun hadn't yet chased away the shadows of the Times Square buildings; the smell of bacon, fried eggs, and French toast made me drool, a real torture, but breakfast was too much of a luxury for me. She approached my table discreetly with a small box filled with butter rolls, which she placed in front of me, her index finger over her lips, "Don't say anything, or the boss will notice," and with that she continued her rounds. Heavy hips, slightly drooping breasts under her polyester uniform, and yet I began daydreaming about her, desire suddenly awakened in me by the attention she gave me. I burned with envy to follow her after work to an apartment I imagined was small, modest, but well cared for. Lace tablecloth, maybe flowers on the table. I'd take a shower, sleep with her, companionship. A momentary pang in my gut as I thought of the one thousand five hundred dollars I'd left with Joe Rousseau, money I saved working hard at the McArdle sawmill. With it, I could have paid for a hotel room for both of us, a luxurious room. I would have brought her out to eat in the finest restaurants, where we would have ordered the best, the most expensive items on the menu. I could tell she didn't look other customers in the eye when she poured them coffee. With me, it was different — she smiled, we exchanged a few words. She volunteered something about a picture in the newspaper I had in front of me, a baby with arms like fish fins, caused by medication doctors had prescribed to pregnant women. "It's horrible," she said, her eyes suddenly clouded. I would have taken her hand to reassure her, but what could I say? Then, not long after, she came back with a plateful of French toast that I ate rapaciously, another secret between us. I told myself that was it, I had won, I'd sleep with her tonight. And then, suddenly, a man's loud voice came from next to the cash register. She stiffened. Jennifer, she was called. An animated discussion between them and she disappeared into the kitchen. I understood. I got up, disappointed at not seeing her again, once more alone in this city I had dreamt of but which had turned out to be nothing at all like my dreams. Once again events forced my hand. *Your courage will come from the choices you can't make.* I could hear Captain Hogan's words from *The Buccaneers of the Red Sea* in my head like a cruel joke. My heart tight, I wandered the humid asphalt of Times Square, thinking of the two guys who'd picked me up as I was hitchhiking out of Mont-Joli, two guys madly in love with two Gaspé girls they'd met in Maria. They'd been far too busy talking with each other to take any interest in me. They didn't know my name, I didn't know theirs, but when they'd dropped me off at the Greyhound station in Montreal, I felt a lump in my throat as if I was saying goodbye to good friends.

The next morning, a thin, persistent rain was falling on Manhattan, and everywhere the bitter smell of tar. I was walking in Greenwich Village, looking for a place to hide without being bothered, when on 13th Street, I discovered a used bookstore with a friendly sign in the window:

FREE COFFEE FOR ALL CUSTOMERS

A labyrinth of dusty shelves and unsteady piles of books of all kinds — bestsellers with well-thumbed pages, reference books, poetry, essays by some of the eternally suspect — Mao, Marx, Rosa Luxemburg — as well as erotic books and, in the back, a small section, "Books in French," where I discovered *Le Deuxième Sexe, The Second Sex.*

"She's right, Simone. *Tous des salauds, les hommes.* All men are bastards."

I stiffened. A man's nasal voice, almost cartoonish. The same guy I'd seen behind the counter at the front of the store when I walked in, with a funny bird's head, piercing blue eyes, and a kind smile. He asked me in French whether I spoke the language. I hurriedly responded that I did, relieved to finally have a conversation with another human being. And he laughed, an open laughter that suited him. Here was this man, not at all put off by my dirty clothes, trying to impress me with the few words of French he knew and delivered at machine-gun speed, "*Bonjour, c'est la vie, la vie en rose....*" A terrible accent, enough to scare off a herd of cows. "*L'amour, l'amour, filles de joie, voulez-vous coucher avec moi?*" We both laughed at that, like boys in the playground at the end of a day. God, it felt so good!

Charlie Moses, with a mug like Bob Dylan's. Thin and nervous, he spoke with his hands. He was two years older than me, and dreamed of becoming a famous writer. In his desk drawer, he had a few half-written novels, but the books weren't quite *there* yet. He warmed to his subject — he was on the right path, he assured me, he was working on a "promising story." To pay the rent he worked part-time in this Greenwich Village bookstore, The New York City Lights Bookshop, a reference to the bookstore founded by Lawrence Ferlinghetti in San Francisco, cradle of the beat movement, which had produced, according to Charlie, the best American writers, including his favourite, Jack Kerouac. He stopped suddenly and asked, excited, "You're French Canadian?"

He barely waited for my answer, and disappeared into the back, then returned with a large blue atlas under his arm. He opened it, his hands shaking, on the page that showed Canada. "Come on, man!" he said, "Show me! Show me where you're from!"

Amused, I pointed at a minuscule dot on the map that he then contemplated with amazement.

"Oh!'"

"Oh, what?"

His eyes moved slightly west, a strange expression on his face. He said, with one finger on the map, "Rivière-du-Loup is right there."

He'd pronounced it *Revere due loop*.

"And?"

He slapped his hand on the table. "Oh man! Oh man! Oh man!"

"Oh man … what?"

He danced around me, slapping his hands on his thighs. "Oh man! You're like Ti-Jean!"

"Who?"

He put on a serious, grandiose air. "Jack Kerouac." His parents and grandparents came from Rivière-du-Loup and had settled in Lowell, Massachusetts, hoping for a better life in America.

"Just like you, man! We had to meet! It was written in the stars! Man, oh man, yes!"

Charlie invited me to share his small apartment in East Harlem, the Hispanic part of Harlem where, he told me with pride, Dean Moriarty had lived for a bit in *On the Road*. He lived in a dark, one-bedroom apartment, its wallpaper stained with moisture, no shower, only an old bathtub. Strangely enough, the bareness of the place didn't seem to affect him at all. In fact, it was the opposite, he seemed to savour it like a privilege. He was living like Kerouac's characters, and so he was convinced he was living a fabulous life, directing his own story, knowing in his heart that he would eventually move from spectator to protagonist.

Charlie Moses. I began calling him Moïse, in French. I can't remember why, but he absolutely loved it.

In the following days he showed me his city with obvious pride, as if he owned it all. Bringing me everywhere, to tourist attractions — the Empire State Building, Battery Park, the Statue of Liberty — and to more sordid ones — the creepy peep-show cabins on 42nd Street and the foul-smelling discharges of the Meatpacking District, where rangy dogs roamed, famished, drawn by the awful smell.

Indefatigable, he frenetically took notes in a dog-eared note-book for his new novel, a sort of *On the Road*, though limited to New York. "New York is a country in itself, a microcosm of future America." Full of nervous tics, Moïse told me that the action would take place in the city's neighbourhoods, with landscapes as beautiful as the snow-peaked mountains of Colorado, and as depressing as dead-end towns like Shelton, Nebraska. No cowboys or feather-capped Indians like in Cheyenne, Wyoming. Or *pachuco* Mexicans like in Fresno. No, none of that, but instead blacks, Puerto Ricans, Jews, Italians, Poles, Irishmen — the poor and the dumb and the full of cash. "New York!"

I watched him in ecstasy before the city he loved so much, feeling such gratitude at having crossed paths with such an amazing man.

On a sunny afternoon, he brought me over the Brooklyn Bridge on foot, cars and the blue waters of the East River flowing beneath us. Moïse wanted to show me the place he was born, "So you can understand what I mean, a bit more." A sad, derelict building, four stories high, in the shadow of the rusting Williamsburg Bridge. Before the bohemian lifestyle he treated himself to in East Harlem, Moïse had been truly poor, the sort of poverty you can't choose. Broke parents who couldn't pay the bills. A sinister apartment, a single room without a bathroom or a bathtub — those were shared, at the end of the hallway — just an old sink with rusty enamel to wash in, robbing you of all privacy. Moïse said, his face drawn, "I was diseased at birth, stricken with a hereditary ill that only the most vital men are able to shake off. I mean poverty — the most deadly and prevalent of all diseases."

He laughed at my bemused air. "Hey, man! Don't look at me like that! I didn't come up with the phrase. That's Eugene O'Neill, the great American playwright. You know him?" I shook my head. "It doesn't matter." He gave me a friendly slap on the back and urged me to the side of the building where he extended his arms, ready to give me a leg up.

"You really want to go up there?"

"I've done it a thousand times."

We pulled ourselves up the fire escape and climbed to the roof. There, Manhattan and its horizon thorny with skyscrapers took my breath away. Lost in thought, Moïse said, "I used to come up here often. I could spend hours here. When you're small and you live in a shitty place and your parents work as hard as possible but still can't make it, and from your own home, from your rotten neighbourhood, you see this, well, you tell yourself, one day, I'll be there." He took in the view. "Look how beautiful it is. Beautiful and terrible. Terrible because it always reminds you how shitty your life is. I came to understand I should never be melancholy about the city. No, I needed the view to inspire me to better things. And that's what it did."

After that, we stayed silent for a while. We could see, in the distance, the top of the Chrysler Building shining in the sun, reminding me of the lighthouse near Métis Beach, where Gail had kissed me for the first time with a desperate energy and something fearful in her eyes.

And this unbelievable story of rape that Frank Brodie seemed to believe entirely. I'd been duped, betrayed.

I felt so far from all of it now that I wasn't sure whether my memories were real or not, whether my past actually existed. Unless my present was the lie — this overwhelming view of Manhattan, the shimmering waters of the East River, sparkling white boats sailing on it, and my new friend Moïse fidgeting next to me. Past and present seemed impossible to reconcile, as if they were two troubling, distinct dreams, dreamt by two different people.

"Hey, man, you okay?"

I staggered, and felt myself growing weak. Lack of sleep and food was getting to me, despite the fact that Moïse had been seeing to my diet like a loving mother — beans, canned spaghetti and stew, its slightly nauseating odour mixed in with the acrid smell of his old gas stove in his seedy East Harlem apartment. I felt like puking.

He caught me by the arm, sat me down on the warm tar roof. "Hey, take it easy, man. Take your time." My eyes filled with water. I began speaking, my throat tight with emotion, of Métis Beach, the village, the cordial relationship, tainted with suspicion, between the English and the French, those summers spent watching the English, envying them. I talked. Talked and talked and the words came to me easily, a constant flow, punctuated with childish sobs: "You see, back home, it's not like here, there's no river separating us, but the border is much more difficult to cross than the East River. I could have never dreamed of saying what you did — one day I'll be there. Just impossible. You're born to a station, and you stay there. That's the way it is in the world I come from. What you're saying, the beautiful and terrible image, it doesn't exist. Or maybe it does, I don't know, but if it does I couldn't bring my eyes to look at it out of fear of being burned...."

Moïse listened to me carefully, his brow furrowed, welcoming my words with small nods. God, it felt good to speak! Without feeling judged. When emotion stopped me, he put his arm around my shoulder, without asking any questions. Moïse still didn't know my whole story; he'd deduced I'd left home like a thousand other boys my age after some violent argument with my parents, and he believed I was waiting for a friend to get back to New York to stay with her until the dust settled. It was what he thought, and I hadn't said anything to make him believe otherwise.

"Come on! There's more to see! You'll be okay?"

We took the subway on Marcy Avenue. The whole way back Moïse didn't stop talking, his hands cutting through the air — his novel would make him rich, finally, and with the money he could stop writing by hand and buy a typewriter, and all of the girls in New York city would fall for him. It would all happen when he became famous. He chatted away, grimacing like a monkey, trying to keep me distracted. "Hey, man, we're in New York! Forget the rest, okay?" And I laughed. He was a ball of energy, Moïse.

My friend Moïse.

Back in Manhattan, we got out at 125th Street and Lenox Avenue, in the middle of Harlem. A total shock to me.

"You think your borders can't be crossed, but wait and see, you might think they're not so bad after all."

He dragged me into a dense crowd, only blacks, most dressed in their Sunday best, walking under a heavy sun, skirting itinerant salesmen selling their goods from blankets on the sidewalk. Books, clothes, kitchenware, radios. Fat women, bunches of kids around their skirts, bartering loudly. A teeming crowd, supervised by heavily armed white policemen as well as images of Martin Luther King and Malcom X stuck to every wall and lamppost.

"Not bad, eh?" Moïse said into my ear.

I looked all around me, read a few titles of the books on the ground, *The God Damn White Man* jumped out at me. Piles of pamphlets distributed on the corner of practically every street. And newspapers as well, "black" newspapers, like *Muhammad Speaks* handed out by young men dressed in suits and ties, members of the Nation of Islam.

Moïse turned towards me, "You've heard of it?"

I shook my head, perplexed. He laughed, and began dragging me along, all the while rattling off his story, "Islam comes from far way. It has no roots in America. That's why it's so attractive to them." He stopped to wipe his eyes filled with fine grey dust that the wind had raised off the dirty streets of Harlem. "Christianity allowed slavery. Christianity determined they didn't have souls. So they invented a religion."

"What does it say?"

"That blacks are the original humans. From which us, the whites, the Asians, and the Indians, all descended. We are inferior races. Wonderful, no?" He laughed. "They say the black man is the begetter of all men. They believe that the place they occupied in the beginning will be returned to them one day." Before my stupefied expression, he chortled, then said more seriously, "God is an invention of man. Humans decide what God thinks of them. Do you understand? So I say that God is watching us from up there, at this very moment, and he's having a good laugh. And by the way, he also says welcome to New York!" And we laughed out loud under the Harlem sun.

Moïse dragged me far from the chaos of 125th Street into a cross street, lined with dilapidated brownstones, windows covered with old sheets. The dust here made us blink, filled our nostrils, and irritated our throats. On the sidewalks, mountains of trash. From time to time we saw a rat scuttling off, as large as a cat.

"Come on!"

We were walking north. Tall, sinister-looking types gave us sideways glances, but Moïse didn't even look at them. He seemed to know where he was headed.

We ended up somewhere on West 129th Street, in front of a door that opened onto a grimy apartment, dark and humid. Moïse looked me over: "You're going to be okay, man? You think you can do this?"

"Yes."

"You sure?"

"Yes."

He smiled, as if to say, *what you're about to see will be with you for the rest of your life.*

In the single room with cracked walls, there was a woman. A young black woman, no more than twenty-five, her eyes sad. Thin and not particularly pretty. Henrietta was her name. A name that carried a singularly joyous rhythm to it, far too happy for the desperate woman before us. She waved in our general direction.

Around her, on the dirty floor, four young children, all her own, slept or crawled on their fat little legs. Henrietta sat, a newborn in her arm, sucking at her breast without much energy. A stink of sour milk and dirty diapers permeated the air, and I felt like I was about to throw up. "Hey, man! You gonna make it?" I nodded, ashamed at being so weak.

Henrietta. Moïse seemed to know her, but from where? He brought a chair over and sat down, placing his notepad and a pen on a sticky table next to him. One of the children caught his ankle. Moïse smiled and picked him up and put him on his knee. The child began laughing, babbling. I stayed separate, attentive, seated on a broken couch. Moïse spoke softly, his head near the young woman. She answered his questions nonchalantly. How was she pulling through? Where was her husband? He left when the youngest was born, no news since. She sighed, plaintive. "Niggers don't make good fathers." *Niggers?* Hadn't Moïse said that blacks hated the word, which was tied to slavery? He didn't seem to notice, continued his interview — did she have family in Harlem? How did she see her children's future? She stiffened at that, "The future?" Moïse could have damned God and she wouldn't have reacted so strongly. "The future is for no one!" she cried, offended. "The future is in God's hands and God's alone."

Moïse smiled. With compassion. He grabbed his pen and scribbled down a few notes on his pad. She observed him, offended or amused, it was hard to say. She moved her hand towards him on the dirty table, as if she wanted him to understand that she didn't want him writing about her. But Moïse persevered, asking other questions, always in that same low, calming voice. Then one of the children began crying, and the young woman got up, the newborn in her arms, its small head hanging limply. She told Moïse it was time to go. Moïse got up, taking the boy he had on his knee in his arms, a small boy, two years old perhaps, who looked at my friend intently. How did he know this woman, for God's sake? Where had he met her?

He asked her whether she could let him stay for a few days. She stared at him with large dark eyes as if he was insane, then glanced at me suspiciously, hoping for reassurance. I shrugged, not knowing what to say. "Henrietta, it's for the novel," Moïse reminded her. *Henrietta?* It was said so … intimately. "The novel

I told you about." She pouted. "I'll pay, of course." And Moïse pulled ten one-dollar bills from his pocket and gave them to her, a fortune for him. The woman contemplated them with her wretched eyes, as if she'd never seen money before. She rolled the bills in her dirty fingers and placed them in her bra, clearly grateful. Then she intoned in a deep drawl, "Gad bless ya. Gad bless America. In Gad we trust."

Outside, as we walked in silence along 129th Street, Moïse turned angry, "Goddamned country! She can't even read, d'you know that? But she knows what's written on a goddamn dollar bill! In God we trust. She could die in her own filth, and America wouldn't give a shit. Her civil rights were taken from her, America doesn't give a shit. But, to her, it's like that betrayal doesn't even exist. She's proud of her country! Because it...." He choked on his anger. "Because it believes in God and prints it on its goddamn dollar bills! In God We Trust. Fuck! That's Eisenhower's strategy to taunt the Communists and get on McCarthy's good side. Capitalist Christian America vs. Atheist Soviet Union! Goddamn this country concocted from God and money! There are still slaves here, for crying out loud!" He kicked a pile of trash, and we heard a tin can rolling down the street. "Fuck!"

That strangely fabulous day in August 1962 would remain carved in my memory forever.

2

The day after Labour Day, I got Dana on the phone. After having tried the number a few times over the course of the previous days — Moïse had found her number in the phone book — and brief, polite exchanges with a person with a strong accent — the maid, according to him — to whom I'd refused to give my name, I finally got Dana on the line. My throat tightened, tears in my eyes.

"Where are you?" She sounded furious, her voice as brittle as glass. A half-hour later I was in Harperley Hall, an Art Nouveau building on Central Park West. The door opened on a small woman with pale eyes, mute with astonishment, with Dana appearing behind her, red pants and white blouse, her face drawn by two long days on the road. "What the hell got into you? Everyone's been looking for you for two weeks!"

"Dana, let me explain...."

But she wasn't listening. She dragged me roughly into the living room, a large space decorated like a museum, great paintings on the walls. She poured herself a vodka, then poured a second one for me without asking whether I wanted it, and pushed it into my hands.

"Have you looked at yourself in a mirror? What have you been doing for the past two weeks? Have you been sleeping in the streets?"

My voice trembled, barely audible now, "I...."

"Is it true, then? What they're saying?"

"No!"

I told her about Frank Brodie, what he had said to my mother, defending myself.

She looked at me, concerned, "What *did* you do?"

"I slept with Gail." She took her head in her hands. "Dana, I swear, I have no idea why Brodie said I raped her."

She said nothing. My breath quickened. My legs were like rubber, I thought of the provincial police agents Brodie had alerted, their thick fists pounding on every door in the village, looking for me. No, Dana said. Nothing like that. Only rumours. The Newells said something about rape, but no one knew whether it was true. The Egans had disappeared like thieves in the night.

"Do you believe me, Dana?"

She didn't answer. Instead, she got up from her seat and began pacing.

"Why did you run away, then?"

The question surprised me. It was clear we came from different worlds. "What choice did I have? Do you really think Robert Egan cares whether I slept with Gail or...."

"He sent Brodie?"

"I don't know."

"And why do you think he did it?"

"I don't know."

Dana struggled to remain calm. She grabbed her pack of Kools off the coffee table, sprung one out of the pack, lit it, blew smoke with exasperation. That untenable silence between us! When the smoke cleared, a discouraged expression on her face — or was it concern? "What's important is that you're safe. That nothing bad happened to you."

On the night Gail and I were together — it seemed so long ago now — Riddington appeared at the Tees' place still in his bathrobe, in a state of panic. Dana hadn't actually seen it, she'd gone home by then. Something had happened to Gail and the dog. Everyone mentioned the dog. "I went to your mother's store, but it was closed.

Didn't open once before I left. I couldn't talk with her or your father. I even rang at the door, but didn't get an answer. The drapes were drawn day and night. But I knew your parents were there. Françoise told me. They're worried sick. Françoise is too. You should have heard her over the phone, she couldn't stop crying."

I kept silent, trying to think, my chest tight. The shock my mother must have felt when she opened the door on an empty room, my window open, the drapes floating in the wind. "My parents, they … do they believe….?"

She shrugged. "I don't know. I can't say." She rubbed her forehead. "What a crazy story."

She poured herself another vodka and asked me whether I was hungry. Rosie, a matronly Irish woman, prepared a plate of cold roast beef and placed it in front of me. I devoured it in minutes as Dana looked on tenderly. As soon as I finished, her face hardened, "You can't stay in New York."

I felt my head spinning again. "Why?"

"Have you thought about your parents? What are you going to do here?"

"You don't understand. If I go back, Robert Egan is going to have me arrested."

"I'll talk to that imbecile."

"No, please! I don't want to go home! Now that I'm here, give me *my opportunity*."

"Your 'opportunity?'"

"Dana, please, I could make a life here. If you just agree to help me a little."

It was late, past midnight. Rosie gathered up my empty dishes. Dana covered a yawn. "We'll talk about it tomorrow. Meanwhile, Rosie, show him his room. There's a bathrobe on the bed. And draw him a bath. It certainly won't hurt him."

The next morning, I found Dana in the kitchen, seated before a bowl of fruit and a cup of black coffee, already dressed, her hair done, made up, with Rosie reading an old copy of the *Irish Times*. She didn't look any more welcoming than the night before, which only increased my apprehension. Before she opened her mouth, I said very quickly, "If you don't want me here, kick me out. I'll figure it out. But I'm staying in New York; I've made my decision." She looked at me, astonished, "Who said anything about kicking you out?" She turned to Rosie. "Did I say that?" Rosie shook her head, unequivocal.

I stared at them.

"Well now," Dana said. "You see? Don't just stand there look- ing at me like that. You've got a big day ahead of you. First you're going to call your mother, she must be worried sick. Then, you'll put on those clothes, if we can call them that." She waved her hand in the direction of my clothes that Rosie had washed, dis- infected, and folded, and now waited for me in a basket on the counter. "Then we'll go out and find some real clothes for you. Now that you're in New York, we'll make a man out of you, a real one, refined and cultivated."

Next to her, Rosie smiled, flashing a mouthful of rotten teeth.

3

"Look at your reflection, Romain. Know that it marks the beginning of your new life."

Dana was laughing, amused by the gruelling game we were playing. An army of salespeople were at our service at Brooks Brothers on Madison Avenue. I was trying to go through the ever increasing pile of clothes in my change room. Shirts of all colours, sports pants, polos, stylish suits, and more, including the one suit I currently had on my back, which made Dana chuckle with pleasure, "Handsome man!" Polite, the salespeople approved with half-smiles as Dana exclaimed her pleasure or displeasure, circling me, examining me head to foot, cradling her elbow in her hand, her finger touching her lips. "Never forget, Romain, Americans believe in *new beginnings.*" Happy words to me. A suit of fine wool, perfectly cut, white shirt, silk tie. I admired my reflection, surprised and enchanted by what I was seeing — a tall, thin, yet elegant boy, hollow cheeks with prominent cheekbones, brown eyes shining with optimism. My future was before me.

I didn't dare ask my mother to close my account with Joe Rousseau and send me the one thousand five hundred dollars. I wanted to save her the trouble — it was hard enough for her as it was. It was easy to imagine that she was watched every time she left home, she and my father both. A boy who abandoned his parents, a sordid story of rape about which no one knew the whole truth but that was told and retold anyway. If he fled like that, for sure he had something to hide. On the phone, my mother was inconsolable, but, at least, she hadn't believed Brodie, and each time we spoke, she would insist, imploring, "You'll come back and explain everything?" *Explain what, Mom?* The truth might kill her as much as the lie.

I called her every week when my father wasn't there. If he was, I heard the front door slam the second my mother pronounced my name. One time he picked up the phone. His large calloused hands grabbing the receiver, and his malicious voice, ferocious, "Your goddamn face, you son of bitch, I don't wanna see it, am I clear enough?" A knife to the heart. Not that it was a surprise coming from my father, but hurtful anyway. My mother informed me he'd lost his contracts — first Robert Egan, then the others, and no one gave him the real reason, because no one knew the whole truth.

"Mom, I have a chance in New York. Dana is helping me. I'm going to school."

"Going to school" might have been an exaggeration, though not by much. Dana had organized private English and art history courses so I could take advantage of New York's museums and understand what I was seeing. What incredible museums they were! The Metropolitan, the Museum of Modern Art, and the impressive Guggenheim, like a ship's hull, a staircase like a propeller that you climbed down slowly, finally reaching street level. "A new museum experience," my teacher had told me, excited. Darren Hunter was thirty or so, with an old patched tweed jacket on his back, messy blond hair, a deep soft voice, and penetrating blue eyes. Together, we walked through the museum's rooms, while he spoke of the various painters' works — Picasso, Braque, Poussin,

Delacroix. Every week, we met up at his place in Morningside Heights, near Columbia University, a small apartment fitted out with a projection room; sometimes there were two or three of us watching his colour slides, the masters' works appeared and disappeared on the walls like luminescent heartbeats. Caravaggio's dramatic theatre of shadows and light, Rembrandt's humanity-filled portraits. I was amazed that the hand of man could so perfectly reproduce the miracle of love in the lustre of an eye.

I liked Darren a lot. He taught me new, surprising things, always respecting the limits of my understanding. He was one of Dana's old friends, and often he invited us to eat at his place on Claremont Avenue, the projection room transformed into a dining room. Happy meals, with no one to make me feel like I was seventeen; the pleasure of being treated like an adult by Dana, her sister Ethel, and their friends was certainly the best way to help me gain confidence in my budding maturity.

When you're expected to be a man, you don't want to disappoint.

One day, in front of a portrait of Genghis Khan at the Met, Darren said, "At fifteen, he was already an infamous warrior, respected. Never underestimate the young." That night, he gave me the honour of being seated next to him, signalling that my conversation was as interesting as anyone else's. He sat at the end of the table, I was to his left, Dana to his right. An older couple was also present. The man was a professor at Columbia — as was Darren — and his wife painted, just like Ethel. I remember noticing Darren watching Dana closely that evening. In the taxi ride back to Harperley Hall, I asked Dana:

"Darren and you...."

"*What*, exactly, Darren and me?"

"You were never ... together?"

"Never! He told you that?"

"No! I just thought that...."

"Don't put your nose where it doesn't belong, young man...."

She glowered, her face turned towards the window. I couldn't decide whether she was angry or upset. If I'd been a woman, I think Darren would have been the sort of man to attract me. But Dana didn't seem to want a man in her life.

With my English teacher, things were different. Ian Dart was a university friend of Ethel's, a young man with thick glasses and fine, bony hands, naturally kind, perhaps a little shy. He came three times a week to Harperley Hall, coached me through my lessons, gave me texts to analyze and essays to write. Most of the time I was free to choose my own topics, except when he decided I should become more interested in a particular subject — current events, more often than not. He taught me about America's domestic issues. I remember well how interested I was in racial integration — the first black student admitted to the University of Mississippi, his admission forced by John Kennedy. Of course, I was fascinated by JFK's promise to send a man to the moon before the end of the decade. I bore down, filled with wonder, telling myself that everything was possible in this country. Yes, everything was possible.

At Harperley Hall, I occupied the guest room, which used to be Mark's room, Dana's son. I vaguely remembered having seen him once or twice at the clubhouse in Métis Beach. He'd been Geoff Tees' age, with black hair and suspicious dark eyes. After his father's death, he stopped accompanying his mother during the summer, preferring to spend his vacations in New York with his grandparents. A strange child, Dana said. He was a homebody. Now he lived in London, and their relationship was stormy at best. Mark was what you might call a fundamentalist Jew whose conversion had been a trial for Dana. She very rarely spoke of it.

My presence at Harperley Hall might have been filling a gap. Dana seemed eager to take care of me like a son, generously paying for everything, from my courses and clothing to my nights out. I was ready to work, but she refused — the important thing was to concentrate on my studies. We'd take care of the work permit some other time. Once she finally got Robert Egan on the line, he'd been so furious he answered none of her questions. "Real accusations, Robert?"

He shouted, "If ever he sets foot back here, I'll have him arrested!" Then he threatened to go after her as well for aiding and abetting. Dana hung up, visibly shaken. "We're in no hurry, Romain. Let's clear things up before we get you your papers. Don't worry about it. I've got great lawyers, the best in New York. We won't be intimated by that bastard."

All I wanted was to believe her. I'd never been so happy in my life.

4

That thunderous character, the *chutzpah* and corrosive repartee, dark eyes that glimmered with thought, and something of Ava Gardner in the shape of her face.

In the pictures she showed me of herself as a girl of eight or nine, Dana Feldman already possessed that shadow of arrogance in her eyes, the arrogance of those who know they'll accomplish great things. I liked it when she flipped through her yellowing photo albums, commenting on the pictures with nostalgia, a glass of something in her hand, always surprised by the distance of memories. Photos of Ethel and her in their family home in Queens, a modest Jewish home — her mother managed a charity, and her father gave private violin lessons. Dana had lacked for nothing, though her parents knew that the environment they offered her — the best schools, opera tickets, diction classes — would end up making her world too narrow. The sisters took me on a visit to the rather dreary neighborhood they grew up in much later, moved to tears by the memories that came to them. They'd been concerned by the growing deterioration since their parents had died — black families had replaced Jewish families who'd themselves moved to more pleasant districts over time — repeating breathlessly, as if to console themselves, that things must have been better back then. The park where the Feldman family liked to picnic on warm summer days had been disfigured when the city cut down all the sick elms, including those on the sidewalk in front of her old home. Their bare stumps were still there. In her old photographs you could still see the stately trees throwing long shadows on the tiny, scrupulously maintained Feldman lawn.

She showed me pictures of her at nineteen and twenty, with her classmates from the class of 1943 at Barnard College. She studied literature, and you couldn't miss her — Dana posing proudly, chin raised, God, she was beautiful, it would be impossible to be modest when you looked like that. She would say, with indulgent gaiety, "The other girls thought I was a real snob, but I didn't care." Even back then she was sure her writing would make a mark. She wouldn't follow the path of the jealous and ambitionless girls who welcomed the self-constructed prison of the housewife, withering like houseplants without sunlight or rain. No, not she, "What can I say, Romain? I was far too serious for my age. And pretentious." She laughed.

Among the other girls, there were pretty ones, but none as pretty as she, and I began looking for those who might have accepted the affront of her beauty and her friendship without succumbing to jealousy. I asked, curious, "Did you have any friends?" She pointed to a tall blond girl with pale eyes and a straight jaw. "Nora Toohey." And saying her name out loud, Dana burst into stories, telling how they both loved to go out and listen to the new style of music that was all the rage in the forties — bebop jazz — music for the war years in Europe, though before the humiliation of Pearl Harbor, before America intervened. It was rapid fire, dissonant, subversive, it transgressed the borders of the predictable, it made her shiver all over, sending her into a trance. Sometimes we listened to some of her old records at Harperley Hall, eyes closed, one foot tapping out the beat — Dizzy Gillespie, Charlie Parker, Thelonious Monk. Magicians of improvisation she saw play every Monday night with her friend Nora at Minton's Playhouse, in Harlem.

"I saw Monk once with Nora at Minton's. John McPhail was there. Do you remember him from Métis Beach?"

No, I was too young, I never knew the man. I expected her to show me pictures of him but instead her face darkened. She shut the album abruptly, as if its contents had suddenly become unbearable.

She'd noticed him, sitting alone at a table in the back of Minton's narrow smoke-filled room. A hint of sadness about him, deep, intense eyes, his head and body moving, letting themselves be moved by Thelonious Monk's disconcerting music. He was the only white man in the room that night, but wasn't aware of it. A young white man with the air of an aristocrat, she saw it in the way he picked up his glass of Crown Royal and brought it to his lips.

"Class, Romain, like I'd never seen."

In the living room at Harperley Hall, she moved to the teak bookcase filled with an impressive collection of albums. "I had to speak with him. As if there was, that night, an opportunity I couldn't miss," she laughed. "I was such an idiot."

She got up from her table, and Nora grabbed her wrists, asking her what she was doing. Thelonious Monk had just begun one of his long silences on the piano, stilling the crowd at Minton's Playhouse. "I was wearing a little red jersey dress, rather becoming. Everyone looked at me and tried to see under it."

She took a record out of its sleeve, placed it on the turntable. "*Epistrophy*, Monk. The piece he was playing that night." She grabbed a Menthol Kool, Monk's music filling the living room. She stood, her eyes closed. "Monk. The fabulous Monk. He still hadn't moved, his hands suspended over the keyboard; the whole room held its breath. No one knew what he was going to do." Apparently, Monk sometimes stopped playing right in the middle of a piece, he'd get up, start dancing or running around his piano, disappear from stage, return, laughing, and continue his piece where he'd left it, with more energy and insanity than before, making the whole crowd go crazy. She continued, still enthralled, "And there he was, sitting, back bent, legs apart, hands hanging in empty space. Then, a victorious smile appeared on his sweaty face, as if he'd just found his way, and he began playing again, kneading every note with his stiff fingers, feverish. And the room went wild."

She stopped speaking, pensive.

"And then?" I asked.

"I took advantage of the applause to make my way between the tables towards John."

Her smile returned and she began speaking gaily again. After having called a taxi for Nora, she and John walked around Harlem, letting themselves be guided by the notes that escaped from behind the closed doors of jazz clubs. Perhaps they were making a show of their courage, demonstrating to each other that they weren't afraid, they were different from the rest, which meant they shared something. After all, whites walking in Harlem at night were a rare sight. John was happy, savouring the autonomy he had won for himself that night, after having freed himself from his father, with the pretext that he was beginning a cold.

She took a drag of her cigarette, poured herself a cognac. "I asked him if his father would be angry when he realized he wasn't in his hotel room. He answered, 'My father stays at the Waldorf; I stay at the Algonquin.' I was surprised, of course. His father loved the Waldorf's ostentation, while he was depressed by it. He preferred the Algonquin, and the impression of being surrounded by the ghosts of all the writers who met there for lunch in the twenties. That's when I told him that I wrote, and his beautiful face lit up. Of course he asked what I wrote about. I was sure I was going to disappoint him, 'No, not novels. I write about women,' I said. 'But publishers aren't ready to take the risk.' He said, 'What risk?' as if he didn't live in the same time and place as I, and hadn't seen the problem! I wanted to kiss him. I said, 'Publishing a critique of a society they themselves endeavour to defend, can you imagine? Publishers are afraid. Timid.' I didn't know why, but I was uncomfortable talking to him about it. I was curious to know more about these separate hotels."

Sudden, violent emotion took possession of her. Seeing her so vulnerable, an incredible desire to hold her filled me, followed by a sort of panic when I thought of Darren, his eyes blind to everything but her that night, fear at the idea that I too would fall under her spell. I chased the idea away by going to grab a beer in the kitchen. Except for a few lamps in the living room, the apartment was dark. Rosie had gone to bed a long time ago.

"So what was the story behind the two hotels?"

She blew her nose. Monk played, accompanied by Kenny Clarke.

"John said that it allowed him to skip out on his duties without having to face the consequences. And go out to jazz clubs that his father called, without a trace of irony, Sodom and Gomorrah." She giggled. "His father suspected nothing. The idea of separate hotels had been sold to him a long time ago. John and his father owned a large steel company in Canada. The Canadian government depended on them for the war effort. Each in his own hotel meant there was no risk — her voice cracked — no chance of both of them dying if there was a fire. It was the same for airplanes. Never both on the same flight. It was their rule."

She was crying now. I didn't know how to console her.

Each time Dana spoke of John, she needed at least two days to get back on her feet. She would seek refuge in her room, blinds drawn, knocking herself out with sleeping pills. Worried, Rosie tapped at her door every two or three hours, walked softly, placed plates of food on the bedside table, taking back the previous plates, still full. Sometimes I'd look after Dana, sit next to her, hold her hand. She'd wake up, groggy, looking at me with wet eyes, her diction made soft by the sedatives: "He hasn't felt a thing in a long time, while I'll be in pain for the rest of my life."

I was eleven when John McPhail died. I had no memories of him, but I could picture the front page articles: RICH INDUSTRIALIST, JOHN McPHAIL, DIES IN PLANE CRASH — MÉTIS BEACH IN MOURNING, THE SMALL COMMUNITY LOSES ONE OF ITS MOST ILLUSTRIOUS MEMBERS. The same blurry picture accompanied every article, a charred mass in the shape of a cross in the snow. Someone had died, burned alive. Someone who spent his summers in Métis Beach. That made quite the impression on me. As usual, father and son were travelling separately, and the son drew the short straw. His small Beechcraft crashed in a snow-covered field in Ontario as he was making his way to the opening of a new factory owned by McPhail Steel Co. This was in 1956. John was thirty-five. The next morning, crushed, Dana had flown to New York, fleeing her responsibilities and abandoning her twelve-year-old son Mark to John's parents. "Take care of him. I haven't the strength." For weeks, she hid in the large apartment in Harperley Hall, the one they had bought together a few years before, when John realized Dana wasn't happy in Montreal. And yet, after their wedding, in 1943, she had had no hesitations about following him to Canada, with war in Europe, fear all around, and the uncertain future making the material world secondary. Dana wanted to be with John, that's all that mattered. But life in Montreal ended up weighing on her.

After her husband's death, Dana wrote frenetically to drive away grief. To drive away the hateful feeling that had grown in her in Montreal — though she had no awareness of it yet; she was suffering too deeply to begin analyzing herself. But later she saw it, that feeling of having lied to the little girl she'd been, the promise she had made. She wanted to make up for lost time, and those long hours spent stooped over her Underwood paid off — *Mademoiselle, Harper's Bazaar*, and *The Hudson Review* published her short stories, all starring desperate women seeking emancipation. Her characters succeeded, though at great cost.

Her story "The Broken Vending Woman" was condemned and acclaimed in equal parts. The story of a woman, Karen, whom Dana compared to a vending machine. You slipped bills into a slot (get the picture?) in exchange for services — a warm meal when you got home after work, child-rearing, meticulously done housework, smiles, cheerfulness, tenderness, sexual relations. Exhausted, Karen cracks. How do you react when a vending machine doesn't work? You shake it; in a rage, you hit it. The seeds of her sensational book *The Next War* had been sown.

5

"Can you tell me what you find so interesting about your friend Moïse? He drinks and lives like a hobo."

A hobo! Hurtful, unjust words! Dana didn't trust him. She disapproved of the power he had over me. "Can't you see he tries to attract attention with his stories of being some sort of wretch? A dirty home, a job that pays nothing. No one with any sense brags about living a life of poverty."

Moïse. As if she were saying: *you don't know how to choose your friends.* Dana could go to hell. Anyway, *The Next War* was taking up all of her attention; she couldn't control my comings and goings.

In our free time, Moïse and I continued our tours of New York — Chinatown, Turtle Bay, the Bronx, all the way to the Lincoln Tunnel, which we walked through, our windbreakers tied around our ears, looking like the Arabs Kerouac mentions in *On the Road* — coming in to blow up New York. We hung out in front of the Chelsea Hotel like groupies, in hopes of seeing Jack Kerouac ("that's where he wrote *On the Road* — *in only three weeks, man!*"), but as Moïse said, we'd have been happy with Allen Ginsberg — Carlo Marx in *On the Road* — or even William Burroughs — Old Bull Lee in the novel — or even, if we had to, a distraught

Arthur Miller (in room 614, the playwright had cried over Marilyn Monroe after their separation).

In the evenings, we hung out at the Gaslight Café in Greenwich Village, where a young singer with an astonishing voice amazed us. "Oh, man!" Moïse exclaimed, tears of joy running down his cheeks. "This guy is just amazing!" Moïse watched him as if he was admiring himself in a mirror. Bob Dylan and Charlie Moses, they were almost twins — the same bird head with soft, tangled hair, piercing eyes of an unreal steel blue, a narrow nose slightly bent at the end over a small sad mouth. "The Doppelganger," Moïse was called at the Gaslight. He dressed like his idol Dylan, wore his hair the same way, studied his movements on stage, trying to imitate them when he walked through Greenwich Village. When girls or guys stopped him on the sidewalk, he laughed as he entertained the confusion, just enough time to see in their eyes an admiration he imagined he himself would inspire one day, when he'd be a famous writer. "I've got to train, man. I've got to learn to be up to it."

Dana locked herself in her office early in the morning and did not emerge until late at night — endless days spent writing and calling her sister Ethel, begging her to come support her in her moments of anxiety. It was a demanding writing schedule, which she had forced on herself after a catastrophic visit from her publisher, one rainy morning in November 1962.

His name was Burke Cole. An affected little man in a three-piece suit from another time, glasses slipping down his nose.

He'd run, the poor man, and couldn't seem to catch his breath.

"My God, Burke!" Dana cried. "What's happened to you? Rosie, take his coat and hat. And bring him water. Water's fine, Burke? Or would you like something stronger."

"Water … Water will be fine."

Dana became nervous suddenly. A bad feeling. In the living room, she poured herself a large glass of vodka and lit a cigarette, her hands trembling.

"What's going on, Burke? You don't want to publish me any-more, is that it?"

Burke shook his head, swallowing his water, his wrinkled neck shivering at every mouthful.

"So why are you here?"

He took a deep breath and announced that a certain Betty Friedan was about to publish a feminist book that was going to cause a stir.

Dana blanched. "You think I don't have what it takes, is that it?"

Once again, Burke shook his head and put on an apologetic air, "We need to advance the publication date for *The Next War*. To avoid Friedan getting all the attention. We need to publish at the same time, or a few days apart."

Dana wasn't sure she had heard correctly, or understood. She said nothing.

"Dana, do you understand me?"

"What are you trying to say?"

"You've got three months."

"Impossible! I'll never be ready!"

"We don't have a choice, Dana."

"We! We! How dare you speak of *we*! We're not talking about you, but *me*! And I'm telling you I'll never make it!"

Burke got up, embarrassed. "I'm sorry, Dana. But I know you. I know you're up to the task."

Betty Friedan published *The Feminine Mystique* in February 1963. Two days before it came out, I found Dana in a state of panic at Harperley Hall, her sister Ethel with her, trying to calm her down. On the living room table, a book Burke had delivered to her, wrapped in hastily torn brown paper. Dana was gesticulating, circling the table, casting angry glances in the book's direction, a fierce beast before her prey, resolved not to let it off easy.

"Everything I wrote in *The Next War* is in here!"

"No!" Ethel said. "You approach the topic completely differently."

"Differently? Are you kidding me? Her approach is far better than mine! A thousand times better!"

"Oh, Dana. Please!"

Dana grabbed the book, opened it, whipped through the pages. "Have you seen this? It reads like a novel! Nobody will be interested in *The Next War* after this!"

"Calm down, will you? My God, it isn't the end of the world. You know very well that you have a more personal approach. This one is more … methodical. More scientific."

"More rigorous, you mean!"

"Of course not! All it means is that feminism is part of the conversation now. That's what's important. And you need a plurality of voices for progress. If there are a dozen women like Betty Friedan, Simone de Beauvoir and you, Dana Feldman, on the case, so much the better! The revolution will only come quicker!"

But Dana wasn't listening. She was pacing, furious, her eyes blurred with tears.

"Did you read her passage on Freud and his ridiculous theory of penis envy, how she eviscerates him? Genius! Relentless!" She grabbed her glasses, put them on. "Listen! Listen to this, 'The fact is that to Freud, even more than to the magazine editor on Madison Avenue today, women were a strange, inferior, less-than-human species." Do you follow me, Ethel? No, you don't. Listen, listen, I'm telling you, 'But when he dismissed women's yearning for equality as "penis envy," was he not merely stating his own view that women could never really be men's equal, any more than she could wear his penis?'" She slammed the book shut, throwing it on the table. "Tell me how can I publish after this? Tell me, Ethel!"

Dana was about to storm out of the room when she saw me in the doorway.

"What the hell are you doing here?"

"Uh … I think I'm going to go…."

"Not a chance!" She turned to Ethel. "Give him the book!"

Surprised, Ethel said, "To Romain?"

"Yes, Romain, who else?"

"Me, why me?"

Hesitant, Ethel took the book, handed it to me.

"Read it," Dana ordered. "You'll tell me what you think. Tell me whether you think it's better than *The Next War*. That's your mission for the next few days."

I was trapped. "Dana, you can't ask me that."

"Go on, get to work. And it'll also get you to stop spending time with Mr. Oh-look-how-poor-I-am."

I took the book, shooting her a dark look.

In my quarters at Harperley Hall, lying on the large bed in my elegantly decorated room, with my soft rugs and a colour TV, I began reading *The Feminine Mystique*. To my amazement, I discovered a world of desperate, miserable women, fighting against a "problem that has no name," women trapped, locked in the role of wife and mother like in a prison that you can never leave. Experts tried to explain away the problem through all sorts of daft theories that Friedan exposed — a problem that came from an excess of knowledge (some proposed to prevent women from attending university), or the shortage of skilled workmen (!) that women depended on to repair their appliances (why not train them to repair their appliances themselves?). Others blamed their monotonous or disappointing sexual lives, with experts encouraging them to spice things up. Betty Friedan didn't agree. For her, the problem was something else, deeper, more fundamental — a visceral need for fulfillment doing something other than being at the service of a husband, children, or housework. A need to exist for who they were. I realized with alarm that this is what Gail had tried to tell me. She was trying to describe this prison for women that she so feared. *You can hope for more out of life. I can't.*

Did I miss Gail? It was hard to say. The powerful anaesthetic called New York had progressively muddled my memory. Sometimes, when I thought of her, I realized I couldn't decide what I had really felt for her. A girl I seduced the way you win a trophy by default.

I later learned through Dana that she hadn't married Don Drysdale. The big wedding at the Ritz-Carlton had been cancelled, and she'd left to live in Calgary to take care of a sick aunt. (I hadn't known that Gail had family in Alberta.) I did feel something when Dana told me, in the summer of 1963, of her union with the heir to Barron cookies (those butter biscuits with their tin boxes, popular among the English of Métis Beach but impossible to find in the Gaspé). He must have had millions of dollars, that young man. "A good catch," Dana said, a half-smile on her face. I couldn't help thinking of Gail's parents, probably overjoyed at their daughter's marriage.

The tone of *The Feminine Mystique* was both measured and persuasive. *The Next War* was vitriolic, almost a pamphlet. Like Betty Friedan, Dana worried as she witnessed young American women deserting the universities, "Almost fifty percent of students were women in the twenties," she wrote. "Today, they make up only thirty-five percent. What's happening?" Later, on page 114, "They tell you that too much knowledge makes you suspect, ladies. Worse yet: undesirable. Think about it for a moment — why would they say this to you?" Or on page 258, "Your dreams are limited to a husband and a nice house filled with children and modern appliances. A lifestyle to fulfill you emotionally and materially. Must we see in America's newfound wealth a trap for women? Are women victims of postwar triumphant capitalism?" (Angry critics would label her a "dangerous Communist" for having dared write those words.)

If reading *The Next War* left me scratching my head, *The Feminine Mystique* devastated me — simply because Betty Friedan spoke of Gail.

"So?"

Two days later, an anxious Dana was staring at me from across the kitchen. I quickly stammered out an answer, "It's wonderful, you complement one another...."

She stiffened. "That's a coward's answer! Come on, tell me — her book is better than mine, isn't it?"

She looked at me, her face tense, veins throbbing. What could I answer? I felt embarrassment redden my cheeks, and Dana noticed, "I knew it!"

"No! It's not what you think...." I wanted to flee, completely aware of the embarrassing inadequacy of my argument. "You're more ... biting. Dramatic...."

A timid smile on her face, like a first dawn. "Be honest, Romain, which do you prefer?"

I bit my lip. "Yours. Of course I prefer yours."

Her face brightened. She came near to me, placed a wet kiss on my cheek, missing my mouth by a hair.

Unsurprisingly, *The Next War* caused a scandal, but not immediately, only after a long newspaper strike came to an end. New York was bereft of papers for almost four months, something never before seen — it was as if you'd turned out the city's lights. Dana had been cross with Burke for having precipitated the book's launch. "It's as if I didn't exist, Burke! As if I did it all for nothing." Reminding her that Betty Friedan was in the same situation didn't change anything, she went on, complaining ceaselessly. The strike finally ended, and when Burke and I wanted to celebrate its end, Dana looked at us as if we'd gone crazy, "Celebrate? What will they say about me now?"

As she feared, the papers didn't spare her. AN H BOMB DROPPED ON MALE-FEMALE RELATIONSHIPS; AFTER THE COLD WAR THE BOLD WAR, the *Daily Mirror* and the *Daily News* titled their reviews. A few weeks later, there were rumours of incidents in Manhattan. A Madison Avenue ad agency was overrun by a pack of angry young women. They gathered at the foot of a building for a peaceful protest, placards in hand: GENTLEMEN, THE NEXT WAR HAS BEGUN! The situation soured when agency employees, young men, as young as the women themselves, came down to the street to harass them. The police intervened, and six young women were arrested for disturbing the peace. Another time, a group of female students jeered at a small delegation of gloved and be-hatted women distributing pamphlets on the ground floor of Gimbels on 34th Street; they were handing out pins with the message: SHAME TO THE FEMINISTS THAT ARE BRINGING OUR NATION TO ITS KNEES. Voices were raised, insults were bandied, and in the kerfuffle, a student pulled on the store's fire alarm, and the whole place flew into a panic. Eight people were arrested.

But the highest-profile of all these protests was, without a doubt, a crusade led by a group that one *New York Times* columnist would call the Freudian Vandals. Every day, for weeks, the city woke in fear — or hope — of a new stunt. Vandalized billboards, sometimes at the four corners of Manhattan, all at the same time, clearly the work of an organized group. At first, the Vandals simply painted large moustaches, à la Groucho Marx, on faces "pink with pleasure" of young women immortalized in advertisements. Quickly enough, however, the Vandals began painting obscene, immense masculine attributes. To avoid shocking the public, television cameras filmed only the crowds reacting to these "acts of vandalism" on Times Square or Herald Square. Close-ups of stupefied and outraged faces, nervous laughter from the few who were amused. Dana and I followed it on television — Mayor Wagner's perplexed declarations, the threatening press conference of New York's Chief of Police. After five weeks, the Freudian Vandals unmasked themselves by exposing the pictures they'd taken of their exploits in a West Village gallery. Huge before and after pictures over which they'd written:

ART ISN'T THE OBJECT BUT THE PERCEPTION WE HAVE OF IT

Soon after, the police raided the Bleecker Street gallery — there were so many cops it was ridiculous. Indignant, we watched the brutal arrest of the gallery staff, then of the four Freudian Vandals, three men in their early twenties and a slightly older woman, trotted out in front of the cameras and handcuffed. "The next war is only the beginning!" one of the men yelled, a thin guy with a ridiculous woman's hat. Dana was disgusted, "They've understood nothing, those idiots. I write for women, not buffoons."

Soon enough, *The Next War* became an expression that feminists and radical youth used in their militant jargon, and that their detractors mocked. Dana was forced to defend her title on every radio and television show, and in every newspaper, No, it wasn't a war against men; yes, it was a war against the stereotypes that men — ad men, writers, journalists, psychiatrists, doctors — maintained to ensure that women remained subservient. On television shows, she responded to ridicule with courage, suffering through interviewers' sarcasm with dignity, "Why do you hate men so?" Or, "In what way is a man like me — clean and well-dressed — a threat to you?" She could have taken the public mockery personally — often the audience at these talk shows was made up mostly of women — but it seemed to leave her unaffected. In the end, all women would come to see the light, she told herself. They would see what they were missing out on.

It wasn't her book that Dana was selling on these talk shows; it was herself. She was a feminist rock star. Her presence at a signing ensured a packed house. "Ask yourself the following question, ladies," she'd say between two autographs, "Are you happy in your marriage? No, no, don't tell me you have a nice house, nice kids, that you travel twice a year. I'm talking about you. Are you happy? Do you feel that your life has meaning? *Meaning*, ladies." You could see them thinking, heads lowered, almost ashamed. "Well, if you answered no to the question, I tell you, go back to school or get a divorce!" (Indignant Oh's! and Ah's! would always be heard here.) "Don't be afraid! You'll be surprised at how you'll build a new life, and the next man you meet will know he's marrying a free woman, not a slave." Shocked, some women booed her, but most of the time their response was anxious silence. In these crowds of distraught women, sometimes Dana would be moved to tears.

Her beauty fascinated. She was sexy, telegenic; she had a quick wit, was very funny, and the media loved her. She didn't have a professorial air like Betty Friedan. She was rich and had, or so the rumours said, an eighteen-year-old lover — me.

6

"They'll hear from my lawyers, those monsters! They don't have the right!"

Dana was shaking with anger, a copy of the *Daily Mirror* in her hands. "Who told them, Romain? Who?"

I was as confused as she was. How had it reached the ears of the damn society columnist at the *Mirror*?

A picture of Dana and me. Taken during a preview at the Leo Castelli gallery, on East 77th Street. Nothing incriminating. Standing next to each other with glasses in our hands. Dana looking straight at the camera, and I looking in the other direction. The caption read, "Dana Feldman and her young Canadian lover." A comment, supposedly humorous, accompanied it, "The masculine version of Nabokov's *Lolita* advances the cause of women."

"Answer me, Romain! Who?"

I didn't know. The same way I didn't know how we had ended up where we were.

Since *The Next War*'s publication, in addition to my classes with Darren and Ian Dart, I acted as Dana's assistant (she hired me after we completed all the paperwork, sorting out my situation with the American authorities; according to her lawyers, nothing led them to believe Robert Egan had lodged a complaint against me in Métis Beach, so I was now the happy owner of a green card). I accompanied her to all her promotional events, looked after her agenda, answered interview requests, opened her letters, sorted them. I read the newspaper for her and prepared press reviews, setting aside hurtful criticism or comments. Twice a day, I made my way to the newspaper stand on Broadway, in front of the Lincoln Center, still under construction, and I bought the morning and afternoon editions. That's how I had come across the *Daily Mirror*'s picture.

I loved accompanying Dana to her events, as much as I loved being in her company when, both of us exhausted, we settled down in the living room, each lying on a couch, shoes off, reviewing the day's events. A new prize, or a lecture, a television interview with one of the great names of television that impressed me so much — Johnny Carson, Ed Sullivan, and the very serious Walter Cronkite, whose tears led to our own a few short months later, the day John F. Kennedy was assassinated.

All of it felt like a dream.

Moïse was put off because I wasn't spending nearly as much time with him. He didn't tell me, but I could feel it. "Don't worry about it, man, I'm writing a lot right now, anyway. You know what? I've got a title. *A New York Tale*. What do you think?"

"Perfect. Genius."

"So can we see each other tomorrow?"

"Don't think so, still got things to do with Dana. I have to be there, you know?"

"The day after, then?"

"I don't know, Moïse, I'll call you back."

And I hung up, feeling guilty. Moïse, my friend Moïse. It took a surprising problem for me to disregard my good friend's needs. Yes, a real problem.

You should have seen her, Dana, speaking in front of crowds in awe of her even before she opened her mouth. Crowds of young women and a very few young men, brought to tears, their eyes shining, impatient for a new world. You should have seen her talk to them with her eyes pulsing like embers, radiant in her small black dresses that showed off her shoulders, her long brown hair cascading down her back, and her flat shoes, ballet shoes in black silk that made her look like a student, even though she was forty-one. Women wanted to be her, men, like Darren, mooned over her. As did I. It was impossible not to succumb to her charm.

"Hey! What are you looking at?"

That morning, Dana would have slapped me if the kitchen table hadn't been between us. Bent over the press reviews I'd prepared for her, glasses on her nose, her bathrobe was slightly open, showing the top of her breasts, naked and full, under her dark blue men's bathrobe bought at Brooks Brothers. (Dana made fun of women's bathrobes — "not warm enough and desperately overdone when it comes to seduction.") She raised her eyes and caught my stare. Immediately, I blushed red.

"Sorry … I was thinking of something else.…"

She drew her bathrobe tight around her. "Something bothering you? You've been strange recently. Problems with Moïse?"

"No, just a little tired."

"Tired? My God! What will you be like at my age?"

She stared at me for a few beats, as if she didn't believe me.

Another time, I can't remember where we were exactly, but there were a lot of people — maybe a dinner organized by her publisher — her eyes intercepted mine, staring at her curves. She furrowed her brow before slapping me, right there in front of everyone. "Hey! Were you looking at my ass?" Embarrassed, I left, feeling all eyes on me, and returned alone to Harperley Hall, hating myself for being so obsessed. *What's wrong with you, man! She could be your mother!*

Things became tense between us. Dana avoided me. And when she couldn't — I was her assistant, after all — she was in a terrible mood. At dinner parties, in taxis, she was distant, cold, carefully calculating her movements to avoid brushing up against me, always with that air of disdain, the same you'd have with a mangy dog: *Don't come near me! Don't touch me!*

The happiness I had built for myself in New York was slipping away.

7

That memorable night at Columbia!

Since Dana encouraged young women to enroll in college, they were particularly generous to her in return. Not a week would go by without Dana receiving honours — diplomas, prizes, decorations — or invitations to speak to enthusiastic crowds of young people. In 1964 and 1965, female enrollment increased, and she was proud of it. That night, in front of a feverish crowd of young women at Columbia University, Dana realized that the promise she'd made to herself as a little girl was coming true. All these young women listening to her with veneration, their eyes wide open, full of light. She inspired them! She could influence them, help them choose paths they might not have taken otherwise. Dana was accomplishing something great!

I was in the back of the room. As had been the case recently, Dana was unpleasant and distant in the taxi. I hadn't mentioned it, but there, on stage, she seemed happy. For a moment, our eyes met and she smiled at me because she knew that I knew something secret about her, and that secret was a shared thing between the two of us. Her voice broke, and she stopped talking. A worried silence fell over the room. Dana lifted her hand to reassure us, took a sip of water, then went on, jokingly, that it would teach her for talking too much, a quip at a *Mirror* columnist who'd written a few days earlier, "Women already talk too much, we shouldn't encourage them." Everyone laughed. She slowly sifted through her notes on the lectern, clearing her throat. Then, with tears in her eyes, she began talking about her childhood, the little girl from Queens raised in a family of modest means. She spoke of her parents' love of music and the arts, a love transmitted to her sister and herself, the confidence her father always had in his two daughters, and the promise she'd made — to carve out a life for herself, to be the master of her own fate. A fulfilling life. She'd been laughed at and teased at Barnard College. But today, she was sure, her life was far more exhilarating than that of most of her old classmates, imprisoned in beautiful homes now emptied of children. "You can do great things with your lives, ladies. Don't wait for a man to start working on your future. You can accomplish big things!" And the auditorium shook with the sound of applause and cries of admiration, and a small group of women intoned "Nellie Bly," and we all joined in.

"Well, that's worth a glass of champagne!"

Dana returned to Harperley Hall euphoric. She had been energized by the crowd of young women. In the taxi, she took my hands and kissed them. "Romain, isn't it wonderful! All these young women with brilliant futures before them!" My pulse quickened, a growing discomfort between my legs. Oblivious, she continued gaily, holding my hands, kissing them — "I'm still shaking all over. What about you?" Apparently she didn't notice the effect she was having on me. *Good God, Dana! What game are you playing?*

Rosie wasn't at Harperley Hall; she was spending a few days with her elderly mother in New Jersey. Left to ourselves, we started going through every cupboard in the kitchen, looking for a bottle of champagne. (Dana giggled when she found Rosie's personal beer stash — a dozen bottles of Pabst Blue Ribbon. "Rosie, my Rosie? Is it possible?") I found champagne in the pantry, Veuve Clicquot, and put it in the freezer to chill. Dana, who wanted a bath, disappeared into her quarters, drunk with happiness. Not even caring to close the door to her room or her bathroom. *What game are you playing, Dana?* I heard her drawing her bath, then climbing into the bathtub. Again, my pulse quickened, and again, that pain between my legs, a match struck. Ten minutes passed, then fifteen, then twenty. The sounds of water, a delightful gurgle, terribly inviting. *Good God, Dana!*

I hurried to the living room, went through the albums and found *Someday My Prince Will Come*. I let Miles Davis, volume turned up high, fill the space, as if I was trying to drown out the last coughs of a dying man.

I returned to the kitchen, my brain buzzing. The bottle! My hands shaking, I brought it out of the freezer; it wasn't as cold as I'd hoped. Too bad. I clumsily popped the cork, which crashed against the wall. Then I had an impudent idea.

"Give me two minutes, I'm not ready."

I knocked a few times on the half-open door to her room, champagne glass in hand. I said, my heart beating in my chest, "I've got a glass for you. You can have it in the bath if you want." She was quiet. I continued in a faltering voice, "It'll help you relax. And delivery is free." But she didn't laugh. "Okay," her tone was dry, suspicious, "leave it on the table next to the door." I slipped into her room, my legs like cotton. A perfume of jasmine and citrus filled the air. In the living room, a Walt Disney tune, played divinely by the great Miles Davis. I placed the glass on the table, hesitated a long time —"Romain, are you still there?" — and left immediately, intimidated.

Back in the kitchen, back at the starting line. My hands trembled, my breath so tense a black veil covered my sight. I poured myself a glass. *What are you doing, Romain Carrier? You're going to fuck everything up!* Then, as if I couldn't think anymore, couldn't reason, I started pulling my clothes off, as if they'd been contaminated by poison ivy. *Naked? Look how ridiculous you are!* I grabbed the bottle with one hand, my glass with the other. I made my way towards her room again, my heart beating, my mouth dry. Her back was to me, her hair held up with clips, in a bathtub filled with foam. She was smiling, maybe even laughing a little at the thought of her unforgettable evening. The young women had saluted her at the end, so moved, some of them with red faces smeared with mascara. I knocked one of her shoes over — "Romain, is that you?" — and I didn't answer. She repeated, worried, "Romain? If you're there, it isn't funny." Then she saw my reflection in her large mirror. She began shouting, insulting me, throwing water in my direction, but it was too late to turn around. I put one foot in the bathtub.... "No, Romain!" And the other foot.... "I said no!" And my calves, and knees, and my thighs, and the rest.... "No!" Then her protests transformed into violent, mocking laughter faced with this tall, skinny, naked boy. We fought comically, like kids, foaming water splashing to the floor.

Miles Davis had fallen silent long ago. The A-side of *Someday My Prince Will Come* was over, the needle floating over emptiness, and it would do that for a long time to come.

"*Shit, man!*" Jealousy burned in Moïse's eyes. "How did you do it? Tell me, man!"

Sitting like a man condemned, at a table under the fogged-up window of the New York City Lights Bookshop, I held my head in my hands. "What did I do ... I'm done. Completely done...."

"Hey, man! Think of how lucky you are! One of the most beautiful women in New York!"

"She could be my mother!"

"Who cares! You know a lot of mothers who look like her?"

"She's going to throw me out!"

"Is that what she said?"

"No. But it can't end any other way. It isn't normal. It isn't moral!"

"Morality?" He laughed. "Hey, man, you're in New York, not the Vatican!"

The next day, Dana ignored me, until we heard Rosie's key in the door; she was back from New Jersey. Dana looked me straight in the eye, her nails dug into my arm, "Nothing happened between us, okay?"

Nothing? Was she joking?

The atmosphere wasn't the same at Harperley Hall. The air had a tension to it that Rosie quickly picked up on, immediately becoming suspicious. Our routine had changed without her knowing why; Dana now took her breakfast before I woke up, and in the evenings, she often went out for dinner — with Burke, apparently. "Ma'am?" Rosie asked, hesitant. Dana responded, "Don't look at me like that, Rosie. There's no problem, if that's what you want to know." Poor Rosie looked at us with her pale, worried eyes, desperately trying to understand, as if we had changed the backdrop when she was away, and she no longer knew where she was.

Despite the toxic atmosphere at Harperley Hall, Dana let me take care of the daily tasks — letters, newspapers, interview requests — but it wouldn't last, I knew it. Good God! I just couldn't forget the night I made love for real, the way a man would, not like it had been with Gail. And those words she whispered to me, "My body feels something again, finally, Romain!" And *nothing* had happened between us?

And then, one night, after an exhausting day, we fell into each other's arms again, and then again, and another time still.

"Enough, Romain! You're eighteen! Do you know what that means?" She looked pale, distraught. Wringing her hands. Her ring mounted with a sapphire that John had given her. As if what we'd done had profaned the memory of her beloved husband. "Of course, you don't care! But I feel like I'm living a nightmare!"

The next night, she didn't return to Harperley Hall, and Rosie refused to tell me where she was. At two in the morning, still no news from Dana. I couldn't wait any longer. I picked up the phone and woke Ethel.

"Romain? Ah, the two of you, I'm sick of it!"

"I'm looking for Dana. I'm worried sick."

"She's okay, she's fine! She's here. She wanted to talk with me. She'll talk to you tomorrow, okay?"

"Is she okay?"

"Yes, yes, she's fine. She's sleeping. Don't worry, she'll call you tomorrow."

"She could have called me to tell me she wasn't coming home."

"She thought you'd be in bed and didn't want to wake you. Come now, go to sleep, there's no reason to worry."

I felt the end coming.

8

"You're disgusting! How could you!"

Mark Feldman. Her son. On the other end of the line. Colleagues in London had shown him (laughing? pretending to be shocked?) a *News of the World* article. His mother, Dana Feldman, and her young Canadian lover. The same picture that had been published in the *Daily Mirror* months before. This time, the copy mentioned her son, describing him as a young, well-connected broker, husband to Sarah Rosner, the daughter of the extraordinarily rich Ab Rosner.

In the kitchen, Dana had collapsed on a chair, her face ashen. Mad with rage, Mark spoke so loudly I could hear every word. I was petrified by his cruelty, "You're disgusting! Your book of feminist nonsense wasn't enough! You had to find yourself a gigolo to soil my name!"

"Your name? Just take your own, then! Your father's name, John McPhail! The one he gave you and you shamefully rejected!"

"Leave my father out of this, will you? We're talking about you. You brought shame on all of us with your pitiful book. And now this ... revolting picture of your ... lover! It's enough to make me sick!"

So, he knew. But that was no reason for Dana to let herself be insulted this way. There she was, curled around her son's contempt. I said, as softly as possible, so as not to vex her, "Hang up, Dana.

You're only hurting yourself. Your son has no right to talk to you in that tone." She turned her anger towards me, dismissing me with an impatient hand. Her anger was clear. She was angry at me, *It's your fault all this is happening! Get out of here!* I left the kitchen.

It was hard for me to understand the nature of their relationship. Dana rarely spoke of Mark, and when she did, it was always with some embarrassment. She had loved her son with surprising ferocity when he was a child, but at puberty, he had become a tyrant. He was only twelve when he blurted out one day, just back from school, "What sort of mother are you?" throwing his schoolbag down with one hand while with the other smashing a small statuette Dana had always been fond of. He was in such a fury, Dana told me, that his face and neck were covered in red blotches, "I'm as Jewish as my friends Marty and Benny! And I'll have my bar mitzvah! And I want to be called Feldman from now on, like you and Aunt Ethel, like Grandpa and Grandma. McPhail is a name for goyim!" And he spat on the ground. Dana's blood turned to ice.

When she was pregnant, Dana hadn't given a thought to whether her child would be Protestant or Jewish. Dana didn't practise Judaism; she saw it as a rich and living culture — birthdays, marriages, funerals, remembrance — the rest didn't really matter. Her in-laws, the McPhails, didn't see things in the same light. They were worried for their unborn grandson. There had been a particularly tense dinner in Montreal one evening that she told me about once, in which her anxious mother-in-law had asked, "Is it true that religion is transmitted through the mother?" Though the question was incomplete, it was recognizable: *Will Mark be Jewish?* In the car that evening, Dana told John, "I don't care if he becomes Presbyterian or Buddhist. All that matters is that your mother leave us be. And that we don't butcher our son. No circumcision under any circumstances."

But John had died. And Dana and Mark had settled down in New York, with Mark attending a school where half the students were Jewish. Peer pressure or the horrible stories of the Holocaust his teacher told, it was impossible to tell what got to him. He progressively became uncompromising — he started refusing to eat certain types of food, demanding a circumcision, visiting the synagogue. Then he began wearing a kippa, studying the Torah. This was followed by a pilgrimage to Israel and his marriage, at nineteen, to Sarah Rosner, the daughter of an extraordinarily rich and influential orthodox Jew from Lexington, in London. "I raised him in an environment I hoped was as liberal and open as possible, and this is how he thanks me. I thought I'd given him a leg up, to make him a man of his age, and instead I made him a fundamentalist who married a submissive wife who wears a *sheitel*. Why do children need to always be at odds with their parents?"

And now, this *News of the World* article that filled her son with such hate. They were still on the phone, the tone had gotten louder, so much so that Rosie knocked on the door to my room, imploring me to do something. Dana shouting, crying now, she just couldn't bear it. I returned to the kitchen, finding a teary Dana, her fingers gripping the phone so tightly you'd think it would crack. "You would have never talked to me like that if your father were still here."

"If he were still here!" Mark choked back a growl. "If he were still here you wouldn't be sleeping with children!"

"Mark!"

"He's younger than I am, for crying out loud."

Mark hung up suddenly and violently; the phone slipped out of Dana's hands and crashed to the floor.

Dana locked herself in her room for the next few days. The pain of having lost her husband returned, almost as strongly as in 1956. In the fog of sedatives, she told us off every time we came to speak with her. Like all the other times, Rosie came into her room every two or three hours to leave food out for her, which she ignored.

After two days of this, I knocked on her door and opened it a crack. The room was dark, filled with a smell of stale smoke and moist sheets.

"What do you want?" Her voice was weak, pasty.

"I want you to leave this room and get some fresh air. Maybe a walk in Central Park would be nice."

"No, leave me alone."

"You can't just stay here in the dark, dumb with sedatives. You have new interview requests."

"Tell them I'm done giving interviews."

I held out my arm to help her get up; she stiffened visibly, kicking with her feet under the sheets. "Don't touch me!" I stepped back. "What a mess! John died seven years ago! And for seven years I didn't touch a man. To respect his memory! And now I fall into the arms of a boy younger than my own son! My God! What must John be thinking of me, up there? What must he be thinking of me?"

She jumped out of bed and staggered into the bathroom. Her hair was dirty, stuck to her skull.

"We can't go on like this, Romain. It needs to stop."

"I ... What needs to stop?"

"You need to go. It's unbearable for both of us."

9

"You need to think about something else, man! You can't just mope around, man."

Moïse playing the father figure. I had spent the evening and part of the night being consoled in his small dirty apartment in East Harlem, as he tried to make me swallow the canned stew he managed to burn in a beat-up saucepan. Around three in the morning, he gave up, exasperated, and began loudly gathering up the dozen empty beer bottles on the table. "Enough, man! Time to go to bed. We only have a few hours to sleep."

My head was going to burst; alcohol made the whole room pitch and reel. I said, my mouth full of cotton, "I thought you weren't working tomorrow...."

"Right. But no way you're sleeping in. I've got a plan. Exactly what the doctor ordered."

"Forget it, Moïse ... I'm too tired."

"Certainly not! You're going to wake up early tomorrow. We're going on a little trip."

"Trip?"

Moïse went through his pockets and picked out some ten-dollar bills. "You got a few bucks?"

"Fuck, Moïse, I'm not moving an inch!"

Furious, he grabbed my vest off the collapsed sofa in the corner of the living room, went through my pockets, and found twenty dollars, maybe more. "Okay. That's more than enough. We're going to Washington, man. We're leaving at dawn."

"And Dana?"

"No way. Don't start!"

I'd never seen so many buses in my life. Besides ours, there were at least a good hundred of them on the Baltimore–Washington Parkway, and the closer we got to Washington, the more buses there were, hundreds and hundreds of them, all heading straight for the capital. It was around noon when we made it into the besieged city. Its great avenues were filled with a dense crowd, seventy-five percent black. Blacks dressed in their Sunday best, with their spouses, their families, or in groups with the rest of their congregation. They held signs in their hands and had pins on their shirts. They came from across the country. Moïse said you could recognize those who came from down South from their sad eyes, since it was in the South that the blacks were the most severely mistreated. Some of them had come to Washington on a Wednesday against the direct orders of their employers. They would pay a price for it when they got back, if they still had a job. That's why they were in Washington that day — jobs and freedom.

But there were no sad faces. People were walking about, most of them smiling, sporting sunglasses and fine hats, as if they were off to a picnic — that's how Malcolm X described the event and had decided to boycott it. The weather was wonderful, only a few clouds in the taut azure canopy over us.

On Pennsylvania Avenue, we saw the Capitol in the distance, shining and majestic, its dome like a wedding cake. With a nudge and a wave, Moïse pointed out the White House on the right, more unreal than on television, and I shivered at the thought of John F. Kennedy being only a few metres away, breathing the same air. I promised myself I'd buy a postcard and send it to my mother.

I was apprehensive at the flood of people marching. As many as two hundred and fifty thousand people, the organizers said. Thinking with some apprehension of the race riots shown on television, and the crowds of peaceful protestors in Birmingham, Alabama, the most segregated city in the country, being pushed back with water cannons, protecting themselves as best they could against police dogs. But that day, it would be different. For once, blacks were in a position of strength, and nothing would happen to the crowd.

Excited, Moïse grabbed me by the arm and pulled me into the still-growing march. With difficulty, we found our way to the Washington Monument. "Freedom! Freedom!" some called out. "Do you want to be free?" Others replied, "Yes!" They all answered. "Freedom, now!" Farther off, small groups sung gospel hymns, calling on Jesus and God in heaven, a wonderful, joyous cacophony. All of these people, robbed of their rights, marching with dignity and good humour, it brought tears to our eyes.

We walked towards the Lincoln Memorial, the end point of the march. The heavy August sun, and nothing to drink. We couldn't reach the great basin to refresh ourselves; everywhere we bumped into a human wall, impossible to cross. "Shit, man!" Sweat running down my face, my neck; my shirt drenched in the back, under my arms. Moïse grumbled. I tried to distract him, get him to think of something else. I feared his tendency towards excess might get us into trouble. "Think of all these people around us. They've got a lot more reasons to be impatient than you and I do." But he wasn't listening, and as soon as the first few notes of folk music drifted towards us, he let out a desperate, animal cry.

"Oooooh, man ... We're missing everything...." First, Joan Baez's crystalline voice reached us; then Bob Dylan's rough one — *Only a Pawn in Their Game* and *When the Ship Comes In* with Joan Baez. Overexcited, he gripped me and climbed on my back, his desperate eyes looking for them in the crowd.

"Stop it, Moïse, you're hurting me." Around us, a few annoyed glances, then disgusted stares as Moïse threw up his breakfast on the ground, splattering our shoes.

With patience and determination, we managed to get near the Lincoln Memorial, or near enough to see Martin Luther King. Moïse had forgotten his misfortunes already. He still looked weak, yet he fixed his eyes on the distant pastor, listening intently, his brow furrowed in concentration, the pastor's voice like an impetuous wind, leaving us shivering. The fear we felt! The fear that he might say too much, and that it would turn against his people. The fear that he might say too little, leaving his people wanting more. But with eloquence and firmness, Martin Luther King found the right words: *Free at last! Free at last! Thank God Almighty, I'm free at last!*

And the crowd roared like a thousand planes taking flight, applause bursting like a rain of shells. Our ears rung from this torrent of freedom that the pastor had shown might be possible — a torrent whose strength would break the chains of injustice, eradicate hate and ugliness. People grabbed the nearest hand and began chanting together. Later, the crowd would start clearing under the warm sun, leaving the ground littered with paper and trash. The crowd fragmented, and smaller groups ventured onto the surrounding avenues. Thousands upon thousands climbed back onto their buses that had besieged the city and that would bring them home, in the expectation of the full recognition of their rights. A year later, President Johnson signed a law that put an end to segregation in public places and workplaces, and then in 1965 another law that removed restrictions on blacks' right to vote.

It was hard to think of Dana and my life in New York in tragic terms. Moïse was right when he said, "When you see all this, you can't really pity yourself over an enviable fate, man. It's indecent."

Moïse decided we should spend the night in Washington; the city still quivered with energy, an effervescence that would have made us regret not staying. After finding a few cans of soda and sandwiches in a grocery store near the station, we found a cool place to sit in West Potomac Park, where Moïse began checking the girls out insistently. He called out lewd comments to every pretty girl who passed us.

"You're gross, Moïse. Stop it." He saw two blondes in twin sets and close-fitting pants, they looked like sisters; he got up, walked towards them with his Dylan walk, passing his hand through his hair to make himself look cool, an indifferent pout on his face.

One of the girls with long hair, pretty, though not as pretty as the one with short hair, approached him excitedly, "You wouldn't happen to be Bob Dylan, by any chance?" And Moïse had them, hook, line, and sinker.

Two nice girls who'd just arrived from Little Rock, Arkansas, both of them with southern drawls. The small blonde with short hair kept smiling at me. When night fell on the Potomac, we invited them for hamburgers. Seeing that behind their innocent airs they had a plan, we made our way to Union Station and found a cheap hotel, where we got two rooms with no bathrooms. The small blonde with short hair was tender, sweet as honey; the day had been so filled with emotion that we spent a good part of the night simply holding each other, without speaking, giggling each time we heard Moïse's wet grunting through the thin wall.

The next day, in the bus driving back to New York, Moïse said, his tone sombre, "If women dream of sleeping with Bob Dylan, it isn't because he's handsome. It's because he's a great artist. When you've got my face, you need to be famous to attract women. That's why I *need* to become famous, man. And that's why you'll never be famous. You're too pretty. You don't need to make an effort. Even rich and famous women ... oh, sorry, man. That's not what I meant to say...."

"It's okay."

He slapped me on the back — "What a night, man! What a night!" — and he squared himself in his seat. I turned my head to look at the moving landscape, and thought of Dana. Back in New York, I would need to have a long discussion with her, and the prospect calmed me. I chuckled, thinking of the young blonde from Arkansas with long hair who would think, for the rest of her life, that she had slept with Bob Dylan on the night of August 28, 1963.

10

"Okay. Good. There's a pile of correspondence on your desk. I haven't touched it. Didn't have the time. At least three large piles, this high. You've got one last chance, but at the first wrong move, you're out. Got it?"

"Couldn't be clearer."

My conversation with Dana had been honest and instructive. She allowed me to return to Harperley Hall and announced in the same breath that she'd begun seeing Burke, her editor.

"You're jealous, man. It's clear as day."

Okay. I might have been. Anybody but Burke! He was one of those asexual figures in a Norman Rockwell illustration. A sort of Mr. Anderson in *Father Knows Best*, though heavy in the belly and bald. A widower, barely older than Dana, but he looked like an old man two steps from a hole in the ground, with his three-piece suits and his embroidered kerchiefs. Imagining them naked made me nauseous. As did seeing his trench coat on the coat peg in the vestibule. Under it, of course, his horrible galoshes.

I couldn't understand Dana — she could have any man, and she chose Burke? Why him? When he spoke, you had to strain to hear, he always seemed to be falling asleep halfway through his sentences. Timid? No, Dana assured me. An intellectual. A scholar. He knew everything, had read everything. She said she loved their long, rich conversations about writers, philosophers, and great musicians.

Another way of saying I didn't measure up. Burke adopted a pater-
nalistic attitude towards me, calling me *Sonny boy*. Then, little by
little, he started taking care of Dana's affairs, accompanying her to
all her events when time permitted. Good God, why couldn't I be
happy for her? Wasn't Burke the best insurance against Dana and
me falling into each other's arms again?

"You need another girl, man. And we'll find you one."

Moïse, restless, had become obsessed with his adventure in
Washington. Obsessed with the ease with which he'd slept with
the girl from Little Rock. In New York he rarely met girls; each
time he approached one, he got the cold shoulder. Too weird. Too
all over the place. As soon as he saw a girl he liked, he spoke too
loudly, laughed too hard, tried too hard. He filled the silences like
a soldier jumping on a live grenade to save his comrades. Perhaps
I was wrong, but I thought the girl in Washington had been his
first time. Since then, he got it in his head that if he wanted to
get with a woman, he had to pretend to be someone else. I saw
him once giving out autographs to women on Washington Square.
Another time as we were drinking a pitcher of Schlitz — Moïse
was twenty-one, making life easier — a girl called out to him, "Hey!
You're Bob Dylan, right?" He motioned me to keep quiet, both
supplication and threat: *please, don't fuck this up for me, I've got a
plan.* His hair all over the place, seen-it-all pout on his face, he was
about to invite the girl to our table when the waiter, who knew him,
called out, "Go on, Charlie! Show us your guitar!" prompting the
surrounding tables to mock and laugh.

Hurt, Moïse turned to me and said, "Okay, man. When my
novel is finally published, and I'm rich, I'll buy myself a car and
go to San Francisco, like Kerouac. There, the girls aren't stuck up.
They're just waiting for it. If you want, we'll go together."

But Moïse wouldn't have time to publish a novel, or buy a car,
or set sail for Frisco.

III

MOÏSE

Summer of 1964, and Dana left me alone in New York. Burke convinced her to spend part of her summer vacation in Métis Beach, which she thought she would never be able to return to after Robert Egan's threats. He had spread the worst sort of lies about her in town. Burke — whom I'd come to call Jurke — usually soft and unpersuasive, managed to convince her. "Don't let your actions be determined by those provincials." I heard the words through the door to Dana's room, words that must have made her lips curl. Was it that they wanted her to abandon the house she loved? Was that it?

"No!" she cried, furious. "That house is mine!"

"So? What's the problem?" Burke demanded. He was certainly not a man who usually turned combative, but this time he fought back against each argument Dana brandished.

"They hate me! I'm an accomplice. A traitor! They're full of hate. I feel like I just can't face them...."

"You? Dana Feldman? Letting yourself be intimidated?"

"You don't understand, Burke."

"You've nothing to blame yourself for. And *Sonny boy* there was imprudent. He didn't act right, but he didn't *rape* her."

So, Burke knew. Dana had told him.

What a Jurke! You should have seen him, like a child all excited with his new toy when he came back from Gimbels with a fishing hat he'd bought for the occasion. "You think I'll cut a fine figure with it, *Sonny boy?*" I gritted my teeth: *You're going to my village, idiot! Not to the Amazon!*

The idea that this man would go to *my* village, admire *my* river, breathe *my* air, and wander in *my* place … it made me sick with jealousy.

August 1964, and Moïse learned his life would never be the same.

We were both glued to the television in my room, which was a complete mess; the carpet strewn with beer bottles that Rosie picked up, shaking her head disapprovingly. We were following the most recent developments in the Gulf of Tonkin — two American destroyers, the USS *Maddox* and the USS *Turner Joy* claimed they'd been attacked by North Vietnamese skiffs. A consensus emerged on television and in the newspapers — humiliation and reprisal. Moïse shivered, "They're gonna send us there, man."

I replied, aghast, "You think so? You think it'll really be war?"

"No doubt. It's exactly what that bastard Johnson was waiting for. Vietnam, for crying out loud! What the fuck are we going to do there?" He sniffed loudly. "Go get us another beer, will you? Soon it won't taste the same at all."

I thought I was safe, but I wasn't. Burke told me that if you had a green card, you could be drafted just like a U.S. citizen, if you had lived a year in the country. "Me in Vietnam?" There were two ways to avoid it — go back to Quebec or enroll in college. "Me? In university?" I couldn't think straight. Dana was nodding, an exaggerated smile on her face, the sort of smile that's trying to convince you of something. My first reflex was to say I wasn't up to it.

Surprised by the reaction, Burke said, "A smart young man like you? With the courses you took with Darren and Ian? You'll do great, I'm sure." He placed his warm hand on my shoulder, and not a *Sonny boy* to be heard this time. Burke, kind, full of good intentions, making me regret having judged him so harshly.

He was right, too. I took an exam and was accepted in Art History at New York University. Classes began in January 1965, right when the first conscripts started making their way to their draft boards. I'd be left alone until I got my diploma, in June 1968. Being a college student didn't exempt you from the draft — the 2-S status was only a delayed sentence, pushing your military service to a later date, though you had to show proof of commitment and good grades.

"Everything will be fine, Romain, you'll see." Dana was confident, convinced this "dirty useless war" would be over by then. I sure hoped so; the idea of having to return to Quebec terrified me.

Dana decided we should celebrate my enrolment with a party at Harperley Hall. Ethel, Burke, Darren, Ian, Moïse — everyone was there. And they were proud of me, happy for me. Going to university — a dream come true, though hard to savour. Moïse drank his fair share and more of cocktails that night, his head deep in his shoulders, fake enthusiasm on his face. "You okay, Moïse? You're not too angry with me?" A stupid question that a friend shouldn't need to ask, but I asked anyway, in anxious expectation of his answer.

He returned a quickly fading smile. "Why would I be mad, man? You're not American. It's not the same."

Moïse wasn't the same either. He quickly became irritable, furious, agitated. He went to any and all anti-war demonstrations in New York — Union Square, Washington Square, Central Park. He was part of every crowd, his sign held high in his arms — FUCK THE WAR! He called out to groups of passing students, with such anger I felt he was hurling his insults at me, "They've got nothing to fear. Our lives mean nothing more than a shit stain on the bottom of their polished shoes!"

"Moïse, you can't really be mad at them…."

But he disappeared into the crowd, shouting, barking with the other protesters — "Hey! Hey! LBJ! How many kids did you kill today?"— shouting at passing students, especially those who seemed to be from wealthy families. He questioned the ones he saw as rich kids, testing their knowledge about Southeast Asia. "An unjust war, you say? Tell me, why exactly?" Some of the students, surprised by his aggressiveness, would look at him confused, then answer, in various incarnations, something like, "We can't kill people because they think differently than us." "That's sentimentalism!" Moïse would answer. He stared at them impudently, with a haughty air I'd never seen on him. He quoted Bernard Fall on Indochina and the French disaster at Dien Bien Phu, reciting, article by article, the Geneva Accords that should have led to the reunification of the two Vietnams and free elections, but that the United States hadn't respected. "Hey! Did you know that? I'm talking to you! What? You didn't take that class yet?" Other times, he recited from memory passages out of *Civil Disobedience* by Henry David Thoreau. "Who said that? Do you know?" Embarrassed, I grabbed him by the arm and pulled him aside. "Why are these idiots protected from the draft and I'm not? There's no justice! I know more than they do, man! My brain is worth more than theirs, those goddamn silver-spoon bird-brain bastards!"

"You can claim conscientious objector status, no?"

He laughed out loud. "You really think that's how it works? That if I say I'm against war, it's done and dusted? No, man. Not a chance. I'm not Rockefeller, Hearst, or Charlie Thurston Moses III, like these goddamn rich kids!"

As the protests grew, Johnson increased the monthly quotas from six thousand to thirty-five thousand, to forty-five thousand… Forty-five thousand kids ripped from their homes every month. For what? To fight whom?

Slowly but surely, the rope was tightening around Moïse's neck. And I began my new life as a student with my enthusiasm somewhat spoiled by the anxiety of seeing my friend go off to war.

Moïse began drinking excessively, sometimes from morning to night.

"Moïse, you can't keep this up." And he cackled, shrugging.

"I'll be in such a mess they won't want me. A goddamn ship-wreck." *A shipwreck.*

"But you're not a shipwreck."

Again that unbearable cackling. "For the bastards, we're all god-damn shipwrecks." He opened another beer, swallowed almost half in a single swallow, and wiped his mouth with the back of his hand. "There's nothing to do but drink until they call me." He got up, staggered, brought a weak hand to his right temple. "Private Moses, welcome to the greatest, most powerful army in the world!" Then he fell on his ass.

One day, at the bookstore, he'd been drinking and customers complained. He got suspended for a week. I found him dazed, sitting on the sidewalk, his back against the storefront. "You're in no state to work, Moïse. Look at yourself."

He replied, "I'm in a state of nothing, man!"

He looked at me without friendly feelings, for the first time since we met. It made me shiver.

A few days later, at his place in East Harlem, he got angry with me, and pushed me, violently. He was drunk again. "Sure," he moaned, waving open hands under my nose. "Can you see it? The grenade in my hand? They pulled the pin out, can't you see? Why can't you see it for fuck's sake! It's right there, man! Look closer!" He pushed me, his open hand against my chest. Surprised, I fell straight on my back, no time to break my fall. The pain was intense, an electric shock. Moïse cackled. "I'm such an idiot.... Of course *you've* got nothing to fear."

You. Said with such contempt. *You.* Another cut, but I was raw with guilt already. I pulled myself up, gasping for breath, tears in my eyes. And Moïse kept tormenting me, "You're no American. You can't understand." And the ridiculous words I'd muttered, as if I were responsible for even a part of this whole goddamn mess.

"I'm sorry, Moïse...."

"I'm the one who's sorry, man!"

That night, I returned to Harperley Hall, my heart heavy, convinced I was losing my friend. *He's got nothing but contempt for you, Romain. He hates you the way he hates rich kids who have peace of mind.*

At Harperley Hall, things weren't much better. As soon as I crossed the threshold, Dana jumped on me, harassing me with questions. "Where were you? What the hell were you doing? Have you been drinking again? Look at you, you look like a lush!"

Since Burke had entered Dana's life, work for me had become rarer. Interviews, conferences, special events — Burke took care of it all quickly and efficiently. Dana never missed an opportunity. All that was left for me to do was to open and sort correspondence, something I'd been overlooking of late. "What exactly am I paying you for, young man?" Shamefaced, I lowered my eyes, knowing I was taking advantage of her generosity, her money, her patience. I'd become a parasite. Dirty jeans, used t-shirts, long hair, not always clean. I was far from the promise that the mirrors at Brooks Brothers had offered me three years earlier, in high-quality clothes that hadn't been out of my wardrobe for some time. "What do you do with Moïse, eh? Drugs?" Angry eyes, suspicious, when I came home late at night, staggering with drunkenness and despair. Rosie shook her head, picked up my clothes from the carpet, and washed them overnight. And in the morning, always the same rebukes, "You're twenty, Romain! You're almost a grown man now. I want to help you, pay for school, some spending money, but you've got to make an effort!" And I shrugged, my mind in a haze. I was aware enough to know I couldn't keep on like this. Moïse was in all my thoughts. He'd put my life on pause.

2

Moïse still hadn't received a draft notice, but he already knew he wouldn't follow orders. "Between a killer and a criminal, I'll choose criminal, man."

He made his decision in the autumn of 1965, when he saw a man in front of a frenzied crowd committing a criminal act. "I'll do the same thing, man! Yes! I'll do the same thing!"

That day, I picked him up at the bookstore, and we took the subway to Battery Park, where we could hear a discordant clamour coming from Whitehall Street. Excited, Moïse walked quickly. He hadn't been drinking yet that day, nor had he drunk the day before. He was full of energy and didn't want to miss a moment of this demonstration, organized in front of the Army recruitment office, a sinister granite and red brick building, the colour of blood and sand. Applause as the first speakers arrived on stage, folk music playing in the background, and police officers all around. "Come, come on, man! Quick!"

Rumours had circulated about what one of the young speakers was about to do. A heroic gesture that a few young men had already committed — in fact, enough had done so for Congress to pass a law increasing the sentence for this crime — but no one had done it so publicly, in front of photographers and television cameras.

That afternoon in October 1965, Moïse seemed to brighten a little and come out of the funk he'd been in.

Whitehall Street was filled with enthusiastic, noisy pacifists, all surrounding a small truck equipped with a sound system, topped with a platform and a microphone. In the crowd, a small group was singing and playing the guitar, though it was hard to hear them over the sound of counter-demonstrators behind a line of police, chanting, "Communists! Go back to the U.S.S.R.!"

All the ingredients were coming together for conflict. Around us, you could see clenched jaws under police helmets, eyes riveted on the crowd. Tension was in the air, an oncoming storm. Moïse was rubbing his hands together.

Everything happened quickly. On the platform on the small truck, one speaker after another was energizing the crowd to make more noise than the counter-demonstrators. "Shit, man! He's there!" "Where?" "There!" A young man climbed the ladder to the roof of the truck. Short hair, dark suit, black tie: nothing distinguished him as one of the activists the White House hated. A serious young man with sharp features, dressed as if he was going to pick up his diploma. A short silence, a sound like machine gun fire from photographers. "Yes!" Moïse shouted, "It's him!"

The next day, images of him on television, in newspapers, would put fear in the hearts of parents with boys of their own. *He looks so serious, can it be true? What about our son? Will he be a criminal too, anti-American?* A striking image of David Miller touching flame to his draft card, an act of courage that thousands of young men would emulate across the country, even if it was illegal. That day, David Miller preferred to show rather than tell. He didn't speak, but his simple gesture, as the crowd applauded and shouted encouragement, would earn him five years in prison. He was arrested by the FBI three days later in New Hampshire, but his arrest didn't stop many others from following his example — we'd be there a month later when five of them burned their draft cards in front of fifteen hundred people in Union Square as Moïse shouted, "Bravo! Screw the bastards! I'll be doing the same!" The same young men Bob Dylan denigrated in an interview in *Playboy*, saying, "Burning draft cards isn't going to end any war. It's not even going to save any lives. If someone can feel more honest with himself by burning his draft card, then that's great; but if he's just going to feel more important because he does it, then that's a drag." Moïse would come to hate his idol because of those words, and wouldn't tolerate anyone saying Dylan's name around him. "What's he gonna do? Tell me! He's gonna go to the front and play the hero? Of course not! He's not gonna do a goddamn thing because he's rich and famous, so he's protected!"

From then on, in every demonstration, as soon as someone came near him to ask whether he was Dylan, Moïse answered aggressively, "No! If I was him, I wouldn't be here trying to save my goddamn life."

He got word from the army in 1966. "The bastards want to give me a medical. Never thought I would hope I'd have some horrendous disease." But he was declared 1-A, in fighting condition. In November, he was called to 39 Whitehall Street. "Ten days, man. In ten days I'll know. And Bob Dylan can go fuck himself!" I was so worried for him, "You're not really thinking about it, are you? Five years in jail is a long time."

"Calm down, will you? If we're ten thousand in jail, twenty thousand, they'll have to stop locking us up." He put his hand on my shoulder, with a smile he hoped was confident. "Remember Thoreau: 'Under a government which imprisons anyone unjustly, the true place for a just man is also in prison.'"

But that tide of young men ready to go to prison never happened. And every day, fear grew in me, imagining my friend in the hands of the law, like a criminal.

3

That day, I dashed out of Harperley Hall, the *New York Times* under my arm. I made my way to Central Park West, out of breath, jumped on the subway at Columbus Circle, and got off at Union Square. On the stairs, I bumped into a man. He started insulting me, and I told him off right back. We began shouting at each other, and it took other passengers to pull us apart. I finally arrived at New York City Lights Bookstore. I was in such an agitated state that Moïse, strangely calm despite the storm around him, said, "What's up with you, man? Got bit by a rabid dog?"

"Read this!"

"Read what?"

"This!" My hand shaking, I handed him the *New York Times* article. "They say hundreds of draft dodgers have found refuge in Canada. Some say there might be even more. Thousands."

He shrugged.

"Moïse, please listen to me for once!" I shouted. Customers turned to look at the commotion. "Why not you?"

"'Cause I'm not a coward!"

"Am I coward because I fled my country?"

"It isn't the same."

"Not the same? So, tell me, what crime have you committed to spend five years in jail, for chrissake!"

"It's resistance, man. Like Thoreau."

"Goddamn it, Moïse! Thoreau spent a single night in jail. Not five years!"

I was furious. He tried to get away from me, and I pursued him into the back of the store. I said, almost hysterical, "Thoreau gives people with nothing to fear a clear conscience. Civil disobedience, my ass! A goddamn game, you mean! The same one Joan Baez and her little friends play. So fucking courageous, like Thoreau, don't pay your taxes to protest the war! They send a copy of his book instead. How nice! How fucking nice! Good citizens, full of righteous indignation! Good God, Moïse, they're not risking much, are they?" He lifted his eyes. "Listen to me, goddamn it!" I grabbed him by the shoulders. "The friend standing in front of me is already a hero, okay? So don't burn your draft card and end up behind bars to prove it. And anyway, who are you trying to impress? Strangers who don't give a shit? Bob Dylan?"

He stiffened, and I took my head in my hands. Only two days left before his life fell apart. Two days and he'd go to 39 Whitehall Street, and replicate David Miller's courageous gesture. He'd disappear from circulation, in handcuffs. How could I convince him to change his mind?

That's when my eyes fell on an atlas like the one he had shown me the first time we met.

"Moïse, get over here!" He turned to me, annoyed. "Come on, now."

Did he remember Rivière-du-Loup, the land of Kerouac's parents? And Métis Beach?

"Yes," he answered, annoyed by my riddle.

"You can go there. No one will follow you all the way to Métis Beach! You could take care of Dana's house!"

I hadn't thought about it before, but for the first time in a long time, I felt hope. "Right!" I continued. "You can go to Métis Beach, until this goddamn war is over! We'll say you're Dana's nephew. What do you think?"

He looked at the map for a long time. "I don't know, man."

4

It was a tough blow, but hardly a surprise.

I'd barely closed the door when Rosie appeared in the vestibule, her face drawn.

"She wants to see you. Right away."

"More complaints from the boss, Rosie? Is that it?"

She didn't reply. I was in a joking mood, full of optimism. "Oh, Rosie! Don't worry!" Rosie, a small, surly woman, with a strong odour of camphor around her, so small she had to go up on her toes to help me out of my coat. "It's okay, Rosie, I got it." But she insisted, pulling on my sleeves with impatience, as if filled with sexual urgency, and that image made me chortle. She stiffened. "Oh, Rosie! Smile! Finally things are looking up! Something good in my life, and Moïse's life!"

I was happy. Surprised I hadn't thought of it before. The empty house in Métis Beach. Moïse could live in one part of it, insulate it, heat it. Not the greatest comfort, but Moïse wasn't the pillow and comforter type. If you'd seen his East Harlem apartment in winter, you'd know that.

Dana would say yes. Dana couldn't say no. Why hadn't I thought of it before?

Poor Rosie! My good mood didn't seem contagious. "Okay, Rosie, tell Her Majesty I'll jump in the shower and put on some fresh clothes. I've got something to tell her. Something important."

She shook her head. "No, now."

Rosie raising her voice? I looked at her more intently. "Nothing serious, Rosie, is it?"

She didn't answer, sighed with annoyance, and my instinct told me something was wrong.

Dana was waiting for me in the kitchen, her face hard. Burke was in the office; I could hear him speaking on the phone. Burke was spending more and more time at Harperley Hall, easily taking over the territory I was giving up. So much so that the whole apartment smelled faintly of his lemony Eau de Cologne. A bit like cat piss.

"You need to leave, Romain."

I wavered. "Are you serious?" Of course she was. "You're choosing to tell me this now? Two days before...."

"It's terrible, I know. What Moïse is going through is terrible, nobody is denying it, but...."

"Exactly, Dana. About Moïse, I wanted...."

She cut me off, annoyed. "You're twenty-one, Romain. You'll be twenty-two soon! It's time for you to become an adult. I'm not asking you to leave right away. In a few weeks. That'll give us time to find an apartment and a job that won't interfere with your studies, of course."

Become an adult. Anger filled me, as it always did when I didn't have a good answer. "Moïse's life is over in two days! And you ... And you...."

She ignored my despair and went on, "You need to pull yourself together." She turned her eyes away from me, took a drag of her cigarette. "I don't want to play mother to you anymore."

Adolescent laughter overcame me. "I can't believe my ears! Play mother to me! Is that what you just said?" I choked with rage, "And what about...." Without warning, her hand whipped through the air, slapping me across the face. I stumbled. Her eyes like burning embers stared me down, defying me to say another word about our little secret. Burke appeared in the kitchen. A dry smile on his face. A comical and awkward character, appearing in a tense scene to draw the crowd's laughter. "Everything okay, here?" He pushed his glasses up on his nose and placed a small, veiny hand on Dana's shoulder. Strangely small for a grown man. She patted it distractedly, without emotion.

"Burke is moving in next month," she said.

Everything became clear — I was the third wheel. "Congratulations, Burke!" I said, as if he just won the lottery.

Dana gave me a dark look, which Burke failed to notice. I moved onto the issue of the house in Métis Beach.

"Not a chance! What made you think that would be a good idea?"

"The house is empty ten months a year."

"It's not even winterized!"

"Moïse will figure something out."

"And what will happen next summer? Burke and I will be one big happy family with him?"

"We'll cross that bridge when we come to it."

"No! No way! I'm not going to be an accomplice! You know what I'd be risking if I helped him be a draft dodger?"

Tears welled up in my eyes, burning, painful. What would I tell Moïse now that I had begun convincing him to leave? *Sorry, buddy. False alert. Back to the game plan.*

"You'd rather see him in prison?"

"Let him go elsewhere!"

"Where, elsewhere?"

"I don't know! It's not my problem."

You disgust me! But the words stayed in my throat. I left, slamming the door behind me, forgetting my vest in the closet, too revolted to come back for it.

5

"*What* did you do?"

I was horrified. I couldn't believe it. Moïse lowered his head, wiped his eyes. It was freezing cold in his small apartment. An acrid smell floated in the air, and the only window was wide open, letting cold wind in.

The night before, Moïse burned his novel. After, he cleaned his apartment and packed his bag. Moïse, exiled from his beloved city, not knowing whether he might return to it one day. Deathly pale, he told me, "I have to mourn, man. *A New York Tale* was my photo album. It was too painful to keep."

What a mess. And Burke had promised to read it. Burke might have published it.

"So what? If Burke sold thousands of copies, it wouldn't change a goddamn thing. Can you imagine? A book written by a coward who abandoned his country. You really think anyone would read it?"

He sniffed. He looked beaten. The wind slapped the drapes around and something rolled on the floor. A cold, heavy rain began falling on the city. Moïse got up and closed the window; when he returned, he put his coat on, "I'm ready."

We had breakfast in a diner on Seventh Avenue. The young woman serving us was so kind we managed to swallow two eggs and bacon, just so she wouldn't ask what was wrong. Moïse, nervous and serious in his dark suit, bombarded me with questions about

John Kinnear, whom I called in a panic in Métis Beach after my fight with Dana. We had stayed in touch despite the distance, and hearing his voice always put a smile on my face. He didn't know anyone who could take in Moïse in Métis Beach, but he offered something better. He knew of a group called the Montreal Council to Aid War Resisters, and told me to call him back later once he had time to find out more about them. I felt a wave of relief, and left for Central Park. An hour later, after my walk, John gave me all the information I needed — the address of the committee, the name of its main organizer, and his phone number. John told me there was great sympathy in Quebec for draft dodgers, that they were welcome. "We don't understand what the Americans are doing in Vietnam. It's not a war for liberation like in '39. It's a useless war."

I was tempted to accompany Moïse (maybe the idea of letting him leave alone was unbearable), and we spoke about it the night before. "I'll figure it out over there. Finish your studies, man. That's what's important right now. We'll see when you're done." I felt relieved. My life in New York, my art history studies, all of it was important to me. But I couldn't help thinking I was abandoning him. Then there were his parents, old and destitute, who wouldn't have him around to support them. "You'll be my link to them. If you really want to help, go visit them from time to time." I learned he gave them a portion of his meagre pay. "They know it's the right thing for me to go to Canada. They don't judge me. But they'll have a few bucks less at the end of the month, you understand?"

I put my hand on his. "Don't worry. I'll take care of it."

He turned his head, his eyes wet. "You're a real friend, man."

By the time we left the diner, the wind was blowing harder. The rain didn't fall on us, it whipped straight into our backs. Armed with useless umbrellas, we walked to the Greyhound terminal at the Port Authority, on 42nd Street. We were an improbable duo, with our miserable faces and drenched clothes. Moïse, small and at least ten or twelve pounds lighter than he used to be, swimming in his dark suit soaked with rain, and his hair cut so short you could see his skull. And me, six feet tall, hair all over the place, about to burst into tears like a distraught girl. A few people looked at us as we passed, but no one could mistake Moïse for Dylan now. Not dressed the way he was and in these circumstances.

"It'll be okay," Moïse repeated, his voice shaking. I nodded, my throat tight, trying to seem strong, knowing that once my friend was on the bus, I'd fall apart. With every step, our wet shoes squeaked, a pathetic noise that made us want to laugh and cry at the same time.

I said, "A picture!"

"What do you mean, a picture?"

Enthused by my idea, I went on, "You remember, in *On the Road,* when Dean Moriarty returns to Denver after his first visit to New York?"

His eyes brightened, a timid smile on his face. "Yes, man! Sal and Carlo Marx went with him to see him off. They go to Penn Station, where the Greyhounds used to leave from! They were saying goodbye."

We began looking for a photo booth; Moïse spotted one on the second floor. "Here, man! Here!" In the booth, he put his faded cloth suitcase on the floor, ran his hand through his wet hair, adjusted his tie, and forced a large smile. I tried to imitate him, hoping it'd be a winning smile, a snub to the tragedy affecting us.

"So we'll never forget each other, man. So we'll never be alone, right?" And like in *On the Road*, Moïse delicately cut the still wet print with a Swiss army knife he pulled out of his pocket. We each placed our half in our wallets. More a grimace than a smile. I still have the picture, it'd break your heart.

"Here's two hundred bucks," I said, handing him an envelope. "It should help you get started."

His eyes misted over. "Thank you."

"You'll find John Kinnear's information inside. You can count on him."

"You're a real friend."

"You too."

We gave each other a long hug, fighting off tears.

"Well, got to go now, man."

I watched him board the bus that would take him out of the great American game. My throat tight, I saw myself four years earlier on the same bus, scared to death. Moïse chose a seat in the back, far from the other passengers. He was alone in the world now. A whistling of compressed air like a plaintive sigh, and the door closed. The motor started with a rumbling like the end of the world and the bus began moving away. Behind the window, Moïse waved, forcing a smile. His face white with fear haunted me for weeks.

6

Two friends, each a refugee in the other's country, trying to save their skins.

In one of his letters, Moïse described our respective exiles: "You left a woman who you stopped loving after she broke your heart, and I'm the idiot still in love with a woman who dropped him like a turd and who still hasn't understood what has happened to him."

Dana was touched by my suffering, though she didn't quite understand its nature. "You look lovelorn, Romain." It was true. I was learning that the loss of a friend could be as terrible as the loss of a lover. Moïse's departure sent me into such a tailspin that Dana postponed the plan of forcing me to find my own place. It was strange to see her suddenly worried about me. Meanwhile, Burke had dematerialized. After three weeks, I packed my bags. Dana seemed surprised.

"Where are you going?"

"Burke is moving in next week. It's time for me to go."

"I've left Burke."

She spoke without regret, almost amusement in her voice.

"Why?"

"It was a mistake. With him, I would have buried myself alive."

She laughed. With cheerful enthusiasm, she took my bag from my hand, opened it, and began putting my clothes back in my closet.

"You're not doing this for me, are you, Dana?"

She laughed out loud and said, a hint of anger in her voice, "Burke is a widower who became an old bachelor. He's full of annoying habits. Let me give you an idea. He needs a daily portion of steak, potatoes, and peas or else he thinks he won't have enough protein. Beneath his calm appearance he's an anxious man. A few times, I had to calm him down like I was his mother because he thought his anxiety was a symptom of a heart attack. How about this: all his underwear is exactly the same. Blue. And filled with sadness. The same kind his mother bought him when he was a teenager. I tried to get him to wear something a bit more sexy — even bought a pair of silk ones from Bergdorf Goodman. He never wore them, not once, but he still put a label on them, like the rest of his clothes. You'd think he was a boy scout off to camp."

I burst out laughing, thinking of Jurke in his scout's uniform, carefully folding his labelled underwear in a drawer.

"I would have gone mad. Or thrown him out of a window."

I started feeling better once I heard things weren't too bad for Moïse. At first, I received dispatches about his goings-on from John Kinnear; Moïse didn't want us speaking directly over the phone in case the FBI was listening. "All draft dodgers are paranoid, man," he wrote in his first letter. He found a room on L'Hôtel-de-Ville Avenue in Montreal in the house of a friendly old woman, though she was a bit cracked, he told me, speaking every night to her husband, who had been dead for twenty-five years. "At least she's got someone to talk to; solitude is the hardest part." But it didn't last. A couple of blocks away he found Ricky Jenkins, a draft dodger from Connecticut who had founded the war resisters committee that John had spoken of. They quickly became friends and Moïse began working with Jenkins, welcoming new arrivals in his busy living room, filled with paperwork. Moïse was doing well, all things considered. Fulfilled by the work he was doing, he'd never felt so useful.

A growing number of young desperate men were arriving from the States, and the committee was becoming bigger. Jenkins, Moïse, and other volunteers needed to find a larger space. They found one on Saint-Paul Street in Old Montreal. A whole team now worked full time, helping incoming draft dodgers. Within a few months, Moïse began receiving a salary, thirty-five dollars a week, enough to pay for his room at the old woman's place. In fact, he wrote to me, he lived better in Montreal than he used to in New York. Life in Quebec was cheaper and not as stressful. "You should see the girls, man! Prettier than in New York. And far less shy. They love draft dodgers! No need to pretend being Dylan, they think we're heroes!"

He wrote pamphlets — "Ok, so the novel isn't going to make me famous" — that the committee clandestinely sent to university campuses in the United States to spread the Good News about Canada. "And fuck Joan Baez!"

His aversion for Baez and Dylan! He would leave a party if their songs came on. "Highly irritating this habit that Québécois have — we don't say *French Canadians* anymore, Romain — of welcoming us with music from the U.S. As if it would help us better tolerate our exile!" Once he heard Joan Baez play in Toronto — she'd been invited to a local church that supported the TADP, the Toronto Anti-Draft Programme. Members from Montreal's committee made the trip, and Moïse agreed to go with them, without great enthusiasm. The night before he was to leave, we spoke over the phone. He said sarcastically, "What new idiocy will she tell us this time?"

"Don't you think you're exaggerating, Moïse?"

I loved Joan Baez — even today, I sometimes listen to her old albums, and they touch me as deeply as the first time I listened to them. Moïse couldn't tolerate her public disapproval of the dodgers' exile. "If David Harris, her husband, wants to go to jail, that's his choice, man! He gets so much media attention, you'd think he was a movie star or something. She'd better not lecture us!" Her visit to Toronto would put the final nail in the coffin for Moïse when Joan Baez invited dozens of draft dodgers to return to America to continue resisting there.

"Grow up a little, Romain," he wrote me after he returned to Montreal. "Dylan, Baez, they're straight out of a children's book. Instead of dressing up and going to grade school, they talk to the crowds as if they were made up entirely of eight-year-olds."

"My God, Canada is pretty far away if you have such a distorted vision of what's happening here. You remind me that I was right to leave." I played a game sometimes by telling him about what his disgraced ex-idols were doing. "Please," he'd reply. "They're passé. Talk to me about Leonard Cohen, a real poet. And Robert Charlebois. You should give a listen to him sometime." And he added, "The only thing that's missing is you, man."

And each time I felt emotion grip me.

I missed him terribly too.

A month after Moïse left, Dana found me a job at the Museum of Modern Art's ticket booth. I got the job through one of her contacts, one of the museum's wealthy donors. Blema Weinberg was a woman wider than she was tall, so covered in jewellery she looked like Tutankhamen. Blue eyelids, and lips as red as an Andy Warhol painting. She spoke endlessly, moved with small determined steps, filling every room she walked in with the smell of her heady perfume. Blema Weinberg was anything but invisible. She was richer than King Midas. Paintings by the great masters covered the walls of her Fifth Avenue apartment — Picasso, Dalí, Matisse. Sculptures by Giacometti and Henry Moore watched over the massive rose bushes at her mansion in Amagansett, in the Hamptons. To earn her place in heaven, as my mother would say — though with Blema Weinberg, guilt probably wasn't a motivating factor — she gave a part of her fortune to the MoMA, was a patron to many young female artists, and helped more established ones find a place in New York's museums. In 1959, she had pushed for the candidacy of Louise Nevelson and Jay DeFeo, the only two women to participate in *Sixteen Americans,* the legendary exposition at the MoMA, beside such names as Frank Stella, Robert Rauschenberg, and Jasper Johns.

She and Dana were thick as thieves from the day they met. Blema Weinberg invited her to lunch one day and made her an offer. She had loved *The Next War* and wanted to publish a book just as powerful about women and art.

"You know what Hans Hofmann said about Lee Krasner's work?" she asked Dana.

"Jackson Pollock's wife?"

"Oh, Dana! Let me tell you, you just fell into the same trap as everyone else. Doesn't Lee Krasner exist by herself? Must we name her husband to give her importance?"

"You're right. And what talent she has."

"Exactly. So, listen to this: Hans Hofmann, who taught her the principles of cubism, said, 'It's so good, you wouldn't know it was painted by a woman.'"

"Disgusting!"

"That's exactly my point, Dana. And you're in the perfect position to help me out."

Dana returned to Harperley Hall filled with enthusiasm. "Find your best shoes, Romain, we're going out tonight to celebrate." In front of an enormous steak, she told me about their conversation, their shared indignation, and she spoke of the unlimited confidence she had in Blema Weinberg. The next morning, she threw herself into this new project.

My work at the ticket booth at the MoMA, in addition to my university courses, kept me busy. I worked Wednesday afternoons and weekends. At first, Dana seemed to have doubts about my ability to keep that pace going over the long term, "Are you sure you can handle it?" I was surprised at how easy my first year at NYU had been. My second year was just as smooth — an A average, with only a couple B+s. Dana seemed surprised, "No homework? No reading?" No. Darren had taught me everything. I was lucky. The lectures in the large amphitheatres filled with students could have bored me to death, but instead every one was like a miracle. I listened to my professors attentively. They had a talent for capturing my attention and amazing me. My favourite was Martin Valenti, a theatrical man, a joker with bulging eyes. The whole class roared with laughter at his analysis of Salvador Dalí's paintings with objects melting like chocolate in the sun, making a parallel with the sexual impotence of the artist. It was fascinating.

That year I left the nest that was Harperley Hall. (Dana was so busy with her work she barely noticed — completely the opposite of Rosie who, in an unexpected moment of tenderness, had taken me in her arms and hugged me tight, her pale eyes blurry with tears.) With Ethel's help, I found an incredible deal on Perry Street in the West Village — an artist's loft with all the modern conveniences and a closed bedroom. Ethel found me a couch, a table, two chairs, and, as a mattress, a large ten-foot-by-ten-foot piece of foam that would undoubtedly impress the girls I'd manage to bring back home.

By now, my English was pretty good. I barely made mistakes and didn't have a noticeable accent. Sometimes girls at the museum would flirt with me, finding me, in their own words, "charming," though it was always painful to hear them absolutely flay my name with a sorry air, *Ro-main Car-ye*, as if they had pebbles in their mouths.

"Sweetheart?" Peggy and Betty, two regulars at the museum, spry eighty-year-olds, their hair always impeccable and their makeup perfectly done. Every Wednesday they had their weekly "cultural visit," as they said. I enjoyed taking care of them, offering my arm for the stairs or taking their coats. They would sit on a bench in front of the same few paintings, chatting softly. "Sweetheart?" And, "What if we called you *Roman* instead? What do you think?" Soon, everyone at the museum began calling me Roman. Roman Carr, like Lucien Carr, Kerouac's friend.

Moïse welcomed my new name. "Yes, man!" He said with a name like mine, I was sure to become famous.

Moïse wasn't trying so hard to be famous anymore. He'd found something better — love. And this time, it was mutual. Louise Morin was her name. She volunteered with the war resisters committee and was a driver for the draft dodgers who, like Moïse, needed to get their papers in order. To do so, they had to be driven out of Canada and back in, as if it were the first time. The FBI knew about the ploy and had agents all along the border.

"I didn't sleep for days, man...."

The day he was to go through the process, he lay sleepless on his mattress waiting for a knock on the door. That was how he met her, and he told me all about it in a long letter.

You shoulda seen the girl who rang my doorbell. An Amazon. Long shining hair like whale skin. A beautiful squaw's face illuminated by eyes of gold. And a voice, man, a voice that caresses you like a warm wind. I was petrified, nailed to the spot, I couldn't say a goddamn word. And you know what she said when she saw me like that? "Oh, so you were expecting a man to drive you?"

"No!" I howled as if my ass was on fire. And she burst out laughing so hard I was laughing too, like a desperate hyena, much too loud, like Jerry Lewis, you know what I mean? An idiot!

"Are you ready?" she asked.

"Yes."

She told me we had to pretend to be a couple on a lover's tryst in Vermont. Shit! What more could I ask for! But what do you think your idiot friend did? His face turned red. Red like a fucking girl! And after? You know what I said? Oh, man, sometimes… I said, as if I didn't care, or worse, as if it bothered me, "Only for the day, I hope." You read right — only for the day, I hope!

She answered, like a little insulted, "Don't you worry." And what did your idiotic friend add to that?

"Gotta do what you gotta do. Anyway, I don't have much of a choice, right?" Oooooooooh.

Honestly, I wasn't as anxious about crossing the border as I was about her! I was as scared and confused as a little boy who just pissed his bed and didn't know how to hide it. Sitting in the Beetle, I looked at the scenery go by in a Shakespearian state of panic and doubt, to hit on her or not to hit on her, with a visceral fear that I was about to screw everything up. My brain was moving at the speed of rust, my mouth was betraying my thoughts. So I shut it to prevent further damage, so as not to look like some dumb fucking American. The silence was so heavy, man, it hurt. No kidding, I still got bruises.

We drove like that for an hour. Oh, she asked me questions all right, from time to time — where I came from, what my life in New York was like, but I was so afraid of saying something ridiculous that I answered with very few words, the worst clichés, and she seemed disappointed. Oh, man! It was getting worse and worse as the Beetle drove towards the line where my fate was to play out, on the snowy roads of Quebec.

As we got near the border, she began fidgeting with the radio buttons. "An American channel," she said. And then Johnny Cash came on, man, his warm, comforting voice that brought tears to my eyes. Louise noticed it and she became all emotional too, I could see it in the way her golden eyes shone. It was magnificent, man. Johnny Cash made an appearance in the Beetle like a genie out of a lamp. It was marvelous, immense, it floated over us, his baritone voice like a thick cover over two lovers' entwined bodies on a winter morning. I got some confidence and looked Louise straight in the eyes and hummed in time with Johnny. She blushed, man! All I had to do was make a wish now.

When we saw the signs for the border, my nervousness returned. They looked like soldiers lost in the pastoral landscape of the Eastern Townships, a real postcard of valleys and homes of the descendants of Loyalists. Louise said solemnly, "Those American colonists loyal to King and Country found refuge here, during the American Revolution." I had a kind thought for those divorcees of America living peaceful lives, having children who lived peaceful lives of their own. Yes, it's possible. Our stories of exile, yours, mine, they might not be so extraordinary after all. They're two among thousands and thousands of stories just like them that were written on the line that has separated our two countries for the past two hundred years. Despite what we believe, we're just cogs in History, passively following the order of its implacable determinism.

"From now on, you'll be Doug," she told me. We were only two miles from the border.

"Doug." I chuckled stupidly. "Always thought it was like a dog's name."

She laughed. "I won't say that to Doug Naylor. You're lucky, I could have been his girlfriend and told him everything." She winked at me; it felt like an invitation, but I just stared at the long road covered in snow, paralyzed by fear.

You should know that Doug Naylor is a Canadian volunteer on the committee. He lent me his driver's licence. Luckily, there's no picture on it. But let me tell you, I look like him like Robert McNamara looks like Happy in *Snow White*. Returning to the States as a Canadian. Then back to Canada as an American. That was the ploy. Louise hid my papers in the trunk, I didn't know where exactly, but she assured me the border guards wouldn't find them. Meanwhile, we had to pretend to be lovers off trekking in Vermont, at Smugglers' Notch, with our snowshoes and boots and winter coats and pants (Doug had lent me his) — all our stuff visible in the back seat, you know. All that was missing was snow-covered pine trees and "Lara's Theme" from *Doctor Zhivago*, man, let me tell you.

We got to the border before eleven. The border crossing is a small red-brick building, flanked by pretentious white columns that patrician America loves. Around us, nothing. Empty. Snow in its virginal immensity, sullied by the presence of these two guys at the border, two fat Yankees with suspicious eyes. "Don't say a thing," Louise said. They asked the usual questions, and she answered all casually, the two guard dogs circling the Beetle, barking orders, "Get out of the car! Open the trunk!" We were outside, shivering, glancing at the two baboons going through our car. I started trembling. Uncontrollably. My heart was beating so hard you could hear it on the vast white plain. And my teeth started chattering. Clack! Clack!

Clack! A sinister woodpecker shattering rotting wood. I saw Louise go white. She gave me a hard look, making it clear I should get a hold of myself. But I couldn't do it. Man, I just couldn't do it. And then she grabbed me by the collar and pulled me towards her and stuck her warm tongue in my mouth. Ooooh, man!

The guards were annoyed, "Hey, you're not at a motel here!" The other one, the fat one, whistled, "Whore!" Not at all abashed, Louise came near them like a queen of light. She said, putting on the voice and face of a girl caught in the act, "You've got to forgive us, sirs. We're getting married in a week."

"Just go on," said the first. "And obey the speed limit."

Starting the Beetle, Louise returned to her professional air, a sublime Mata Hari, "The first step. We're not out of the woods. There are cops everywhere." I was blown away. Just blown away.

I was back in my country, but I didn't know this part of it at all. Tiny villages filled with invisible souls, houses, their fronts like the sad faces of abandoned children, car graveyards, and cemeteries, as if people died here more than in other places. This is America. Real America. Not Manhattan. Not the one out of Cecil B. DeMille's movies. I wouldn't have known it if it weren't for the American flags everywhere.

We drove west, straight west, towards New York state. Lake Champlain offered up its frozen beauty impudently, peppered with wild islands. I thought of the incident at the border, Louise's mouth tasting of peppermint, an ancient glacier on an erupting volcano, and that goddamn swelling between my legs.

We stopped in Champlain, just before the border. Louise grabbed my papers out of the trunk. "Whatever

else," she said, "don't lie." She made me repeat what I
needed to say to Canadian immigration. I had a copy of
a letter of employment from the *Montreal Star*. I've been
working there as an assistant for a few weeks already (in
addition to the work with Jenkins). A boring job, but it
might pan out into something else. We'll see. The *Star* sent
a letter to my parents in Brooklyn, and they forwarded it
to me. This is the other part of the ploy — getting into
Canada with an employment letter sent to an American
address, like an economic immigrant. To increase my
chances, it was written to give the impression that I was
going to be a journalist.

I looked behind me, whipped by icy wind, before
climbing back into the Beetle. The place didn't look like a
country I was leaving — an empty white plain like a clean
plate. Not exactly the type of image you want for your
last look at home. I cried a tear or two, and I prayed that
time wouldn't fade my memory too much, the only photo
album I'd bring with me.

After that, everything went quickly. First, the interview with the immigration agent, a guy with soft, sincere
eyes. He took my documents and disappeared into another
room where we heard him type on a machine. After half an
hour, he returned, a warm smile on his face, wishing me
welcome to Canada. I almost burst into tears.

Then, on our way back, to my new life as a Canadian
permanent resident — yes, man! In five years I'll be as
Canadian as you — I asked Louise to stop. She smiled a
complicit smile, and I knew she wanted the same thing I
did. We took a small country road lined with pine trees.
We stopped the car on the shoulder. We laid down on
the back seat and made love, in the middle of nature that
welcomed us with open arms.

The tension was gone all of a sudden. When we got back on the road again, I had no fear, no regrets. It was the start of a new adventure, and Louise is its most beautiful promise.

Your friend forever,
Moïse

7

I was seeing a girl, too, but it wasn't the same. Judy Stern, who worked as a guide at the MoMA. She was small, with short brown hair, pretty and brilliant, and she gazed slowly and intently at everything, as if a secret lay beneath all things — a chair, a piece of trash in the street, a Mark Rothko painting. She analyzed the world through extra-clear eyes, devoted, fierce affection for Nietzsche, her conversations sprinkled with, "As Nietzsche said," "According to Nietzsche," "Nietzsche believed." A real intellectual. With diplomas. Together, we spent a lot of time just talking at my place especially, in my ten-foot-by-ten-foot bed, covered with a pretty Indian spread I had found in a store in Greenwich. In bed too, everything was slow and measured; she could spend hours over me, inspecting me like a dissection in a laboratory, with precision and attention to detail. She never laughed. She said that humour was offensive to intelligence, a loathsome aspect of human nature. "There is only one world, and it is false, cruel, contradictory, seductive, and without meaning." Nietzsche, of course. "Obviously," she said. "Nietzsche claims that man suffers so deeply that he had to invent laughter. I know, I know. But, you see, this is why I don't laugh. Because I look at the world the way it is. I don't need medicine to tolerate it. It is there. I am here. That is all." My eyes closed, I listened to her words while her hands took care of me, and I felt I was the subject of some divine experiment.

In my letters to Moïse, I described Judy differently. I said she was tender, joyful. I described our relationship as being serious ("a little bit like you and Louise"). I knew Moïse. If I told him the truth, he would have said, "Except for fucking her, man, I don't know what you're doing with a girl like her. She seems like a manic-depressive to me."

What attracted me to Judy was her knowledge. She was brilliant and intuitive and knew so much about philosophers and their schools of thought. I loved listening, and drinking my fill of all the incredible things her head contained.

She encouraged me to apply for a part-time guide position at the MoMA. This was in May 1967; I was in my third year at university, and classes were getting harder, forcing me to study for long hours.

"Why don't you drop a few of them?" Judy suggested. "You can take them next year."

It was a good idea, but I had to run it past the folks at the local draft office. It was said they followed your progress carefully and could, if they didn't think it up to par, take away your 2-S status whenever they wanted. I scheduled a meeting on West 61st, my designated draft board, and found myself before two unfriendly grey-haired men in their sixties, volunteer civilians doing their patriotic duty, like on every board. They were committed to war, though some of them denied it. They listened to me, their faces hard, took my file from a cabinet and examined it carefully, impassively. I attempted to explain as calmly as possible that I needed to work to pay for the rest of my studies — which wasn't entirely a lie. In the end, my arguments won out, and they gave me a reprieve.

I'd just won another year in New York. I got the job as part-time museum guide and dropped two courses.

I would have never thought so, but I enjoyed speaking in public. I liked the attention. Young and old, housewives and businessmen, workers and tourists, they all listened to me with almost religious attention, their brows furrowed, hands behind their backs. I was more than a simple museum employee, I was a somebody! Somebody who knew more than they did, who had knowledge they would never have. Sometimes they were like children, trying to impress me with their questions and comments. "Excellent point," I answered. Or, "A very judicious remark." If I felt like flattering someone, "Oh, dear me, we have an expert here. Are you an art historian, by any chance?" The person would deny it, a triumphant smile on their face, and discreetly offer me a few dollars at the end, "Oh, Roman. I had such a wonderful afternoon. This is for you. You deserve it."

My favourite moment? When I gathered them around a Jasper Johns painting, his series on American flags. Immediately, I noticed the mocking looks — *This is art?* I would grab the attention of a man in a suit or an older woman who I thought might have voted for Nixon. "What do you feel when you see an American flag? Pride? Patriotism? A sense of belonging to a great nation?" Eyes rooted on the piece, they nodded enthusiastically, while the rest of the group — young people, blacks, students, hippies, foreign tourists — stiffened. I turned towards them next, "And you? What do you see? Our engagement in Vietnam? War and the dead? Racial segregation?" And they would nod in turn, glad to have their thoughts validated, as the other group looked on, confused. The more my protégés let themselves be taken in, the more success I had with my little routine. "And yet it's just art!" I said to make the atmosphere less tense. "And that's Jasper Johns' genius. Through the representation of an ordinary object, so present in our lives, he manages to stir up such contradictory, powerful emotions. Come, now, follow the guide...."

It was going well for me, as it was for Moïse. He'd left the war resisters committee, and was working full time for the *Montreal Star*, where he'd become a reporter. He moved in with Louise, in her apartment on Hutchison, in Outremont, and was waiting for the right moment to ask her to marry him. "Can you imagine, man! Me, Charlie Moses, joining the ranks of married men!"

I envied Moïse. Louise was beautiful. A healthy, pretty woman, you could see it immediately in the pictures he sent me. There was one, so touching, of them holding each other — Moïse, blissfully happy, eyes like fireworks, the perfect image of matrimonial bliss.

As for me, why exactly was I with Judy?

"Come on, man. Send me a picture of her." I can't remember how many times Moïse asked the same question, and each time I answered that Judy hated being photographed, a sort of reflex — even her mother didn't have a picture of her as a child. "Bullshit," Moïse replied. "It's got to be one of two things — either she doesn't exist, or you don't love her."

Dana liked Judy. "Supremely intelligent," she declared, "though a little ethereal." Once, after supper at Harperley Hall, Dana pulled me aside in the kitchen. "With Judy, it's as if gravity has no effect on her, as if her head is about to float off her body, you know, like a Chagall character. Are you happy with her?"

"Do I look like I'm not?"

She looked at me, surprised. "If you're trying to be convincing, you probably shouldn't answer a question with a question."

Was I happy with Judy? The sex was okay, our discussions amazing — enough for me to become attached. But happy? I didn't know. In love? No. For now, it was good enough. It suited me.

I was delighted for Moïse, and he was delighted for me. But what had to happen, happened: our lives were so different now, and slowly we began to drift apart. Moïse didn't know much about contemporary art, and I didn't understand the country he was describing to me, my own, with its bombs, its F.L.Q., the dreams of independence, it all seemed so weird to me, as if he were talking about the Prague Spring. On the phone, our conversations weren't the same, punctuated by awkward silences. Our letters took strange turns sometimes — "Ha! Ha! You're stuck with that whore Nixon. We've got Pierre Trudeau!" Moïse absolutely fawned over the young Prime Minister, sympathetic to the cause of draft dodgers, having publicly declared that Canada should become a refuge against militarism. "Oh, man! The right hook he just gave that shit-for-brains Nixon!"

But when Trudeau sent the army into Quebec, I would write to him, "Trudeau against militarism? And what about the tanks in the streets of Montreal? What are they for exactly? Your favourite Prime Minister's new game?"

He wouldn't answer that one.

Were we moving apart?

"I miss you, man," Moïse wrote at the end of each letter. I thought of the words a husband says to a wife he doesn't love much anymore, yet tries to reassure. "Miss you too," I answered, feeling a little bit sad.

8

I began my fourth and final year at NYU in a near panic. *And after this?* I had to start thinking about returning to Quebec — it was that or the draft, like every other boy of twenty or twenty-one with the ink on their diplomas still fresh, off to do office jobs in the Army. For us, an office job was as bad as being sent to Southeast Asia to kill innocents. No one wanted to contribute to this monstrous war.

Complaining would have been indecent. I had the option of leaving, a back-up plan most people didn't have.

While my situation might have been better than most people's, I was in a constant state of agitation. Though, in truth, who wasn't in some form of distress or other in 1968? The murders of Martin Luther King and Bobby Kennedy, only a couple of months apart. Across the country, riots were sparked by King's murder. Every night on the news more dead, more wounded, in the United States and abroad. Not to mention the endless aluminum coffins unloaded from planes. The quagmire thickening. A majority of Americans now said they were against the war, convinced that Washington was headed in the wrong direction. At NYU, despair was the commonest emotion on campus, classes emptying as young men and women abandoned classrooms to go out and demonstrate, most of the time with their teachers' blessings. From time to time, a young man whose draft deferral was about to expire simply vanished. And while entire families were facing real tragedies, presidential candidates distributed handshakes, small talk, and warm — or falsely empathetic — smiles when snot-nosed babies were thrust in their arms. Nixon's appearance on *Rowan & Martin's Laugh-In,* over a laugh track, made us want to puke. A number of young people were now disgusted at having given him their trust when he'd promised he had a "secret plan" to end the war.

In the middle of this maelstrom Dana completed her book, *Women and Arts.*

She was surprisingly calm about the whole thing, almost serene. A sea-change compared to her insecurities on the eve of *The Next War,* her editor at Harry N. Abrams had done solid work, been patient and confident, and she no longer feared the critics, "I'm not putting forward my own self. I'm highlighting the mission of a handful of artists and Blema Weinberg. It's so much simpler!" And she laughed.

Simpler? "I know, Romain. Times are tough. But art and beauty can help us pull through."

The book was spectacular. A large, beautifully bound volume with colour illustrations on high-quality paper and an audacious choice for the cover — *Slightly Open Clam Shell* by Georgia O'Keeffe, showing a shell that suggests the image of a woman's vulva. The critics lauded her work, and the launch at the MoMA was a roaring success — some three hundred people including artists, patrons, journalists, New York celebrities like Jackie Kennedy and Gloria Vanderbilt, and, of course, loads of champagne. Her face burning with excitement, eyes as deeply coloured as a boxer in the twelfth round, Blema Weinberg waddled from group to group, the book cradled in her bejewelled arms, as if she were holding a child. Dana stood a bit apart from the crowd, slightly pale as a result of a cold she was fighting but happy and fulfilled, scanning the room with an amused air — all these people were impressed and awestruck by … *her book?* Judy spoke into my ear, "I've never seen her so beautiful." And it was true. Dana was staggeringly lovely in her small black dress, flat shoes, hair back in a bun.

The following Saturday, to celebrate the launch, Blema Weinberg invited us to a garden party at her mansion in Amagansett. That morning, Dana woke with a bit of a fever, but there was no way she'd cancel on Blema. Ethel was ill as well, probably with the same virus. She declined the invitation; despite being the subject of a long paragraph in *Women and Arts*, she stayed at Harperley Hall with Rosie. Judy couldn't come either, since it was her mother's birthday. "Do you want me to go with you?" I asked with as little enthusiasm as humanly possible. She seemed disappointed at first but ended up shrugging her shoulders theatrically. "Don't worry about it. Go with Dana. It'll be a lot more fun than with my parents. You know the menu at casa Stern — disappointment, lamentations, guilt, and roast chicken."

So we went, just Dana and I, like in the old days, when things weren't quite so clear between us.

I got behind the wheel of her new Austin-Healey 3000 so she could rest. She was pale, her skin almost translucent like those cold, melancholy women in Italian Renaissance paintings. In the elevator in Harperley Hall she wavered on her legs a moment, and I had to hold her so she wouldn't fall. She tried to reassure me, claiming it was a side-effect of the codeine Rosie had given her; she'd be fine by the time we got to the Hamptons. Shouldn't we stay home? "Not a chance!" Sea air would do her good, she claimed.

It was sunny out, and warm and humid. We cut through Central Park, went south on Fifth Avenue, then east on 42nd Street. On I-495 we sped towards Long Island, roof down.

It might have been the air, it felt fresher with every mile that took us farther from New York. Or maybe it was the sweet image of Dana dozing in her seat, her shoulders turned towards me, like a sleeping spouse. Perhaps it was the sun on my skin, the wind in my hair, or "Mrs. Robinson" jingling on the radio. I was overcome by a sudden and blind confidence in the future — I'd return to Quebec in December and find my friend Moïse. We'd have long, lively conversations together and he'd introduce me to his beautiful Louise, and he'd be so proud it would bring tears to my eyes. I'd find work in a museum in Montreal and wait out the war. I'd come back to New York eventually and return to Dana, Ethel, and, perhaps, Judy. Things weren't so bad after all. I was lucky, luckier than most boys my age.

"What are you thinking about?"

Dana had woken up, her head turned toward me.

"Nothing."

"Liar. It's impossible to think about nothing…."

I smiled, took her hand, and said, "Thanks. For everything."

She took her sunglasses off and gave me a long look. I continued, my voice filled with emotion, "If you hadn't been there, I don't know what would have become of me."

She straightened in her seat and blew her nose loudly. "What are you talking about?"

I smiled. "You remember that timid, ridiculous boy who knocked on your door with a box of Tampax hidden under his shirt?"

She burst out laughing. "My God! Ethel and I laughed about that for days. You were so sweet!"

It was funny to remember that fifteen-year-old, so insecure, his face purple with embarrassment. On the road to Amagansett, the blue sky veiled with humidity, I remembered that stick of a boy, wondering what he would have thought if he could see me now, twenty-three years old, happy and optimistic, at the helm of a red Austin-Healey, racing towards the Hamptons. *That's me? You've got to be kidding.*

"If I hadn't had you, Dana …" my voice broke.

She brushed my cheek. I took her hand in mine and brought it to my lips. A tender kiss, not sexual at all. There was no more sexual confusion between us, no more desire, not even the memory of desire. I was simply filled with a soft, sweet feeling. She giggled like a little girl. "If you hadn't had me, Romain Carrier, you would have become a little pervert!"

We laughed. Then I apologized for our fights at Harperley Hall and my sometimes disrespectful attitude. "I love you, Dana."

Her eyes filled with water, and she told me to shut up before she cried.

That morning, on the road to Amagansett, I told myself that life had really given me all its blessings. I felt I had a future, a real one. My studies, my work at the museum, it wasn't an end in itself, but they would bring me further, I knew it. Judy wasn't an end, either. I'd cross paths with other incredible women, I knew that too. I was free. Free. A flight of birds turned above our heads, and Dana laughed again. We were as happy as children on summer vacation, our hair in the wind. On the road to Amagansett, I surfed on this sudden happiness, like light bursting through clouds, almost mystical, without thinking of its colour, or the dimension and magnitude of the wave that was carrying me, nor the great treasure and disaster that would come in its wake.

9

A mansion. A castle. Twenty-six rooms in all, without counting the guest pavilions. Blema Weinberg's manor was built on dozens of acres with a stunning view of the Atlantic. You visited a dozen countries in as many minutes as you walked through the gardens. Rose bushes, grandiose sculptures signed Henry Moore, Giacometti, Louise Bourgeois. A Calder, light and ethereal, welcomed guests at the entrance. Dana and I were stunned.

Blema Weinberg came to meet us in a white silk caftan. She was drenched in makeup, all but bent in two under the weight of emerald necklaces, a grotesque copy of Liz Taylor in *Cleopatra*. She gesticulated with excitement, clucking with pleasure, "Welcome! Welcome, my dear friends! Oh, I'm so happy to have you with us! Isn't it wonderful? What a beautiful day! How was the drive?" She turned to Dana and rushed towards her, arms open, "Oh, Dana! Wonderful Dana!" She pulled her so tight against her that her perfume clung to Dana for the rest of the afternoon. "Come," she insisted. "Come, I've something to show you."

When she entered the great hall, Dana cried out. A dozen of the works reproduced in *Women and Arts* were hanging from the walls. Blema Weinberg had had them brought over and installed by the museum staff. Works by Krasner, O'Keeffe, Escobar, Nevelson, DeFeo. All it took was a phone call, and an exhibition was set up

in her house. Guests walked in and whistled, impressed; Blema
Weinberg chuckled triumphantly.

Artists, including the women featured in *Women and Arts*,
chatted next to the pool, champagne glasses in hand. Blema introduced us to Roy Lichtenstein and James Rosenquist. A handful
of guests were amusing themselves in the hedge maze. You could
hear them call out, "Is someone there? Where are you?" Under
tall, white tents, giant tables dressed for a royal wedding buckled
under the weight of the victuals — smoked salmon, blinis, caviar,
chicken skewers, salads. A feast. Excited, Blema Weinberg pulled
us aside, Dana and me, for the guided tour. She spoke of her husband, dead after a long illness; he had the mansion built for her.
She had three boys, all married, with kids. They came from time
to time to Amagansett, but certainly not often enough. "And yet,"
she said, as we were walking through a labyrinth of rooms on the
second floor, "there's enough room for everyone." I was counting
them, actually. Eight. Eight bedrooms, each as richly decorated
as the next, with four-poster beds and massive hangings. "Sleep
here tonight," she begged, "it would make me so happy. I love it
when the house feels inhabited." But Dana, still looking rather sick,
delicately blew her irritated nose, and declined the invitation. In
the state she was in, she preferred to sleep in New York. "I don't
think I'll be staying very late, Blema. I'm truly sorry. Romain will
bring me home as soon as I feel too tired."

"Oh, poor Dana! Of course. I understand completely." She
continued covering her disappointment, "What a beautiful day,
my friends! What a wonderful day, right?"

In the garden, a jazz band was warming up the crowd. Blema
Weinberg laughed and clapped her hands. Dana joined a small
group chatting around the pool — Marisol Escobar, Jay DeFeo,
Dana Feldman — three beautiful brunettes with embers in
their eyes, talking passionately about art. What a scene! I took
advantage of the action to disappear, pulled towards the ocean

— crashing waves, agitation, the sheer immensity of it. Living in New York, sometimes I forgot about the sea. But seeing it before me, I realized how much I missed it.

The great river of my childhood, so wide we called it the sea.

I walked to the end of the garden, went down a small pine stairway and took my shoes off, feeling warm sand between my toes. Children were playing in the waves; men and boys tossing a ball; women tanning in the sun, glistening like sardines in oil. A breeze brought a waft of coconut to my nose. I sat in the sand and watched the sea, greater than my own sea in Métis Beach, and closed my eyes. I scanned my memory for an event that might make me feel nostalgic about my past, but simply couldn't find one. I recalled Gail's face, replaying the film of that night in 1962, and I felt no sadness, no guilt. No more than a neutral spectator. Was I cured? The scar gone? With closed eyes, I savoured this moment of fullness, letting myself be lulled by the calming thunder of the Atlantic.

"May I?"

I opened my eyes. It was one of the girls at the party who had accompanied Lichtenstein and Rosenquist. A small blonde, her blue eyes painted in the latest style, with a thick line of khol.

"Please."

She sat next to me, watched the sea for a while, then said, with an accent à la Petula Clark, "What's your name?"

"Romain Carrier."

"Felicia Jackson."

"A pleasure."

She had a small, vague smile. "Do you want some?"

In the palm of her hand, a cigarette she had pulled out of nowhere.

"What is it?"

"Hashish."

I said sarcastically, "And you're going to smoke that in front of all these nice families?"

She shrugged. "All of them are drinking, aren't they? Alcohol is socially acceptable, but it's far worse for you. I know a thing or two about that, I'm British, after all." Her face darkened for a moment, as if a bad memory had suddenly caught up with her. She put the cigarette in her mouth, wet it with her tongue, "While this doesn't hurt anyone."

She turned her back to the wind to light it. I'd never smoked hashish before, not even at university, not with Moïse either who hated the smell — "It smells like degeneration, man, like camel shit." I had had plenty of opportunities in Washington Square, but the idea of swallowing smoke — like Dana with her Kools, all day long — put me off.

"Come on, try some, you won't regret it, I promise."

Her flirtatious voice. She scooted towards me, held out the joint. I took a few puffs, I didn't want to look like a guy who wasn't hip. The acrid smoke burned my throat. She grabbed the joint from me and took a long drag before offering it to me again. I was about to refuse when she placed a hand on my shoulder, and slipped it onto the back of my neck, through my hair, and I felt myself fall forward, too excited to resist, and found myself kissing her, her mouth, her lips, her tongue, and she kissed me back with such avidity it felt like distress, and a mad desire, irrepressible, to take her breasts in my hands, to feel them, to suck on their hard nipples under her dress, to stick my fingers inside her to make her come, there, on the beach, in front of all these people. She laughed, dancing eyes and dilated pupils, and I laughed too, filled with voluptuous stupor, my brain hazy from my first joint, and now the second she was lighting.

"Where were you?"

By the pool, Dana, her skin pale and her eyes feverish, caught me by the arm.

"You look terrible. Go clean up. We're leaving."

"Now?"

She stared at me, suspicious. "What's going on with you? You've been drinking?"

"Did you see me drink?"

"Don't answer a question with a question!"

"I was on the beach, I didn't have a single drop."

She mumbled something, blew her nose. "Fine, so what's wrong with you then?"

"Nothing. I'm fine, okay?"

"You'd better be. I'm tired. That was our deal."

But I wasn't okay. My heart was beating too quickly. A strange sensation in me, almost worrying, oppressive. Felicia disappeared after that man had begun yelling at us, a crowd around us suddenly, men and women, their mouths open as if they were lost, scared children peeking from behind them. My shirt was off, my pants undone, my zipper down, we'd been messing around for almost an hour on the beach. "Go on, say it again, sweetheart! Say what you just said!" A man with black trunks was shouting at us, a tall guy with thick legs.

"Go fuck yourself!" Felicia shouted. "You heard what I said, dumbass!" With a strong arm he grabbed me by the belt and pulled me to my feet.

"You get the fuck out of here with your whore, or I'm calling the cops!" Felicia laughed, and I did too, an uncontrollable, convulsive laugh, like the grinding engine of an old car, and we ran back towards the garden, stumbling on the burning sand. Once we arrived on Blema Weinberg's property, Felicia was gone.

Around the pool, the guests were watching us, and I had the clear impression they were judging me severely, reading my thoughts. Dana got up and handed me the keys to the Austin-Healey. "Oh, no! Already?" Blema Weinberg was disappointed to see us leave so soon, though glad her party had been so successful.

She accompanied us to the Austin, saying the same thing a hundred different ways, how happy she was with *Women and Arts* and how she had other projects for Dana. Her constant clucking made my head spin. Dana gave me a suspicious look each time I lost my footing on the gravel driveway. I followed the women, trying to walk as straight as possible, wondering how I'd manage to drive.

Dana kissed her goodbye, and we climbed in the car. My trembling hands took a few moments to find the ignition, and Dana seemed exasperated. The motor finally came to life, and she sat back in her seat. Blema Weinberg waved at us from the top of the steps to her manor; the illuminated Calder floated like a gigantic butterfly in the humid, foggy air. Night was falling.

My legs thick, my heart beating in my ears, I carefully brought the Austin onto the road and turned right on the 27. I was dizzy, like I was in some slow-motion film. I was cruising at fifty-five miles an hour, feeling I was driving through butter, then I reached sixty, sixty-five, seventy, and still that feeling of not moving at all. The windshield wore a sheen of humidity and dead flies. The moon was shining, but not enough to illuminate the road. "Hey!" Dana straightened, her nails dug into the dashboard. "Slow down, for God's sake! What are you doing?" She grabbed my forearm, frightened. "You're going too fast! Pull over onto the shoulder, now!" I couldn't react; my brain, my arms and legs, simply weren't answering my orders. Dana was shouting, hitting me with her fists. My clumsy feet were looking for the brake. Or was it the accelerator? The Austin-Healey began careening along the road. "Brake, for God's sake! Brake!" In front of us, a seafood restaurant. "Stop here! Here, I said!" The Austin careened again, skidded on the gravel and turned circles before stopping against a line of trash cans, not far from a cook, who'd witnessed the whole scene.

Dana got out of the car, hysterical. She was trembling with fear and anger. "You could have killed us! Is that what you wanted? To kill us? You're in no shape to drive! Get out of there!"

With difficulty, I managed to pull myself out of the car. I moved around it, holding onto the body, and fell into the passenger seat.

"Idiot!" Dana shouted at me one last time before getting behind the wheel and driving off.

After that, I don't know what happened. I remember waking up as the car careened from side to side. In front of me, another car flashing its headlights at us desperately, honking. Dana had fallen asleep, her chin on her chest. With a quick gesture, a reflex, I grabbed the wheel and pulled us to the right. Dana was startled awake, howled in fear, and the Austin-Healey zigzagged on the road. In the distance, headlights flashed, insistent, blinding. Then our shouts of fear, the howling of rubber tearing itself apart on pavement, and the crash of metal.

Then, nothing.

10

"What happened, Romain? For the love of God, tell me!"

I couldn't give Ethel, who was inconsolable, a clear narrative of the tragic events. Just flashes. Furtive memories, scattered, like a deck of playing cards thrown about by the winds of fate, without pity. I awoke in a ditch. Sticky, warm blood on my face and in my mouth. A thick silence, then a sinister screeching in the darkness — the Austin-Healey's wheels turning in the air, the car on its back. "Dana? Dana?" The slow breathing of the sea nearby. Mad birds cackling as they flew in the dark. I hurt everywhere. Couldn't get up. No, wait, I could, walking slowly. Towards the road. A strange music playing in the air saturated with humidity. I didn't know where it was coming from, "Run, run, little horse … run, run, little horse…." Waiting for help. Headlights in the distance, I waved to attract attention. I was lucky — a patrol vehicle. (Later, I'd be told that the Suffolk County cops found me unconscious in a ditch.) My eyes veiled with blood, barely able to make out a figure slumped against a tree. I shouted to the cops (again, fruit of my imagination), "Help her, quick! It's Dana Feldman, the famous feminist!" with a touch of vanity in my voice. The two cops looked at each other, intrigued? Horrified? The birds cackled louder. "Dana? Dana?" My eyes couldn't see. A cacophony of sirens and loud voices scared the silence out of me. Ambulances shrieking. The serious faces of the paramedics, their movements precise, quick. The clacking of stretchers being opened. Comfort from a blanket draped over my prone body. I was cold though it was warm out. They were moving me to the violently lit emergency room of Good Samaritan Hospital, in West Islip. Orders being shouted, quick feet moving around Dana's stretcher. I couldn't see her, though I knew she was there. We were separated. I wanted to protest but didn't have the strength. Lying on my stretcher, I didn't have as large a crowd of doctors and nurses around me. They were calmer with me, much calmer. Standing over me, checking me out, asking questions. I answered yes, no. I was naked, didn't know how my clothes had been taken off.

"You're lucky," the doctor told me. A deep cut on my forehead needing a few sutures, contusions on my arms and legs, a slightly more serious injury in my right eye, a laceration on my cornea.

And Dana? "You need to rest now, you're in shock."

I didn't like the doctor's answer. "Dana? How is she?"

"Don't worry about it. We're taking care of her."

With a soft but firm voice he ordered me to turn on my stomach, and stuck a needle in me. Two cops walked into the room. They wanted to talk to me. They asked me if I was a family member. No, I answered, but we practically were, in truth. I wanted to say more. Explain that I was like a son to her, that we loved each other, that we used to be lovers, it was even in the papers, but fatigue crowded out my thoughts. "We need to talk with a family member," one of the officers said. "Do you know her parents? Brothers, sisters? Children?" The voice was insisting, almost threatening. My mind was getting hazier: whatever the doctor hit me with was having an effect. The doctor encouraged me to answer. With a thick, weak voice, I told them Dana's parents were dead but that there was her sister Ethel, and I gave them Harperley Hall's number, where Rosie was taking care of her. The other cop took notes in a little notebook. Feeling myself falling into unconsciousness, I managed to hold on for a moment and shouted, "Why?" The two cops avoided my eyes, and I knew what that meant.

Dana's funeral took place according to Jewish tradition, two days after her death. Thirty-six hours, to be precise. Everything happened very quickly; her son Mark made sure of it. It was quick, hurried. A train you needed to take but that didn't stop at your station.

Judy, herself a non-observant Jew — "'A person's intelligence can be measured by the quantity of uncertainties he can bear,' Romain" (Kant, this time) — knew that among her people, you didn't waste time with the dead. She told me Ethel had called Mark in London, who contacted a rabbi in New York, who himself gave guidelines to the Suffolk County cops as well as the personnel at West Islip hospital — the body was to quickly be sent back to Manhattan, there was to be no autopsy (out of respect for the body), no embalming or cremation, no open casket or flowers (there was no point in killing God's creatures to honour the dead). Quickly, everyone close to her was informed. Mark and his wife Sarah arrived from London that same night, and the next morning we were all together at the synagogue on Lexington Avenue, shocked, faces drawn, eyes red. When the rabbi's chanting filled the room, Ethel, already weakened by her cold, fainted. Two women ran to her with water, and I fell apart as well and cried — every tear I had in my body.

I would have accompanied Ethel to the cemetery, but Mark — whom I was meeting for the first time — convinced me otherwise with a single look, cold and pitiless. Clearly, I wasn't welcome in the Feldman limousine. So I joined Judy in her father's Ford Fairlane, and we followed, as the rain began to fall, the long procession to the Machpelah Cemetery in Queens, where Dana's parents had been buried.

My forehead bandaged, my right eye covered, I felt my head was about to burst — lancing pain that the doctor's pills could have softened had I not thrown them out in an effort to punish myself. I was suffering from panic attacks since the accident — cold sweat, my heart beating irregularly, a weight on my chest. And Dana's voice, tormenting me, impossible to silence, *Have you been drinking? You're in no shape to drive!* I kept revisiting the last image I had of her, which might haunt me to end of my life, perhaps the fruit of my imagination, who knows, but so real, so terrifying: a doll cast against the tree, its neck dislocated, lifeless. Enough to make you go mad.

"I think I'm going crazy, Judy."

At the wheel of the Ford Fairlane, Judy turned to look at me, her face a mask of empathy.

"No, Romain. It's called sadness. You're hurting, you're in pain, but you're not crazy."

With the same awkwardness shown by the few people who embraced me at the synagogue (friends of Dana, including Burke), she tried to comfort me. "It's not your fault. It happens to thousands of people. It could happen to us, here, now. It was just an accident." She turned to look at me. "Are you okay? I've never seen you so pale. Do you want to stop and grab something to eat or drink? You haven't eaten anything in two days."

The mere idea of food made me want to throw up.

In front of us, a black Cadillac filled with Dana's cousins or uncles or aunts — I didn't know anymore. Behind us, Blema Weinberg's silver Bentley, driven by her chauffeur. At the synagogue, she barely acknowledged me, that dark look she gave me, a knowing look. She was sure it wasn't *just an accident*, as the rabbi — and everyone else — kept repeating. She'd seen me stagger, she'd seen my hands tremble as I had tried and failed to find the ignition.

Drops of rain exploded on the windshield, immediately whisked away by the wipers. I closed my eyes. The Austin-Healey had been rammed off the road by a Dodge pick-up, or so a witness swore. The cops were still looking for it.

Just an accident? All these people who loved Dana — I was lying to them. I couldn't imagine this nightmare ending.

Judy said, "You know what Nietzsche said about death?"

"Please, Judy. Forget Nietzsche and the others. I don't give a fuck about their philosophies. I'm going crazy, for crying out loud!"

She stiffened, her eyes fixed on the road. She said in a small, hurt voice, "I'm grieving as much as you are. What do you want me to say? It's a nightmare? It's the end of your life? You won't live through it?"

"Please, Judy, shut up."

We made our way in silence to Machpelah Cemetery, on Cypress Hills Street, without another word. At the end of the afternoon, she dropped me off in front of my place, on Perry Street, in the West Village. I got out of the Ford Fairlane without kissing her or saying goodbye.

II

"Stay with me, Romain. Don't go. Hold me."

Ethel was living in my loft now. She couldn't be alone at her place or at Harperley Hall, surrounded by Dana's things, even if Rosie would have taken care of her like her own daughter. I made us spaghetti and grilled cheese with Campbell's soup and dry biscuits, but we weren't hungry. We drank a lot: Schlitz in the morning, vodka at noon, sometimes earlier.

I asked Judy to tell the museum I was quitting. She tried to dissuade me, "They'll give you as much time as you need. Don't be an idiot and throw it all away on a whim." I couldn't go back to my old life as if nothing had changed. I wouldn't allow myself to be happy, either. I told Judy it was over between us.

"You can't isolate yourself, Romain!"

"I can, Judy. That's what I need. To be alone. I don't deserve anyone."

The only person I saw was Ethel. She was still sick and spent her days in my bed. She called to me from time to time in a sad, hoarse voice, and I went to her and lay beside her. We spooned, listened in silence to the muted sounds rising from the streets — garbage trucks, deliverymen, and sometimes, not far away, children playing and laughing. Life going on. We were outside time, in another galaxy, in our grief that no one could take away from us. We made love a few times, crying. We were trying to lose ourselves in each other, trying to find pieces of Dana. We made love, and then I told

Ethel I couldn't continue. Ethel looked at me, tears running down her cheeks, and lowered her eyes. She understood. She wasn't angry at me. She knew it was the right thing to do. We both knew.

"We have to accept her death," Ethel said, inconsolable. "I don't know if I can, Romain …" She coughed. A harsh, deep cough, "You really think it was Dana's time? That's all it was? And we shouldn't try to understand?"

Her time had come. When she got a hold on herself, Ethel held on to those empty words like a rotten plank in a stormy sea. They seemed to comfort her. Who was I to take that away from her? What right did I have to tell her the truth?

All that was left was to live with my secret.

It was my penance.

Terrified, I sat with the others in the law office of Sam Waller. Austere, proud, like a James Wood painting. He was to reveal to us how Dana had evaluated our position in her life. Isn't that the accounting we do when we inherit from someone — don't the largest pieces go to those they loved the most?

"No, Ethel, I can't."

"What do you mean, you can't? They're Dana's last wishes! Have some respect, please!"

"I'm not strong enough. I shouldn't be there. Please don't force me to be there…."

I killed her, for God's sake!

"It's hard for everyone, Romain Carrier!"

Waller had barely opened the door, and Mark and Sarah made their way to the leather seats near the window, without a handshake or a nod. They sat down before everyone, and as soon as the rest of us had found a chair, Mark began talking about me as if I wasn't in the room, but simply some manifestation of a bad smell, "What's he doing here?"

Immediately, I wanted to run. Ethel must have felt it, because she grabbed my arm and held on tight. Waller coughed, blew his nose, and formally declaimed that he was executing the wishes of the deceased and that "Mr. Carrier is one of her legatees." Mark made a face.

Mark's resemblance to Dana troubled me. His eyes especially. Black, penetrating. He was a handsome man, clearly used to authority, you could feel it in the superior way he carried himself, making it clear that he would aggressively defend his ideas, his way of life, his God. Dark clothes, beard, kippa. His wife was soft, fat, without beauty (twenty-five years old and already four children). She wore a wig. The way their hands played with the leather armrests, you could tell they were nervous.

Seated in the half-lit room on East 33rd, we listened, tense, to Waller, the third of his name and a third-generation lawyer — it was proudly noted on the wall behind him — as he read the document in a neutral tone, sometimes getting hung up on words, though never numbers. I could hear the blood beating in my temples as Sarah and Mark Feldman stared at him offensively, as if he expected a confession.

Dana had a little more than two million dollars, a fortune for the time, and I felt my stomach churning.

To her son and grandchildren, Dana left more than a million dollars in cash and securities, and Ethel would say later, frothing at the mouth, "Okay, sure, it's his father's money, but still!" You should have seen their triumphant air, Mark and his wife, their satisfied smile. It would soon be erased however. In his drab voice, the lawyer declared that Dana had left to Ethel her Harperley Hall property and everything it contained, including a few very valuable paintings — a Braque, a Soutine, a small Dalí, and a few Franz Klines — as well as seven hundred thousand dollars. "And to Romain Carrier, I leave ..." My name said out loud felt like a punch in the face. Words, numbers, a fog. How much? A thousand? Ten thousand? Thirty? No.... *One hundred thousand dollars!* A hundred thousand dollars like a hundred thousand cuts to the heart. And what's more, the house in Métis Beach, the Victorian mansion that Grandfather McPhail had built and that Dana loved, "So you might always have a connection with your home...." Touching words from Dana, read by a stranger in a monotone.

All of it ... for me? *Punish me, please! Don't reward me!*

"No, please ... I can't accept...."

"They're Dana's wishes!" Ethel cut me off.

Deaf to our reactions, the lawyer continued his reading of the will through his thick glasses, turning the pages with a finger he first wet in his mouth, as if he could taste Dana's life in the description of goods, money, property.

Ethel received the rights to *The Next War* and *Women and Arts*, which would ensure her a certain stability for the rest of her life. Mark, who already felt — counted, probably — the immense pecuniary potential of his mother's books, protested, encouraged by Sarah, "This has to be a mistake...." Ethel turned red, outraged, "A mistake? Is that what you just said? The books you claimed were *feminist drivel?*" Her whole body shook with disgust. She coughed, then said, "*Aleha ha-shalom* — may peace be upon her."

The lawyer was now speaking of things that didn't concern us, a life-long pension for Rosie, a few debts that needed to be settled. Then he stacked the papers on his desk, the signal that he was done with us. He got up, offered his hand, which Mark and Sarah refused. "Everything will be done and distributed according to the wishes of the deceased."

"Not before my lawyers get involved," Mark said.

Waller had a tight smile, "It is no longer my business, Mr. Feldman. If you so wish, go to the courts. They'll decide."

He opened the door. Ethel grabbed my hand and pulled me out.

"Hey, gigolo."

Gigolo? Is that what he said? I pretended not to hear, and kept walking towards the exit.

"Leave us be," Ethel said.

"Hey!" Mark insisted. "I'm not done with *him*."

I was about to step into the elevator with Ethel when I felt his hand on my shoulder, firm, hostile. I clenched my fists. "You really think you're going to get away with this? My grandfather's house will never leave the McPhail family, you hear?"

Ethel spoke up, "Ah! And when's the last time you were there? You always hated the place! A yokel's house in a yokel country, you used to say!" She was hysterical now. "How dare you claim your grandfather's name when you renounced it, *Mark Feldman*!"

She took me by my arm. "Come, Romain. Forget them. This is the last time we'll ever see them." The elevator doors closed. Annoyed, Ethel began furiously pounding the button, calling it back. "Come on! Hurry up!"

Mark kept going, though, his voice threatening. "I'm not done with you. I know you were at the wheel that night."

I became white as a sheet.

"Come on, Romain. Let's take the stairs instead."

But Mark, while shorter than me, was larger, and blocked my way, a vengeful finger pointed under my chin. "Blema Weinberg saw you leave. She told me you looked strange, not normal. I asked the cops to open an enquiry. You killed her. You killed my mother!"

"No!" Ethel howled, "It was an accident!"

I clenched my jaw. The police knew I'd gotten behind the wheel in Amagansett. I told them that Dana had taken over after a few miles since I'd had too much to drink, the only lie in my deposition. The police even questioned the cook who'd been smoking in front of the seafood joint. All of it had been corroborated. For the police, I wasn't a suspect. For them, it was "just an accident."

But what difference did that make? *I was guilty anyway.*

"You killed her! And you're going to pay! Justice will be served, and you'll know God's wrath!"

"Shut up!" Ethel was shouting, "*Shut up!*"

I saw black and red and then nothing. Violently, I pushed Mark against the wall, and Sarah began to shout. Waller appeared from behind his door, furious, and ordered us to leave immediately. Shaking, Ethel grabbed me by the hand and pulled me down the stairs. I heard Mark shout one last time, "You won't get away with this! I swear to you, you won't get away with this!"

12

Since she refused to fly, I went to Grand Central Station to fetch
her, a bouquet of carnations in hand.

Downtown was a mess of traffic, tourists, and subway stations bursting with people. On Fifth Avenue, the Columbus Day
Parade was petering out, the clamour of the marching bands had
passed 67th Street already, and stone-faced municipal workers
were already on the job, cleaning up the streets. Watching the
crowd disperse, I thought of Moïse who, every year, would say,
"Do these people even know what they're celebrating? Christopher
Columbus? The first illegal immigrant to America."

The train from Montreal spilled out its passengers, and still, no one
who looked like her. What if she'd changed her mind? Did I have the
time wrong? The day? Despair began to filter in when, suddenly, through
the crowd, something familiar attracted my attention — her horrible
yellow wide-brimmed hat that she only wore on special occasions.

For the most exotic trip of her life, my mother had dressed
herself to the nines.

I rushed towards her. She saw me, and her uncertain smile
wavered. I opened my arms, and she drew back like a trapped
animal. We hadn't seen each other in six years, and I'd forgotten
that we didn't hug in our family.

I grabbed her old fake leather suitcase that had never gone
farther than Quebec City. She said, as if I was a child who had

dirtied his Sunday best, "Your forehead. What's wrong? And your eye?" "The accident, Mom." She took a step back to look me over, then judged that I was pale, I'd lost too much weight and my hair — cut only two days earlier — was too long. "Tomorrow we'll go to the barber, I'm paying. You'll see, we feel better in our pain when we clean ourselves up a little."

I was freshly washed, shaved, wearing clean clothes I'd just bought, stinking of expensive cologne I had bought just for her, and she was talking to me about the importance of feeling clean? Only a mother.... But after the difficult weeks I'd lived through, I was ready to be treated like a boy.

She was wide-eyed in the taxi that brought us to the hotel. She watched every pedestrian, stared impudently at blacks and young women with short skirts, exclaiming, "God in Heaven!" She raised her eyes, stretching her neck to catch a glimpse of the top of the Park Avenue buildings, "All these people living on top of each other?" She clicked her tongue, turned towards me, incredulous, "How do they do it?" I laughed. Yes, for the first time since Dana's death, I laughed. She seemed offended by the suite I'd reserved for her at the St. Regis. The bellhop closed the door once he had his tip in his pocket, though not after some consternation as he tried to find a place in the richly decorated room, already bedecked in roses and lilies, for the pitiful carnations I'd bought at the train station.

"It's insanity!" The suite was luxurious, with two large bedrooms and a living room, decorated in European style, with golden moulding and the ceiling painted like the Sistine Chapel. "I never asked for this! It's far too beautiful!" She moved from one room to the next, with that rolling gait her swollen legs gave her. "It's ... it's....!"

"What do you want me to do? Tell them we're leaving?"

She wasn't listening. Talking to herself, indignant, as if she had just discovered some hidden scandalous secrets in a teenager's room. "My God! I don't believe it! The bathrobe is as thick as a rug! Bouquets as big as in a funeral home! A television ... a colour television! Two king-sized beds! Two! And two marble bathrooms! And chocolate! I don't believe it!"

"Ma, please. Sit down, just for a couple of minutes."

As calmly as possible, I told her we were in New York and that in New York, that's the way things were. I was happy to spoil her. I wasn't going into debt. It was a gift for myself as well as for her. She calmed down a bit. A bit.

She changed and we went to the hotel bar. There, I actually succeeded in the herculean feat of getting her to have a drink, a Bloody Mary, the house specialty created in this very bar, the King Cole, in the thirties, something the staff was very proud of. But no one had told her there was alcohol in it, and I was certainly not going to be the one. It was far too funny to see my mother this way, glass in hand, my mother who never drank, oh, once she might have wet her lips with a glass of champagne if the Tees had been insistent enough. She drank all of her Bloody Mary, noisily biting into her celery stick, and licking the halo of celery salt around the glass. I laughed; she seemed to calm down a little, her mood getting warmer, her cheeks reddened, and we spent a lovely first night together at the Tavern on the Green in Central Park, where she ordered another Bloody Mary, and drank it with as much delight as the first. I remember her sceptical look, soon aghast, when I told her it contained a little alcohol, "There's drink in this?" Once we left the table, she pulled a cinnamon candy out of her purse and popped it in her mouth, mindful of her breath.

Early the next morning, she knocked on the door to my room, ready to bring me to the barber's. "You didn't forget, I hope?" She looked at my head. "Can you believe it? It's worse this morning."

"Ma, I'll get a haircut later, okay? We've only got three days. It's nice out. Let's go see the Statue of Liberty instead, okay?"

"Not a chance. I'm not walking around with you looking like that!"

And so, after breakfast (which was brought to her room — "Can you believe it? Silverware! Crêpes! Whipped cream!"), she brought me to Tony's, a barbershop the doorman had told us about, only a block away.

Tony was a proud Italian with dyed hair in an exuberant pompadour, a black silk shirt, and a silver lock in the shape of the cornucopia around his neck, as big as a shark's tooth. He fell victim to my mother's "charm" — it reminded him of his own mother, who had died just last winter. He offered her coffee, though my mother didn't drink that either. Tony insisted, saying his coffee was the best, not like the dishwater served everywhere else. "This coffee, it's the coffee of the Madonna!" He pointed to a large plaster statue of the Virgin Mary on the counter in the back. "Yes! The *Caffè della Madonna!*"

My mother accepted for the Holy Mother. A dark, thick cup of coffee that gave her energy all the way to the evening, making her forget her legs that had been so painful only a few hours before. "Strange, I don't hurt anymore, the coffee of the Holy Virgin, maybe?"

We laughed together. The coffee had done such wonders for her pain that the very next morning, before leaving for the day, she insisted we stop at Tony's place. Tony was overjoyed to see her, "Ah! Signora Carriera!" Tony took advantage of my mother's visit to inspect the back of my neck, which he'd meticulously shaved the night before, his thick, warm Italian hands on the back of my head making me shiver.

Now was my chance to catch up with the lost time I'd never had with my mother.

My mother who, her whole life, believed in the virtue of frugality and penitence, was now filling her memory with images, music, and pleasure. Ice cream at the Plaza, where she thought she saw Doris Day. A shopping spree at Saks, where I bought her a beautiful Pierre Cardin wool suit that she proudly wore that same evening to Broadway, where we listened to *Gilbert Bécaud Sings Love*. Her eyes, filled with wonder, on the edge of tears.

I showed her the university at Washington Square and one of the great amphitheatres where Martin Valenti spoke of Dalí and the surrealists with such fervour. I hid the fact that I hadn't gone to a single lecture since classes resumed in September. Since Dana's death, I couldn't concentrate on my studies, not with the headaches and anxiety attacks that overcame me, and the impossibly painful memory of Dana in my heart, a picture of her at every street corner in New York. And yet, physically, I was fine — the deep cut on my forehead was scarring over; the sutures had been removed. As for my right eye, my vision was permanently affected, but with the help of my left eye, my brain could mask most effects. If I returned to class, I'd need to sit in the first row to see, but that was a moot point. I was done. It wasn't important anymore; I wouldn't go back to school, my decision was made, and my mother didn't know it yet. In the amphitheatre, wider than it was deep, our voices traded secrets with their echos; I pointed out the screen where the slides of the great works of a thousand painters and architects scrolled by. And while she looked around, respectfully silent, I grieved the end of my three happy years there.

My mother suddenly said, as if scolding me, "You still haven't shown me your museum!"

Your museum wasn't *my* museum anymore. But she didn't know that either. We hailed a cab on the corner of Avenue of the Americas and 4th Street, and went to the MoMA, where I hadn't set foot since the accident — there were still too many cruel memories there.

"Roman!" Peggy and Betty, on their weekly visit. Overjoyed at seeing me, warmly introducing themselves to my mother, asking her all sorts of questions about her visit, alarmed at the scar on my forehead, my damaged eye, and my haircut. Peggy said, disappointed, "Where have your nice brown locks gone, Roman?" Betty quickly said, with a smile for my mother, "Come now, Peggy, mothers prefer their sons with short hair." "Well, I don't!" Peggy said, vexed at being associated with traditional mothers. And my mother, dizzied by the conversation, not understanding everything that was being said, smiled, intimidated.

They let me be her guide, as if I was still working there. I took my mother by the arm, leading her through the exhibits. She was sceptical of the Rothkos, Jasper Johns, Motherwells, and Picassos. But she listened anyway, attentively, and ended up saying, with pride in her voice, "You know all these things, do you?"

On our last day together, she just wanted to relax. We went for a walk in Central Park, admiring the fall colours. There was a surprising sense of closeness between us, something I had never felt before, even when I was small. We remained silent, each in our own thoughts, certainly miles and miles between those thoughts, a solar system between them, but still, we were close, closer than we'd ever been.

Suddenly she began speaking about Moïse.

"He calls the house from time to time, asking how we're doing. He speaks good French for an American. It's sad that his country wants to send him off to war. Why don't they let kids be? War … It makes you do stupid things."

"You're talking about Moïse?"

She sighed, "No. About your father and mother."

My father. I felt a chill come over me. I would have preferred to leave the subject be, though I knew there was little chance of that.

She took her gloves off and opened her coat. It was a warm afternoon. Her cheeks pink from our walk, she told me they married in 1942 so my father wouldn't need to go to war. It was after the plebiscite on conscription. My father worked as a radio operator on merchant ships and, for a reason that wasn't entirely clear, he lost his job and returned to the village. My father, an old bachelor, knowing he'd be called to war sooner or later, especially considering his good health and knowledge of ships, began looking for a woman to marry, "any woman." My mother said it without a trace of irony. "You know your father." She sniffed, blew her nose. "I was the oldest,

I was twenty-nine. An old maid doomed to take care of her young brothers and sisters because mother had a bad heart. The smallest effort tired her out. At the end she had to stay in bed, all day long."

I realized I never knew how my parents had met. The war forced a lot of young people into each other's arms, without a thought for compatibility. With his savings, my father bought the building where they'd been living since, with the store on the ground floor and in the back the woodworking shop he built for himself. Once tied to the moorings of marriage, my father was forced to give up the sea — a difficult thing for a sailor. Maybe that helped explain his anger.

My mother wanted to stretch her legs. We made our way towards the lake.

I thought of those three pictures my father kept in his workshop, nailed to the back wall. That's all that was left of his life before my mother. As a child, I spent hours in front of those pictures, intrigued. The first picture showed my father on the radio on a ship, smiling vaguely, a cigarette in his mouth. The second was an older man in a captain's uniform, skin like parchment and piercing eyes — a friend of my father's, perhaps, or his boss. And on the third, a picture my mother had torn up and that my father had carefully restored — my father, laughter in his eyes, a young man accompanied by a friend and a very pretty brunette in a light dress. They were on a paradisiacal beach complete with palm trees and, behind them, a tall ship flying a British flag — the *Sofia Ann*, you could read on its side with a magnifying glass.

My mother, convinced that my father had had his fun with "that … that!…," ordered him to hide the picture. Each time, he repeated, "No, Ida. It was the other guy's girlfriend, how many times do I have to tell you?" But my mother refused to listen. One day she had enough and ripped it off the wall and tore it in two.

"Give it to me, Ida."

"No! None of that filth in my house."

"It isn't in the house, it's in my workshop."

"You want to humiliate me in front of everyone, is that it?"

"Give it to me, Ida. I won't ask again."

And my mother gave him his picture back. He stuck it back together and pinned it on his wall. A long scar disfigured the young woman now: her breasts and her thighs, once ideally round, had lost some of their depth, flat now like a cubist painting. To buy peace, my father pinned a fourth picture, small and yellowed, of a woman of eighteen or nineteen, rather pretty, in a far more modest summer dress.

"You're going to get into trouble, Dad."

He looked at me with that permanently exasperated look of his. "What? What do you want?"

I said, sincerely worried for him, "It's about Ma. You know she can't stand pretty girls."

"That's not a pretty girl, for chrissakes! It's your mother!"

My mother stiffened as soon as I spoke Dana's name. When I called home — I was always the one who called, never my mother — I avoided mentioning Dana, suspecting she thought the worst of her. *That...! That...!* What? *Woman? Feminist? Jew? Who slept with her ... son?* She couldn't know the truth of it, but she might have intuited something. We sat facing the lake, eating hot dogs we bought from a cart. The wind had picked up, the lake's surface quivered, and the oaks and sycamores and hackberry trees trembled. I spoke carefully, as if walking barefoot on glass. "They buried her so quickly that, in the middle of the night, I sometimes wake up thinking none of it happened. I wake up, sure she's still there. I start breathing again, easily, like before. A moment of relief. I cry with joy until the truth hits me, all over again...."

It was the most intimate conversation I had ever had with my mother, and it embarrassed her, I could tell. Her brow was furrowed, she fidgeted on the bench, a drop of mustard from her hot dog fell on her skirt. She grimaced, tried to wipe it off with her handkerchief, then asked, nearly mumbling, whether we could return to the hotel so she could change.

"Ma! I'm talking to you!"

She bit her lip, "You're sad. It'll pass. It always passes."

I knew that was the best she could do, and that there was nothing else to say.

As we turned towards Harperley Hall, I could feel she was nervous. That strange dry cough she had, when she was worried or bothered. "Are you okay, Ma?" Her legs seemed better, the walk seemed to have helped, but she was complaining anyway — her skirt was dirty, her fingers sticky, she wasn't presentable. "You'll freshen up at Dana's. In the bathroom that used to be mine. You know, I had my own bathroom there." I was watching her from the corner of my eye and saw her stiffen. She coughed again, then took my hand and said, "Okay, it's okay." Suddenly I felt like my heart was lighter, like things would start to get better.

"Mrs. Carrier!"

Ethel was radiant in a light blue dress, with her smile of happier days and her short brown hair, which she had cut right after Dana's death. Ethel who, after tea, took my mother by the hand and showed her around the apartment, presenting the Braque, the Soutine, the small Dalí, and the handful of Franz Klines — which had all been Dana's — as well as her own paintings here and there on the walls, including one of her series that would become famous, *Nordica: Ocean Stillness*, inspired by the tumultuous and changing waters of Métis Beach. My mother nodded, a perplexed look on her face. Ethel then brought her into the office, took a small oil painting off the wall, a still life with a dark background, composed around a bouquet of peonies. My mother exclaimed, embarrassed, "No, Ethel! I can't!"

"Please. It's one of my first paintings. I was fourteen. Take it; it makes me happy to give it to you."

"Take it, Ma, it's a gift."

Her eyes filled with tears. "It's too beautiful.... I ... I don't know what to say. Thank you!"

On her last evening, I invited her to a restaurant that was all the rage: Ocello's, on West 56th Street. It was owned by two flamboyant Italian brothers, intimate friends of Tony the barber. On the menu, dishes costing more than four dollars (thankfully my mother received the ladies' menu, which had no prices on it). What can I say about our evening out? No doubt we stood out in the fancy pretentious crowd. My mother, proudly wearing her Pierre Cardin suit, with her son, black jacket and pants, black tie and white shirt, buzz-cut inspected by Tony that very morning who, after coffee, recommended the place to us. This place? Had he gotten the name wrong? Thought it was a family joint? With girls like in the magazines, dresses so short you needed all your will power to keep looking them in the eyes. My mother observed the scene, shocked. "Do you want to leave?"

"No! Mr. Tony told us that...." The din in that place, like a stormy sea, and music, much too loud.

"Are you sure you don't want to leave?" She shook her head energetically. No. What kept her there was the hope of seeing some of the famous regulars; Tony had mentioned Frank Sinatra, Princess Grace, and Jackie Kennedy.

To my great relief, we were moved to another table a bit off the main floor. Apparently, at Ocello's, if you mentioned Tony's name, they treated you like royalty. My mother spoke freely of the village, the house, the store that Françoise was minding in her absence. "She works well, that girl. She keeps saying we should 'modernize.' I don't know what that means exactly, but she helps me order new stock, 'young' clothes, like she says, and it works with the English. We had a pretty good summer last year."

We were seated near the aquariums, and the music wasn't so loud there, nor could we hear the bursts of laughter from the noisy tables next to the windows.

I announced, "It's our last evening. A glass of champagne?"

"No!"

"Come on! Just a glass!"

She looked like a girl caught with her hand in the cookie jar when she finally relented. On her first sip, her cheeks flushed.

"I've got good news, Ma."

"What?"

"I can stay in America as long as I want."

She wavered. I went on, "They don't want me. The army, I mean."

She looked appalled, "The army? You said you'd return to Montreal in December, after classes. So you wouldn't need to go to war. What are you saying?"

"The accident. You see my eye?" She nodded, hesitant. "There's a small scar on it. It won't go away. I'll have it forever."

She paled, "That's what you call good news?"

"The cornea was affected. Depending on the angle, it deforms my vision. I'm also hypersensitive to light. It's permanent."

She seemed to be wondering whether I was pulling her leg. I went on, trying to be as reassuring as possible, "The doctor was the first one to tell me. He said it disqualified me automatically. I went to my draft board, and they gave me a test. Classified me 4-F. That means I'm 'unfit for duty' for medical reasons. In other words, I'm free. Isn't it wonderful?"

"Romain!"

"I'm not suffering, Mom. It bothers me a bit, but I'll get used to it. There's far worse. Like returning from Vietnam in a wheel-chair, or in a box."

She shivered. "So you'll never come home?"

"That's not what I said."

"Yes, that's what you said. You've been gone six years. You never think about your mother?" Her lips were trembling. "If you'd only listened to your father, none of this would have happened."

Of course, back to that old chestnut — my father. I was giving her good news, and she needed to bring me down. "I thought you'd be happy for me."

She stiffened, "Happy, why?"

Things weren't going as I had hoped.

Our meal arrived, veal scallopini for my mother, penne alla vodka for me, and a bottle of Chianti I'd be the only one drinking. I was in a sour mood now. I emptied my glass of champagne and started in on my bottle of wine.

"Romain, you drink too much...."

I ignored the remark. I continued, annoyed, "You'll tell him about Robert Egan? You'll tell him that the police, the real police, never looked for me? That Robert Egan did all of that to scare me. That I'm not a criminal." She paled. "That's what he thinks of me, isn't it? That I'm a scoundrel, a screw-up. I'm sure it's convenient for him, for the old man, to think his son is worthless. He always hated me. I could barely walk, and he hated me already."

"Romain!" she exclaimed, indignant.

"I didn't rape Gail! It isn't that hard to understand!"

"Shush! Not so loud!"

"Nobody can understand us!"

She closed her eyes, and wavered. I tried to calm down, despite the blood pounding in my ears. I said, "I share Dad's anger. Robert Egan invented everything and then made sure he lost his contracts. What a bastard...."

"It's been hard on your father since then. You should understand...."

I clenched my jaw, "I do understand! That's what I'm saying!"

"Lower your voice!"

"I understand very well, and I also know Dad. I know that if Robert Egan offered him a job tomorrow, he wouldn't hesitate to kiss his...."

"Enough! You can't talk about your father like that!"

I grabbed the bottle of Chianti and poured myself a large glass. "How can you live with such a coward, Ma?"

"How dare you say something like that!"

"I'm not trying to insult you, I'm just asking."

"You should know, young man, that I learned what duty means! You accept your problems, and you deal with them. We didn't run away from them like … you kids."

"Is that a personal attack?"

"I'm not insulting you, I'm just saying how we do things."

She shoved her plate away from her. "I'm not hungry anymore. I want to go back to the hotel."

"You're not going to leave like that, are you? You barely touched your plate." I took her hand, but she freed it impatiently. "I'm sorry, Ma. You know I get so mad when I talk about Dad. Ma, please!"

Furious, she grabbed her handbag off the chair, got up, and made her way to the exit.

"Ma! Wait for me!"

The waiter grabbed me by the arm. "Hey, now! Leaving without paying?"

I didn't sleep all night. My mother didn't either. More than once I heard her turning on the tap, and the water running down the drain. The next morning, she barely touched her breakfast and refused to get a coffee at Tony's, despite having promised him the day before. All my half-hearted apologies fell on deaf ears. Letting her leave this way broke my heart. "Ma?" Again, she simply shrugged. Her luggage was ready, and she waited out the morning in the small living room, her eyes dark. It was quarter to eight. Her train left at ten.

"Ma?" She ended up bursting into tears, saying that she understood what I was feeling, but my father wasn't the monster I thought him to be.

"Okay, Ma."

Before leaving the suite, she covered her head with her horrible yellow hat, the one for grand occasions. I took her luggage; she insisted that she carry Ethel's small oil painting, carefully covered in brown paper.

We were quite the sight on the platform at Grand Central, both stiff with embarrassment. As if the past days spent together hadn't brought us closer at all. A hug? Not a chance. Two noisy little kisses on each other's cheeks. I helped her get on board, placed her suitcase in the luggage compartment.

She seemed sad to see me go, "When will you come home?"

"I don't know. Soon, perhaps."

A shadow of disappointment veiled her eyes. Dana's house in Métis Beach? I'd talk to her some other time about it. Moïse might take care of it when he went up there with Louise. For now, it would be best to just leave it at that.

"Come for Christmas at least. I'll make you *tourtières*."

"Maybe."

Before returning to my place in the West Village, I had a meeting in Flatbush, in Brooklyn. Some long-haired guy was trying to sell his 1966 Westfalia. I'd seen the ad on a bulletin board in a Village coffee house. The van was in almost mint condition, a beautiful velvet green. I paid nine hundred dollars cash, filled out the paperwork, and drove back to Manhattan.

I was thinking about my mother. She simply couldn't understand my need to move forward, not backwards. The events in Métis Beach in 1962, and now Dana's death in New York. I needed to move on to something else. Breathe and live a little, breathe and be fully alive. The St. Regis, the gifts and moments spent with my mother, I gave them to her knowing I'd be leaving, even farther this time. It was the last time we saw each other. She died three years later, at the age of fifty-eight.

I packed my bags, gave the loft keys to the doorman, leaving everything inside. I was rich and free. In my 1966 Westfalia, heading west, my heart filled with promise, I glanced in my rear-view mirror. Behind me,

> *Gloomy, crazy New York was throwing up its cloud*
> *of dust and brown steam. There is something brown*
> *and holy about the East; and California is white like*
> *washlines and emptyheaded — at least that's what*
> *I thought then.*

You couldn't have said it better than Jack Kerouac....

IV

KEN, PETE, BOBBY, AND THE REST

I

Two ghosts, their heads smooth like bowling balls, desperately waving their arms, covered in mud, stinking of sweat and fear, terrified by what they'd seen in Fort Lewis. The summary execution of a soldier from their company, a simpleton (yes, the army drafted them too), barely eighteen. His crime had been to steal a grenade from the munitions dump and threaten to pull the pin.

I picked the guys up on Route 160 south of Sacramento. Two GIs on the run, AWOL — deserters, in other words. They appeared out of nowhere, in the rain, and jumped in front of the Westfalia which, by chance, hadn't been going very fast. They'd scared me shitless! I slammed on the brakes, and the Volks skidded on the wet pavement. They slammed their dirty hands against the windows, which I was not opening. *What do you want?* I quickly understood they were at their wits' end, begging me to let them climb aboard. So I did, though not without a certain pang of emotion when I saw them dirty my backseat with their muddy boots and soiled clothes. Relieved, grateful, they told me, still in shock over what had been done to the poor guy, a young black killed right in front of them in Fort Lewis, in Washington state. One of them, the one called Pete, said, "He was like a seven-year-old, in his head, I mean, for God's sake!" The other, John, added, "He should have been in an asylum, not in the army! But it's like the rest of it, they don't give a fuck!" Pete took over, breathless, wiping his eyes with his large, dirty hands,

"John and me, man, we tried to reason with him, but he was laughing and shouting, 'Boom! Boom!' pretending to pull the pin. I was going to go for him from behind, to neutralize him, you know. But that goddamn sergeant ordered me to stand down." He caught his breath and went on, his voice racked with emotion, "And the motherfucker shot him down in front of us. Like he was a wild turkey."

I had saved their lives, or so they kept telling me as the Westfalia cut through the night and rain, as dark and wet as their soiled clothes. They knew they'd find a friend in a Westfalia, "a hippie van," you could see it coming down the road even in the dark by the shape of its headlights. They asked me where I was going. "San Francisco? Great." They mentioned some party in Berkeley, as excited as teenagers, "You absolutely have to come with us. We want to thank you." A madhouse of a party, they said. They'd go wild for a night or two before slipping underground, free from goddamn Vietnam, the goddamn army, those goddamn madmen.

Between Sacramento and Berkeley, I became their *Canadian friend*. They slapped me on the back, we laughed together. "Canada? God, you're lucky!" We got into Berkeley late, driving through poorly lit streets lined with modest houses. They told me to park the Westfalia in front of one of them, stucco peeling. Impatiently, they dragged me inside, a dirty place heavy with cigarette smoke, pot and hashish as well, and the stench of unwashed bodies. Throbbing music — the Doors — loud enough to tear your skull into a thousand pieces. On all sides, young men and women lay slumped, eyes staring emptily, others were fucking in rooms around the house, in twos and threes and more. One guy was vomiting in the toilet (it might have been a girl, it was hard to tell). "California hospitality!" Pete laughed at my astonished air. He draped his arm around my shoulders and led me to the tiny kitchen littered with empty bottles and old pizza boxes; both he and John grabbed a beer and offered me one. "Our way of saying thanks," Pete said. "You can drink what you want, fuck who you want. Here, that's all the girls are waiting for." Pete and John were already on their second beer, then third, then fourth. Ready to get back to civilian life, though sentenced to living underground. They pulled their shirts off to reveal muscled chests and started cruising for available girls. It wasn't my sort of place, my sort of thing, my sort of people. A few guys were looking at me as if I'd just gotten off a spaceship, with my short hair and the back of my neck shaved. I was about to thank Pete and John and get back on the road for San Francisco when a girl threw herself on me — "Hey, you, handsome!" — her hand already in my pants. Pete burst out laughing, "Welcome to California!"

The next morning, I opened my eyes, head pounding (something slipped into my drink?). The girl with whom I'd supposedly spent the night, a vague memory, was gone now. My head heavy, ready to explode, I got up, got dressed. I found the girl in the living room in the arms of another guy, both of them naked and sleeping, mouths open. I left the house, my ears buzzing, ready to drive to San Francisco, when a guy called out to me on the street.

"Yours?"

He was contemplating the Westfalia, circling around it, limping, a penguin's gait.

"Yes."

"Nice wheels."

He glanced at the licence plate, furrowed his brow.

"New York state?"

"New York City. Got in yesterday."

He smiled. Turned his eyes back to the Volks, as if I had just made him an offer and he was thinking about the price. Then he glanced back at the house I had come out of. The rain had stopped, the sky was clear.

"I'm here to see a friend. You were at the party?"

I nodded. He barked a disdainful laugh, "I hate those happenings."

And I thought, *me too.*

Pete came out of the house, bare-chested, his combat boots unlaced, and they fell into each other's arms. Pete told me they were childhood friends, had grown up in the same neighbourhood in Oakland, their fathers had worked in the same factory.

He was called Ken Lafayette. A face half-angel, half-devil. A hungry mouth, a turned-up nose, round cheeks like Jon Voight — with whom he also shared his feminine blondness and intense stare, always teasing. He studied sociology at the University of California at Berkeley and led the antiwar committee on campus. "He's incredible," Pete said. "He's the best."

His voice filled with gratitude, Pete told him how I'd "saved" them, John and him. (Apparently, someone was supposed to pick them up north of Sacramento, but he never showed, forcing them to hitchhike, a risky proposition for two AWOL soldiers the FBI would soon be looking for.) Their reunion quickly turned sour. "So what should we have done?" Pete asked. Ken shook his head, annoyed. And Pete, trying to calm down, told Ken how lucky they'd been to have come upon me. "Roman is Canadian and has an American friend who fled to Canada."

Ken ran his hand through his hair. "Really? You're Canadian? Travelling?"

"No. I'm a permanent resident. Have been for five years. Medical exemption. Eye problem. An accident."

He stared at me. Intense, judging eyes, separated by two hard lines between his eyebrows, as if he was constantly fighting a headache.

"And what are you doing here?"

Forgetting New York, I thought. Instead, I said in a falsely joyful tone, "I came to see California. Spend a bit of time here. Maybe settle down in San Francisco. I don't know yet. I've got all the time in the world."

He didn't want to know more than that. He turned towards Pete, slapped him on the back. "Well, this morning I've got to take care of Pete and John. But after, come and see the committee. I'll show you what we're doing here."

Despite his eyes, dancing with strange fire, I agreed. Ken Lafayette was one of those rare people with an unexplainable, powerful magnetism.

2

My visit to the antiwar committee should have been my first warning.

We agreed to meet at his place, a large apartment on Le Roy Avenue, with tons of books in every room and little furniture. I got there on time, two o'clock in the afternoon. He opened the door, his chest bare. He seemed surprised to see me. "Ah, yes," he said after a moment. "I know who you are. The Canadian. Okay, well, no matter. I need to go to the committee today anyway. Give me a minute, let me find a shirt."

We walked along Hearst Avenue. Ken kept talking, walking quickly, despite a pronounced limp. One of his legs was shorter than the other, at least I thought. It gave him that singular walk. With pride, he told me about his latest action on campus — "under my orders," dozens of students had barricaded themselves in a building to protest the refusal of the board to allow Eldridge Cleaver to hold a seminar on racism.

"You know who I'm talking about?"

"The Black Panther."

"Exactly. You know what Ronald Reagan, our benevolent governor, said? If Cleaver was allowed to teach students, they'd go home that night and slit their parents' throats!" He burst out laughing. "But we won! Cleaver will come to Berkeley, as it should be. We'll see if the blood of infidels is spilled behind the white picket fences!"

I shuddered, thinking of the women Cleaver admitted to raping in *Soul on Ice*, written in prison. "Rape was an insurrectionary act." White women, but black ones too — he had trained and perfected his technique. Dana read the book before tearing it apart, page by page. "The monster! The bastard! And the pathetic intellectuals praising him! They should all be hung by the *kishkes*!"

"The what?"

"The balls, Romain." Furious, she began writing a long opinion piece that the *New York Times* published, "What would Cleaver say if we trivialized the situation of blacks the way he trivializes rape?" In the days that followed, she received hundreds of hateful letters for having dared attack a charismatic leader of the black resistance.

"You'll come and listen to him?" asked an enthusiastic Ken. "You can't miss it."

Bow down to an impenitent rapist! Never!

But instead, like a coward, I blurted out, "You're right. Can't miss it."

At the committee office, a handful of volunteers were talking all at once. Phones ringing off the hook, a dense cloud of cigarette smoke in the air, thick enough to cut with a knife. As soon as they saw Ken, they rushed to surround him. In the confusion, I learned that one of them had just been arrested; it seemed serious, they spoke of accusations of sabotage, a factory whose production had been interrupted, injuries perhaps? Workers evacuated?

"Shut up!" Ken ordered. "Can't you see I'm with someone?"

Silence fell. They lowered their eyes. Ken introduced me, the Canadian. I wanted to disappear. A tall guy with long hair and a dishevelled beard said, almost supplicating, "You need to call the lawyer. It's serious, this time." "Later," Ken shut him up. "It can wait." Resigned, the guy mumbled, "Fine, you're the boss." And the crowd around us dissolved, returned to their desks.

"Listen, Ken," I said, embarrassed. "We'll catch up some other time. They seem to need you."

"If they don't have the nerve, they should go back to their mothers. Courage isn't given to everyone, right?"

"But we're talking about one of your activists, no?"

"We need arrests. We need trials." He spoke with enthusiasm, but sounded almost annoyed. "It's the means we have to make sure they talk about us, to spread our ideas. We're fighting imperialism. The greatest revolutionaries all spoke from prison cells." Paraphrasing Henry David Thoreau, as if the words of the great man were his own.

He invited me to stay in his large apartment on Le Roy Avenue. It was generous and unexpected coming from a guy who showed so little regard for those around him. I accepted, thankful; it would let me explore the city, its surroundings, as well as San Francisco some twenty minutes away. It would give me time to decide where I wanted to settle down. To my great surprise, I discovered an affable, solicitous young man; he let me stay in the larger of the two bedrooms, the one with a window at the back and not on the street. We spent hours talking together, discussions that seemed more like political science lessons than an exchange of ideas. He gave me all sorts of suggestions about what to read — Marxist philosophers, those of the Frankfurt School in particular — and his house was full of them, I could stretch out my arm out and grab one from the numerous makeshift bookcases, old boards lying on bricks. There were magazines as well, *Monthly Review*, and *Radical America*, and *Ramparts*, rather off-putting and ponderous reading, which I suspected students on campus read the way others start smoking cigarettes, to look cool, to be part of a group, not to be *suspect*. "Marxism is the unavoidable philosophy of our time," Ken would repeat. Though he never mentioned the origin of that gem, Jean-Paul Sartre. But I listened to him, impressed to an extent that surprised even myself. He was so knowledgeable, and he had this way of talking to you, looking at you straight in the eye as if hypnotizing you, manipulating activist jargon with disconcerting skill to win you over to the Cause, which he called *The Big C*, or better yet, make you look like a fool if you didn't have the right opinions.

He showed me around Berkeley, and got me to visit the latest coffee houses. Brought me to assemblies where he was a star of the New Left. His speeches were passionate, and always well attended. The first time I saw him talk I remember thinking, *I share an apartment with the guy*, with a sort of unhealthy pride that would have alarmed me if I hadn't been so fragile. He'd been incredible, magnificent, really. We were at Sproul Hall. Some fifteen hundred, maybe two thousand students were listening to him. Tension was in the air, and the cops seemed nervous. Powerful in his eloquence, he had the crowd under his spell from the very first second, "We no longer want anything to do with this war! Four years, my friends, it's been four years! Four years we've been fighting against it by any means! Four years and no one listens in Washington! What else do they need? Riots? Violence? Bodies in the streets? Have we become outcasts in our own land? Have we? Outcasts?" The crowd roared its agreement. "Oh, they would love to get rid of each and every one of us...." His eyes, filled with fire, scanned the assembled multitude. "To kill their own citizens, like they send others to be murdered over there for their own interests!" Thunderous applause broke out, eliciting in him a devilish smile. He gestured towards the crowd, you could barely see his handicap then, hands joined together, index finger pointed towards us, as if holding a gun. And the crowd began to chant, "*Shoot us! Shoot us!*" And he pretended to shoot us down, one by one, his eyes like embers now. "That's what they dream of in Washington, to eliminate us! All of us! One by one! To have their path free and clear and pursue their imperialist mission. But we are Reason, my friends! The conscience of this nation. And to do nothing in these troubled times is a form of violence in and of itself."

And the crowd, in a frenzy, chanted all over again, "Shoot us! Shoot us! Please shoot us!"

Life in Berkeley was exhilarating. Intriguing youth, arrogant, not exactly like New York. Here, young people were kings in their own country — demonstrations, sit-ins; they filled the streets by the thousands — angry, determined, and they could paralyze the life of an entire community without warning. They were certain they were giving birth to a new society, pacifist, egalitarian, as if the previous generations had never thought of doing the same or simply didn't have the same intellectual and material capabilities. The Vietnam War gave them this platform, an opportunity to be heard, to show their superiority. Their feeling of superiority could be seen everywhere — in the speeches, in the eyes of Ken Lafayette, in the relationship the activists had with authority figures and police. A supercharged mood that I tried to describe to my mother in our phone calls, but that she simply couldn't understand, "You're being careful, Romain? It sounds dangerous." My mother suffered, knowing I was so far away. "California? What about your diploma in New York?" She cried, making veiled accusations of having abandoned her. Her health was declining; like her own mother, her heart was failing, her legs had begun to swell again. Pockets full of change, I called her every week from a phone booth on Telegraph Avenue, describing what I was seeing around me — sometimes a demonstration was taking place, and she could hear the police sirens and the deafening growl of helicopters overhead. "Romain, it sounds like war." I reassured her as best I could, and each time, the same question, "Where is Berkeley exactly?"

"On the other side of the continent, Ma. I told you."

And I told myself: far enough for me to start feeling lighter again. I realized that my headaches and anxiety attacks were growing further apart. I was still fragile, certainly, and prone to terrible fits of sadness, but I was doing better, trying to live one day at a time, trying not to think too much about the past or the future.

Ken's mood changed; the honeymoon hadn't lasted long. At first, I didn't understand. "Ken, is there a problem?" He'd make a face.

"Problems? There are problems everywhere! That's all there is!"

I was stunned. "Did I do something to annoy you?" This fear I had of indisposing him was insane.

Again he made a face, "Please, don't be like the others. All those people at the committee who are scared of me. It's pathetic."

I was concerned. He had charmed me with his ability to talk brilliantly about any subject, his status as the star of the antiwar movement in Berkeley, his face in the newspapers — and now that he had nothing left to tell me about himself, it seemed I didn't deserve his attention. Was that it?

He was constantly picking fights. Once it was a shower, too long for his taste. "Hey, petty bourgeois," he shouted, slamming his fist on the bathroom door. "This is no palace here!" Oh, and the groceries. He had offered me a place to stay, so I bought food to thank him, an exchange of services he seemed to appreciate until he began inspecting every bag I brought back from Lucky Supermarket. "What's *that*?" Once, it was a roll of Saran Wrap. I thought he was going to punch me.

"What do you mean, *that*? You're holding it, you know what it is."

"That shit's produced by Dow Chemical! Napalm, you fool, does that mean anything to you?"

Furious, disgusted, he pulled out toothpaste, jam, toilet paper. "All of this trash is made by companies on the blacklist of criminal imperialist conglomerates that have a financial interest in the war. None of it can enter this apartment, you hear? Since you're not intelligent enough to understand that, from now on you go through inspection before putting anything away."

I don't know why I didn't just say, *Go fuck yourself! Buy your own shit!* The shame and self-loathing I felt! Why did he turn me into a goddamn child?

Then there was Pete. He was arrested in a bar in Oakland, completely drunk.

"What the hell was he doing in a fucking bar?"

Ken learned about it from a guy who was with Pete that night. After half a dozen beers, Pete got into a fight with another customer (over a woman, maybe?), the bar's owner called the cops, who quickly figured out they had an AWOL soldier.

Pete was sent to the Presidio in San Francisco, a military prison with a sinister reputation.

I said, horrified, "We've got to get him out of there."

Ken snickered. "Yeah? And how are we going to do that? We're not in a Walt Disney movie!" He kicked the couch in the living room and disappeared into the kitchen. A few minutes later, he reappeared, his hair a mess, as if he'd been holding his head in his hands.

"Well, let's see the good side of this mess. Better in prison than running to Canada."

"You can't be serious.…"

"Of course I am! It might be difficult to drill into your bourgeois head, thinking about saving your own skin, that's your first goddamn thought!" He shook his head with disgust. "What a pathetic reflex. To save your own life. Just like your friend *Charlie Moses*."

I could barely choke out the words, "What the fuck, man!"

"Oh, and now you're crying over the fate of your little friend!" On the coffee table, the newspaper with the day's tally of the dead in Vietnam. He picked it up and threw it in my face. "For each guy who flees to Canada, another will have to replace him. Do you think about the man who will get his brains shot out of his skull instead of your coward of a friend?"

Coward! "You have no idea what you're talking about!"

"Of course I know what I'm talking about! People who shit their pants in fear, I see them every goddamn day. Not everyone is a hero, unfortunately. You should know, what with your friend *Moïse*."

And you, you should know, protected by your limp. Are you a hero? But I stayed silent. Once again.

Weeks later, desperate knocks on the apartment door. It was past midnight, and I was in bed with a book. I heard Ken swear in his room, and then his feet dragging to the door. "Pete? What are you doing here?"

Pete? Out of prison?

I ran to the living room and found a horrifyingly skinny Pete, his skin waxy. He staggered to the couch, and fell on it. I ran to the kitchen and grabbed him a beer, which he drank thirstily, his eyes closed. We watched him. "Pete? What happened?" Ken asked impatiently, "They let you leave the Presidio?" Pete shook his head weakly. No. "So?"

"Escaped."

"Escaped? Shit!"

His hands and face were covered in scabs. His clothes smelled like urine. Mould. Barely audible, Pete told how, in his section, they discovered that one of the guys had hepatitis B. "We threw ourselves on him like vampires. Cutting him with our nails, with stones, whatever we could find to make him bleed. Then we cut ourselves and we mixed our blood with the guy's, like brothers making a pact. We waited and soon enough we were trembling all over and shitting ourselves. They waited a few days before sending us to the hospital, just to make sure we weren't acting. Then they realized we weren't. There were five of us transferred to the hospital, and I managed to escape with another guy."

"If they catch you," Ken said, "you'll be in for fifteen years. We've got to get you to Canada."

Stupefied, I stared at Ken, who averted his eyes. He had spoken with disgust, shaking his head, as I'd seen him do so many times. Pete, a desperate case that you gave up on? A problem to be gotten rid of in Canada? I shivered.

Why didn't I leave, right then and there? *Why?*

3

Pete needed a driver to cross the border. I offered without hesitation.

It was one of those cold and foggy January mornings. A humidity that put a chill in your bones. The sun giving half-light, barely warm at all, as if covered in plastic film. The air hung heavy, and we breathed even more heavily.

That morning, Ken hardly helped us at all, saying something about some emergency or other at the committee. I grabbed him by the sleeve as he was leaving the apartment. We could hear poor, sick Pete savouring a last warm shower before the great departure, at least as much as he could savour anything in his current state. I was angry.

"He's your friend, Ken!"

"That's how it is. Nothing more to say."

He left, not bothering to shut the door behind him. Flabbergasted, I watched him go down the stairs, limping, one hand on the railing. A few minutes later, Pete appeared in the living room, bare feet and a towel around his hips, revealing a thin figure, his back and arms covered in infected scabs.

"My God, Pete. We'll need to find you a doctor soon. We've got to take care of you."

He shrugged and his eyes glanced towards the open door.

"Where's Ken?"

It was just too cruel. "He left. An emergency. He couldn't wait. He's sorry, really. He said he was sorry. He wants us to call him as soon as we're in Vancouver. He'll never give up on you. He promised."

A tired smile on his face, "I knew it. He's the best. You can always count on him."

I spared him the truth, and returned a smile. All the while cursing Ken Lafayette.

We drove north, towards Canada. A pit in my stomach and Pete in the back, on the Westfalia's cot, under heavy blankets, a shadow of his former self. It had been only three months since that rainy evening in October 1968, on Route 160, south of Sacramento. His long scraggly figure, waxy skin, and that old Giants baseball cap Ken gave him to hide his shaved head that marked him as a GI. So weak and feverish I had to help him climb down the three stories of the Le Roy Avenue building. His burning skin gave off a strong smell of infected flesh. He was wearing my clothes, and looked like a kid in them.

It wasn't entirely certain that Canada would welcome Pete. Ken knew it and hadn't cared. After all, a key portion of the immigration process was the medical exam.

I got a first laugh out of him in downtown Seattle when I gave him a handful of Canadian bills, about a hundred dollars that I had exchanged at the bank.

"That? Money? You just got swindled, buddy!" He put the bills on the cot, laughing like a kid as he examined their colours. "It's like Monopoly money!" Then, intrigued, "Who's the chick with the uppity air?"

"You're kidding! You don't know who that is?"

He shook his head weakly, "Should I know?"

"That's Queen Elizabeth II."

He coughed, sniffed. "What's she doing there? She's the Queen of England, right?"

"Ours as well."

"Hey, we fought a war in 1775 to get rid of her!"

"Well not us."

He looked at me, confused, as if I was telling him that we were off to Siberia. The ignorance of Americans always astonished me. As if Canada was a building, or the name of a horse, of no interest at all. A banal, ordinary thing they paid no attention to. Oh, sure, they'd been told once it was another country, but that hadn't stuck.

We were a few miles from the border. We drove through breathtaking landscapes. Pete saw none of it. He slept, interrupted by episodes of delirium, and that goddamn fever that didn't seem to be letting up. "Pete, we're getting closer. You need to sit up front." I helped him sit up, got him out of the Westfalia. He drank a bit of water, pissed on the side of the road; he seemed lost. Night had fallen, it was past eleven. We were betting the border guards wouldn't be as curious so late, hoping that Pete's state wouldn't seem suspicious. I washed his face, got him into clean clothes and threw out the ones he'd been wearing since we left. He moaned, but let himself be moved this way and that. He said, a small smile on his pale lips, "Don't worry, it'll be fine."

Yet the battle was far from over.

Our anxious faces at the Douglas border crossing. That great white shining arch, illuminated at its base, the Peace Arch on which both flags flew, carried by the wind, dancing, synchronized. The inscription at the arch's base read, MAY THESE GATES NEVER BE CLOSED. Pete took it as a promise.

A first stop, then a second. I lowered the window. A thin guy, some forty years old, "What brings you to Canada?" I could feel my heart beating in my chest. I said, my voice choked with nervousness,

"We're coming to spend a few days with friends in Vancouver."

He stared at me impassively. "American?"

"No, Canadian." And without him asking for it, I offered my birth certificate, immediately regretting my hurry, which might look like an admission of guilt. He seemed surprised, looked at the document.

"And you?"

As we'd hoped, the darkness worked to Pete's advantage. "No, American."

"Anything to declare?"

"No," Pete said, his voice surprisingly strong.

"Alcohol? Cigarettes?"

"No," Pete said a second time.

"How many days in Vancouver?"

"Three days," I said. "We'll be back on Sunday."

"Have a nice visit."

And that was it. We drove the next few yards in incredulous silence. When we got far enough and the light from the Peace Arch couldn't be seen anymore, Pete began to cry.

Georgia Street, East Vancouver. Abandoned buildings for rent, small sad, worn-down houses, and heavy low clouds, the colour of lead.

The war resisters committee was easy to find — a ground floor office in a beat-up brick building that had, at one point, been of a definable colour, posters mounted in dirty windows shouting their slogans, exclamation marks punctuating them like explosions: STOP IT! U.S. OUT OF S.E. ASIA NOW! ENDLESS WAR IS ENDLESS DEATH!

Pete was becoming weaker by the hour. He could barely cross the street to the office. I had to help him up the couple of steps until a guy inside the office saw us and ran outside to help. What a welcome! A handful of friendly volunteers, far more relaxed than those who swarmed around Ken Lafayette. We were invited to sit, served coffee and cookies. While we were introducing ourselves and getting to know one another, a doctor, whom one of the girls had called, arrived at the office. He was a young guy with long hair.

He took Pete aside, examined him before prescribing a long list of medicines. "Enough to treat a whole Marine battalion," Pete said.

The committee's volunteers gave us the address of a cheap hotel to the west on Georgia Street. While Pete — knocked out by the doctor's pills — was sleeping like a baby in our room, I visited an apartment not too far away with one of the committee members. Three clean rooms, well heated. We went out to buy some furniture that we transported in the Westfalia, and filled the refrigerator. I paid a year's rent to the owner, a dry, haughty woman who looked at me with suspicion until I pulled out my stack of bills. "Oh! If only all young people were like you!" I said nothing, simply shaking her hand with the lease in my pocket.

Pete thought the apartment was perfect. "This is home? I've never had anything like it. How can I thank you, Roman?"

"By getting back on your feet as soon as you can, and accepting this envelope without saying a word."

He opened it, and his eyes went wide. There was a thousand dollars in it. Dana's money. He began crying again.

The next morning, I returned to Berkeley, feeling empty. After everything that had happened with Ken, I didn't feel like going back to the apartment on Le Roy Avenue. I still had Pete's pale face in my mind's eye, worrying about his friend, "We promised Ken we'd call him when we got here. We need to tell him everything's fine. I know him, he must be worried sick for me." Ken? Worried for someone else? What a joke! Why, for God's sake, did Pete have such a distorted impression of his childhood friend?

The Georgia Street volunteers let us call Berkeley. Each time, Pete would get a busy signal, or someone who promised to pass the message on. But Ken never called back. "He's got lots to do," Pete said. "It doesn't matter. We'll end up talking to each other sooner or later." I could tell he was dejected after he hung up. On the morning I left, he came to me, "Tell Ken I'll call him at the apartment Saturday morning, okay?"

"Okay, Pete. If I have to, I'll tie him to the bed before he wakes up." He smiled and gave me a hug. I climbed into the Volks, full of hate. Things were beginning to affect me.

I arrived in Berkeley two days later, late in the evening. The apartment was dark; Ken wasn't there, to my great relief. I hurriedly gathered my things — some clothes and books — and left a note on the table, which I hoped was biting:

> Ken,
> Pete is in good hands, at least for now. He's courageous, despite what you think. He'll call you Saturday at 10 a.m. You know, some have been thought brave because they were afraid to run away.... Time for me to get back on the road. Thanks for your hospitality.
> Roman
>
> P.S. – The phrase on bravery isn't from me. It's from Thomas Fuller, in case you want to use it in one of your speeches.

4

Ethel had given me the contact info of a friend of hers whom she'd met in New York and who'd been living in San Francisco for a few years now. I had thought of calling him a number of times when I was in Berkeley, without ever having gone through with it, maybe to prove to myself that I didn't need anyone's help. "Go see him," Ethel had told me. "He's charming. He'll help you sort yourself out over there. He's expecting you."

His name was Bobby Spangler. We met up in a coffee place on 5th Street, right next to the *San Francisco Chronicle*, where he worked. Warm and polite, he wore large steel-framed glasses, spoke slowly, choosing his words carefully, his fine hands constantly in movement. As a journalist, he covered cultural events. At twenty-six he had his very own column, called "Sounds and Music," which offered read-ers intriguing encounters, both improbable and innovative, such as comparisons between the Beatles and Schubert, Pink Floyd and Mussorgsky. Born in Brooklyn, Bobby had studied music at Juilliard before dropping everything to move to San Francisco. "The only thing that's ever mattered to me is to build a life without having to make too many compromises. Painful compromises." He fell silent after those words, as if meditating on his past, on the tragedy of Vietnam.

He was surprised at my guess. "Oh, no! Not the war!" He flashed me an enigmatic smile. "No, that problem solved itself."

"They'll leave you alone? You'll never go?"

"Never."

"How did you manage that?"

Bobby was homosexual. He stared at me from behind his glasses, waiting for a reaction. What was I supposed to answer? *I don't give a shit? It doesn't bother me?* I said nothing. He took a sip of coffee, wiped his mouth with a paper napkin. "It's surely the only time that being a homosexual in America has had a positive aspect. This country is mad."

Bobby ordered us two pieces of carrot cake as if our conversation had stimulated his appetite. He went on, "In New York, it's either the lie or the provocation. There's nothing in between. Either you hide and you make up a girlfriend for social respectability, which is what most people do, or you strut your stuff grotesquely, a middle finger to society. Here in Frisco, a community is taking shape. Sure, nothing is won yet, it'll take time, but we'll get people's respect sooner or later. It's the inevitable law of numbers." He swallowed a piece of cake and smiled. "And you, what brings you here?"

I shrugged my shoulders, "I'm not entirely sure. Hopefully, some guiding light, some revelation to show me how to rebuild my life."

He pushed his glasses up his nose.

"What are your interests?"

"Art, generally speaking. But what to do with that?"

He laughed. "Your road has brought you to San Francisco; it seems to me you're right where you should be."

Bobby Spangler was probably the best thing that had happened to me since Moïse. Our conversations about painting, music, literature — God, how I missed the MoMA in New York now! — were so much happier than those about war, imperialism and Communism, and the rest of that garbage, all part and parcel of living in Berkeley. Bobby brought me to the opera, to the movie theatre, to the San Francisco Museum of Modern Art. I had the feeling I was regaining some stability.

I moved into a three-room apartment on the corner of Post and Taylor, in the Tenderloin. I liked the anonymity offered by the six-story building, filled with tenants, every one more ordinary than the next, living typical lives far from the chaos and effusion of arrogant youth. Ten streets away, on Columbus Avenue, stood the bookstore founded by poet Lawrence Ferlinghetti, City Lights Books, which Moïse had so dreamed of visiting. ("Oh, man, I'm so jealous! Who did you see there? Ginsberg? Burroughs? Kerouac?" "Just Ginsberg." "Ginsberg? What's he saying, Ginsberg?" "What do you mean?" "You didn't speak to him?" "What would I have said to him?" "Oh, man! There are *so* many things to say to Allen Ginsberg!")

Bobby found me a job as a low-level assistant at the *Chronicle*. I didn't need the money, but I was interested in seeing how a newspaper worked. My job was to hand the reporters wire service dispatches that were spit out day and night by the telex machines parked in a large air-conditioned and soundproofed room. I loved the infernal machines beating out the rhythm of the planet — war, diplomacy, results of great sporting events, the stock market. The feeling of tearing that still-warm paper along the dotted line, sep-arating carbon copies and bringing them to the reporters at their desks — Vietnam, local news, politics, sports, economy. I was the one who "distributed work," and the reporters jokingly began call-ing me *boss*. I felt like I was part of a family.

Quickly, rumours about Bobby and me made the rounds. Bobby told me about it one evening, after work. He was mad as hell. He asked, "You think I'm hitting on you?"

"I...."

"Forget it. You're not my type. You never will be."

Apparently, a guy at the local news desk, Nolan Tyler, had begun the rumours. The sort of guy who was always talking about his sexual prowess, always had a new story to tell, always smutty and unbelievable. The next morning, Bobby called him out publicly, in front of the whole *Chronicle* staff, "What about you, Nolan?"

"What about me?"

"As far as I know, you don't have a wife or girlfriend, right?"

"What are you saying, friend?"

"Well, maybe you too could be...."

"Shut up, Bobby, or...."

"Or what, Nolan? Why are you getting angry? I'm using the same logic as you are. And I'm not checking my facts."

Nolan, a tall, strong guy, his back bent, broken in a long-ago car accident, stood up. Bobby said to him, "Why don't you leave us alone, Roman and me. Because I can start a few rumours myself."

And that was the end of that.

One morning in April 1969, the words *deserter* and *Vancouver* attracted my attention. A news item from UPI, the paper still warm, all the way from Blaine, in Washington State. I read it three times, my hands shaking. The worst possible scenario, right there, in black and white. The item was about Pete. Canadian authorities had thrown him out of the country, something to do with drugs, heroin he had tried to buy from an Indian prostitute in Vancouver's Downtown Eastside. I turned pale, *What got into you, goddamn it?* He'd barely stepped on American soil, and the FBI put handcuffs on him. Stupefied, I re-read every word of the dispatch, hoping I'd gotten something wrong — the name, the age of the perp, but no, it was him: Pete Dobson, born in Oakland, twenty years old, escaped from Fort Lewis, Washington state, and the Presidio in San Francisco. I looked for my name there, but didn't find it, to my great relief. The dispatch didn't mention the circumstances surrounding his arrival in Vancouver. His trial would soon begin; he was facing fifteen years in prison, perhaps more. I brought the dispatch to Nolan. He covered stories on deserters for the *Chronicle*. He saw my face and said, "Hey, anything wrong?" I mumbled, "Another guy who got caught." He went through the text quickly, "Well, he broke the law!" I knew I could never have that conversation with Nolan Tyler.

Poor Pete. The news of his arrest had me in the dumps for days. I thought about what they'd do to him, the treatment he'd receive in prison; they weren't kind with recidivists in military prisons. And Ken Lafayette? How would he react? Did he have any compassion for his childhood friend?

5

For the first time ever, I remember thinking, *There, that's what I want to do with my life.*

We were outside the Castro Theatre. Bobby and I had just seen *Midnight Cowboy*. The theatre was emptying out, and we stood steady, like boulders in the middle of a river as the crowd flowed around us. We were quiet, still filled with that improbable but touching friendship between Joe Buck (Jon Voight) and Ratso Rizzo (Dustin Hoffman) in the New York Moïse had helped me discover. My throat was tight. I had the uncanny impression of having seen us, Moïse and me, on the big screen. It was almost our story. The story of our providential meeting and our indestructible friendship. For the first time, a film was showing me myself. For the first time, they talked about me in the movies.

(Bobby told me it was a gay movie, but I didn't believe him.)

"I want to write movies, Bobby."

He pushed his glasses on his nose, and stared at me with his clear blue eyes, looking for confirmation that I was serious. Around us, the flow of moviegoers was dwindling.

"If what you're saying is true, you've got to work hard," he told me. "First, you've got to start writing."

A few days later, he came to my house with an old Olivetti he had found at the *Chronicle*. With a few adjustments, it worked perfectly. "If you really mean it, you'll get on it as soon as I'm out the door."

And that's what I did. For days and weeks and months, I kept my ass in the chair like Bobby had told me to. "Hook your brain up directly to your fingers. Don't let the keys get between you and your ideas. You'll see, you'll be surprised by what comes out of ..." — he put his finger on his temple — "here."

Finally, I had a goal, a real one! I'd be a scriptwriter! I began organizing my life around my exciting, motivating promise, working by day at the newspaper, writing in the evenings at home, going to movie theatres at least three times a week, where I savoured the latest productions — *Easy Rider, They Shoot Horses, Don't They?*, Costa Gavras' *Z.*... I came out of the theatres at midnight or later and rushed to the apartment to begin writing, all through the night until dawn, and then made my way to the *Chronicle*, dead tired but satisfied and perfectly ... happy. Yes, happy! My life had meaning — I was more than comfortable financially (I'd wisely placed my inheritance in the bank and in bonds), my work at the *Chronicle* wasn't an obligation, I could have left, now that I had this new occupation, but as Bobby said, "Ideas appear in contact with others." Sometimes I got contracts with advertising agencies to write scripts for television — one for pantyhose, another for lipstick; they gave me a concept, and I wrote a short story. It was fun and paid well. For the rest, "the serious projects," I sent my scripts to Hollywood or producers in San Francisco, following Bobby's advice. It was one disappointment after the other on that front, but Bobby encouraged me, "Don't give up. One day you'll make it." I could only hope he was right.

Then, my mother died. Moïse told me over the phone. I'd spoken to her not too long ago, and an edge to her voice had told me something was wrong.

"Ma, is everything okay?"

"When are you coming to see me? You've been promising me for years."

"Ma, things are complicated for now. There's work, my movies."

"It's been three years since I came to visit you in New York. I don't think I can hold on much longer."

"Hold on? What do you mean by that, Ma?"

"Your mother is feeling her age, Romain. That's all."

The guilt I felt, the guilt of not having seen her one last time.

6

*There, over the horizon, sun rising after a long night,
returning to the country of his youth. A strange language
spoken around him, sounds he had lost somewhere on
the side of the long road that leads to exile. His travel
bag in his hands, he strides through the hallways of the
Montreal airport, his ears raised like a nervous dog, his
throat tight. He listens for a dancing voice he's missed,
he scans the crowd for a friend he hasn't seen in five years.*

A scene out of a movie? No — September 1971.

"Hey, man? Is that you?"

I couldn't believe it. I'd gone past the man at least twice.

"Moïse?"

I had to pinch myself. He'd put on weight, cheeks full. He
had a moustache like Dennis Hopper and an impressive afro. He
countered my astonishment with his own. "And you! With your
beard and your hair, you look like you just came out of Manson's
compound! Come here, buddy!"

And like in our best days in New York, we burst out laughing
and fell into each other's arms, our eyes wet, fighting off tears. "Man,
man, man! Five years! It's so good to see you!"

Yes, it was good to be together again.

He hurried me to the airport parking lot where Louise's Beetle was waiting for us, the same Louise of Moïse's impassioned letters. He grabbed my bag, threw it on the back seat, opened the door and invited me to climb into his car, holding my hand as if I was his girl on a date. "Quit screwing around, Moïse!" He laughed. His moustache danced beneath his nose. He started the Beetle and we drove off towards Métis Beach.

"I can't believe you're here, man! It's a dream! A goddamn dream! How does it feel to be going back home?"

Yes, how did it feel? "I don't know ... I'm nervous ... I should have come back earlier. When she was still alive. When it mattered...."

He placed a hand on my shoulder. "Hey, you couldn't know, man. You're being too hard on yourself."

"It's too late for her. She can't care anymore...."

Moïse gave me a worried look, then turned his eyes back to the road. We were driving past the suburbs, a blue September sky above us and already the trees taking on autumn's dress. It was strange to have been gone all these years and not be able to say how I really felt. Finally, I spoke, "I'm going to have to face off with the old man. That's what makes me the most nervous, I think."

Moïse laughed. "Don't worry about it. Your father's a harmless old man now. You might not even recognize him." He turned towards me, "I'm happy you're here. I know you're sad, but you'll see, Louise and me, we'll get your mind off things." On the highway, the wind was buffeting the Beetle, and Moïse kept his hands firmly on the wheel. "Shit, shit, shit, and shit! So many things to tell you, man! Oh! I'm so happy!"

It was almost four o'clock in the afternoon by the time we got to the funeral home. Moïse put an arm around my shoulders and guided me through the crowd, perhaps thirty people in all. Suffocating heat, disparaging glances, muted whispers. *It's him! Are you sure?* If Moïse passed the decency test with his dark suit, I failed miserably with my dirty jeans, my fringed vest, my long hair, and beard. *That's him? That's Romain?*

I found my father prostrate before the coffin. Moïse was right; he was an old man. His back bent, a bald and wrinkled head, thick glasses that magnified his eyes. The whispers in my wake alerted him. He turned and noticed me. He pulled himself to his feet, walked towards me, close enough for me to smell the alcohol on his breath. I didn't say anything, and he didn't either. Around us, the crowd fell silent. I didn't know what I had expected, certainly not reconciliation, perhaps a sort of truce. His vehemence put ice in my veins, "Go get changed and put on a tie, for God's sake. You're burying your mother!"

I tightened my fists. Discreetly, Moïse encouraged me not to make a scene. I said, as calmly as possible, "Hi, Dad. You could say hi before losing your temper."

His face contorted. That evil, threatening look he had like that time I almost broke my neck falling on the Egans' garage roof so many years ago. He told me off that time, instead of worrying for his son — yes, *his son!* — who could have injured himself seriously, fallen to the ground, broken an arm or his back.

"Did you hear me? Go get changed!"

"It's all I have with me. It'll have to do."

It wasn't true. I had a suit and tie in my bag, for the burial.

"Get changed, or get out of here!"

In the room, a stupefied silence. I was too astounded to recognize any of the faces staring at me. Jean? Paul? And over there, Françoise's imposing figure? Outraged, hostile looks. I turned towards Moïse, "Okay, Moïse. Let's get out of here."

"Whatever you say, man."

I turned and was about to push my way through the crowd when I felt his calloused hand on my shoulder, "It's your fault she's dead at fifty-eight! You broke her heart!"

I turned and faced him in a blinding rage, "What do you want to do now, eh? Hit me? How long have you dreamed of it? Go ahead! Go ahead, hit me!"

Fire in his eyes. He was about to take a swing, but Jeff Loiseau placed himself between us.

"Drop it, Albert. Think of Ida. She's probably making a scene about this, up there."

He mumbled, and cussed him out. Limped to a chair along the wall and fell onto it. The only sound was his ragged breath.

Rattled, I made a beeline for the exit, Moïse right behind me. How could I not despise him? How could I not despise myself? After all these years, for God's sake, nine years of exile trying to become a man, and I still couldn't face my father. I was fifteen all over again.

In Louise's Beetle, I couldn't speak I was so upset. We passed my mother's store. I barely glanced at it. That's where her heart had given out on her — just like her mother's had before her. In the middle of helping out a customer. I was tired. Tired and broken-hearted. We drove in silence down Rue Principale through to Beach Street, past the majestic pines and spruce, the ancient cedar rows, and the grand summer homes with their tennis courts. I hadn't missed any of those things, even if, seeing them up close, so different from my memory that had faded with time, I felt a pang of nostalgia. Everything was like before, except perhaps the vegetation, which seemed denser, more vigorous. Moïse told me that Frank Brodie, the policeman who had appeared at my door on the morning of August 19, 1962, had been forced into retirement after Métis Beach fell under the jurisdiction of the provincial police.

Then, Dana's house.

"It's your house, Romain. In Métis Beach. Your house."

Moïse got out of the Beetle and watched me, smiling, as if he'd surprised me with a gift. My house. The one Dana had given me so that I might always be close to my native soil. It was more beautiful than I remembered, with its two towers, each a separate wing, dazzling under the still-warm September sun, its freshly painted veranda, its shingles washed by the salty air of the sea. Oh, Dana! I would have paid a pretty penny to see her nestled in one of the Adirondack chairs in the garden, in canvas pants, a large sailor's sweater, and dark sunglasses, reading *Life* or a good novel, raising her eyes from time to time towards the sparkling sea before her. She would have heard the gravel on the driveway crackling under the Beetle's tires, she would have turned her head and said, "Romain, is that you?" She would have gotten up, walked towards me barefoot in the grass as she loved to do; she would have opened her arms, taking in the space around us, "It's your house, now." She would have held me tight against her, placed her lips on my forehead, and I would have smelled jasmine perfume on her. "Yes, your house. The one in which I was so happy with my wonderful John."

I'm so sorry, Dana. You can't imagine how much I miss you.

"Isn't the house wonderful?"

I was thankful that Moïse and Louise had taken such good care of it. Louise walked towards us and offered up a soft, sweet-smelling cheek for a kiss, the seductive Louise I was meeting for the first time and whom I kissed in front of Moïse, who might have been jealous. He quickly showed me the ring on her finger. They were to marry soon. In two months, as soon as Moïse got his Canadian citizenship. I was happy for them, and I was happy to be with them, here, in Dana's house.

"Are you okay, man? You're going to pull through?"

By this time, they were probably putting my mother in the ground, without me. Not after what happened at the funeral home.

We sat on the veranda facing the sea. Louise brought us a few beers and a couple of wool blankets. The September air cooled quickly, as soon as the sun began setting on the other side of the river. We were in for quite a show, one of those burning red sunsets. I was cold, still trembling from the confrontation.

Louise left us alone on the veranda; we had so much to catch up on, and she knew it. Before she left, Moïse asked her for a kiss — "I love you," he said. She gave him a smile, then smiled at me, and I felt the faintest touch of envy, a small twinge. "Right, man, how lucky am I?" he asked, as if reading my thoughts. He burst out laughing, and I joined him. His eyes filled with tears, and mine too.

Bloody Moïse. What a joy to be with him again.

He took a sip of beer, wiped his moustache on the back of his sleeve, suddenly serious. "Okay, man, let's talk frankly. Time to organize your grand return."

"Forget about it. Every one of your letters says the same thing. You sound like a Jewish mother trying to get her son to visit."

He ignored my remark. "Incredible! You just can't see what's right in front of your eyes! What are you hoping for? What are you fucking doing over there?" He sighed loudly. "Look. I did my research. They're looking for someone at the Musée d'Art Contemporain in Montreal. It would be prefect."

"I've got my job at the *San Francisco Chronicle*."

He snorted, "You're a goddamn assistant, man! It isn't serious! You can do better!"

"It's exactly what you were doing when you started at the *Montreal Star*!"

"Sure, but I had bigger plans — to become a journalist. Is that what you want?"

"How many times have I told you in my letters, I'm writing scripts."

"You've never sent me one."

"Fine!" I said, frustrated. "I'll do it as soon as I get back to San Francisco."

"You'll never do it."

"And why not?"

"Because you can't. And each time you fail, you fall deeper into despair."

I said, cut to the quick, "What do you know about that?"

"Look at you, man! You're at the end of your rope."

Above us, the sun was sending down its last rays. I was thinking of my mother in the small cemetery at the end of Rue de l'Église, and I promised myself I'd go tomorrow, with flowers, red carnations, her favourite. After the fight with my father, I had taken a quick glance at the coffin and noticed that she was wearing the Pierre Cardin suit I'd given her in New York. The furtive image troubled me, like a playing card seen in the middle of a shuffled deck. I came all the way from San Francisco, and saw her for only a few pathetic seconds. A long trip to hear Moïse lecture me and denigrate my work as a scriptwriter.

"And you," I asked, irritated, "where's the novel that'll make you *so famous*?"

He began to laugh, an amused laugh, the sort an old man might have, remembering his past mistakes.

"I don't have the time, man. I have responsibilities now. You have to waste your days dreaming if you're going to write."

"I can't believe what I'm hearing! You sound like another goddamn capitalist!"

"Maybe I'll get back to writing someday. After I retire."

"Goddamn it, Moïse, you're only twenty-seven! What's going on with you? You, the writer!" Where's your love for Kerouac and the others? An accountant! That's what you sound like!"

"You'll see, man, when you have a real career."

A punch in the gut. I grabbed my beer and got up. There were limits to tolerating such stupid conversation!

"Hey, don't take it that way! Come on, be serious for a moment. Look at your life! An assistant's job and dreams you'll never achieve! One day, you'll wake up and realize that you've lost years of your life. We need to build a solid foundation at our age, or else everything will fall apart later. You also need to come to terms with what's happened here, man. You need to come back. Or you'll never be able to move forward. And you know what else? With your mother's death, it might be time to reconcile with your father."

"Are you kidding?"

"Do I look like I am?"

"You don't understand a goddamn thing."

Furious, I rushed down the steps towards the sea. The salty, cold air, heavy with humidity, slapped me in my face. What had happened to my friend Moïse? From a volcano, an inch away from eruption, he had turned into something tepid and flat. "Romain!" I turned, shivering. Moïse had followed me onto the beach, a wool sweater over his arm. "Put this on, man, you're going to catch your death." He helped me put it on, patted me on the back. "Hey, man, we haven't seen each other in five years. We need to talk. That's what friends do, no? Come on, let's eat. Louise made something good."

Moïse was at the table. His back straight, a napkin on his knee. Louise had prepared us beef with carrots and mashed potatoes, set in the centre of the table. He got up, served us without spilling anything, reasonable portions, well placed on the white plates, whiter than white. Sparkling. Even his table manners — which used to revolt Dana — had become miraculously refined. I smiled. He looked like a goddamn aristocrat. Impossible not to think of the old Moïse, who ate with his fingers, mouth open, talking, spitting, and burping because it was funny. I was stunned.

And my anger faded.

"Still seeing that fucker Ken Lafayette?"

In my letters, I often spoke of Ken, and Moïse had warned me off fanatics.

"I haven't seen him in more than two years. Sometimes his name pops up in the newspaper, but I'm not telling you anything you don't know when I say I don't miss him one bit."

I spoke of his scandalous attitude towards his friend Pete. They listened to me attentively, shocked. I told them of a particularly awful moment at the Berkeley antiwar committee office. Ken had gone after a guy who was about to be drafted into the army. For the guy's father, who had served in the Second World War, it was all about honour. Ken decided to "have a little fun" with him, because he came from an illustrious Republican California family.

"What did the bastard do?"

"The guy's father was close to Governor Reagan. The guy was pitiful. Both rebel and daddy's boy. Drug problem and in to sports cars. Terrible self-esteem but a big mouth. He wanted to know how to join "the Resistance." Join the Resistance! Like in Nazi-occupied France! He was ready to renounce his family, his family's money, and his Porsche 912 to live clandestinely. Ken told him that to get his help, he had to pledge allegiance to the Maoist cause in front of at least fifty students and sign a $2,000 cheque over to the Cause."

"No!" Louise exclaimed.

"Oh, yes! Within twenty minutes, Ken gathered fifty students on campus. Everyone was in on it. Ken gave him a megaphone and the poor guy stammered out his love for Mao. Everyone was laughing. It was cruel."

"The guy's a criminal!"

"Did he sign the cheque?" Louise asked.

"Yes. But I don't think Ken put any money in his own pocket. Someone at the committee told me the money would help to buy supplies."

"Supplies?" Moïse asked. "What kind of supplies?"

"I don't know."

"I swear, that guy could be making bombs as we speak."

"On that, Moïse, we disagree. The guy's a manipulator, but he's non-violent."

"I hope you're right."

After the meal, Moïse invited me into the living room. Grand Marnier in crystal glasses, the same ones Dana used to drink her vodka from with Ethel, in this room that once was so full of life, and smoke. Seeing Dana's furniture and Ethel's paintings on the walls, I felt my chest tighten. Dana, and now my mother. Disappeared, and only their belongings as testimony to their lives. Dana had been dead for three years. It was like an eternity had passed. The sadness I felt when I thought of her was still as strong, though not as intense, like the shape of something far away. With sudden acuity, I realized I was afraid my memories might simply fade away. It was a paradox. But that night, with Moïse and Louise, in the fabulous, warm home, good memories chased away the bad. "To our reunion!" Moïse exclaimed. We raised our glasses, brought them together. A tender look passed between them, and I thought, *He seems so happy! Such a simple, serene life!* I thought of my own life, seemingly slipping away, a series of fortuitous accidents over which I had no control. Sipping my Grand Marnier in front of the fire Moïse had lit, I surprised myself as I began to consider that it was time to find a place to call my own, and build a future on a more solid foundation. *But where, how?*

"Good evening."

The voice paralyzed me. A voice I immediately recognized. A voice that brought me back to the past like an old scar cut anew. At a loss, I gave Moïse a questioning look. Embarrassed, he didn't look at me.

"Gail?"

7

She was smaller, more melancholy than I remembered. With a disconcerting fragility in her eyes.

She had come to Métis Beach by herself, as she did sometimes, when her parents weren't there and her husband was busy at work. She liked the solitude of the village, the long walks on the beach.

She had learned about my mother's death and wanted to offer her condolences. She had thought of coming to the funeral home, but thankfully had decided not to. "Your father wouldn't have taken it well, I think?" I was speechless. An awkward silence fell over the room; Moïse and Louise were smiling dumbly. Gail said, "Everyone's talking about you in the village. The prodigal's return." She watched me with a mixture of amusement and confusion. "Your beard, your hair, I would have never recognized you."

Louise invited her to sit down and offered her a drink. Moïse quickly said, "We met Gail last year at the clubhouse. Louise and Gail get on well with each other."

Why hadn't he said anything in his letters? He could see I was upset, and laughed nervously while Gail, still shocked by my appearance, repeated, "Oh, Romain, you've changed so much."

Her voice was softer, more resigned than in my memory. There was some openness about her, not like that night in August 1962, with her caustic laughter, eyes filled with a disturbing fire, and that photo of Don Drysdale she stuck under my nose as a challenge, or perhaps to humiliate me.

Do you love him?

I don't know, maybe I do, maybe I don't, but that doesn't matter right now.

The memory of having been manipulated, ridiculed.

But the young woman who appeared in Dana's house looked nothing like that. Long dirty blond hair safely tied back into a bun, white pants and a black vest, shadows under her eyes that her light makeup couldn't hide, an angular face, pale lips. As timid as a little girl, she said, "All that time … So many things have happened to you…. Wonderful things, according to Moïse."

"Is that so?"

"New York, California. A degree in Art History."

"I don't have a degree. Quit before I got it."

She forced a smile. "Moïse said you write for the movies, is that true?"

I gave him a dark look. What had he said about my projects? Had he been sarcastic or respectful?

"Yes, it's true."

"That's fantastic, Romain. I'm very happy for you."

She got up, took something out of her bag, and held it in her hand. I saw she had a slight limp. She presented me with a hand-painted card, a watercolour condolence card, a child's drawing, with animals. I was touched that she had thought of me and my mother. She was no longer that young seventeen-year-old girl, disturbed and egotistical, who lured the naive and fearful adolescent I was into her bed, making him believe that she was actually interested in him. I thanked her, put the card back in the envelope. "And you?" I said. "What's been going on with you?"

She shrugged. "Me? Nothing extraordinary."

"I hear you married the heir to Barron cookies."

She laughed. "You say heir like it's a royal title."

She sat back down, and there was something fleeting and veiled in her eyes. "Yes, he's my husband."

"So?"

"So, what?"

"Are you happy with him? Do you have children?"

Her face darkened, and I felt Moïse and Louise stiffen. She said, with poorly hidden disdain, "Oh, no. And it's better that way."

What could that mean?

We spoke for a time of Métis Beach — Gail told me about Mr. Riddington, whose health was declining. As for the Babcocks and McKays, they sold their properties after the car accident that cost the lives of their children. Art Tees bought the Babcock property while the eldest Hayes girl bought the McKays'. Gail spoke with surprising detachment of the whole affair, her eyes sometimes seemingly empty of emotion, and a constant trembling in her hands, like someone on mood-stabilizing drugs.

Moïse tried unsuccessfully to hide a huge yawn. "Man, with all that road we covered today, and all the emotions, I'm beat. Off to bed for me." Louise followed him, leaving us alone, Gail and me. I was sorry to see them go upstairs; I too was dead tired. Gail offered an embarrassed smile, and poured another glass. I went into the kitchen for a beer.

Then she began telling me about her misfortunes. She showed me the bruises on her arms, a red mark on the back of her neck. I was horrified and astounded at the ease with which she confided in me, as if there were nothing appalling about what she was telling me, and she had never thought of putting an end to it.

"He beats me."

They'd been married eight years, and for the past eight years it had been hell.

"What are you waiting for? Leave him!"

A bitter laugh. "I'm the wife of a very rich and very influential man, who would never let his wife leave like that. And anyway, what would I do, all alone? I don't have a degree, or my own money." She gave a fatalistic smile. "I'm trapped, Romain."

I couldn't accept her defeatism. Not doing a very good job at hiding my anger, I said, "This is 1971, Gail, not the fifties. Women can divorce, build a new life of their own. Your parents can help you, can't they?"

She took a long drink, her hands shaking. "My parents? You know them. If I'm still with Howard, it's partly because the marriage is important to them."

I shook my head. "You're twenty-six, for God's sake! Who gives a shit what your parents think!"

She drew back, lowered her eyes to the ground. "It touches me to see you lose your temper for me."

Except that she didn't seem touched. She seemed elsewhere. It was late by the time she left. I slept poorly that night.

The next morning over breakfast, I questioned Moïse. He was on the defensive, "I didn't know how you'd react. Louise and I, well, we crossed paths with Gail a few times over the summer. We never saw each other in Montreal. I thought it was best not to tell you, I didn't want to stir up old memories. I thought I was doing the right thing."

"She has friends?"

"I don't know. Like I said, I don't really know her."

"She told you about her husband?"

"She talked to Louise about it. Louise is trying to get her to leave, but it seems to be complicated."

I had a headache and had barely slept a wink. "She's taking all sorts of medication, Moïse. She must be, to let that bastard keep beating her and not fight back. All drugged up, no wonder she doesn't."

Moïse put his cup on the table and gave me a worried look. "No, man, don't tell me that...."

"I didn't say anything. I didn't even think anything."

"Yes, you did. And you shouldn't. She's too fragile. And you're more fragile than you think too."

Gail and I spent the next afternoon walking on the beach and talking in the warmth of the heavy sweaters Louise had knitted, sitting comfortably in large chairs on the veranda. Her hands weren't trembling like the night before, her eyes had recovered some of their sheen, but she was still a broken woman, defenceless, who needed protection. She told me surprising confidences, without shame — their unhealthy sex life complicated by the infirmity of her husband, his legs paralyzed by polio. He wanted children; he harassed her. She didn't want any, didn't let herself be touched on the critical days of the month. So he beat her. She said, as if it was a clear victory, "It's the only power I have, to make sure he doesn't have children." I didn't try to contradict her. She spoke of their life in public, her being forced to parade on his arm and look like a loving and devoted wife. Sometimes, a few hours before a society event, she numbed herself with Valium and barbiturates and ended up in such a fog that Howard left without her, furious, promising to show her when he got back home. Her mother-in-law commented on her flat stomach every time she saw her. She used crude words, one time, "You just have to spread your thighs, my girl. It's a question of willpower." Another time Gail inadvertently picked up the phone and caught a conversation between her husband and his mother, as he gave her a detailed report on their sexual interactions and their frequency.

I was shocked. "Why did you marry him?"

"Because I didn't have a choice."

"You said the same thing about Don Drysdale. But you didn't marry him."

"I ... You can't understand. I don't want to talk about it...."

She went quiet. I wasn't going to force her to confide in me, what she had said already was difficult enough to hear.

The wind was rising, clouds were gathering on the western horizon, black almost, heavy with rain. "When Frank Brodie came to my house that morning, why did he mention rape?"

She stiffened. "I'm sorry, Romain. I had nothing to do with that. My father sent him."

"Why *rape*? Who spoke of rape? You?"

She protested, hurt, "No!"

"Who, then?"

"My father learned we slept together that night. And he went mad."

"You told him?"

"No! He deduced it. Remember — the dog, poor Locki ... And my shouts on the veranda.... The Riddingtons heard me shout, and they saw you running on the beach. They alerted my parents at the Tees' place." The air was getting cooler. Gail shivered. she sought warmth from her own arms. "When my mother and father came home, I was in such a state of shock, I could barely breathe. Locki wasn't dead, he was choking on his own blood. I was staring at him, crouched down, powerless, terrified. My father took me by the shoulders and ordered me to go back inside. I saw his work through the window — he took Locki's head in his hands and broke his neck in one swift motion. To stop his suffering. I cried so much, Romain, I cried and cried. It was simply awful."

Rain had begun to fall, tearing the still surface of the river. I was thinking of Louis, my fists tight, *Why had he gone after the dog, for God's sake?*

"Remember, I was naked under the sheet. I couldn't think straight, I didn't know where I was, what I was wearing. At first they were alarmed, then they became furious. They mentioned you, asked if you were responsible, for the dog, I mean. I swear, Romain, I told them nothing, I denied everything. But they didn't believe me."

She was shaking all over now. Her revelations weren't unexpected. Still, I was deeply moved, embarrassed when I thought of the insensitivity I had shown, preoccupied with my own misfortune, never hers.

She snuggled into her chair, looking for heat. "My father wanted to scare you, to push you away as far as possible since the marriage with Don was getting closer. He succeeded, didn't he?"

Her voice was filled with derision. "What comforts me, the only thing, is that you've made it. I envy you." She gave a small, resigned laugh. "For me, everything went downhill from there. A bad dream I've never woken up from. But I asked for it, didn't I?"

Our conversation stirred something in me. In the disorder of my inner life, I felt a responsibility towards her. "What sort of responsibility?" Moïse asked later, concerned. It was hard to say. Maybe because she didn't have the same opportunities I did. She never met someone like Dana, someone who could have helped her. "It isn't a good idea, man. She needs psychological help, not a good guy like you. You're naive if you think you can save her."

On the second night, we made love. Gail was tender, soft, affectionate, and it made things more confusing. "Sex gives the worst advice," Moïse warned me. Perhaps.

But I invited her to come with me to San Francisco. "I have money. You can get a law degree, like you always dreamed of. After that, you'll be able to make your own decisions, and not depend on anyone. I'm not asking you to love me, or even live with me like an official couple. You'll be free, freer than you've ever been. Like I've been, since the summer of 1962."

Her eyes filled with tears.

"I'm serious, Gail."

8

In San Francisco, we emptied out my Tenderloin apartment in a single day. The next day we moved into a place on Telegraph Hill, far more spacious and luxurious, its large windows looking out onto the bay. If you craned your neck a little and looked west, you could see Alcatraz on a bright day. Gail would shudder when she looked at it, or laugh, depending on the day. A beautiful apartment on Calhoun Terrace, with high ceilings and rooms filled with sunlight. So it was far too expensive, four hundred dollars a month, but why not — I had the money — and Gail seemed to be happy there, at least at first.

I realized soon enough that she was in a pitiful state.

She cried often and couldn't explain why. She could sleep twelve, fourteen hours a day, barely getting up. Other mornings, she'd jump out of bed like a dynamo, ready to go out and conquer the world. I dreaded those mornings. She insisted I accompany her to all her "activities," which this time, she assured me, would be "the right ones" — yoga, meditation, purification, prayers and incantations, hypnotherapy, mystical clubs.... In a childish voice, she begged me to call in sick at the *Chronicle* — where I'd been moved over to page layout, a job I enjoyed — and she dragged me out of the city for a rejuvenating hike or a treatment at Shasta Abbey. She abandoned her designer clothes from Holt Renfrew for cheap peasant dresses and knitted shawls into which she disappeared like an old woman hiding from the cold. The pills she'd brought with her ended up in the toilet

— Valium, Tofranil, barbiturates, drugs that kept her in a zombie state but regulated her moods. At home, she imposed new diets — tofu, algae, vegetable concoctions. With single-minded enthusiasm, she experienced every type of guru California had to offer, convinced she'd end up finding the panacea that would heal her of despair.

During that time, I stopped writing. I just didn't have the time or concentration to do it, and Bobby criticized me.

I quickly began regretting my decision. Regularly, and kindly, I hoped, I suggested she should begin thinking about applying to a university, but she always put it off, always something else to do, to try, a need to claim her newfound freedom, or so I guessed.

I feared there might be problems with her husband, but to my great surprise, he made himself known only once, through one of his lawyers he sent to San Francisco. Gail told me about it after the fact, as if it was a detail, of no importance. She met with the lawyer one afternoon at the Sir Francis Drake Hotel; he presented her with a pile of documents, divorce papers, and she'd signed them without reading a word. "What did you do?"

"I broke my chains. He's out of my life."

"And he's not giving you anything? You didn't negotiate at all?" She shook her head, victorious.

"I don't want a penny of his dirty money." I was astonished and sceptical; I never knew whether she told me the truth or had invented the whole story. With Gail, I couldn't be sure.

Her relationship with her parents was a total catastrophe. The few times she called them, they hung up on her. She learned through a cousin that to save face (after all, hadn't Gail followed her "rapist"?), they told people their daughter was staying at a retreat in California to treat severe depression — something she did indeed suffer from. Her charming family attributed her depression to "her infertility that makes her suffer so."

"What they didn't know," she said, disgusted, "is that I had to climb on top of Howard like an animal to satisfy his needs."

She sent them wild letters, filled with rebellious poems. Ginsberg, Orlovsky, Gregory Corso. "They say I'm crazy. I'll prove them right." She wrote that she took drugs and loved getting raped in the streets of San Francisco. It made me mad. I no longer knew whether she was playing a game or truly falling into insanity.

In the evenings, she'd sit in front of the television to watch the news with an unhealthy obsession. I couldn't understand what she was getting out of it. She would sit straight up on the couch, hands on her thighs, rocking softly like an autistic child, as she watched, eyes wide, the chaos flashing on the screen — bombings in Vietnam, dead, mutilated bodies, antiwar protests that turned to violence, the Weather Underground's bombs. One day, a bomb blew up not far away from our place, in the parking garage of the federal building on Washington Street. Two employees, two young women, were seriously injured. It was all they talked about for days on television and in the papers. Gail was terrified. "How can they target innocent people? I don't understand this country, Romain, it scares me." Her whole body was shaking, as if she had a fever.

"It'll end soon, Gail. It can't last forever."

She cringed, "I don't think so. This violence isn't a temporary aberration. It's rooted in this country."

One of the young women died of her wounds. Gail stared and stared at the pictures of her that appeared on the front page of the *Chronicle*, a pretty young woman, twenty-five years old, a mother of two young children. Underneath her picture were the photos of the three Weathermen the FBI was looking for, though their responsibility was never confirmed. She said, scared, "It could have been anyone. Including us. Do you understand?"

"And we could die just crossing the street."

She gave me a dark look. "You've been living here for too long. You don't see how sick it is." She turned her head, bit her lower lip, "I want to go back to Montreal."

I'd been expecting it for weeks but, strangely, it angered me. "You're serious?"

"I want to go home. All this scares me too much."

"You're not going back to Howard, are you?"

She shrugged.

"Gail, you're not going to go back to that son of a bitch?"

She didn't answer. Her eyes were sightless, as if lost in the fog of her mind. I got on my knees and took her hand. "Okay, I'll take care of it. If that's what you want."

She never mentioned going back to Montreal again. She even began the process of enrolling in the law faculty of the University of California at San Francisco. I would pay for everything, we'd agreed.

She made a friend, Susan, whom she met in an art school in North Beach — a young, energetic woman with red hair and a loud, kindly laugh. They became fast friends. Susan gave watercolour and pottery classes at the school. She had fled her husband, a controlling man who didn't allow her to work. She'd been devastated when the court gave him custody of their children. *Adultery* was a rather big word for what she'd been accused of — a few times she had gone to a neighbour's house in Dale City for comfort, when she just couldn't handle being with her husband anymore.

One night, Gail said, "Susan left, she was afraid of nothing. She even abandoned her children." Her face darkened, "Abandoning your children, do you know what that does to someone?"

I was confused. How could I know? How could she know? We didn't have children, either of us.

And she began crying. There was something painful she couldn't bring herself to tell me. Like a secret. *Gail had a secret?* When she got hold of herself and wiped away the tears with the back of her hand, she said, "If Susan wasn't afraid, why would I be?"

"Afraid of what, Gail? I don't get it."

"Afraid of everything. Of other people. Of not having enough money. I don't trust myself. I don't think I can do it by myself."

"Do what? Your studies? You'll be fine. There's no reason for you not to succeed."

"You really think so?"

"I don't doubt it for a second."

But I didn't believe what I was saying. Maybe at one point I had thought I could help her, but I knew now she was a lost cause.

By the summer of 1972, Gail still wasn't enrolled.

We hit the road with Susan in my Westfalia, for a sort of Woodstock in Ahwahnee, in Madera County, at the foot of the Sierra Nevada. A great gathering of hippies. I abhorred their sexual and communal promiscuity, but Gail was enthusiastic about going.

The party, if you could call it that, brought together a menagerie of half-naked and intoxicated hippies. We were supposed to celebrate the summer solstice according to some druidic tradition. The festivities were to last three days, and I couldn't see how I was going to make it all the way through.

"Romain, stop pouting!" Gail chided me. "You'll see, you'll feel much better afterwards."

And that's what worried me, this naive belief that we would emerge from this masquerade purified and energized. I don't know who had convinced Gail that these ridiculous rites — which were, to me, only a pretext for these insufferable hippies to get high and fuck — would make our lives better or show us the path to our dreams.

"Why do you always have to criticize everything, all the time?" she asked. "Just look around you."

She was right. The site was magnificent. Hills covered in grass the colour of gold, sparse vegetation, ash-green trees and shrubs, almost muted, and soil the colour of blood. In the hollow of the valley, a swollen, bubbling creek, around which a few cows grazed, answering each other's calls, while Yosemite's Blue Mountains hung in the distance with their serrated peaks, slashing the radiant sky. We got out of the dusty Westfalia and were welcomed by a bare-chested guy with long hair and dirty fingernails trailed by two children as dirty as he was, their blond locks washed out by the sun.

"They're adorable," Susan said, melancholy in her voice, "Are they yours?"

The man snickered, pushing his hair back behind his shoulders. "Children aren't our property." He played with one of the boys' hair. "They're individuals in their own right. The community is their true family."

To my great consternation, Gail nodded. Later, she said, "What he said was beautiful, wasn't it? He saw the truth of it — children aren't the property of their parents."

"Do you know why he said that?"

She stiffened. "What sort of idiocy are you going to come out with this time?"

"He said that because he can't claim paternity over them." She shrugged and turned to Susan to tell her not to listen to me. "It's true! With hippies, and their stories of free love, mothers are the only ones who know who their children are. The guys, well, they're never sure of anything, so they comfort themselves with meaningless phrases."

"Oh, you're just speaking nonsense!"

In the hills, dozens of tents had been erected. Between them, children were running and playing. Branches and cut-up bushes had been piled here and there, pyramids of dried vegetation that would be set alight once darkness fell. "The summer solstice," Gail was repeating, excited, "marks the victory of light over darkness." All night, these pyres would light up the sky.

We began a series of processions and ridiculous rituals. We had to fill a basin with cut flowers, and place them in another basin at the other end of the site. Women got naked and wandered about to ensure their fertility. The smell of marijuana and hashish was floating everywhere. As the sun set, we were told to run, hand in hand, around the tents, yelling, "Light! Light! Light!" until the sun, red-dening, disappeared behind the copper-yellow hills. Then the men lit the pyres, and the sky blazed, bringing cries of astonishment from children's throats. "Isn't it wonderful?" Gail asked. "We are going to spend the night under a fiery sun." She took my hand. "Come!" — and dragged me towards a series of more modest fires next to the river. A bunch of naked hippies were walking over scattered embers.

"Our turn!" Gail exclaimed.

"No way! I'm not going to grill myself like a sausage."

She began taking her clothes off. "Come on! We'll purify our-selves. Start a new life. Turn a page on our shitty past."

"Our" shitty past? Was that what she said?

She tore her clothes off, threw them in the grass. "Come on, join us! Get naked!"

Susan stripped as well. It was the first time I'd seen her without colourful layers of shapeless clothing. Feeling watched, she crossed her arms over her generous breasts. Gail was becoming impatient; she grabbed her arm and both of them, hand in hand, jumped over the flames that licked at their calves, shouting in raw, reverent voices, "Light! Light! Light!" Flames on every hill, roaring from all the bonfires, a fireman's nightmare in the middle of a thirsty, dry country.

Then came a grotesque series of two-bit rituals, including a pathetic moment where each was invited to throw into the fire some-thing they considered the principal barrier to their happiness. Everyone began searching the desert scrub for an object that might represent their obstacle. An emotional woman spoke of incest by her father when she was eight; she threw a mouse's corpse into the fire, and the crowd applauded. Feverish, Gail turned towards me and asked me for my wallet. I thought she was joking. She insisted, "Give it to me, please."

"No."

"Give it to me!"

Something angry in her eyes, uncompromising. She seemed ready to explode. I gave her my wallet, thinking she wouldn't dare.

But she dared. She pulled out every single bill, showed them to the assembly.

"Please, Gail…"

She looked at the crowd and said, "Hello. I'm Gail."

"Hello Gail," they answered together.

She raised her head, pushed her long blond hair from her face. She was naked, like most of them. The prominent bones of her pelvis practically tore through her skin. Displayed like this, for all to see, I didn't find her quite so desirable. She disgusted me, even. *We can't keep going on this way, both of us.*

She brandished the bills, shook them in front of the flames. "This money perfectly symbolizes my family and my ex-husband. Rich people who never have enough. They have no qualms about breaking the lives of those around them to get even richer, just a bit — scandalously — richer.…"

Applause, words of encouragement, "Go for it, Gail, we're with you!" She smiled, counted out the money — two hundred dollars. The crowd purred with pleasure.

"Gail, don't be ridiculous … Give me those bills back.…"

She snickered, staggered, her small breasts quivering like boiling water. "You're rich too! You have to be, to be carrying this much money!"

"Yeah! Go for it Gail!"

I gritted my teeth, grabbed her by the arm. "Tell me, how are we going to pay for gas on the drive home?"

She moved away from me brusquely, barked a sarcastic laugh. "You're ruining everything with your capitalist preoccupations!" Spoken with the same tone as Ken Lafayette.

I said, trembling with indignation, "Capitalist? Who's been taking care of you since you got here? Who's going to pay for your studies?"

She choked, "Ah! See that? You keep telling me it makes you happy to do it! But you're lying! You were just waiting for the right time to criticize me! Just another form of control. You think that by paying me you'll be able to put me in chains?"

Around us, the crowd was stirring. "Leave her alone!"

"Yes, leave me alone."

"You don't know what you're saying. You smoked too much hippie grass."

"That's none of your business!"

"Fine, I'm going to go get some air. Better put an end to this discussion. You might regret what you say."

"Regret what I say?" She mocked my inflection. "I'm telling you what I think — at last! I can't breathe, Romain Carrier, because of your false benevolent attentions!"

Like a knife in the gut. "Fine! Go back to Montreal! I'm not your goddamned jailer!"

"Yes, you are! You just don't realize it!"

A sensation of vertigo, nausea. She challenged me with her eyes, took the two hundred dollars, and threw it in the fire. Shouts of joy and incantations. The bills burned, quickly reduced to sparks carried by the wind. Gail was laughing, her head thrown back, triumphant. On her moist skin, shining with sweat, the flames danced, reflected like in a mirror. She turned her feverish eyes towards me, and we knew, at that very moment, that something had been irreparably broken between us.

A guy with long hair, completely naked, placed a hand on my shoulder. "It's only money, man. Don't take it that way." He pointed at Gail. "Tonight, you helped her free herself from her demons. That's worth all the gold in the world." He slapped my back and made his way towards Gail, leaned towards her and said something in her ear. She burst out laughing. He took her by the waist, the bastard, and she let herself be taken, all the while looking at me straight in the eyes, a vengeful smile on her face — *I'm not your thing, your property*.

And suddenly, a light burst into the sky, burning like a giant comet. Flames exploded from the other side of the hill and thick smoke began to rise, covering the light of all the solstice fires. Thick black smoke. And shouts, enough to put ice in your veins.

"What ... What is it?" Eyes filled with fear. Someone said something about coyotes, there were quite a few in the sector. "No!" a woman shouted in terror. "No! The children...."

A cacophony of shouts, mixed in with the roar of fires, amplified by the echo of the valley. We began running, climbing the hill. All these intoxicated people, falling, naked men and women, shouting in horror. At the top of the hill, we could see the downwards slope, and a terrifying spectacle — the great tent was burning. "How many children? How many are there?" a man was shouting, disoriented. Five? Eight? Ten? Twelve? "I ... I don't know," a woman said, crying. Some of the women were distraught, on the edge of fainting, calling for their children, frenzied, looking for them, the children they'd forgotten were there. A few children stepped from the darkness, their faces fearful, and hugged their relieved mothers. The rest of us watched, horrified, powerless, as the nightmare unfolded. Cries, shouts, tears. "How many children? Can someone tell me, for God's sake!" Ten? Twelve? The flames were too high, too wild for any of us to get close.

Gail was shaking like a leaf. "Susan," she sobbed. "We need to find Susan." Her distraught eyes searched the crowd. "Where are your clothes?" I asked her. She didn't know where she'd left them. Too bad. I put my vest over her shoulders and ordered her to follow me. We found Susan near the stream, in a state of shock. She had put her clothes back on and couldn't stop sobbing. "Tell me it isn't true ... that it's a mistake, that it's a dream...." I felt nauseous, a wild buzzing in my ears. The fire. The cries. The cries of *dying* children. I took both their hands; they let themselves be led to the Westfalia.

The night was deep by the time we left that twisted place. We saw the emergency vehicles arrive, two fire trucks and four ambulances. But it was too late.

A deserted road, no light but the moon. My wallet was empty; we would run out of gas soon. Anyway, where would I find gas? No service station would be open at this hour, but I drove on anyway, no faster than twenty-five miles an hour, with tension in my neck and an incessant drumming in my skull. To flee that place, to get as far away from it as quickly as possible, to no longer see the gruesome glimmer in the rear-view mirror.

In the back seat, Gail and Susan had fallen asleep, knocked out by emotion and the grass they'd smoked. After twenty minutes, I saw a neon Mobil sign on Route 49, shunted this way and that by the wind. Relieved, I slowed down, brought the Volks into the gravel parking lot, filled with weeds. My headlights shone on a beaten-down building, with what seemed like a single lamp inside. I parked the van, cut the engine, and waited for the owner. Around six in the morning, an old pick-up parked next to me, and a guy in overalls climbed out. I woke Gail up.

"Give me your watch."

"Where are we?"

"I said your watch."

"Why?"

"To pay for gas."

She shrugged, turned towards Susan. "Don't you have any money?"

"No, Gail. Leave Susan out of this. I want your watch."

She stiffened. Her hair was dirty, her forehead stained with ashes.

"Are you crazy? It's worth a fortune! Howard gave it to me. You could buy a car with it."

I exploded, "You're crying for a watch that your husband who beat you gave you? I can't believe my ears! You should have thrown the goddamn watch into the fire! Not my money! I wasn't born with a silver spoon in my mouth!"

She smiled unkindly. "But you didn't mind taking the millions that Dana Feldman left behind, right?"

I choked back terrible words, "What's Dana got to do with anything?"

She didn't answer. "You know what?" I continued. "I learned at least one lesson from this night with your gang of idiot friends. You'll always be a daddy's girl who expects to be treated like a princess."

"I hate you!"

"Enough!"

Susan raised her voice. "Cut it out!" Exasperated, she put her hand in her bag and pulled out a fistful of bills. "Go, take them, for God's sake. And for the love of God, shut up!"

When we got to San Francisco, Gail took refuge in our bedroom and stayed there for the rest of the day. At supper time, I knocked softly on the door; she pushed me away with an "I'm not hungry!" That night I slept on the couch. Early the next morning, she was waiting for me in the kitchen, ready to leave.

"What time is it?" I asked.

"I called Susan. She's coming to drive me to the airport."

9

After Gail left, I wandered through the city until late at night, then returned to Telegraph Hill, exhausted, upset, and relieved all at once.

A full moon overhead, mottled with filmy clouds. A late June heaviness hung in the air; it was humid, and a handful of boats could be seen on the bay, their owners taking advantage of the summer heat. The apartment was bathed in darkness. I threw my keys on the table in the vestibule and flicked on the light switch for the ceiling light — nothing happened. Same thing for a small lamp on the table, the living room lamps, and my office lighting. A power failure? I could see light pouring out of the windows of my neighbours' place on Calhoun. Maybe a problem with the fuses. I groped forward in the dark, the only light coming from the moon. Then I saw the fan turning in the bedroom. *So not an electrical problem. What's happening?* My heart began beating faster. In front of me, at the end of the corridor, the kitchen window was completely open, its drapes dancing in the wind. "Is someone there? Gail? Is that you? Did you come back?" I entered the kitchen and saw that the chairs around the table had been moved and lined up along the wall, all except one.

"Gail, if it's you, well … this isn't funny.…"

Then a noise from behind, startling me, followed by a croak of laughter.

"Ken, what the fuck are you doing here?"

"That's no way to welcome a friend."

He was standing on a chair, behind the door.

"How did you get in here?"

"Through the window."

"Why?"

"Why not?"

"Why did you come in here, like, like ... why did you break in?"

He chortled, "Break in!"

"What did you do to the light bulbs?"

"Unscrewed them."

"Why"

"Simple precaution."

"Precaution for what?"

He came down from his perch, his shorter leg almost tripping him up. He dug one hand into his pocket, and pulled out a light bulb that he screwed into the lamp over the table. Raw light exploded on his sweaty face; he was panting as if he'd been running, and I wondered how he'd managed to climb the outside wall and through the window. *An accomplice?*

"What do you want from me?"

He ignored me, scanned my kitchen. "Nice place," he said. "And here I was thinking you were in some wretched state."

"Who gave you my address?"

"They say she's pretty, the girl you were living with."

"Bastard!"

He grabbed my hair, pulled it back. I screamed in pain.

"Let me go, for God's sake!" He let go, pushed me against the wall. "What's wrong with you? Are you crazy?"

Stunned, I watched him limp to the refrigerator and grab a beer. He opened it, dropped the cap on the floor. "I'm talking to you, Ken!" He closed his eyes, took a long swig. His face was strained, his hair greasy and long, his clothes wrinkled, a stale smell came off him. He wiped his mouth with his hand, and said in a soft voice, "Sit down. I'll tell you."

The FBI was looking for him, for having set up a GI coffee house at Fort Ord, south of San Francisco. GI coffee houses were opened by civilians just outside military bases, where soldiers could get together, listen to music, get drunk, smoke, and, especially, talk freely, without a sergeant's gun at their temple. In that smoke-filled atmosphere, a mix of students and soldiers congregated, and an abundance of subversive and revolutionary literature circulated that had convinced more than one GI to try insubordination, even desertion. The authorities petitioned the courts to close the places down.

"The cops came in two days ago. All the employees were arrested for public nuisance. Now they're looking for me. I need a place to stay for awhile."

I paled. "You're welcome to stay tonight, but after...."

"After what?"

"You'll need to find something else. You know the risk I'm taking by sheltering a man the FBI is looking for."

"You're not understanding me, Roman. I'm asking for hospitality. The same I offered you in Berkeley."

He's serious, the son of a bitch? I had to stop myself from laughing.

He continued, "If I'm arrested, I might go in for six years. Imagine, you brought tons of GIs to the other side of the border...."

I stiffened. *Pete talked? Pete told the FBI about going to Vancouver?*

"What do you mean tons?"

"It's your word against the committee members in Berkeley, if you know what I mean. A simple phone call, and...."

He's trying to trap me, the bastard!

"You disgust me."

"Come now, don't be that way. You let me live here a while. You act as if nothing is happening, you buy enough food for two, like in the good old days." He laughed. "You'll see, we'll find common ground, you and I."

"Go fuck yourself."

I let him stay, unable to defend myself after ten months spent with Gail. She'd burned me out, emptied me. I'd lost almost twenty pounds and begun suffering from insomnia again. My eye was weaker, it tired more quickly, especially when I drove, leaving painful headaches during the day. I was in a pitiful state, and Ken understood that quickly enough. His daily threats, barely veiled, put me constantly on edge, "You know, a lot of them know all about your little trip to Vancouver," and my name, he repeated, would come out during Pete's trial. I could only stare at him, fearful.

I made every meal, and he never lent a hand. He would serve himself huge portions and bring them to his room. He never brought the plates back to the kitchen, just left them there to dry out until I picked them up, filled with rage, and tried my best to clean them. Sometimes, weary looking guys came over to the house. They spoke softly, one of them had maps with him, maps of San Francisco and California, which he rolled out on the living room floor and studied closely. If Ken really was on the lam from the FBI for his GI coffee house, they never spoke of it. They talked about the great coups they might organize — occupations, blockades, climbing tall towers, suspending banners. And, perhaps, acts of sabotage. But I didn't want to hear any of it, and so I tried not to listen.

Ken Lafayette had been holding me hostage for two weeks, and Bobby still knew nothing. He often asked me questions, worried for me. "What's up with you? You're not doing well, I can tell. Are you sick?" I started avoiding him, and he held it against me. "What did I do, for God's sake, for you to run away from me!" One afternoon, as I was about to leave the office, he made a beeline for me. His face was hostile and his eyes threatening behind his glasses. He told me to go into the small room reserved for microfiche archives, and closed the door behind us.

"Okay. Enough games. Tell me everything, and I'll leave you the fuck alone."

"Bobby … I'm just not feeling all that well. That's all."

"Take a few days to rest, then."

His voice was dry, without compassion.

"No!"

He blinked at my tone. "No?"

"No. I'm telling you I don't need a day off."

He sighed, and gazed at me for the longest time, suspiciously. "As long as you don't tell me what's going on, we're not going anywhere. We'll spend the night here if we have to. And the next one too."

"I don't see what's so mysterious, what you need to know. Gail left, I'm sad. You can understand that, right?"

"You're not telling me the truth. I know there's something else. You're jumpy. As for Gail, I know as well as you do that you're relieved she's gone."

I said nothing. He put his head in his hands.

"Please, Bobby. Let me go."

The door opened and Nolan Tyler appeared, breathless, looking worried.

"What's he doing here?" I asked Bobby.

He ignored my question, turned towards Nolan. "So?"

Nolan came in, closed the door behind him. He flashed a half-smile, showing stained teeth. "Oh, we got a few bites, all right."

Bobby looked at him, attentive. "Go on, we're listening."

"I was just at your place, Roman."

I jumped up. "My house?"

"I saw your guest through a window."

I swallowed. I could hear my heart beating in my chest.

"So who is it?" Bobby asked.

"Ken Lafayette. The FBI is looking for him. He's a suspect in a bombing that killed a woman and injured another on Washington Street, two months ago."

"Bomb?" I protested. "No way! They're looking for him for public nuisance, something to do with a GI coffee house."

"Is that what he told you?" Nolan asked, surprised.

"Yes."

"Well, he lied to you. The guy's wanted for murder."

I felt the floor opening up underneath me. I said, panicking, "I never heard his name associated with that story. They said it was the Weathermen...."

"You're wrong. The police don't think it was the Weathermen. They say they've got proof against your friend...."

My friend!

"How come I never heard about this? I work in newspaper, right, just like you! I should know this, shouldn't I?"

"The police asked us to keep it close to the vest. So he doesn't escape."

"But he knows he's wanted already!"

"Let's say he suspects it. He's no idiot."

Bobby fell into a chair, his face drawn. "You told me you weren't seeing that piece of shit anymore!"

"I wasn't seeing him anymore! He came to my place one night, and he...."

I fell silent.

"And he what?"

My blood was pounding, as if it was about to burst. "He threatened me...."

"Threatened you with what?"

"He said he'd squeal on me. For having driven a GI to Canada."

"That true?" Nolan asked, his brow furrowed.

"Yes."

"You did that?" Bobby said.

"Yes! Okay? Yes, I did, three years ago, when I was in Berkeley."

"That's it?" Nolan asked.

This interrogation was beginning to make me angry. "Yes! That's it!"

Nolan rubbed his hand across his wrinkled face. "We need to send the cops to your house, Roman."

"No, you can't do that...."

"We don't have a choice," Bobby added.

"They'll link me to him, and I'll be an accessory to murder. They'll accuse me of...."

"No," Nolan said. "It won't happen. I'll take care of it."

"Please...."

"If we do nothing, you'll risk far more. You'll be an accomplice. Listen to me: we'll tell the police that as soon as you learned about what Lafayette was actually wanted for, you called them. I'll take care of the rest. I promise, you've got nothing to fear."

"He's crazy. He'll try to get revenge ... accuse me of all sorts of things."

"His word is worth nothing," Nolan cut in. He's a murderer, a manipulator." He opened the door, motioned for me to walk. "Come on. Let's go call the cops."

V

LEN

I

"Do you believe in God, Mr. Carr?"

People often asked me this question now, and always with a knowing look. As if they knew I was an impostor. After all, wasn't not believing in God in this country akin to anti-Americanism?

The first person to ask me was Christie Brenan, a journalist with the *Los Angeles Times*. She appeared on my doorstep on Appian Way, in a perfectly fitting jacket and skirt, impeccable hair, high heels. A photographer accompanied her, a bald guy about my age, his face far more lined than mine. I invited Ms. Brenan to sit in one of the comfortable armchairs in the corner of my office where I held meetings. She squirmed in her narrow skirt as she looked over the questions she'd prepared and transcribed into a spiral notebook. Like a handful of other journalists chosen by It's All Comedy!, she had received the first two episodes of season two of *In Gad We Trust* "under embargo," and I couldn't help thinking, *Did she like them? Hate them?* I discreetly looked for something in her eyes that might say yes, she had liked the episodes, but she wasn't smiling, and her serious, fixed expression resembled a mask. Ms. Brenan was above it all. Ms. Brenan had power and she enjoyed it, you could tell by the way she ordered the photographer around, a guy far older than she, and suddenly I felt vulnerable, at the mercy of this arrogant journalist, the sort of ambitious young woman who wouldn't hesitate to betray a colleague to make it. She ignored me, her nose in her notes, leaving me completely helpless with the photographer and his sustained clicking, coming nearer and nearer with his device, making me more self-conscious — what image was I projecting? Determination? Vulnerability? My hands were moist, my mouth dry. *In Gad* wasn't just a television show, it had become an *issue* in certain circles, a subject debated with passion and animosity in local newspapers, on radio stations, and on television, leading to thousands of complaints. Meanwhile, at the head of It's All Comedy!, there'd been the whole fiasco that forced Josh Ovitz to intervene in the production, that line of dialogue I'd been forced to change — though Trevor had tied the scene together well in the end. Matt, the director, had pushed the right buttons, and I was willing to admit that the scene was better without the mention of God, but there was no way I was going to make any more concessions. The ratings were excellent, a handful of episodes in season one had attracted almost three million viewers, a more than respectable figure for a cable channel.

I was prepared to face Christie Brenan's questions about Chastity and her abortions, and the other controversial aspects of the series. Despite what Josh might think of me, I would think twice before I spoke. "That's all I ask," he had told me on the phone the night before. "We don't need a new controversy." Annoyed by what I interpreted as a lack of trust, I answered dryly, "It's all comedy, Josh. Not politics." There was a long silence on the other end of the line. Josh was involved in Bill Clinton's re-election campaign, and I was certain his newfound hesitations were in part due to his political activities, though he wouldn't admit it.

Before pressing "Record," Ms. Brenan complimented me on the house and the décor, and I wondered if she was sincere or it was some sort of manoeuvre to get my guard down. "You should tell Ann," I said, trying to look relaxed. "She found the house and decorated the whole place."

She smiled vaguely, as if she didn't believe me, or didn't care. I immediately regretted not having pushed for Ann to be present. Had we been two, the whole thing wouldn't have been as stressful. But over the phone, Ms. Brenan had been inflexible, "It's your name that appears in the credits, isn't it?" I argued, explaining that without Ann there'd be no interview because without her there'd have been no *In Gad We Trust*. She sighed loudly, and I gave up. And anyway, Ann didn't like to be the centre of attention.

I answered the questions calmly. On abortion: a woman's inalienable right, *Roe v. Wade* had closed that debate, there was no reason to open it up again.

"The sheer number of abortions she undergoes — isn't that a kind of provocation?"

"It's a caricature, and caricature exaggerates features. You could also see it from another angle — you sometimes hear that some women see abortion as a method of contraception. Perhaps Chastity, Gad Paradise's daughter, is a foil to denounce that idea as well."

"Chastity pays her doctor with money taken from the faithful, the followers of the church. There's a character, pious old Mrs. Wilcox, who is completely unaware that her money is going to Chastity's abortions. That's a bit shocking, isn't it?"

"The televangelist Jim Bakker personally appropriated millions of dollars from his followers. He even bought Jessica Hahn's silence with their money, the woman who had accused him of rape. I'm not inventing anything."

Ms. Brenan was taking notes. I told her how *In Gad* was a satire of those merchants of faith who had fallen into disgrace, of their financial and sexual scandals, all the while questioning the gullibility of people who financed their empires, those poor followers like Mrs. Wilcox.

Her lips twisted in a half-smile, "One could accuse you of making money on the back of Christians as well. By mocking them, I mean."

"I'm not mocking Christians. I'm mocking con men who use religion to take advantage of naive people."

"Sure. But there's something in these 'naive people,' in your words, these Christians, that seems to bother you more than most. You're not defending them. It's obvious, your body language speaks for you. You're a liberal, and liberals generally don't have a very good opinion of Christians. An obvious intolerance, even."

I laughed. "Intolerance? Which side is more intolerant, do you think?"

That led me to tell her about the context of the summer of 1988, when the idea for *In Gad* first came to me. Ms. Brenan was too young to remember. Los Angeles was besieged by thousands of angry Christians; they were arriving by the busload from all over California and the United States to protest against *The Last Temptation of Christ*, the Martin Scorsese movie, which no one had seen but about which everyone had an opinion. You could see them on every street corner, in supermarkets, Bible in hand, getting petitions signed. All summer, demonstrations on Lankershim Boulevard. Page after page of newspaper copy dedicated to the culture wars; it was, indeed, *a war*. Calls for boycotts against Universal and the mothership MCA. Executives at Universal were receiving death threats, their home addresses published in the Christian media, including Lew Wasserman's address, the big boss, whom Josh knew well. Dead pigs were found on their front porches, packages with voodoo dolls in their mailboxes. Thousands upon thousands of protest letters, and thousands upon thousands of calls, causing outages on MCA's phone system. I had just met Ann in the summer of 1988; we took long walks everywhere together, often meeting people protesting under a hot sun, signs in hand, their messages in large block letters: NO TO THE SCORCESE MOVIE — REMOVE ALL SEX SCENES — WASSERMAN, DON'T TOUCH MY JESUS! And of course: THEY KILLED JESUS ONCE. WASN'T IT ENOUGH? An allusion to "Hollywood Jews." Sometimes the signs were accompanied by caricatures of Hitler and the gas chambers. Ann was disgusted, and so was I. It was just a movie, for God's sake! While this was happening, there was a long Writers' Guild strike, the longest in the Guild's history, five months on the picket lines, thousands of people out of work, Hollywood and the big TV networks all paralyzed, an endless stream of stories reporting bankruptcy and personal tragedy. I'd seen friends lose their houses, others their wives, some both. I often met couples who both worked in the industry, and some of them hadn't been able to withstand the pressures of suddenly finding themselves without income. The strike hadn't affected me that deeply, I had my job at the Kyser Gallery, a house I fully owned in the Fairfax District, a bank account and judiciously placed investments that made me free from financial worry. I hadn't been directly touched by the events, but morally affected, yes, by the impression that we were returning to the Middle Ages. I couldn't accept that people — I was about to use the term "with retrograde values" in front of Christie Brenan, but checked myself — who campaigned against the rights of women and gays could impose their backward vision of the world on everyone else. Dick, who knew quite a few people at Universal, told me that they were all devastated over there, and were even thinking of not distributing the movie at all. Some distributors and theatre owners decided not to take the risk, fearing acts of vandalism. There was an astounding sense of violence in the air. Ann and I were just getting to know each other, but that summer's events brought us together. We shared the same beliefs, the same indignation. Ann was finishing her studies, a doctorate in Film and Television Studies at the University of Southern California, and the attempts to censor Scorsese and Universal Studios disgusted her.

"Do you know the last time there was any sort of comparable upheaval surrounding a movie?" Ann asked me one night as we were having supper in a small Italian place in Venice Beach. "1915. *Birth of a Nation*. A silent film. Ever heard of it?"

It was the first time I'd heard the title. She spoke passionately about this foul, racist movie on the Civil War and its consequences. Blacks were depicted as animals and rapists, to be lynched without hesitation. A Confederate point of view that would make you sick, an apology for the Ku Klux Klan. A horrible movie, banned in numerous cities, that had raised the ire of blacks and caused riots. "And you know what?" Ann said. "The movie is, cinematographically, a masterpiece. It's avant-garde, innovative, and it inspired a number of filmmakers. Problematic, right?" I was impressed by her knowledge and the way she had of expressing it. She continued, her eyes burning, "Can the quality of a movie excuse its racist content? Of course not. But should it be censored? I don't believe so. Art doesn't need to be acceptable. Films are a product of their time. Consensus isn't proof of quality, or truth."

I gave Ms. Brenan Ann's perspective, which I shared a hundred percent. The story of *Birth of a Nation* captivated the journalist. Then I told her about the Nikos Kazantzakis novel that had inspired Martin Scorsese, "I read the book in 1963. It was placed on the Index by the Vatican, but everyone was reading it in New York. For Kazantzakis, Jesus was a man, with his weaknesses, his cowardly moments, his dreams, and fantasies, a man whose divine mission terrorized him. It was a revelation for me. I had just arrived from a small town in Quebec, in the Gaspé region, where the Catholic Church decided whether it would rain or not. What a surprise to realize that there were places where it didn't have a complete hold! In New York, nobody cared about the Vatican's orders. It was hard to believe at first. A place of total freedom. For a whole generation, *The Last Temptation of Christ* was the cool book to read. And now, thirty-five years later, fundamentalists were ready to set fire to movie theatres, to injure people — which actually happened in France — just to prevent Hollywood from making a movie. That reality cries out for an explanation."

Ms. Brenan offered a wide smile. I wasn't sure how to interpret it. She said haughtily, "A score to settle with your Catholic education?"

"Of course. But first and foremost a question of free speech. I'm besotted with freedom and will fight for it, always."

The recorder stopped loudly. Christie Brenan took the tape out, and flipped it to the B side. We'd been speaking for an hour already. As she consulted her notes, I thought of Ann and our long conversations in the summer of 1988. By God, I loved her; I was charmed by the brilliant young woman who, one night, as we left that Italian restaurant on Washington Boulevard we enjoyed so much, told me with the passion that alcohol feeds so well, "Write, and I'll help you." And that night, in my house on Gardner Street, after having made love in a warm wine-soaked fog, we wrote the first two scenes of *In Gad We Trust*, which would much later be filmed exactly the way we'd written them. The only part of the production that was shot in New York went like this:

Episode 1 / scene 1: Exterior, Brooklyn Street – Day

(We are watching the "conversion" of Gad Paradise, forty-one, a man who has spent twenty-five years in the service of the Brooklyn Mafia. A man on his last legs, walking the streets of his neighbourhood, his back bent, limping slightly, his face covered in bruises. People he meets wave at him as if there's nothing wrong — he's known in the neighbourhood — but he doesn't wave back, absorbed in his thoughts.)

GAD PARADISE
(Voice-over. The narration is illustrated by familiar neighbourhood scenes.)
As a boy, I had two possibilities – the Catholic Church or the Mafia. My mother, like all good Italian mothers, would have cried tears of joy to see her son wear the cloth like his cousin Paolo. You should see how respected he is in the family, in the neighbourhood. Always Paolo, Paolo this, Paolo that. As if he was a saint. Well, I had the spirit of a businessman. That's what Dad said, born Pardes, it means "paradise" in Hebrew. Dad is Jewish, but doesn't practise. The hassle of religion isn't for him, he always left

that to my mother. At eleven, I had learned how to extort money from the neighbourhood store-owners to help Big Joe get that much richer. Dad held Big Joe in the highest esteem – the only one in the entire neighbour-hood to drive a beautiful white Cadillac. At his place, there was furniture covered in gold leaf, the kind you'd find in the Pope's apartments in the Vatican. Even my mother thought Big Joe was a respectable man, always ready to offer financial help when the church needed it. Big Joe gave me my chance. For him, I started doing dirty work, then the dirtiest work. But Big Joe isn't Joe Bonanno – he never was able to get his business going outside the neighbourhood, and now, we've got Puerto Ricans aching for a slice of the pie. So Big Joe sends me to bring them a message.…

(Close up on his face: broken nose, black eyes. He takes a handkerchief from his pocket and wipes at a forehead still covered in blood. This time, he's not going back to Big Joe to give him the news; this time he's going to church, determined to end it all. Before going in, he makes the sign of the cross.)

Scene 2: Interior, Church – Day

(The church is empty, to Gad's great relief. He will be able to pray alone. He walks up to the altar, takes out his gun and places it on the altar. On the verge of tears, he calls on the Holy Father, his head lowered, hands together, beseeching Him.)

GAD

(Voice-over)
I asked the Lord to help me. I asked Him to become my new boss. He told me, "Go far from here, bring your family, share the story of your conversion, spread the Gospel." I thanked Him, "Thank you, Lord. I shall see to it, Lord." And I left Him enough so that he could live in style, at least for a while.

(Gad replaces the gun on the altar with a stack of cash, then leaves.)

We were excited by the project. Ann was sure we would be able to sell it. I gave a defeatist laugh, and she seemed surprised. Attentive and empathetic, she listened to me as I told her how, in twenty years of relentless work, I had never managed to sell a single script. I had worked for others, had written for Aaron Spelling, but my own creations had only met with rejection. I wrote dark comedies that Dick characterized, with utmost seriousness, as *subversive* and *anti-American.* She laughed. Ann was an optimist. She was absolutely convinced that the large networks would be eclipsed, over time, by young cable outfits. "You'll see, their potential is enormous." Over the next few weeks, we developed *In Gad*'s characters — Gad Paradise moved to a small midwestern city, where he built his own church, created his own television show, and swindled his followers. In the La Brea studio, we were amazed by the brilliantly conceived sets that were centred around the gun displayed in Gad's anti-glare Plexiglas case, a symbol of his newfound conversion. Special effects, mechanized platforms, exuberant music. Amazing work done by the technical staff. Each episode started with the same scene — a close-up of the Paradise family members counting the money they had swindled from the believers the previous night. Meanwhile, we followed Gad, whose mafioso habits were hard to break; Mrs. Paradise, bored to death, slowly succumbing to alcoholism; their daughter Chastity, obsessed with being thin, whiling away her days with fashion magazines, getting one abortion after the other because "the pill makes you fat"; and Dylan, young Dylan, trying to cope with the tumult of puberty, searching for his sexual identity. But no matter, as long as the money keeps rolling in. Gad promises to return to New York as soon as they get rich, something that would never happen. And so everyone agrees to play their part in the great comedy of God.

Ms. Brenan was about to start recording again when Ann knocked on the door. She was leaving to take her mother to the doctor's for a routine check-up. She shook hands with Christie Brenan and the photographer. The photographer wanted to take a picture of the two of us together, but Ann protested gently. She didn't like to be in the limelight. Often, with indulgent gaiety, she would say she was a theoretician, not a celebrity, "While you, honey, interviews and all the rest, you just seem made for it."

Me? Certainly not. But it was an obligatory ritual of success, one I would have been glad to avoid.

Ann left, and Ms. Brenan offered a tight smile. While she gave new instructions to the photographer, I thought of Dana whom I'd seen in action countless times when I accompanied her for the promotion of *The Next War*. That admirable talent she had for answering questions with a triumphant, almost cheeky smile on her face — she could be so funny! Everyone was always charmed by her. "More than anything else," she explained once, before an interview, "don't say too much; limit yourself to short, catchy answers — reporters love it — and don't forget to be funny. People like you when you make them laugh, they just want to give you a hug. Add a dash of sedition, not too much, just enough to create ambiguity — is she being serious? Is she joking? Do you understand, Romain?" I nodded, astounded by her poise and intelligence.

In the midst of my reminiscing, Ms. Brenan asked her last question, the gotcha question, a challenging tone in her voice. "Do I believe in God? No. But as a child I did. Because of the endless death threats."

She raised her eyebrows, "Death threats?"

I smiled, proud of the effect. "When you keep telling a child he'll burn in hell, that's a death threat, isn't it?"

She looked me over with her carefully made-up eyes, encouraging me to continue.

"I stopped believing in God when I started thinking for myself."

She smiled with satisfaction — the interview had gone according to her plan. Her voice revealed the pleasure she felt, "You might call that a rather pretentious attitude."

"To fight against lies is pretentious? No, I don't think so. Pretentiousness is making up a God to give yourself a convenient alibi. When you think about it, God is the best excuse man ever gave himself for war, domination, and greed. You know as well as I do, the worst atrocities are committed in the name of God."

This time, Ms. Brenan gave me her warmest smile, and I felt a shiver of triumph. I had just given her the phrase she'd been looking for, the one the *L.A. Times* would print on the front page of its culture section a few days later — *In Gad We Trust* — *God: Man's Best Excuse to Do Wrong*. A subversive headline for a flattering article (and a flattering picture):

> *With his incisive pen, Roman Carr holds a mirror to our moment in time. Seeking redemption at any cost, for a hundred, a thousand, ten thousand dollars.... American society shouldn't be surprised that it has made religion into a lucrative, hard-nosed industry. In Gad We Trust, a brilliant reference to our national currency, shows us that religion and money, in this country, are inseparable....*

A more than welcome article only days before the start of the second season. Josh didn't like the headline, though he was relieved by the content. Ann was overjoyed — "You see? That's a nice change after all the complaints."

I was awaited on another front now, and rather apprehensive about it. Only three days before the second season was scheduled to start, I was expected in Calgary. "Everything is going to go well," Ann reassured me. "He's your son, Romain. Len is your son. He's been waiting for this moment for a long time."

2

He arrived fifteen minutes early. He too was visibly nervous. About my height, maybe a little bit taller; he was at least twice my weight, a giant. His jacket wet with snow open on his wide chest, his face flushed, he was trying to catch his breath, as if he had walked too quickly out of fear of being late.

I could have gotten up and waved to him with the eagerness of an old friend; I decided instead to observe him, realizing with unease that nothing in this big man, his features, his way of holding himself and moving, connected me to him. He moved gingerly among the tables of the Westin Hotel bar, where he had told me we could meet. The place was packed on a late afternoon during a snowstorm, minus eighteen Celsius outside the pilot had announced, almost amused, as we were landing in Calgary.

He froze when he saw me, and emotion overcame me. *My son? Is it possible?* To make my discomfort worse, he had something of Gail's father in him, without me knowing exactly what; I hadn't noticed it in Montreal when Gail, in her hospital bed, had introduced us to each other, her voice so weak we could barely hear her. I retained a hazy memory of an obese young man, stressed out and awkward, who, once the secret of our filiation had been revealed, mumbled a few inaudible words and offered a moist hand, disagreeable to the touch, the same one he was offering now in this Calgary hotel bar, filled with businessmen and a few women dressed to attract attention, like those two blondes at the table next to ours who'd glanced at me a few times already, perhaps hoping I'd join them. While Len was taking his coat off, I wondered whether they might be checking out both the father and the son, an idea that would have amused any father, but I was far too tense for that.

"Hello. Have you been waiting long?"

"Only a few minutes."

He laughed nervously, and so did I. Then he looked embarrassed when he saw the copy of the *Calgary Herald* I had bought at the airport and read through in the taxi, hoping to find an article written by him. I found one in the business pages about the tar sands in northern Alberta; it was well written and contained just enough commentary to communicate his knowledge. I was surprised to feel pride like a normal father would; it both troubled and reassured me.

Gail had died almost three months ago. His business card had spent those three months lying in my desk drawer — Len Albiston, Reporter, Economic Affairs, the *Calgary Herald*, with his home phone number written down by hand. How many times had I picked it up, then put it back in the drawer, thinking, *What are you going to do with this thirty-two-year-old son? What does he expect from you? What if you can't love him?*

"You don't have the right to stop your son from knowing his real father," Ann had told me.

And Dick had given me a lecture, "He's your flesh, your genes. You can't pretend that's worth nothing. If I discovered I had a son, you can be sure I would want to get to know him."

Irritated, I answered, "You? You're always saying that you got snipped to make sure you wouldn't have any!"

He made a face. "Whatever. If it happened, I'd be a great father."

I laughed. "Oh yeah? And what if he was a homosexual with pierced nipples who voted for Ralph Nader?"

Instead of getting mad at me, he looked me straight in the eyes, dead serious. "I'd kick his goddamned ass and make a man out of him. I'd help him, like you can help Len."

And Ann agreed, hoping that with Len I might discover a paternal instinct. After all, she'd been talking about children for a while now, despite our agreement at the beginning of our relationship, "A child, Romain, why not?" Each time she talked about it — seriously, but not too much, so she wouldn't alarm me, since we'd seen couples break up over the same issue — I could see the young, determined woman who had charmed me years before say, "I don't have that narcissistic ambition to reproduce, if that's what you want to know." But she'd been only twenty-eight at the time; she was thirty-six now. The maternal drive was like an animal impulse; there was nothing rational about it. She wanted to convince me, but wanted the decision to come from me. Except that I wouldn't change my mind. Not at my age. Not with *In Gad*, which left us not a single minute to spare. And now that Len had suddenly appeared in my life, I could see her eyes burning with envy, almost like an accusation, *You have a son. I don't have anything.*

Len sat down in front of me, smiling. A big guy covered in sweat despite the cold weather. He had hurried between his car and the hotel. He said, hesitating, "I'm happy you're here.... Happy you called.... I was starting to lose hope, in all honesty." He laughed to make sure it didn't sound like an accusation. "Thank you."

To overcome our embarrassment, we talked about the weather, the snow, the cold. Len warmed to the subject, explaining that the chinook, the warm wind blowing over the Rockies with a constant whistling sound, melted the snow at a dizzying pace, creating differences in temperature of up to twenty-five degrees in a manner of minutes. I listened, or tried to, trying to figure out where the similarity with Robert Egan came from, perhaps the same reddish brown hair, or his eyes, an iris encircled in white that gave him a permanently angry, surprised look. Len steered the subject of conversation. He talked about his work at the *Calgary Herald*, the article he had to write for the next day, a major acquisition in the petroleum industry, as if that's all there was in Alberta, oil. He glanced at my empty glass, the beer I had finished too quickly before he arrived. He offered me a drink, it was a surprise, he said, looking for a waiter. The bar was full of workers, one more drink before going home, their voices loud, excited by the snowstorm raging outside. "So what's the surprise? Nothing too strong, I hope?"

"You'll see," Len said. "It's something rather special, for us. A source of pride."

"A Canadian Pride?" I said, looking for the name of the cocktail on the menu. I must have looked so confused that he burst out laughing — a deep laugh, straight from the belly that rang out in the packed bar. The two girls next to us, now accompanied by two guys, turned their heads unexpectedly, as if they had heard a gunshot. "What's with them looking at us?" I asked Len, and he only laughed harder. There was something special happening between us, and it delighted me.

What followed was even more incredible. The waiter, his tray heavy with glasses, placed two drinks before us. Nothing extraordinary at first glance — two Bloody Caesars with their celery sticks like flagpoles. Len got excited all of sudden, telling me how this drink, drunk the world over, had been created in this very bar, in 1969, housed in the very same hotel, though called by a different name back then, the Calgary Inn. I felt overcome with weakness, thinking it must be a joke. His eyes widened when I told him about my mother at the St. Regis in New York in October 1968. The mother and son enjoying a Bloody Mary, the specialty of the house at the King Cole bar, the famous drink invented by one of the establishment's barmen in the 1930s. Two hotels, three thousand kilometres and twenty-eight years apart. As if, in our family, there were powerful rituals to be repeated, without our knowledge. The striking coincidence was too extraordinary to be true, a prodigious roll of the dice, a sign we couldn't ignore.

Moved, I raised my glass. "To the Bloody Caesar, to the Bloody Mary!" And Len added, his voice cracking with emotion, "Like the blood that runs in our veins!"

Yes, the father and the son.

3

After two Bloody Caesars, Len began telling me about his childhood in Lethbridge, in southern Alberta. An only child, protected and pampered by his parents who were much older than those of his friends, a bit over forty when they adopted him. A childhood that was neither sad nor happy but terribly boring, so much so that his acceptance at the University of Calgary had been a liberation, far from his parents, in an apartment they paid for despite their modest means. "They made sacrifices for me, and I felt relieved when I left their home. It was a strange feeling. I felt like I was betraying them. They were hoping I'd visit them in Lethbridge on weekends, but I never went. And they never dared visit me in Calgary, because I never invited them. The perfectly ungrateful son, in other words." An expression of remorse on his face. "They're still there, in the same house. They're old now, and barely ever go out." He fell silent for a moment, then continued, a guilty smile on his face. "I'm a better son now; I visit them from time to time."

The bar was raucous with laughter. I understood his interest in his biological parents: raised by people who could have been his grandparents, a generation earlier, a father probably too old to take him to the baseball diamond or the football field, and a mother who might not have known how to react to this large boy living through the pangs of adolescence. I imagined a sad and gloomy home, smelling of old rugs and disinfectant.

He enrolled in economics, and quickly became intrigued by what he called the geopolitics of oil. He said, suddenly energetic, "Alberta was humiliated by Pierre Elliott Trudeau. The arrogance of centralization." He barked a rough laugh. "He forced us to sell our oil below market price so the eastern provinces like Quebec might have an advantage. The resource is ours, it's Albertan. What did Quebeckers do to thank us? They held two referendums, in October 1980 and now last year. Each time, the whole country quakes in its boots." He shook his head. "Spoiled children. You must know all this already."

Surprised by his vehemence, I said, smiling, "Oh, it's been such a long time. To be honest, I'm don't know much about Canadian politics."

He blushed. "I'm sorry. We're barely getting to know each other, and I'm boring you with my stories."

"It doesn't matter. I can tell you're a passionate young man."

He turned even redder; my remark pleased him.

I thought of Moïse. His long letters filled with savoury and enlightening anecdotes, thanks to which I was able, in the seventies, to follow the rise of the Parti Québécois and its yearning for independence, which Moïse and Louise supported. "Quebec has nothing to do with the rest of North America," Moïse would say. "It has its own culture, man, awfully courageous." Even though he returned to New York in 1977, Moïse liked to give me lessons about my own country, which he knew far better than me, I had to admit.

What of it was left in me? Childhood memories? Impressions? As for the rest, politics, social issues, the *national question*, as it was called, well, I didn't know much about it.

Len took a picture out of his wallet and showed it to me with pride. "My family." Next to him, a plain woman, rather chubby, and in front of them two red-haired children, as speckled as trout — a boy with a timid face and a girl with an impish smile in a mouth filled with holes left by her missing baby teeth.

"Cody is nine, Julia is seven."

"They seem adorable."

"Oh, yes, indeed, they are! I'd do anything for them. Do you remember Garp, the father obsessed with the security of his children? Well I'm his twin." He looked at the picture, his face softening with emotion. "When I had them, I felt the need to connect with Gail."

Gail. The way he said her name, a mixture of respect and affection. I thought, *he was close to her, closer than I ever was.*

"You know, I learned early on that I was adopted. My parents never hid it from me. My mother kept the adoption papers, in case I ever wanted to find out more. After Julia's birth I asked to see them. I'll always remember it. She smiled like she'd been waiting for that moment for the longest time. She got up, very dignified, disappeared into her room and came back with a large envelope that she gave me. She said, 'This is yours, my son. It's your story.'"

His eyes filled with water, and I choked up.

Thanks to the documents, Len found a nurse who worked at the Lethbridge hospital where Gail had given birth. She spoke to him about a Miss Egan, that's all she remembered. A Miss Egan from Montreal.

"But Gail stopped using the Egan name after I was born, in 1963. She took Barron, the name of her first husband, and then, when she married Jack, she took his, Holmes. I couldn't have known. I called every Egan in Montreal, without results. Someone finally led me to a Robert Egan in Toronto. Her father."

I shuddered; Len didn't notice. He said, anger simmering under the surface, "I can't say I received a warm welcome... 'My daughter,' he said, 'What daughter? You've got the wrong number, young man.' And he hung up on me. What an idiot. You know, he never even made the trip to see her one last time at the hospital. It's so cruel."

He rubbed the back of his neck. He was angry, but making an effort to contain himself. We were getting to know each other; it wasn't the time for either of us to become aggressive. Knowing we shared the same distaste for Robert Egan was enough. It reassured me.

"Finally," he continued, "my mother advised me to sign up with the Alberta Post-Adoption Registry. You sign and you wait. Nothing happens unless the biological mother consults it herself. Unless she signed up as well. You see?"

"Yes."

"And you know what? Gail had registered years before. She'd been searching for me since 1975. It was 1989 by then." He grabbed his glass and seemed surprised to see it empty, a surprise he'd display after every glass that night. "So we were put in contact. And that was that." He wiped his eyes, "It was as if we had known each other forever. It was extraordinary."

Shook up, he ordered a third Bloody Caesar. I didn't join in; clearly, my tolerance for alcohol was lower than his.

I wanted to know more about the first time they met, and began asking questions. Len smiled, laughed, and spoke quickly, animated. "I went to Montreal. It was fantastic. Jack was incredibly kind. They have a beautiful home in Baie-D'Urfé on Lake Saint-Louis, with a large garden and magnificent trees. I went there a number of times. Five hundred dollars every time I flew over, it became pretty expensive, pretty fast. My wife Lynn doesn't work; mine is the only salary. The frequent flights ended up becoming a burden, especially once Gail got sick. The last two years, I was going there once a month. I had to go into debt to keep going there. Lynn disapproved. I couldn't really blame her, she was worried about us. She's always been insecure about money, perhaps because she doesn't work. We met at university; she was also studying economics. We got married immediately after we graduated, and since we wanted children as soon as possible, we agreed it didn't really make sense for her to look for a job. Anyway, I spent all this money on plane tickets, and in the end, she wasn't very happy about it: 'You're neglecting your own family here in Calgary! We haven't gone on a trip in two years!

And what about the pool you promised your children!' It was true, my reunion with Gail made me neglect my family, but there was so much to catch up on, and Gail knew she didn't have much time left. I asked Lynn to give me a chance. 'She doesn't have long to live.' 'And what if she lives longer than expected?' she answered. 'It's not an unheard of thing for cancer patients.' I was surprised by her insensitivity, and I told her that if that happened, I'd take a second mortgage on the house. After all, I was the one paying for it. I don't need to tell you how she reacted to that...."

I could see the sadness in his face. He seemed like a man burdened with a mediocre marriage. He took a long drink and said, "Gail left me a small inheritance. I'll be able to pay for the pool that Lynn and the kids want next summer." He gave me a melancholy smile. "Will you come visit?"

His question caught me off guard. "Um ... yes. I'd be happy to."

He beamed at me. He emptied his glass and looked at his watch. "It's past seven already. Are you hungry? I know a good French restaurant not too far from here. You'll love their fettuccine Alfredo and their garlic bread."

"Alfredo and garlic bread in a French restaurant?" I asked, trying not to offend him.

"Yes, and they're excellent! It's called the Café de la Paix." He pronounced it *de la Paiks*. "Come on, I'm buying."

"No," I protested. "Let your father take you out."

The words came out of my mouth without premeditation. My eyes filled with tears. Len's smile wavered. He coughed and mumbled something that sounded like *thanks*.

We left the Westin in the snowstorm. The restaurant was a few blocks away, so we decided to walk; there were no taxis anyway. Luckily, I was wearing the winter jacket Françoise had forced me to accept in Métis Beach; it was warm and windproof. I dug my hands into my pockets and had a thought for Françoise, and that aggressive, supplicating tone she'd taken, *No! I'm telling you, it's a gift!* She had inherited my mother's store. So what? I couldn't care less. Françoise didn't need to feel guilty.

"Are you okay?" Len asked. "Cold enough for you?"

The glacial wind whipped the snow and sent it screaming every which way. A snowstorm like in my memories of Métis Beach, and I thought of my last winter there, when I was seventeen, more than a year before Len's birth. It was hard to believe. There was something unreal about letting myself be guided by *my son* in the streets of Calgary — he looked like a 4 x 4 ploughing a snowed-in street with his half-open coat, his massive, warm body that you wished you could snuggle up to. It was hard to believe he was mine, as inconceivable as a giant elm growing from a fragile seed, yet there he was, the result of a reckless night, when his mother and I were still children.

A few minutes later, we reached 7th Avenue. Staggering slightly, I followed Len into the deserted avenue and almost lost my footing when a CTrain appeared out of nowhere, shining its threatening headlights on us like a predator's eyes. Len laughed. "Don't worry. It moves slowly." My heart beating, I climbed onto the sidewalk, and then into the Eaton Centre. Restless, he pointed out the architectural elements. Calgary had a few hidden gems, like this luxury mall, a ceiling made of vaulted glass, walkways suspended between buildings so you never needed to go outside. "Ingenious," I told him. Len smiled with pride, as if the compliment was directed at him. We returned to the blizzard through another door, ended up on Stephen Avenue, the downtown core's pedestrian street, still illuminated by Christmas lights, lined with deserted restaurants.

We'd arrived.

The Café de la *Paiks* was a hodge-podge that pretended it was French. The only authentic thing about it was its owner, Michèle, who had arrived from Marseilles fifteen years earlier. A menu without surprises or interest. I had hoped for something a little more exotic, like frog's legs or sweetbreads. "Ah!" the owner exclaimed, "We used to have them on the menu, but no one was interested. We had to adapt our cooking to local tastes. But things change. Oil brings money, and money brings more refined tastes."

Len raised his glass, "To Alberta's oil!"

He ordered the fettuccine, I chose the rack of lamb. Michèle suggested a red wine, an honest bottle that paired with both dishes. Our time was fleeting, and still so many questions to ask Len.

"Did Gail tell you about us? I mean, the two of us?"

He seemed embarrassed, hesitated before answering, "She was rather discreet on that topic. She said, among other things, that you were both too young for what happened."

I couldn't tell whether he had finished his thought and decided to stop there. Trying not to be too insistent, I asked, "Did she tell you what happened?"

He shook his head. "Only that you were both seventeen, and it happened in Métis Beach."

So she hadn't told him about the so-called rape, which relieved me. Still, I couldn't hide my disappointment, "That's all?"

"I also know she stopped having regrets when we reunited, she and I. That's what she told me."

"Regrets?"

"At having gotten pregnant so young."

I lowered my eyes, suddenly resenting Gail. Why had she hidden all of that from me? Why hadn't she told me when we were living together in San Francisco? Was it what she had been trying to say that time, when she was crying over her friend Susan and the children she no longer had custody of? *Abandoning your children, do you know what that does to someone?* Was that it?

Len continued, "She was supposed to marry this guy Don Drysdale. She told me she liked him well enough but wasn't ready for married life." He laughed nervously. "Apparently, I saved her from a marriage she wanted no part of."

"When did she learn she was pregnant?"

"Two weeks before the wedding, which was then cancelled. Her mother cried and wailed to the heavens. Her father drank a bottle of Chivas Regal." He grabbed a couple of pieces of garlic bread and buttered them generously. "That's what she told me. You know Gail, she could be theatrical."

It was said without anger, more like affection. I said, almost in the same tone, "Ah, true enough!" trying to avoid thinking of our ten months together in San Francisco.

He laughed, delighted we shared something else — having faced Gail's rather singular character.

His eyes lit up when our plates arrived. As we ate, the discussion lost focus. Len asked questions about New York; Gail had mentioned my time there. His surprised look, almost disapproving, when I mentioned Moïse and his exile in Canada. "Moïse, a *draft dodger*?" I immediately went on the defensive, and it showed. "He received Jimmy Carter's presidential pardon, like every other draft dodger. He returned to New York in 1977. It's ancient history now."

Surprised by my tone, Len looked guilty. He seemed suddenly so distraught! I apologized. "Sorry. It brings back memories ... and anyway...." I pushed back my wine glass. "I should go easy on this stuff. Talk to me about Gail instead. Where was she for the pregnancy, exactly?"

He told the story enthusiastically and with plenty of detail — he knew more than he had let on at first, it turned out. For Gail's parents, the problem had to be solved quickly. The solution, a Doctor Ziegler, in Côte-des-Neiges in Montreal, who would make her respectable once more for the modest sum of four hundred dollars. "Her mother escorted her to the clinic so that she couldn't sneak off. Gail was terrified."

I wasn't sure I had heard properly, "Her parents were going to make her get an abortion?"

He nodded with a sort of childish cheerfulness that confused me. "She even described the place to me. A dark, peeling apartment. Nothing outside could have hinted there was a clinic inside. The medical personnel spoke softly. In the waiting room, sad young women wrung their hands in anxiety.

I was astonished he knew so much, as if he'd been there himself. "Gail told you all this?"

He didn't seem to see the absurdity of the situation. He went on, as if it were the thing to say, "Talking about it was a sort of therapy for her. But don't worry, the story ends well." And he burst out laughing as I looked on, uncomprehendingly.

I forced a smile, even if there was nothing amusing about this story. Len took it as encouragement and told how Doctor Ziegler had taken Gail into a small room and told her mother to stay in the waiting room. "He asked her whether it was her choice. He was a good doctor and cared about patients deeply. They were the ones who counted, not their parents. Gail immediately felt she could trust him." He took a sip of wine. "So she refused, and I was born. Gail fought so I might live."

I was speechless. An abortion story that ended well. Len told it like it was someone else's story. He grabbed the bottle of red and poured the little that was left into our glasses. "Should we get another?"

I didn't know what to say. "And then what?"

"And then? Someone told her about a woman in Lethbridge, a widow my parents knew. Her name figured in the document my mother gave me, a woman called Pinker. By the time I began my search, she'd been dead for a long time. Mrs. Pinker hosted a home for teenage mothers, helped them during their pregnancy, and accompanied them until birth. My parents adopted me a week after my birth." There was a long silence. "For Gail it was much harder."

I look at him with apprehension, "Harder?"

His face darkened. "You know, Gail was sick. After she gave birth, she was diagnosed as manic-depressive. She received electroshock therapy. Four times." He seemed apologetic. "I don't think she ever mentioned it to you. She didn't speak much about it. With me, it was different. It was a way for her to warn us, me and my children. What she suffered from can be hereditary. Thankfully, no one at home got it...." He broke off, emotional. "By the time we got to know each other, she was being monitored by doctors and therapists. She was treated the way she should be. She even told me, one day, that she was happy for the first time in her life."

It shouldn't have come as a surprise to me, and indeed, I wasn't taken aback. Yet I couldn't help feeling sad. And guilty. I didn't understand mental illness, and I was the sort of person who believed that if you worked harder, you could overcome it — that mental illness *affects* erratic people instead of *making* them erratic. Gail *was* sick. Of course I knew that — the way she had of pushing happiness away like a threat, her despair at times, so deep it banished all positive thoughts. And yet I always judged her harshly, with barely any compassion at all.

I must have looked miserable, since Len asked me whether I was okay. I reassured him with a smile I hoped was as cheerful as possible. I said, "Did she ever tell you why she didn't mention you to me?"

He looked as if he was trying to remember a specific conversation they had had, making a point of recounting it word for word. He said, kindly and seriously, "She felt like she was solely responsible. You were living your life in the States, and she didn't want to bring you into hers, a life that was topsy-turvy. She said you were living a life you couldn't even have dreamed of as a child. She thought she didn't have the right to make you miserable. That's what she said."

He looked at me and shrugged.

Michèle appeared with the second bottle. Len took advantage of the break to change the topic, "Let's talk about your work. I'm very curious, how did you end up writing for television?"

Len listened attentively. How I reached Los Angeles in August 1972; my meeting with Dick Mercer, a producer friend. Bobby put us in touch; he and Dick met at the premiere of a movie in L.A. and became fast friends. I couldn't imagine them together, two opposite ends of the spectrum until, one day, I saw them debating movies. Actually, they were debating the underbelly of the movie industry. Stories of power, alliances, and big money. Dick was the one who told Bobby that Francis Ford Coppola had been forced to agree to direct *The Godfather* to clear up a debt with Warner Bros. Bobby described Dick as the best connected guy in Hollywood. The right man to give me a hand.

"And was he?" Len asked.

I laughed. "Dear Dick. Always criticizing me for my dark, complex scripts. Modern humanist fables, social criticism. He used to say, 'We're in L.A. here. Not Germany or Sweden. If you want to make art' — he practically winced when he said the word — 'go back to New York with your neurotic pal, Woody Allen.'"

Len laughed, a child's explosive laughter, encouraging me to continue. Alcohol made me talkative and funny. The first time Dick agreed to meet was on Sunset Boulevard, a bar next to a succession of gas stations and fast food drive-throughs. He was waiting for me, sitting in a poorly lit corner to observe me as I walked in. It was as dark as a coal mine in there. You walked in from the blinding sun into that smoky grotto, rather depressing, reeking of cigar smoke — his cigar, incidentally. "Hey, kid, over here." Dick decided that since he was five or six years older than me, he had the right to be condescending and decide what I'd drink. "I'd prefer a beer," I told him politely, eyeing the twin dry martinis in front of him. He laughed. "Why force the waiter to run around for no reason? I'm making his job easier. I'm sure he appreciates it." The two martinis were for him. He ordered two beers.

Len was having fun. These were the sort of stories he liked — about people who drink too much. He wiped his plate with a piece of bread, poured himself another glass.

I went on, telling how Dick intimidated me with his way of looking at me like I was an idiot. He gave me the old sermon about how "many are called but few are chosen" — all the while staring me down to make sure I was sincere. I also had the pleasure of listening to his rant about taxi drivers "who all have a script to sell in their glove compartment." As well as the usual warnings, "Here in Hollywood, there's no room for romantics. Life is hard, everyone is competitive." His first martini downed, he asked to see my papers, as if I was an illegal immigrant; bemused, I handed them over. Dick is a man who demands, a man you obey. His wrath is a thing to behold. You should see him on set … He took an interest in my name and read it, grimacing. "Ro-main Car-rier…." He shook his head. "Ro-main Car-rier…." I blushed.

"You can call me Roman Carr," I told him. But he wasn't listening. He was making strange sounds with his mouth, his eyes fixed on the ceiling, as if he was gargling mouthwash.

"No, no. It needs to roll off the tongue. You need to be able to recognize it, to remember it."

"People have been calling me Roman Carr for years." There was no point in arguing, he wasn't listening.

"You need to change it. People shouldn't think you're from elsewhere. Canada! A country full of socialists! Not good at all, that. And, you know, worst of all, it lacks style." He took a drag off his cigar, blew smoke in my direction. "I got it! Roman Carr!" He said it, savouring the sound. "Ro-man Carr! What do you think?"

At the Café de la *Paiks*, Len's laughter resonated through the restaurant.

"That's Dick," I told Len. "He can be sold on the best ideas, as long as he thinks they came from him."

The second bottle of red was gone. Len ordered two cognacs. I protested vigorously, but he insisted. He was buying.

"And then?" Len asked. "I want to know what happened next."

"Well, Dick was right. Hollywood is a jungle. None of my scripts got sold. Dick reviewed them and demolished them. Then, one day, he told me, 'Why don't you try television?' 'Television? Dick, be serious. I write for the movies, not for...' He cut me off, 'Right! *Art!*' Still with that disgust in his voice. And so he introduced me to Aaron Spelling."

"No! The real Aaron Spelling?"

"In the flesh."

Len was like a little boy now, elbows on the table, his eyes filled with wonder. I said, "He's a nice guy, Aaron. Always willing to give an opportunity to someone who's willing to work. He agreed to try me out on *Chopper One*, a show about police helicopters that protect Los Angeles from bad guys. It lasted a season. It wasn't very good, and it wasn't the contract of the century; we were a handful of writers on it. My name wasn't even in the credits. But it was a first, important step. After that, Aaron Spelling trusted me. Not long after, he hired me for *S.W.A.T.*, then *Fantasy Island* and *The Love Boat*."

"Oh!" Len exclaimed, "The shows from my childhood. If I'd known there was a bit of my father in them...."

I thought he was going to start crying. We'd both become emotional, what with all the alcohol.

"Then he got interested in *In Gad*."

"How did that happen?"

I told him about the summer of 1988, *The Last Temptation of Christ*, how I came to know Ann, and the way I convinced Dick to invest in the project.

"Dick? How did he react?"

Michèle appeared, all smiles, and offered us dessert. Len scanned the menu, his brown eyes vaguely reminiscent of Robert Egan's. He took time to scrutinize mine as well, darker than his. He asked questions about the greyish scar I still had on my right eye since the accident in 1968. I spoke to him about the effects of it — my vision deformed depending on the angle, hypersensitivity to light — but very little about the accident itself and nothing about Dana. It was still too early for that.

He ordered tiramisu and seemed disappointed that I didn't join him. "Nothing for you?"

"No, thanks."

"You're watching your weight?"

Yes, but since I didn't want to insult him I simply said, "I'm going to burst if I eat anything else." It had the merit of being true.

He said, embarrassed, "I'll have to take care of my weight one day. Now that I have a model to follow, at least. I've got someone to measure up to."

I smiled lamely, though emotion welled up in me. He got up and said, as if he was afraid I'd escape, "Wait for me a couple minutes. I need to take a piss. I want to know how he reacted, your friend. I like this Dick. He has personality."

Only a few tables were still occupied at Café de la Paix. A Thursday evening, a snowstorm, the streets almost empty, the yellow warning lights of ploughs splashing through snow banks in hypnotic, revolving colour. I was thinking of *In Gad*, Chastity's abortions, and what Len had told me with a sort of detached amusement — Gail and Doctor Ziegler, her parents wanting her to have an abortion, her desire to keep the baby, to keep Len. I was surprised to realize that I had, until now, seen the right to abortion as something theoretical, enshrined in law and needing to be protected. And here was Len, my son, a counter-fact to that idea.

"And so, Dick?"

Len was back. He'd splashed water in his face. Impossible not to be charmed by this smart young man with his contagious enthusiasm.

I talked about the plan I conjured up to convince Dick, despite the fact that my friend hated surprises. I picked him up at his place in Beverly Hills on a Sunday morning during the Fourth of July weekend. I drove a used Mazda at the time — I'd never been the type to go into debt for a car. Dick was nervous, his mood sour, "Where are you bringing me? Not to church I hope!"

"Maybe."

"Very funny. Seriously, tell me where we're going."

"You guessed it, church."

"You're joking, right?"

"No, I'm serious."

"Stop the car right now! I've never set foot in a church, and I won't start today."

"It'll be an experience, Dick."

"An experience! Stop the car or I'm throwing myself out."

"Calm down. I want to show you something."

He had cursed me out when I'd refused to take his Mercedes, "No way. I know you, Dick. You'll be yelling at me the whole way and end up driving yourself."

He had grumbled, "If you'd listened to me from the start, you'd be rich today. And you'd be driving something less pathetic."

In the end, he had climbed into my Mazda, grimacing in distaste. And like every time he was annoyed, he lit a cigar. Without asking whether I was okay with it.

We exited the Hollywood Freeway and got on the I-5 going south, always south. The more we drove, the more Dick groused, his eyes fixed on the endless display of billboards beside the highway, advertisements from the benign to the refined to the gaudy, promising to serve you as if you were a celebrity. Welcome to Los Angeles! Dick found his smile when I drove down Disney Way — "Ah, now you're talking!"

— but immediately lost it when I turned towards Garden Grove.

"Patience, Dick. Patience."

Len was listening, rapt. His tiramisu finished, he attacked the glass of cognac I'd given up on. "You're sure you don't want any more?"

"No! Or you'll have to carry me back to the hotel." Once again, his tumbling laughter resounded in the restaurant.

In Garden Grove we drove down Anaheim Boulevard and then Haster Street. Large nondescript streets, lined with ordinary houses, small shopping centres. I turned left onto Chapman Avenue, a faithful replica of the mediocrity that had preceded it. Suddenly, on our right, a surprising, shining edifice, glittering from a thousand reflections, hard to look at, like staring straight up on a cloudless noon.

"What the fuck is that?"

I was speechless myself.

"Can you tell me what the hell this is?" Dick repeated.

"Robert H. Schuller's Crystal Cathedral."

"Whose what's what?"

I parked the Mazda in the huge parking lot, filled to one-third capacity. Dozens of people were converging towards the astonishing glass building, a hundred and thirty feet high. Others were welcoming them by the entrance, smiling warmly. I caught Dick by the coat and pulled him inside; we were both struck with vertigo, sucked upwards by the immensity of the cathedral in the shape a four-pointed star, made of ten thousand panes of tinted glass, held together miraculously by a fascinating set of steel beams. It defied all earthly laws, could withstand earthquakes, or even divine punishment. A cathedral bathed in light, its vault California's blue sky. A pool of water, fountains, and behind the altar a majestic organ like a great ship in an ocean of glass. The televangelist Robert H. Schuller had bought himself quite the cathedral, for seventeen million dollars.

"Okay, so it's impressive," Dick said. "But we're not going to attend the service."

"Why not?"

"No way! I'll wait for you outside."

"Make an effort for me, Dick."

We sat apart from the crowd. The organ, the gift of a rich patron, began playing "Ode to Joy" accompanied by a choir of twenty? thirty? fifty people? The music reverberated in the space and in our bodies and hearts, and we felt we could almost fly in the palace of glass around which palm trees danced, cradled by the wind. Suddenly Dick began sniffling, and furtively wiping his eyes with his hands. Embarrassed, he hid behind the Ray-Bans he pulled out of his vest pocket. I smiled. Dick, emotional! Before us, a camera was sweeping the room. Dick didn't notice it. We were live on *Hour of Power*, and he didn't know it.

Tears began streaming down his face when young men and women began arriving from the four branches of the star carrying flags, a forest of red, white, and blue flags floating in the immense, celestial luminosity of the cathedral. Then Doctor Schuller in his academician's robe, silver hair, and golden-rimmed glasses came out, welcoming the flock. Apostle of positivism, more motivator than pastor. ("Look at this wonderful church, we did it! Tell yourself that all of you, here, you can all do it! Yes! You can succeed too!") His theatrical sermon exuded patriotism. It was written for the Fourth of July and given on Independence Day weekend every year. *I Am the American Flag*, it was called. He personified the American flag, embodying it using the "I" with excessive affect, punctuating his speech with orotund exclamations, painting a picture of America since its foundation.... "I have known forty Presidents....", "I have earned the right to be heard....", "I have earned the right to speak...." Extolling the greatness of America and its exceptional generosity towards other nations. Referring to its sins with a contrite air, its mistakes.... "Show me any other country that is stainless, shameless, spotless, or sinless over whose people I could fly with greater honour...." "I am proud to fly over my imperfect America...."

Hidden behind his dark glasses, Dick stifled a sob while a giant American flag was raised to the ceiling, the symbol of God and country in the church. Spellbound believers shouted spontaneous "Ohs!" America casting a shadow over God. America looking at God, haughty.

Driving back towards Los Angeles, Dick, who usually could only describe emotions in derisive terms, was shaken up, "I'd follow Doctor Schuller anywhere."

At the wheel of the Mazda, I turned my head, looked him straight in the eyes, "I finally have my idea for a TV show, and this time it's the right one."

He furrowed his brow, "What do you want to do? Tell Doctor Schuller's life story?"

"No, it'll be a dark comedy about God and America. And you'll like it, I'm sure."

"A comedy? I don't see anything funny in what we saw. It commands respect. R-e-s-p-e-c-t, in the words of Aretha."

"Trust me, Dick."

"You say that every time! I can't imagine what you could do with Doctor Schuller's life story in a comedy, except mock him."

"You saw the palace he built with money from his flock?"

"You Catholics built your sumptuous cathedrals the same way, no?"

"Dick, look at yourself! Schuller's got you good. I bet you'll send him a cheque."

"And why not? There's nothing wrong with it. As far as I know, no one put a gun to my head and forced me to give." He took another cigar out of his pocket and lit it. "Doctor Schuller brings the Good News, the one of American success. You can't be against that. Imagine if everyone followed his advice. Imagine how rich society would be. No more crime, no more poverty, no more dirty commies. I think it's far more inspiring than hearing someone like...."

"Like?"

"Like all these goddamned idiots who criticize the way we Americans live."

I didn't react to his insult. "Okay," I said. "Doctor Schuller isn't a fundamentalist. It looks like he's got no skeletons in his closet. Perhaps he even does good, all things considered...."

"The man has my complete admiration."

"But what about con men like Jim Bakker? Or that pitiful moralizer Jimmy Swaggart who pays for whores in seedy motels and confesses in tears on his show because he knows his sexual obsessions will lead to his downfall? 'I've sinned against You, my Lord!' Hypocrites, all of them!"

Dick shrugged. "So they're clowns. Pathetic clowns."

"These clowns have the politicians' ears in Washington. The clowns and charlatans of faith who haven't yet fallen from grace have powerful networks. They can bring down a president. You saw how Reagan was willing to kowtow to them. Remember how he began praying publicly all of a sudden? He did it to mollify them. To have them on his side. You know what they're looking for, besides screwing over the little guy? They want to bring us back to the right path so Jesus will come again and walk the earth. That's what they say, Dick! But it'll only happen when humanity has washed itself of its sins. Meanwhile, they've taken on the mission of cleansing the planet of everyone they hate — liberals, atheists, feminists, gays. Everyone who isn't like them and doesn't think like them. They invest in power, the courts, schools — they reintroduce prayer in classrooms, make Darwin's theory heresy, eradicate homosexuality, take away a woman's right to choose. These people, Dick, want to bring us back twenty years, destroy the rights we fought for in the sixties, the years you might hate but that made the world a better place. Shit, Dick, you see them everywhere in Los Angeles, ready to lynch Martin Scorsese and the bosses at Universal! They want to dictate their vision to Hollywood!"

In my rusted Mazda heading for Los Angeles, I was angry, indignation in my throat. Dick was chuckling, smoking his goddamned cigar.

"Aren't you worried?" I said, insulted by his attitude. "I am!"

"Of course you're worried: you're Canadian. Feminists, homosexuals, socialists, peaceniks, and abortion doctors are normal for you. Meanwhile, good and honest Christians who work in their communities for the good of all, and practise their own faith, for you guys, they're all idiots."

"You're an asshole, Dick."

It was past midnight, and the Café de la Paix was empty except for us. Politely, Michèle made it clear it was time to close up shop by placing the bill on our table. I grabbed it before Len could. It was our agreement — the father was taking his son out, like any father would. Grateful, his eyes wet, Len thanked me. I got up unsteadily, "I'm sorry. I feel like I'm the only one who got in a word."

"Don't be sorry! It's fascinating! You can't imagine how proud it makes me."

I smiled. Michèle brought us our coats, helped me put on mine. My God, so much alcohol! As we got to the door, I told Len, a hand on his shoulder, "As soon as you've got a couple of free days, come visit us in Los Angeles. Bring Lynn and the kids. Ann would love to meet you. I'll show you around the studio, and you can meet the actors if you want."

"That would be wonderful."

Before leaving the restaurant — and facing the snow that was still falling — Len took a blue envelope out of his pocket.

"It's from Gail. She asked me to give it to you."

I staggered. "Gail? An envelope? Why?"

Len shrugged, embarrassed, "I don't know."

I took it, tucked it in my anorak. We shook hands like businessmen, then judging it wasn't quite the way a father-son relationship should go, I opened my arms and Len opened his, and we hugged. Tears in our eyes, we said goodbye. I jumped into the taxi that Michèle had called for me and headed for my hotel.

In my room at the Westin, I quickly undressed and got into the hotel's cotton bathrobe. I was dizzy enough to be slightly nauseous. Still, after a moment's guilty hesitation, I poured myself a St. Leger from the minibar. It was one of those nights.

I sat on the bed and took a deep breath. The envelope. What could it contain? Its blue paper was like silk, so thin it might have been empty. Another sip of St. Leger, and I opened it.

It was a picture of the two of us. In Métis Beach, in the Egans' garden. "August 1962," Gail had written on the back. A few days before *the events*. Our tense smiles, our eyes squinting into the sun. Gail wore a white tennis dress, and I had a pair of awful brown pants, too short for me, and a matching rayon shirt. My mother sold clothes, yet I looked like I was dressed from the Salvation Army. I didn't know whether I should feel pity for myself or laugh. Why would such a pretty girl, with the face of a princess who reminded you of Grace Kelly, be interested in me? Timid, almost frightened, I looked at the camera Françoise was impatiently holding; it was that time Gail had made her take a picture of us, an obsession that had gotten her overexcited, *It'll be a small victory, Romain. A small victory for my independence. Do you understand?* She wanted the picture to look at in the moments of boredom once she was married to Don Drysdale. She would hide it from him so he could never find it. *Do you understand?* The same picture that had pushed Françoise into telling on us out of revenge. She gave the signal that sent Robert Egan on the warpath, armed with a golf club, in the messy garage my father and I had repaired years earlier.

I finished the St. Leger and put the picture back in the envelope, unable to understand what Gail had hoped for by giving it to me.

4

While Christie Brenan's article in the *Los Angeles Times* was positive, it didn't have an effect on the number of complaints we received; on the contrary, they were growing, but so were the ratings. Enough to delight the team, Josh, and the It's All Comedy! investors.

A second season, new viewers each week, the sales and advertising division going wild over their loyalty. "Money is telling us we're on the right track," Dick said. "Not the handful of bigots with their threats and insults." We started believing we were heading towards a record audience for a cable show with almost five million viewers for an episode in late February 1996. The team was ecstatic; we celebrated at Josh's place, a large house in the Bauhaus style on Wild Oak Drive — garden, pool, open bar. I was happy, savouring the moment. Years of work finally rewarded.

"To Roman! To Ann!" Then, "To the team! To the actors!" A night of self-congratulation, a time for celebration. The contagious gaiety of the actors that night — Avril Page (Chastity), Bill Doran (Gad Paradise), Kathleen Hart (Martha Paradise), and Trevor Wheeler (Dylan) — whose careers were now launched thanks to *In Gad*. After the six seasons we were planning to shoot, they would be able to choose their projects, offers would abound, perhaps even in the movies. All four hoped one day to make it into the movies. I was certainly proud of their accomplishment. To have given an opportunity to Avril and Trevor, two young, talented actors, and to have helped Bill and Kathleen, both in their forties, whose roller-coaster careers had long forced them to pick poorly paid side jobs, felt great. They could relax now — if everything continued to go well, of course.

The night was warm, the moon high in the sky like a benevolent protector. That state of grace you reach when everything comes together in your life; you hope beyond hope that your existence will continue to look like this moment, that nothing will change or move out of whack.

Following Dick's suggestion, for a laugh, we toasted the *Ayatollah's Komedy* on the great terrace that overlooked the valley. That's what he called the censors at the Parents Television Council (PTC), a new organization in the American TV world. People who had nothing else to do than watch, listen, and scrutinize everything broadcast on prime time, tracking with inquisitorial zeal every swear word, blasphemy, moment of nudity, and scene of sex and violence. No surprise we were on their blacklist; already they'd begun putting pressure on our advertisers, threatening them with a boycott campaign. But our advertisers targeted younger viewers, and were impervious to these sorts of threats. It's All Comedy!, a cable network dedicated to comedy shows of all stripes, as its name indicated — series, variety shows, shows for teenagers — jealously defended its independence. If the Big Three (ABC, CBS, and NBC) were more receptive to pressure applied by the PTC, It's All Comedy!'s trademark was boldness, and the advertisers knew it. "Free to laugh!" the network's advertisements stated, a rather clear reference to the sacrosanct First Amendment.

"To the *Ayatollah's Komedy!*" Dick exclaimed, already tipsy. Dick never missed an opportunity to toast something. Josh and his wife, Adriana, were making the rounds, bottles of champagne in both hands, filling our glasses, which we quickly emptied each time. We clinked and raised them in unison. Laughter and jokes. Feverish, contagious gaiety. The women were pretty in their

lightweight dresses; the bluish mirror of the pool reflected speckled, dancing light; Ann, as always, was the most beautiful of all.
A memorable night.

Josh Ovitz had made a daring bet when he bought *In Gad We
Trust*. It was in 1992, two weeks after Bill Clinton's election. I was
fascinated and soon charmed by this young Harvard man, not very
tall, a healthy glow to his skin, black hair and the expressive eyes of
a curious child. You might not have suspected that the thirty-one-
year-old was a shark of a businessman and a multimillionaire. He
looked like a student — washed out jeans and Harvard t-shirt. He
had made his fortune through investments in the ad industry before
moving to It's all Comedy!, a network he bought with his father and
developed into what it was today. He invited us to his place, Dick
and me (Dick put up, as producer, half of the show's budget), to
this incredible house on Wild Oak Drive. That such a young man
could own a magnificent house like this impressed me. He ushered
us into the living room with the confidence of a much older man
who'd seen it all. Tall windows like in skyscrapers, a room decorated like a magazine — Italian couches with pure lines, varnished
furniture, and silk rugs. On the living room table, newspapers and
magazines all open to pictures of Bill Clinton. Josh was close to the
Democrats, who had recently won back the White House, crushing
the Republicans who had been in power for twelve years with their
"moral and economic obscurantism," he told us, emphasizing every
word. He had the aplomb of an older man who gives his opinions
and doesn't expect to be contradicted. He poured us each a scotch
as he enthused about the November 3 victory as if it had been the
best news of his life. He was overjoyed, floating on a cloud, so much
so that I later thought that he might not have taken the risk with *In
Gad* if the project had been offered to him at another time.

Josh mentioned that with the Republicans' debacle the
religious right had seen the doors of power close on them in
Washington, "neu-tra-li-zed!" He spoke as if tasting fine wine,

though he mimed slitting his throat. No doubt, according to him, fundamentalist Christians were destined to be marginalized. "They're the ones who led to the Republicans losing. The electorate understood the danger they represent."

Then we spoke of *In Gad* — he mentioned he was charmed from the very first pages — God, America, money, "the three pillars of American wisdom," he said ironically. And *The Last Temptation of Christ*, "What Lew went through, it was just awful." Lew Wasserman, the big boss at Universal who'd been in the eye of the storm in 1988. A good friend of his father's. "They banged him up good. Dragged him through the mud in every paper. Those fundamentalists are trying to shut us up with their vicious anti-Semitic attacks. Never again," he'd said, shaking his head, "Never again." A promise he made, and I was happy for it, except you never know what's around the corner. Josh learned that lesson the hard way with *In Gad. These Hollywood types* — *always going after Christians but never Jews. Why is that?* Attacks directed at his name and that of his ad director, Michael Hausman. His right-hand man, Ab Chertoff, his father, Sam Ovitz. It had been quite a blow for Josh. He would lose that confidence that had so impressed Dick and me on that afternoon in 1992.

He wasn't as tense now that the success of *In Gad* seemed assured. He was enjoying himself that evening, at this celebration in his lush garden smelling of orange blossoms. Matt was horsing around. He fashioned a crown of thorns — no idea where he found that — and placed it on his Knicks baseball cap, which was never very far from him. A funny guy, Matt. Tall, talented, and sensitive, with a strong New York accent. He might have been the most exasperated among all of us with the constant complaints and criticism. The explanation was his childhood as an Irish Catholic which, from the little I knew, had been far more difficult than mine. The crown of thorns he had on his head, it was to fuck with them, he told me, so each time he went through the small group of people camping out in front of La Brea studio, he could see the shocked faces of the pro-life demonstrators, their moral repugnance clearly showing. I ignored them — they weren't aggressive yet, though the slogans on their signs were — SHAME ON YOU! ABORTION IS MURDER! — and passed them without looking at them. It was important not to make them feel important. Matt and Dick couldn't help themselves and would often engage with them. Dick especially, with his taunting questions, "Don't you work? Who's paying you to be here? Unproductive people like you, we should get rid of all of you!"

"You don't seem to be affected by it," Matt told me once.

"Why would I?" I answered. "That's their opinion, I've got mine. That's all."

He looked at me, confused, his Knicks cap raised on his forehead. "How do you do it?"

I needed only to think of Dana and her admirable courage to be immune to the noise and scandal surrounding *In Gad. The Next War* had sparked much worse. With a bit of perspective, I understood how hard it must have been for Dana, a feminist in a hostile world, surrounded by men jealous of their prerogatives. She'd been hated, ridiculed. Alone and fragile, yet she had resisted. Such hateful copy in newspapers, messages in the mail, death threats, sarcasm on TV.... She had faced so much! That's what I thought of when I saw the demonstrators on the sidewalk, their closed faces, their indignation painted on signs; it was nothing at all compared to what Dana's book had caused — arrests, demonstrations, the Freudian Vandals. That's what I thought of when Chastity's abortions led to attacks against us in the media — always a passionate topic, and no different on that night at Josh's place when Dick, his speech slurred from drink, said, "Chastity's the one who brings us the most money. People are glad to see we've got balls." He spoke coarsely, gesturing with his hand to make sure we knew where his balls were, without thinking of Avril only a few feet away. In the garden, under the soft light of small lanterns, I saw Avril blush. She was a discreet young woman of nineteen, with beautiful blond hair. She was young to be facing such pressure. Ann and I wanted to protect her; we helped her choose which interviews to do — the media were interested in her character most of all — and sometimes we accompanied her. I had to be strong to make her comfortable. When we wrote the series, Ann and I knew it would cause a scandal, and we were ready to face the music — like Dana had done with her formidable ideas, audacious for her time.

"What about your son, Roman? What does he think about it all?"

My son? The words were still too new not to cause a shiver of surprise. Ab Chertoff was asking the question. Ab Chertoff, an affable man the size of an offensive lineman.

"Len?" I said. "He likes *In Gad*. He says his father is a genius."

I laughed, and so did he.

"We're happy for you. A son well established in life. Good for you."

Ab had two sons, one of whom had caused all sorts of trouble as a teenager. I thanked him, and he placed a heavy, warm hand on my shoulder. There was no jealousy in his eyes, only solicitude.

I was staring at the pool, thinking of Len. Our long discussions over the phone about *In Gad* and American politics. My son was on the right of the political spectrum and spoke openly about his admiration for Ronald Reagan. I wasn't surprised, but disconcerted, yes. Over the course of our conversations, I discovered our opinions were starkly different, and that forced me to be more open. It was the same thing when it came to abortion, a sensitive subject for him, for obvious reasons. Next to me, Dick laughed. He told Ab, as if he could hear my thoughts, "Sure, his son was raised right. But he lights candles for that failed actor turned president anyway." Dick was drunk; I hated seeing him like this. "Hey, Roman! Tell us how you managed to make a right-wing son? How did you do it?" To make sure we understood what he was alluding to, he'd gestured graphically, aping with unbounded energy a sexual act.

"Dick, shut up."

I didn't like it when people mocked Len.

5

No way I'd be skimping on the welcome for Len's first visit to Los Angeles!

Flowers in the guest room, a refrigerator filled with goodies — my son was a giant! Eggs, bacon, ham, potatoes, plenty to make delicious hamburgers on the grill at lunch, and two good bottles of cognac — Courvoisier XO — only the best for our long discussions after supper. Dizzy with it all, Ann told me to relax. "You're going to embarrass him, the poor man!" But I wasn't listening, determined that everything be perfect, a success, spending plenty of time on the phone reserving tickets for all sorts of things (theatre, concerts, the Dodgers' season opener) and a table for two, father and son, for a dinner at Spago's. It was the "place to be" in town, just filled to the brim with celebrities. The best tables going according to your *value*. Dick brought me there to celebrate when we sold *In Gad We Trust*. Full of pride, he gave the good news to the legendary owner of the restaurant, Wolfgang Puck. Soon after, I became a regular at the most desirable tables, right next to the window. "Roman Carr," Dick told him, "remember that name."

I would definitely impress my son.

My God, that first time! Len was as excited as a child. He simply couldn't hold still in the Pathfinder, amazed each time he recognized a landmark from hundreds and hundreds of movies. L.A. isn't Paris or London or New York, with their grandiose, distinctive monuments. No, in L.A. things are different. It's a more subtle experience; constant impressions of déjà-vu, as if you had lived in the city in another life. The great boulevards lined with palm trees, the Hollywood Hills, floating over the smog, the freeways (is there anything uglier in a city?) cutting through the megalopolis. Len knew their names by heart — Hollywood Freeway, Ventura Freeway, Santa Ana Freeway —from having read them in Michael Connelly novels.

My God, that first time! We were both so nervous at the idea of spending three days together — and what if we disappointed each other? From the airport to the house, Len couldn't stop talking, as if he feared silence between us, naming every movie he ever loved that had been shot in Los Angeles — *Lethal Weapon, Heat, Dragnet, Terminator* …. I was a bit disconcerted, *My son? That's the type of movies he likes?* I would have preferred if his list were more like mine: *The Graduate, Barton Fink, Chinatown, Pulp Fiction.* But why not? He seemed so happy! There was something touching in his child-like enthusiasm, while I, his father, was already trying to find excuses for him, *He's my son, he can like whatever he wants. And have his own opinions.*

Len loved the house on Appian Way, way up in the Hollywood Hills. Large, comfortable, simple. A two-storey stucco home, its back against the hill, meaning we didn't have a garden, but we did have a large terrace over the garage that offered a fantastic view of the valley, which, far out to our right, cut a path towards the skyscrapers of Los Angeles as slender as wild reeds. They were perhaps the strangest element of this town of excesses, especially for a New Yorker. (Yes, strangely enough, after all these years in California, I still thought of myself as a New Yorker.) Our reward was to our left — round hills the shape of a young woman's breasts, Hollywood's name tattooed on them.

As if by magic, Len's arrival in our life put an end to Ann's obsessions with maternity. I don't think she was conscious of it at first, nor do I think she would have agreed with my interpretation of the changes in her behaviour. But his presence — and through him the presence of his children — seemed to satiate her, at least temporarily. It was her attitude towards herself that changed first — she stopped comparing herself to women of her own age who had children. Then, her attitude towards our relationship changed — we began making love in a way that was so much more carefree. I hadn't seen her so calm in a long time, without a nagging thought in the back of her head cutting her off from her own pleasure, spoiling our moments of intimacy. We went to Calgary a few times to visit our grandchildren. Ann was overcome with a deep and sudden affection for Cody and Julia, calling them from L.A. often. She would send them books, VHS tapes, even toys sometimes. "Grandma Ann! Come play with us!" And she laughed. The children were simply marvelous, always happy to speak to us, bringing tears to our eyes when they said, "I love you, Ann, I love you Romain." Filled with boundless gratitude when we sent them gifts, "Oh, it's so beautiful!" or wisely puzzled, "How come a gift? It isn't my birthday." They were at odds with the children of friends and neighbours in L.A. — like one of Ann's nephews, a boy named Judd who was a little older than Cody. His mother, Ann's sister, had spoiled him silly, then abdicated, terrorized by this child, capable, when angry, of holding his breath until his eyes rolled back in his head.

When Len visited us in L.A., he always came alone, never with the kids or Lynn. It was his decision, he said, to catch up on lost time, as he'd done with Gail. He would come in on a Friday evening and leave early on Monday morning, going straight to work in Calgary from the airport.

"Lynn doesn't object to it?" I asked him, once.

He smiled. "Oh, she says that it's my new pretext to be away from home. She also says that when I'm done with you, I'll find brothers or sisters — new alibis."

"Lynn doesn't seem very happy for you."

He shrugged. "She sees it as a threat, I think. I've come to understand that housewives, when they lose control, they feel their backs against the wall."

"And do you see it like that? Like a way of escaping?"

He lowered his eyes. "I don't know, Romain."

Another time, when we were having supper with Ann near Rodeo Drive, he declared, taking in the place with his arms wide, "You know, when I see all of this, I feel like my life is pretty dull. This city is both as unreal as a fairy tale and at the same time, because of movies and television, as familiar as an old shoebox full of family pictures. Los Angeles disorients me. I never know what state I'll be in when I get back to Calgary."

"Why don't you bring Lynn with you?" Ann asked. "Come with the kids, spend a week or two. There's more than enough room at home. I'd like to see Cody and Julia. I miss them both so much. You could borrow one of our cars and maybe drive up the coast, to Santa Barbara, or farther. Why not? You'll see, it's spectacular over there."

"And for the kids, there's Disneyland and Universal Studios," I added. "And if you're worrying about money, Len, your father's here for you."

He blushed with embarrassment, making me immediately regret my tactlessness. Ann kicked me under the table.

"He's a man!" she shouted at me once we were back home. "With a good job. Why did you have to humiliate him? You could have waited until you were alone, and offer it like a gift, without mentioning his finances. Now that you've got so much money, you're forgetting what it's like to live in the real world."

Being a father was complicated.

A few months later, Len came with Lynn, but without the kids. There was no way Cody and Julia could take time off school. Ann was disappointed. Len had paid for their plane tickets, and I hadn't insisted. But it bothered me so much! To make amends, I reserved all the movie tickets, the shows, I brought them out to fine restaurants almost every night and when Len tried to pay, I would tell him firmly that it was my treat, that it wasn't negotiable, that it was a father's right. He smiled, embarrassed.

As much as I loved Len and the kids, I found Lynn depressing. Oh, sure, she was a kind young woman, without malice, an excellent mother to Cody and Julia, but as a wife to a husband? Plump and hung-up about it, she didn't speak much, avoided our presence when she could, found refuge on the terrace or in their room. In the mornings, she waited for Len before joining us for breakfast. She simply never interacted with us on her own. Between them, you could feel a constant low-level tension. Impatient gestures, an annoyed clacking of the tongue, sighs of exasperation. She wasn't happy about the trip, it was clear, and she kept complaining that she missed the children. Before we left for the airport, Len took me aside.

"I'm sorry, Romain."

"Sorry for what?"

"Lynn isn't the best travel companion. She's more of a homebody."

"She has every right. She'll always be welcome."

He gave me a strange smile. His thoughts were elsewhere.

6

"Len, is that you?"

In front of me, Len, but not exactly Len. Lean, his skin tanned from being outdoors, in an elegant grey suit, his hair cut short, almost shaved, making him look a bit like Yul Brynner. He had just got off the plane from Calgary, his travel bag in hand, fresh as a rose, not at all exhausted like the other times he'd come. The three-hour flight was usually an ordeal for him, since fitting his huge frame into a tiny seat was no easy task.

"You look like you've been working out."

Embarrassed, he mumbled something that sounded like, "It was time for me to get in shape.... Isn't that what you've told me a hundred times?" He didn't look me in the eyes. In the Pathfinder, he chatted distractedly, without his usual enthusiasm, glancing this way and that. He answered my questions — How are Lynn and the kids? Work? — with an almost inaudible mumble, "Good ... good ... everyone's good. Work is fine...." I felt hurt at his refusal to tell me what was wrong. *Len are you sick? If so, would you tell me? You'd tell your father, wouldn't you?* But his tanned features certainly contradicted my worries. His skin was glowing. So what was the problem?

A woman, he ended up admitting. Behind this surprising transformation, there was a woman. What else could it have been?

"I know what you're going to say," he mumbled. "That it's a cowardly thing to do, cheating on your wife. You're the first person I've told."

I was touched by it, really. Flattered that he had shared his secret with me, a secret which brought him joy and pain in equal measure. Isn't a father supposed to be there for his son in his most difficult moments?

I said, trying to be neutral and reassuring, "What do you intend to do? Is it just a passing thing, or does it mean your relationship with Lynn is shaky?"

"I don't know, I really can't say for now. The only thing I do know is that I'm happy about it. I feel like I'm alive."

Len had transformed into a seductive young man. He looked good in his new role. The price to pay seemed high, though — torn by guilt when he thought of Lynn and the kids. Otherwise, he spoke with pride of the hours he spent in the gym, of the fact that he barely drank anymore, of his new dietary habits. "Fried foods are out, forty-ounce steaks and fettuccine Alfredo down at the Café de la *Paiks* are gone as well!" he said, laughing. Fish, white meat, vegetables, and salads. A radical diet that had helped him lose forty pounds and reveal a beautiful face enhanced by prominent cheekbones and a square jaw.

"He looks exactly like you," Ann sad.

During the weekend, as we were out in Beverly Hills — Len was looking for a gift for Joan, the woman behind his transformation — I was surprised by our reflection in the mirror of a clothing store; Len and I, next to each other. Ann was right, we looked exactly alike. Father and son, no one could doubt it now. Moved, I put an arm around his shoulder and said, a bit awkwardly, "I love you, son." He bit his lip and turned his head away, to hide his tears.

"You think Lynn suspects anything?"

"No, I always have a good alibi."

"Be careful, Len. You're playing with fire. Sooner or later, you'll have to make a decision. You can't cheat on her indefinitely."

"I know, I know. But I can't just leave my children."

Len didn't need to make a decision in the end; Lynn took care of it for him. Despite what he believed, Lynn had been suspicious for some time. She confronted him one night when he came home late. That night, like almost every other time, he said he had some event to cover for the *Calgary Herald*, but Lynn knew he lied by the smell of his shirt, that persistent smell she'd been noticing for weeks, a female smell she even detected in his underpants. Not able to lie anymore, Len admitted everything, and she threw him out. That night, he called me from a hotel in Calgary, crying.

"I'm an idiot, Romain. A real idiot. What will the children think of their father?"

The following afternoon, he arrived in L.A. in a pitiful state. His clothes wrinkled, eyes red, a two-day beard, and smelling of alcohol. I picked him up between two scenes we were shooting at the studio. Ann kindly offered to go pick him up, but I refused, knowing what state he'd probably be arriving in — his tears, on the phone, the night before, had been enough to break your heart. So I went to the airport, dragged him into the Pathfinder trying to console him, brought him home and put him to bed in the guest room, knowing he would get up as soon as I left and pour himself a drink.

Len hadn't loved Lynn in years; that was no secret. The problem was he couldn't do *that* to Cody and Julia, the children he loved more than anything.

After having spent the night crying and feeling guilty, he got up the next morning with a strange light in his eyes, his face serene. He ate a light breakfast of fruit and cereal, and called Joan, in Calgary, to tell her that it was over between them.

"I'm going to get Lynn back," he declared, after hanging up. Incontestable truth, that's what it sounded like, his eyes shining with an excessive confidence that alarmed me, having seen the same light in the eyes of his mother in moments of euphoria. Perhaps I was wrong, perhaps my interpretation betrayed an irrational fear in me — *illness can be hereditary* — and Len, though troubled by his marital problems, would end up finding the right path. I just needed to help him a little.

"But you're no longer in love with her, Len."

"So what? I need to do it for my children. At least until they're of legal age."

"Len, it doesn't work like that."

"No? And what would you know? Do you know what's it like to raise children?"

Hurt, I wanted to tell him, *I've got you, now. And I've got the impression, right now, that you're not much older than your children.* But, of course, I said nothing.

Lynn didn't want to hear about reconciliation. She swore she'd take him to court if he didn't give her full custody of the children. His infidelity, she promised, would play against him. And Len was doing worse by the day, drinking more and more, putting weight back on. "The bitch!" he lamented. "She's going to take away my children, my own children!"

Traumatized, Cody and Julia refused to speak to him over the phone. His voice, the tone he took when he drank, scared them. Meanwhile, Lynn was keeping notes on his reprehensible behaviour "so the day you force me to get a judge's order, I'll be ready to make sure you never see your children again." And Len couldn't get a grip on himself, shut away in his pathetic basement apartment on 11th Avenue, which I got the address for from Lynn. She was so desperate over the phone. Desperate and filled with rage, "How could he have done this to us!"

I arrived in Calgary the next day — Dick was becoming more and more annoyed by my repeated absences — and found him in his apartment. The place was absolutely filthy. He was slumped on the couch, two empty bottles of Jack Daniels at his feet. He was dead drunk. "Wh ... What ... What the fuck are you doing here?" He mumbled, his eyes glassy, his face swollen, shining with sweat. His clothes were dirty, covered in grease and ketchup stains. He hadn't shaved in days, his hair was oily. How could he give up like this? *My son?* Len was losing his children and his job — Lynn told me the *Calgary Herald* had put him on indefinite leave — and he wasn't fighting back for God's sake!

I grabbed him by the collar and dragged him into the grimy bathroom. I turned the shower on, helped him out of his clothes and put him in the bathtub. He tripped, swore. As soon as the cold water touched him he cried out like a wounded animal, long, supplicating shouts. He didn't fight though. After ten minutes, I stopped the water, helped him dry off a body that had reverted to being flabby and immense. Staggering, he disappeared into the living room, reappeared with clothes that were far from clean, his face contrite. I called a taxi, and we went to the Westin.

"You're taking me out for a ... Bloo ... Bloody Caesar?" he mumbled, an idiotic smile on his face. I said nothing. "Yes ... yes ...," he insisted, his head lolling. "A Bloody Caesar, just ... just like ... the first time!"

"The first time, I was with a respectable man," I cut him off. He froze, looking at me, incredulous. "Look at yourself goddamn it! If you keep going like this, you'll end up in the street! Is that what you want, Len?"

7

Two weeks later, Len called me in Los Angeles to tell me he had joined Alcoholics Anonymous.

His voice didn't waver. He almost sounded cheerful, "You'll see, Romain, it'll soon be ancient history. Cody and Julia will get their *real* father back."

And I could only be happy for the excellent news, relieved to finally see my son take control of his life.

One thing was certain, Len was doing better. At work, his boss decided to give him a second chance, chalking this unfortunate episode up to the shock of separation. Lynn calmed down and accepted shared custody without going to court. However, she was demanding exorbitant alimony, which Len conceded without protest.

Len settled down in the apartment we found together during one of my trips to Calgary, a five-room apartment on the eighth floor of a newly built building, a deal at only seven hundred dollars a month, just off a busy street, not too far from the Bow River. We spent a weekend shopping for furniture, kitchen equipment, sheets, bedding, and a stereo, before decorating the smallest room, the one in which Cody and Julia would sleep when Len got better. In the children's furniture section at Sears, he broke down in tears, "Do you think they'll want to see their bastard of a father again?" I consoled him by repeating what Ann had told me in L.A., when I'd been a little worried about Cody and Julia's reaction towards their father. "Children are far less resentful than adults, and their memories are more selective. It's what saves them."

One day at a time. That was the daily prayer that helped Len rebuild his life. He stopped drinking completely, lost all the weight he'd gained, began working again, even accepted new editorial responsibilities at the *Herald*. I was incredibly happy for him. And then he met Melody.

Melody was a self-assured young woman. That much we could tell from the picture Len sent us. Brown hair, eyes almost black, a confident, satisfied smile. On the back, Len's words, scratched down quickly like a forced confession, which should have made me happy but instead left me perturbed. "I found my soulmate." Len had met her in a Baptist church. Over the phone, my son's voice had regained its composure.

I said, surprised, "At church? I thought you weren't religious."

"Oh, of course," he said, sounding hurt. "I knew my father was as allergic to God as an asthmatic to dust, what with *In Gad We Trust*."

It was the first time he'd spoken of *In Gad* with such disdain.

"No, Len … I'm only … surprised. Whatever makes you happy, son.… You know I'm just happy to see you happy."

My tone wasn't very convincing. Annoyed, he said, "I needed to get back to my roots, Romain. I need spirituality to clean up my life, to get to know myself better. A member of my AA group invited me to join him one Sunday. I was right to go. That's where I met Melody. She introduced me to wonderful people who are helping me find myself. Good people, who only want to help others. Do you understand? People who don't chase after money or fame, because they've got God, and that's enough."

Of course, that last remark was aimed at me. But had he known it? Had he tried to hurt me? *Money and fame, two worthless things that will only rot your soul.* Is that what Len believed?

I hung up, astounded.

"Let him find his way again," Ann said. "It's a phase, he needs to rebuild himself."

Len brought Melody with him to Los Angeles a few weeks before Christmas in 1997. The show was on hiatus, we had shot all of season 4, which would be broadcast starting in January. Ann and I were free to spend all of our time with them. It should have helped take some of the pressure off, but instead their visit was making me nervous.

I far preferred Lynn to this young woman — so full of herself, always ready to judge others with her small malicious eyes. We ate at home on the first evening. Ann had prepared a wonderful dish, a lemon chicken, which Melody had sniffed at impolitely.

"Is there alcohol in there?

"Oh no!" Ann exclaimed, unsure whether to be embarrassed or insulted. "Romain and I know Len is sober."

Uncomfortable, Len lowered his eyes. Under the table, Ann's foot was calling me to the rescue. As surprised as she, I tried to restrain myself, "We know Len. No need to remind us."

Melody emitted a small nervous laugh and Len blushed. To try to lighten the mood, Ann wished us all "*bon appétit*" with forced enthusiasm and an exaggerated smile that didn't do much to hide her disappointment. I placed my hand on hers, which caused Melody to give another small impertinent laugh I chose to ignore. To show my gratitude for this meal she slaved over to welcome Len's new flame, his "soulmate," I attacked my plate with enthusiasm. My fork was halfway to my mouth when that little piece of work glared at me and insolently said, "I'd like to thank God before seeing you swallow a mouthful...." She then turned to Len, looking for reinforcement. He hadn't said anything yet. "Right, Len?"

Uneasy, Ann clumsily knocked over a glass of water. (We had banned alcohol from our meals with Len. I couldn't even imagine what absurd thing Melody would have said if there'd been wine at the table that evening.) She immediately apologized, wiped the table off with her napkin, and disappeared into the kitchen. I would have followed her to take her in my arms and help her calm down if I hadn't lost my own temper already.

Trying not to yield to anger, I told Melody that it wasn't our custom to say grace, and if it was important to her, she could do so on her own. Then, defying her with my eyes, I swallowed a first mouthful, which was welcomed with another one of her small nervous laughs. Len, who still looked as annoyed as when he came in, judged that it was the right time to get involved, but not in his father's defence. "Romain, it's just a moment to take a break in our day, to be mindful of how lucky we are to live …" his arms wide, he took in the dining room with its view of the Hollywood Hills, "so comfortably."

Of course, money — it rots the soul.

"Romain, please." Ann had returned, her hand on my shoulder. She was right. No one wanted to spend an uncomfortable evening. I put my fork down and Melody, who now had an aggrieved look, threw the blessings in our faces like a handful of pebbles.

The next morning, she barely said good morning to us; the only thing that interested her was the location of the nearest Baptist church. I was about to tell her I didn't spend my days tracking churches, but Ann, trying to avoid a confrontation, pointed one out on the map of Los Angeles we had lent them. Selma Avenue, a few streets away from Grauman's Chinese Theatre. I had never noticed it.

Melody grabbed her vest and Len and left. From the living room window, I watched them climb into Ann's Passat, Len at the wheel, Melody next to him, speaking animatedly, making large, forceful gestures, her brow furrowed. Len buckled his belt impassively, not at all bothered by Melody's shouting, or at least what seemed to be shouting. Then I saw him smile, and laugh, and that hurt me. Not too long ago, we were the ones having fun together, he and I.

He started up the Passat, and headed down Appian Way. Len was letting himself be dragged to church, like any other man would let himself be dragged through the stores on Rodeo Drive by his wife. It bothered him, but he accepted it. There was something shocking in his mute approbation, his shrugs of capitulation. *Sure she leads me wherever, but I don't care.* I couldn't understand it.

Ann appeared, relieved at having a moment or two to breathe. I said, "What the hell is he doing with her?"

"It's just a phase."

I hoped she was right, but I didn't believe it. Len had changed too much, as if Melody had cast a spell on him.

Early the next morning, with everyone still asleep, I surprised Melody in my office. She was sitting at the chair in front of my computer, holding the tickets I had purchased for an event being put on by amfAR, the American Foundation for AIDS Research, a few months away.

"What are you doing here?" I demanded, furious.

"Nothing, just visiting." She turned her head. "The view is really nice from up here."

It was a clear morning, the sky electric blue, still streaked with yellow and pink over the hills, an effect of air pollution.

"You're in my office without my permission."

"Oh! I didn't know this was a private area."

"It is. The door was closed."

"I'm sorry."

With a haughty air, she got up and stopped to look at pictures of *In Gad* on set. A few frames up on the wall, a present from the production team. Finally. We were going to get into it. An opportunity to address the elephant in the room, which we'd all avoided so far. She stared at the pictures stiffly. The production team on break, laughing, making faces for the camera. She was holding onto the amfAR tickets so tightly I thought she just might shred them. Without turning her head to face me, she said, "Don't you hear all the anger around your show? All these people you offend in their deep convictions, their religious beliefs … does it make you laugh? What is everyone smiling about in these pictures? Who are they mocking?" She turned, glaring at me. "I can't understand why Len has any admiration for you."

The sheer brutality of her insult took me by surprise. Panicked, I imagined what she might be saying about me to Len, maligning me to him to win him over to her own hatred. I was filled with an irrational fear of exacerbating the problem, *How could I do that, exactly?* All I managed was to say, "Give me the tickets. They've nothing to do with you."

She examined them, put them back on the desk. "Twenty-five thousand dollars for a table of ten … That's what? Two thousand five hundred dollars a meal? So much money for AIDS when there's so much need in the world — poverty, famine, war. AIDS isn't an accident or one of life's trials. It's God's just punishment, Romain. These people spread the plague, and you want to encourage them?"

"Get out of my office, now!"

"You provoke each other," Ann said. "Stop being so curt with her."

"Curt! You should see what she does!"

"Len isn't wrong when he says that *In Gad* made you allergic to God. You can have faith, practise your religion, and be intelligent. Look at your own son — faith put order back in his life. Cody and Julia have their father back, isn't that important?"

So it was *me* who was curt with *her*? *I* was the one who was intolerant towards people who practised their religion?

I wanted to show them around L.A., but in the end I was relieved to realize that Melody was avoiding us. Why had she even agreed to come to L.A.? To taunt us? To demonstrate the prodigious influence she had over Len? As if she were saying, *I'm the one who made him better, not you! I know how to help him, so leave him alone!*

Ann and I had wanted these five days to be all about family. Well too bad. I gave them a pair of keys and the alarm system's code. "Give them to Melody instead." Len said. "I'll just lose them." Melody carefully wrote down the code, took the keys, and put them in her handbag. Next to her, Len looked like a puppy, wagging his tail, perpetually waiting for her orders and perhaps even her strokes, which I imagined were rare. My doubts were confirmed that very night, after Melody had gone to bed — she would disappear into her quarters early, around nine. We were both sitting in the living room. Timidly, Len told me he hadn't been following *In Gad* for a while now. I pretended to be surprised, "Really? Do you want me to give you a copy of the series?"

He seemed uneasy, "Maybe we could just watch a few episodes?"

"Tonight?"

His face lit up, like an adolescent hearing his parents will leave him the house for a night. "We've got all night, no?"

I didn't know what to think. "You're serious?"

He nodded. "Well, sure. Why not?"

I walked to the television set. Thinking of the unpleasant conversation I had had with Melody that morning, what she had said about his admiration, just thrown it in my face, something that hurt more than any physical blow. At least Len had some autonomy left — she hated the series, he still liked it. Len wasn't as easily influenced as I thought, the complicity between us was still there. I just needed to watch him on the couch, smiling to his ears, to realize it. Ann was right. I'd been too tense since they got here, making a scene out of everything, which was out of character for me.

Animated, Len told me he stopped watching the series almost a year ago. I picked the right tape. As I slid it into the VCR, my back to him, I tried to gauge his reaction, "Not Melody's sort of show, right?"

"Oh, if you knew what she thought of it, terrible!" He laughed, I didn't. "You know, she works for a pro-life organization. It's important to her, very important. No need to tell you what she thinks of Chastity."

"And what do you think?"

He laughed again, though not as heartily. "Let's just say Gad is my favorite. Chastity, I mean, I can laugh, of course, it's comedy and all, but...." He searched for his words, couldn't find them. After a moment, he continued, "You know, Melody keeps telling me I almost wasn't born. You can't say she's wrong about that."

I shivered. No, you couldn't say she was wrong on that point. Gathering my courage, I said, "Why are you with her, Len?"

He hesitated for a moment, then looked me straight in the eyes. "She's helping me pay for my sins. She helped me fight my demons. She made me lose all the anger I had in me. Things are better with Lynn, and I've got Cody and Julia back. You should see them when they spend the week with their father. Melody helps me feel less guilty about what happened. She helps me to do good, something I never really did in my life. Do you understand?"

What could I reply? That Melody controlled him to such an extent he seemed only a shadow of his former self? A weak, castrated man? Who might just wake up one day more miserable than he'd ever been with Lynn?

He added, "You'll never believe me, but we haven't slept together. We're waiting until marriage. We're going to get married and have children. I'm getting a new beginning, Romain!"

"That's ... wonderful ..." I stammered.

Shook up, I pressed play. Season 3, Episode 4. Coincidentally or not, the show opened with Chastity and her father Gad.

"You want me to fast forward?" I asked.

"No way!" He pointed his finger towards the ceiling. "I'm free tonight. She's sleeping."

8

Len and Melody were married in the spring of 1998. It was an intimate affair, Len explained, embarrassed, over the phone. Only his adoptive parents and Melody's parents would be there. I was understanding, "Of course, yes, I see ... Anyway, Ann and I are so busy...." With just a bit too much enthusiasm to hide my deep disappointment.

A son marrying, not inviting his father.

"Where did I go wrong, Ann?"

Ann was as surprised as I was. And deeply saddened at being separated from Cody and Julia since Len had taken up with Melody. Sometimes she sent them a note and a little present when they were at Lynn's, or spoke on the phone with them, unbeknownst to Len, of course. But it was a balancing act, as Ann would say.

"You didn't fail, Romain. Len is still fragile. He's getting his life back on track. Let's just hope he isn't as sure about the decision he's making as he looks. Maybe that's why he doesn't want us to be there."

"But I'm his father; I should be there to help him see what he's getting into."

"He isn't twelve, Romain. He's thirty-five."

After the wedding, Len became even more distant. If I called him — them, now — I could tell by his tone whether she was behind him telling him to hang up. I encountered constant excuses

— "Melody needs the phone" or "I'm waiting for a call from work" or "Sorry, Romain, I need to go to the other end of town, I'm expected." Or worse still, "The garbage truck is coming, and I need to take out the trash." I'd seen his building — I'd found his apartment for him! — and you put the trash down a chute at the end of the hallway.

After a time, Len stopped calling.

There was no way I was going to give up. Every week I called him at different times, and on different days, so that he wouldn't be able to think, *It must be Romain; I'll let it ring.* But nine times out of ten, I'd get the answering machine: "Hi, you've reached Len, Melody, Cody, and Julia...." And each time, it felt it like a blow.

Then, one morning, at seven, he picked up immediately, like a child hoping for a surprise.

"Hello?"

"Len?"

A long silence. "It's early, Romain. Melody and the children are still sleeping."

"We need to talk. We can't keep up like this."

"There's nothing to say. You're busy, I'm busy."

"Bullshit! You're avoiding me, Len! And I don't understand why!"

He sighed loudly. After a time, he said, "Listen, I need to tell you something...."

I thought I was dreaming. My son, finally receptive? Len, I wanted to say before he could go any further.... Len, my son ... What about all the great time we spent together? Remember how you loved coming to Los Angeles.... Our nights out in great restaurants ... Dodger Stadium, chowing down hot dogs, our shouts and jeers.... And your sincere laughter, the laughter of a man who knows how to enjoy himself.... Len! Shit! What's going on with you, son! This woman is going to kill you! And while all these thoughts were going through my head, a storm in my mind that I didn't want to reveal for fear that all my words would rush out at once, Len admitted, stammering, that he'd written an article on *In Gad We Trust.*

"How could you have written an article if you haven't been watching it?"

"It's about the reactions of parents in Alberta."

"I guess it isn't very flattering?"

"You could say that."

"That's your right." Again, a heavy silence. "Can you send me a copy?"

"If you want. I need to go now. I'm expecting a call."

I never got the article. I asked Moïse at the *New York Times* to get a faxed copy from the *Calgary Herald*. He sent it to me with a note. "In terms of journalistic rigour I've seen better." Indeed, Len could easily be accused of conflict of interest — he didn't even mention that he was my son or that he had close ties to evangelical churches.

In Gad We Trust: An Offensive Show
By Len Albiston

"Blasphemous." "A bad example for our children." The Hollywood TV show *In Gad We Trust* is raising the ire of Alberta parents.

"We are determined to prevent this poison from entering our homes and infecting our defenceless children," says pastor John Reimer, the man behind a petition circulating throughout the province, which has accrued some thirty thousand signatures so far. Yesterday, hundreds of scandalized parents demonstrated on his initiative, in front of Zion Evangelical Baptist Church in Calgary. They denounced the trivialization of abortion that the series promotes.

"Chastity's character is criminal!" Helen Daly, of the Family Research Council, says. "It turns the clock back decades on the efforts to get adolescents to treat their sexuality seriously. How many times has Chastity suffered through an abortion since the beginning of this scandalous show? Ten, fifteen times? It's completely irresponsible!" …

Over the next few weeks, demonstrations against *In Gad We Trust* will be held in Calgary, Edmonton, Red Deer, and Lethbridge. Meanwhile, pastor Reimer is inviting parents to cancel their subscription to It's All Comedy! and send their complaints to the cable network's advertisers.…

Does television threaten the moral values parents try to inculcate in their children? Yes. An example? It's All Comedy!, Wednesdays at nine.

Of course, the article infuriated me. I was shocked, even. Impossible to not think of his happy laugh that night we watched *In Gad* while the girls were sleeping. Only Melody could have pushed him down this path.

The next morning, at six-fifty, I called him. As I hoped, he picked up on the first ring.

"Have you seen the time?"

"I read your article, Len.…" On the other end of the line, silence. "You know, I'll survive.…" And I continued, speaking calmly but at length, not giving him time to interrupt me. Weighing my words so as not to insult him. A father speaking to his son. A father trying to bring his child back "on the right path." Explaining that it didn't seem like him, writing such an article, so far removed from his talent as a journalist, and that, in my opinion, there must have been "a little" of Melody behind it, and that.…

"Leave Melody out of this, will you?"

"Len…."

"Whatever Melody does, you've always got a bone to pick."

"Len, I'm your father, and…."

"And what?"

And I don't know why — frustration? anger I had contained all this time? — I said that as far as I was concerned, Melody was destroying his life, like the bottles of Jack Daniels used to. He didn't say a word, I could only hear him breathing heavily. I knew I'd done irreversible damage. I looked for something, anything to say that might erase the words I'd just spoken. I didn't have the chance. Len declared, in a voice as cutting as broken glass, "You just insulted the woman I love. We've got nothing left to say to each other."

And he hung up.

Len had just kicked me out of his life.

9

"We've got nothing left to say to each other."

As if he'd said, *I gave you a chance, and you screwed it up.* Or, *I owe you nothing....*

I was down for days; Ann was as devastated as I was, trying to console me, "You'll end up talking to each other, and everything will be like it was before." But I knew it wouldn't happen. That Len wouldn't come back.

I was broken.

I'd become more and more preoccupied since the publication of Len's article. Obsessive even. And so I asked to see all of the complaints It's All Comedy! had received about *In Gad*. Josh, Ab, Michael, all of the higher-ups at the network told me not to do it, "It's our job to deal with complaints, Roman, not yours." But I insisted, became aggressive about it. Dick told me that "all of the bullshit is going to influence you. You'll start censoring yourself." But I was stubborn, and I read piles and piles of complaints, some polite, others insulting, some threatening. I read through them quickly, almost absent-mindedly. I was looking for ... *what?* I needed to know ... *what exactly?* Two-thirds of them were about Chastity, some focused on Dylan, her gay brother, and the rest on the show more generally, deemed offensive to all Christians.

Was Len right to be angry at me? All these people agreed with him!

"Stop worrying about it," Dick said. "You're seeing problems where there are none. It's normal to receive complaints. Everyone has a right to their own opinion. It's the sign of a healthy democracy."

And so I re-read the scripts for season 1 (1995), 2 (1996), 3 (1997), 4 (1998) and counted the number of times Chastity had gone to Doctor Feltheimer's office.

How many times has Chastity suffered through an abortion since the beginning of this scandalous show? Ten, fifteen times?

No. *Five* times. The woman Len interviewed had exaggerated the facts, and he hadn't taken the time to correct her.

Of course not, it made for a better story that way.

I told Dick, "And what if Chastity no longer had any abortions? What if she became an advocate for celibacy? I mean it's in her name, right?"

"If you do that, you'll give these fucking idiots the win."

My son? An idiot?

"Have you thought of the women who want children and aren't able to? How do you think they feel about Chastity?"

"Roman, you're losing it. You need to rest, to get out of your own way. You need to forget Len a little. We're making a comedy for fuck's sake!"

10

Was it fatigue? Overwork? For a short moment, I even thought it might have been hallucinations.

Season 5 of *In Gad We Trust* represented new challenges for the team. We had to refresh our ideas, avoid repeating ourselves and especially avoid going for the cheap laugh. We needed to push the plot forward without using over-the-top scenes, and we wouldn't give up on Chastity's pregnancies. Josh and the others had warned me, "The ratings are holding. We're not changing a winning formula." Bill Doran, the actor playing Gad Paradise, also needed to be better directed — over time, he had started playing a caricature of his own creation, and the character lost credibility because of it. I was exhausted. Exhausted from writing scene after scene, always under pressure. Exhausted by It's All Comedy!'s constant requirement. Exhausted at having lost Len without ever having an opportunity to explain myself, face to face. Exhausted to the point that I was thinking of just dropping everything and taking Ann for a long vacation. But Dick, always full of energy, kept telling me, "We need to aim for a sixth season. It's been the plan all along. After that, you'll be a free man."

It was almost noon, on a warm summer day. As I left the studio in

La Brea, my eyes were drawn to a strange woman in the parking lot behind the building. A youngish woman — though it was hard to say at a distance — with long red hair, wearing a diaphanous white dress with kimono sleeves, the kind of caftan that a goddess might wear in a Greek tragedy. Her back was to me, near the Pathfinder, as if she was leaning against it for fear of fainting. I hurried towards her, asking her in a loud voice whether she needed help. She turned to me brusquely, her eyes hidden behind large black glasses, an enigmatic smile dancing on her face. I noticed the round belly of a pregnant woman, but there was something that didn't fit, I couldn't quite say what, a visual hitch the size of a hibiscus flower but dark red, almost brown, there under her belly, right at the pubis. It was too strange for me to look away, and by the time I understood what was happening, that this woman was losing her baby right before me, my God, I ran towards her to help, she turned and fled towards a nearby supermarket. A delivery truck passed between us, and I lost sight of her. The woman simply disappeared in the landscape of asphalt and concrete, like a fleeting thought soon forgotten.

How could a woman having a miscarriage run like that? Had I scared her? *Had I dreamt the whole thing?*

I couldn't say.

Deeply shaken, I spent the next few days combing over the few blocks around the studio, looking for clues and drops of blood. I scanned the local news pages of every newspaper, fearing that I would see a headline like: WOMAN FOUND AFTER BLEEDING TO DEATH IN ALLEY or WOMAN'S BODY AND HER FETUS FOUND DEAD BY PASSERBY. But nothing.

"Stop thinking about it," Dick said.

"You think I'm going nuts?"

"No. You're just working too hard. Success can lead to exhaustion. It happens to sensitive people like you. Come on. Let's go eat at Spago's. It'll make you feel better."

Then, a few days after the mysterious apparition of the red-headed woman, the demonstrators in front of It's All Comedy!

grew in numbers and aggression. They were different from the passive, innocuous people who'd been there for two years now, with their faces that had become familiar, their signs and the pamphlets they distributed to passersby on La Brea when they weren't talking with one another, sitting on iceboxes or folding chairs. We had gotten used to them, didn't see them anymore, sometimes even waved at them when we passed. Dick and Matt no longer insulted them as they walked by, and hadn't in a while. But these new demonstrators were of a different breed. Younger, more aggressive. *Pro-life* activists — what a ridiculous title they gave themselves, as if they were for life and others were against it — carrying horrifying signs with pictures of dismembered babies, bodies without heads. The same sort of people you find standing in front of abortion clinics across the country, shouting, intimidating medical staff and patients, finding out where doctors live in order to harass them, or, in some cases, kill them. In Florida, Massachusetts, New York State, and, most recently, Houston, Texas, doctors had actually been murdered. In Texas, the killer shot and killed a doctor through the window of his home, in front of the man's seven-year-old daughter. When it was reported in the news, I couldn't help thinking of Melody. Wasn't she an activist for a *pro-life* group? Had she been disgusted by the murder? Or did she believe, like some activists interviewed on television, that the Houston doctor, "murderer of thousands of babies," had reaped what he'd sown?

And what did Len think of all of this?

All day, in front of the La Brea studio, there were a dozen men and women taking shifts under an intense sun, their signs enough to send a shiver down your spine: ABORTION IS MURDER! IN GAD WE TRUST IS INCITEMENT TO MURDER! We walked through the thicket with our eyes down, as they stared at us, faces contorted with hate.

"Bums," Dick said, indignant. "Nothing else to do but bother honest people trying to work for a living."

We were wrong to think they were harmless. The white stucco building gave us a false sense of security — we called it The Bunker, after all. At one point a group of lunatics managed to break into the building and find the stage where we filmed the scenes that took place in Gad's ministry. The altar, the pistol in its Plexiglas box. No one was there at the time, except for a janitor who alerted security guards and the police. Five people, two men and three women, were arrested.

Then they went after Avril Page, the young woman who played Chastity. Poor Avril. A talented young woman, soft-spoken, completely transformed in front of the camera. It was strange to see her play the insolent, arrogant Chastity with such ease when we knew that in "real life" she was a timid girl, constantly afraid she was bothering other people, a rare quality in an actress. We attributed her lack of self-assurance to her youth, and worked to help her gain confidence. "Impostor's syndrome," Ann diagnosed. Indeed, her parents told us that a lot of students were jealous of her at school and Avril, who hated confrontation, usually reacted by belittling what she did.

And now she played the most controversial and thankless role in the show, the one that led to the most complaints, some bad enough to send a shiver down your spine. There was even talk of putting us under police protection.

She wished she could give a piece of her mind to these lunatics, but she simply couldn't. She was paralyzed by the fear of offending them.

In the darkness, they lay in wait for her in the parking lot. Avril had left by the back door, like we all did now since the demonstrators had set up camp on the sidewalk. We couldn't move them; they were protected by the First Amendment. Since the incident in which a handful had breached the building, It's All Comedy! had hired additional security guards, there twenty-four hours a day, but where were they that night? *Where were they?*

Avril had finished her scenes for the day, but we still had one to shoot without her, so she was the first to leave. "You'll be okay, Avril?" Ann asked. "Sure, sure. Don't worry on my account. See you tomorrow!" She gave us a radiant smile, despite having worked for ten hours straight. She grabbed her white Ralph Lauren bag and left.

Two women and a man were waiting for her. They appeared out of nowhere, Avril would later tell the police. A woman of about forty and another, younger woman, more aggressive. They were accompanied by a wild-eyed man, clearly of limited intelligence, who kept repeating, non-stop, "Abortion is murder.... Because of you, America will feel the wrath of God's judgment...."

"Leave me alone," Avril replied.

But they followed her. When she stepped up her pace, they stepped up theirs. "Please, I'm only an actress. Leave me alone." They continued their pursuit anyway, and the incantations of the young man became more feverish. She was about to run, but fear paralyzed her. She thought of calling us on her cell phone, but didn't dare. She didn't want to offend them. "Offend them?" I would later say, furious. She continued to walk quickly towards her car, trembling like a leaf. The three lunatics followed her closely, threatening, and the inhuman voice of the simpleton became a desperate moan that covered her in a cold sweat. "Because of you, America will feel the wrath of God's judgment...."

Her hands shaking, she opened the door of her Honda Civic and found refuge inside. The two women began slamming their palms against the windows, insulting her. Terrorized, she felt a scream bubble up inside her. She thought of calling the security guards. That's when she noticed something on her hood, something strange and shapeless, something wet, sticky ... Blood? Something that looked like ... a *baby*? Like those pictures on their signs. *An aborted baby?*

||

There were about a hundred people that evening in front of the Beverly Hilton, where the amfAR gala was taking place. A worthwhile gala, despite the price tag — twenty-five thousand dollars a table. I could still remember how offended Melody had been months earlier. *AIDS isn't an accident or one of life's trials. It's God's just punishment.* The revolting things Melody had said repeated here by dozens of lunatics, loudly and furiously invoking the wrath of God, "AIDS is the punishment! Repent and you will be saved!"

Along Wilshire Boulevard, policemen were waiting in their cars to intervene if needed. Meanwhile, amfAR's guests in their evening wear hurried into the hotel, heads held high, pretending that God's troublemakers didn't exist.

"Come on!" Ann said, pulling on my arm. "They're waiting for us in there."

I couldn't stop staring at the crowd of lunatics, perhaps unconsciously looking for Melody and … Len? (Would Len participate in such a demonstration? To make Melody happy? The idea sent a shiver down my spine.) I also thought of Avril, whom the security guards, back from a break at a nearby Taco Bell, had to rescue in the poorly lit parking lot. They were only gone five minutes, ten at most. "You were shooting a scene," the two imbeciles pleaded. "We couldn't know the girl would leave." They found Avril in her Honda Civic, in tears, almost hysterical, and hadn't been quick enough to arrest her three tormentors who fled on foot. They were fired on the spot and replaced the very next day by ex-Marines who had fought in the Gulf. "They've got blood on their hands, those guys." Dick had said. "It should reassure us."

Reassure us?

Then, a familiar silhouette dragged me brutally out of my thoughts. There, in front of the Beverly Hilton, in the middle of the crowd.

"Romain, what is it?"

Before Ann could stop me, I ran, blood rushing to my temples. *Who is she? What is she doing here?* The same white dress with the kimono sleeves. The same red hair, gleaming like a helmet. The same face hidden behind black glasses. The same round belly, *stained with blood?* "Romain!" Ann howled. Alerted, the redheaded woman ran down Wilshire Boulevard. I thought only a man could run that fast. A black car with tinted windows was waiting for her, she jumped inside, and the driver sped off.

"Romain, what are you doing?"

"The woman, Ann ... The woman I spoke to you about...."

"What woman?"

Ann was losing her cool. I felt shaken to the core. Who was this grotesque character? And what did she want of me? Suddenly, a group of demonstrators surrounded us, brandishing horrible signs showing monstrous fetuses, their shouts amplified by a megaphone, "Murderers! Murderers! Let him who sheds innocent blood for gain be damned!" I felt a heavy hand on my shoulder. "Hey, don't just stand around here." It was Dick. "I don't think you want to speak with them...." He gestured towards a handful of photographers and cameramen not too far away from us. "And you don't want to be on the news for this. Getting shouted out while you stand around in a tuxedo. So please, come with me."

That night, at the Beverly Hilton, while everyone was having a good time, while movie stars were hobnobbing with rich donors, while Liz Taylor, a tireless sponsor of amfAR, outrageously made up and covered in jewels, spoke in front of a crowded room, I simply wasn't there anymore, wasn't listening.

I'd been so happy to buy the expensive tickets for my friends. We were supposed to spend a nice evening together, Ann, Dick, my friend Bobby from San Francisco and his friend Dwayne, as well as Josh, Adriana, Matt and his wife, and Ab Chertoff.

From time to time, Ann, sensing my distraction, would glance at me questioningly, *What's wrong?* Ann had been in a great mood for the past few weeks, loving, full of desire for me, but I was so preoccupied with the demonstrators, I was barely receptive to her at all. Ann was radiant, serene. And she had a curious attitude recently, as if she wanted to tell me something, but couldn't quite find the words. "Romain?" "Yes?" A moment's pause, "Oh, forget it," with an enigmatic half-moon smile, as if she had a surprise in store for me.

Her eyes, that night! And that black dress with an open back that fit her marvelously, fit her beautiful hips and that small, sexy midriff of hers, which seemed slightly swollen that evening, though it didn't seem to bother her. She spent so much time at the gym to keep it flat! The small suggestive roundness charmed me, enhanced by her shimmering dress bought just for the occasion. Men looked at her, devoured her with their eyes. Ann Heller. My woman. The woman I loved. Why weren't we married? It had never seemed important, but perhaps we'd been wrong never to discuss it. "Romain?" She said. "What's wrong? Smile a little. It's a nice evening." I smiled at her. Bobby and Dwayne were talking about the house they had just bought in Russian Hill in San Francisco, showing off pictures, while Dick mined his abundant repertoire of old bachelor's jokes, "My wife? She's at home. Someone's got to wash the floors, right?"

I was probably overreacting. This wasn't the first time someone was tarred and feathered publicly for a work of art. What about Martin Scorsese and Universal, or Salman Rushdie, condemned to live in hiding for fear of being assassinated? I shivered. *We live in a civilized country. It isn't the same thing.* Though was that really the case? Who was the redheaded woman? A man in a dress? A madman after me? Someone who could go after Avril?

"Romain? Make an effort, you look bored."

"Sorry, Ann."

I forced a smile and turned towards my friends to suggest a toast, but ... to what? "To freedom of speech!" Dick offered. And everyone together, "To freedom of speech!"

I let Ann drive home. "Too tired," I said. She looked at me without speaking for a moment, worry on her face. "Romain, you're letting yourself be affected by these people. Don't give them importance they don't deserve."

She started up my new Audi with an exasperated look. Next to us, Dick waved from his Mercedes. Bobby and Dwayne had gone up to their room.

Wilshire Boulevard, Santa Monica Boulevard ... in the rear-view mirror I watched headlights trailing us. *And what if we were followed?* What did I think I would see? Actually, what was I afraid to see? The black car the redheaded woman had jumped in? It was far too dark to see anything, anyway.

"Romain?" Ann said. "Yes?" I answered, my thoughts elsewhere, my eyes on the rear-view mirror. Once again, she repeated, "Oh, never mind," this time with a note of anxiety in her voice.

I said, "What? What do you want to tell me Ann?"

She hesitated for a moment before saying, "Oh, nothing. I just wanted to say that Bobby and Dwayne seem to have a beautiful home. It would be nice to visit them in San Francisco, right? It would do us good to get out of town."

Is that really what she wanted to tell me? I answered noncommittally, "Yes, sure ... it's a good idea...."

She turned left on La Cienega Boulevard before taking Sunset Boulevard, and, to my great relief, the car that had been following us continued along Santa Monica Boulevard. I tried to laugh about it, telling myself, *What's going on, old man? Get a grip!* Ann looked worried now.

Why didn't you tell me, Ann? Why did you wait until it was too late?

Yes, we need to fight for what we believe in. But what happens when it isn't you who suffers, but those you love?

At the gala at the Hilton, I began making modifications to the next episodes of *In Gad* in my mind. Whatever Josh and the others might think, I would make changes to Chastity's character, put an end to her repeated pregnancies and abortions. She'd become an advocate for abstinence. Yes, Chastity Paradise, missionary for chastity, going around to schools to preach the good news. Avril and her parents would be reassured, the public and the critics would say it was a stroke of genius — Roman Carr denouncing the sexual counter-revolution in American schools. Yes, that's what I would do.

At the house, all the way up Appian Way, Ann turned pale when she realized the alarm system hadn't been activated.

"Did you forget, Romain?"

"No, I don't think so…. Listen I can't remember … I probably thought I put it on and then forgot."

"Forgot, that would be a first."

I was convinced I had set it. "I forgot," I lied. "I remember now."

In truth, I had no idea.

"I don't like this, Romain…."

"There's nothing to be afraid of, Ann."

We walked into the house, hesitant. I went first, to reassure Ann. Looked through every room and closet, discreetly, so as not to scare her. Thinking of the redheaded woman and the lunatics that had begun gravitating to me.

That night, it took me a long time to fall asleep.

That night, my mind wasn't easy at all.

12

"What a feast!"

The next evening, we invited Bobby, Dwayne, and Dick for supper, and I promised myself I'd be in a good mood. Ann had worked hard to prepare a fantastic meal.

"I want it to be a celebration, Romain!"

"Why? It's nobody's birthday."

"And why not? And anyway we almost never see Bobby."

It would have been hard to not be in a good mood surrounded by Dick and Bobby, jokingly chatting about the Lewinsky affair. Far away in the valley, the smog that covered L.A. had been set alight by the setting sun, about to dip into the Pacific.

"Monica Lewinsky. Paula Jones. The uglier they are," Dick said, "the more that idiot Clinton goes after them!"

"Ugly?" Bobby said. "He doesn't care. He just closes his eyes. We men have a great talent for abstraction when it comes to sex."

Next to Bobby, Dwayne pretended to be offended. Bobby went on, "Kenneth Starr and his gang of inquisitors believe they'll have Clinton's head. I think it'll just turn against the damn Republicans."

"Republicans!" Dwayne rolled his eyes. "Why is no one making a racket about Newt Gingrich's infidelities?"

"Because he isn't the President of the United States of America," I said.

Dick continued, excited, "Jack Kennedy did far worse. Sam Giancana got his women for him. Everyone knew it, the reporters knew it, but it wasn't judged to be of public interest, and I agree."

"But it is of public interest!" Ann countered. "If the President uses his penis before his brain, anyone can blackmail him. Our enemies across the globe have certainly learned a lot thanks to this pathetic story."

Dick shook his head. "Reason will prevail in this beautiful country of ours. The goddamn vultures will never successfully excommunicate Clinton. Americans are happy about what he's done for the economy. Our country has never known such prosperity, not since the Second World War. I raise my glass to Bill Clinton."

And we all raised our glasses to Bill Clinton.

"Come on," Ann whispered in my ear.

I followed Ann, particularly radiant that evening, into the kitchen, smelling her perfume in her wake, looking at her back with desire, the nape of her neck exposed by the bun she made with her hair. I wanted to kiss her. There was something flamboyant in her eyes, in her smile, like a warm afternoon sun. "I love you," I said. She turned and giggled with pleasure. In the kitchen, where she had spent the day working, the makings of a feast were revealed — foie gras, oysters, prime rib, and almond chocolate cake she had just taken out of the oven. I was extremely hungry all of a sudden. "Romain?" This time she didn't say "never mind." No, this time she said in a small, uncertain voice, "I've got something to tell you, but not now. Tonight, when everyone's gone." Worried, I asked, "Nothing serious, I hope?" She smiled. "No, you'll see. It can wait."

It can wait.

Someone rang the doorbell.

"Who is it?" Ann asked, surprised.

"I don't know."

"At dinnertime?"

"I'll go see."

I kissed her and left the kitchen. From the terrace, Dick shouted out.

"With the money you're making, maybe it's time to get some help, eh?"

"I won't change my habits for money, Dick! Being bourgeois kills creativity!"

Laughter. The bell rang a second time. "Coming, coming...." Who could be so irritating at supper time?

I opened the door. There was no one there. The neighbour's kids, probably. They used to be nice, well-mannered kids but had transformed into bothersome teenagers. Last week, they had set fire to the garbage can of another neighbour. A garbage fire in New York isn't a big deal, but in L.A., swept by the warm, circular Santa Ana winds that get their energy from the deserts, a garbage fire can burn down an entire neighbourhood, threaten lives.

"Who is it?" Ann said from the living room.

No one, I was about to answer, until I noticed the front steps.

Blood. A viscous mess of blood, spreading so quickly I backed up as you do when a sudden wave crashes at your feet with unexpected strength. In the middle of the puddle, something shapeless, sticky ... a sort of dog without hair, with hooves ... a calf fetus? Like the one on the hood of Avril's Honda Civic?

Suddenly nauseous, I was about to step back into the house to alert the cops when the woman appeared at the bottom of the steps, the same redheaded woman with her heavy belly, her white tunic stained with blood and her black glasses. My heart was beating frantically. What was she holding in her hands, pointed at me? A ... gun? A real one? Behind me, the sounds of a door being pulled open. "Romain? Who is it?" A glimpse of Ann's stupefied face. My legs buckled under me, the shock of my torso hitting the blood-covered cement. The sounds of shots, one, two, a deafening crack. I felt Ann's body collapse on mine.

VI

MOÏSE

I

My jacket collar was raised against the chill as I walked in Central
Park. Quick steps, hands balled up in my pockets, with no other
goal but to reduce my blood pressure, which I kept under control
only through medication. Almost five years and these little green
pills — and other pills too — were saving my life, apparently. Since
Ann's murder in 1998. It was now 2003. Years had passed, meaningless time, a new millennium entered without a hiccup, despite
the anticipated computer apocalypse. For me, the blow had come
before, after which the world had stopped. It could have been six
months or twenty years since I'd been back in New York. Time
meant nothing to me now.

To calm myself, I slowed down as I approached the Jackie
O Reservoir. The most stable element of my life at that point
might have been this great stretch of water, which I likened to an
inland sea. I gazed on the waters every day from my apartment
on the ninth storey of the St. Urban on Central Park West. It was
April, the cherry trees in full bloom, a miracle each spring, the
pink spots before the leaves came, like a female presence. Joggers,
their ears covered with headphones, didn't seem to notice life
blooming. I was cold, but shook with anger. Because of Moïse.
Another one of our fights, this one more serious. Since September
11, to my astonishment, I had discovered a reactionary side to
my friend — "They don't bring the war to us! We bring the war

to them!" Moïse had become radicalized, letting his emotions cloud his judgment. You could chalk a lot of things up to the attacks, a break in History, like the ones the world wars had produced. There was a before and an after, a pre- and a post-, and in the after, it seemed like some New Yorkers had lost their ability to think critically. Moïse was one of them. This cynicism, this arrogance of his, it was a typical New York thing. And until then, it had protected the inhabitants of the city from the daily aggressions of a place that was, in truth, infernal. But all of it had fallen down with the Twin Towers, making room instead for fear and a desire for vengeance.

"You can't understand! You're *not American!*"

That's what he had yelled at me an hour earlier at my house. God only knew that in these times of suspicion and exaggerated patriotism which had reached new heights since George W. Bush had declared his absurd war in Iraq, being told that you weren't American was nothing less than an insult, or, worse still, a curse. I'd been living in the States for forty years — been a citizen since 1979 — and Moïse had the nerve to tell me I wasn't American, exactly like he had done in 1966 in his East Harlem apartment, when he pushed me with a sneer as he waited, terrorized and dead drunk, for the army to hand down his sentence. Part of his life's work had been to denounce that war. So, what about this one?

"No? Not American? So what I am then?"

He hadn't answered, preferring to stare at the tips of his shoes. I continued, furious, "If I don't think like you … *Americans*, I'm not one of you, is that it? Either *with you* or *with the terrorists*, like your good friend George Bush so eloquently put it!"

Incensed, Moïse grabbed his coat and left, slamming the door behind him. I heard him get into the old elevator at the end of the corridor, then from the window watched him jump into a taxi, full of rage, gesticulating like a broken weather vane.

A part of me was simply stunned, the other tried to comprehend: Moïse the pacifist, Moïse the draft dodger, giving his support to this warmonger obsessed with Iraq and its oil? Because they were afraid, because they'd been hit *on home soil — you can't understand, you're not American!* — Moïse and a majority of Americans were ready to accept as incontrovertible truth the damned lies about Saddam Hussein's weapons of mass destruction, impressed by Colin Powell's wild demonstration at the UN, and despite the UN inspectors saying that Iraq was collaborating with the inspection, that there was no need to get carried away. And Moïse, a reporter at the prestigious *New York Times*, was only asking me to believe. How could it be?

"My God, Moïse! Remember the Tonkin incident in 1964! You were the first to say it was all lies! Same shit, different day! It smells even worse today than it did then!"

He was pacing in the apartment. His eyes didn't leave the copy of the *New Yorker,* which he had brought over and thrown on the table, eyes filled with rage, as if to say, *how could you do this to me?*

I said, trying to stay calm, "I wrote what I think — that this war is as dirty and immoral as Vietnam."

"It isn't the same! We haven't been attacked like this since Pearl Harbor!"

"Who attacked us? Bin Laden and Al-Qaeda! So why go into Iraq? What does Saddam Hussein have to do with Bin Laden?"

"They want to destroy us! They want to destroy America!"

Had I heard him right? I couldn't believe my ears. His eyes glowed with rage, his almost bald head covered in sweat. I continued, outraged, "That's precisely what all these people you hated back in the day — LBJ, McNamara, Agnew, Nixon — said about *Communists,* 'they want to destroy America.'"

He stiffened, waved me off, as if he didn't want to waste another minute with an imbecile. "Stop bringing everything back to Vietnam! This time we're not killing innocent farmers! This time, we'll destroy their weapons, hit identified targets."

I burst out laughing, "You, the reporter at the *New York Times*? You believe that?"

That's when he tightened his fists and looked at me, full of contempt, "You can't understand, you're not American!"

Had the heavy cloud of ash and smoke that covered New York after the fall of the World Trade Center altered the judgment of its inhabitants? Had the dust as fine as talcum powder that stuck to our hair, our skin, our clothes, that we had breathed and eaten for days, that we later learned was toxic, lethal and that had, in fact, led to the deaths of dozens of firemen, made thousands of people sick, had this apocalyptic dust made some of us mad?

That fateful morning, deeply distressed, Moïse and I had spoken briefly on the phone just before the city's communications infrastructure went down. Outside, the deafening scream of thousands of sirens. From my window, southern Manhattan and part of the sky disappeared in a heavy cloud of yellow smoke, while footage of the two planes smashing into the towers played in a continuous loop on my television, the second plane destroying all doubt about the first.

"I ... I can't believe it ..." Moïse said. "It's a nightmare...." He was interrupted, someone at his office at the *Times* began speaking to him, the panicked voice of a man. "I've got to go, Romain. It's madness here. I've got a lot of work to do...."

It was impossible to speak to him after. He spent the rest of the week working and sleeping at the *Times* office. I managed to speak to Louise. She went to Staten Island to a friend's house, unable to sleep alone in their own home. I told myself she might have liked to stay at my place at the St. Urban, in my eight-room apartment I still hadn't had the energy to furnish. But who would have wanted a depressed man to console them in September 2001?

In the days following the attacks, I left my place, at 88th and Central Park West, walked to Ground Zero — at least as far as they let me — stupefied like everyone else, lingering around the pictures of the missing posted at major intersections, thinking obsessively of all these men and women who died there, their bodies never to be discovered, gone in the smoke that floated over the city. So many innocents killed, like Ann, another innocent, had been killed. My distress mixed with the distress of the families and loved ones of the three thousand people who had died. Survivors staggering, their eyes tormented, waiting … *for what?* Wondering, simply, *why?* But there was no answer. Among the pictures, hundreds of young women of Ann's age, someone even looked like her a little, her eyes and smile filled with the same light of life, and I thought of Ann, feeling so close to her, as if I needed the horrible event to help me truly begin the grieving process, to actually accept that she wouldn't come back, more than three years after her death.

Federal agents had worked well and quickly. James F. Lovell was arrested a few days after the murder, in a motel in New Mexico. I was shocked to discover the face of her assassin. Twenty-seven years old, his cheeks covered in pimples, the frail body of a prepubescent boy, almost a child. Images replayed constantly on the television, enough to make me crazy, but I couldn't look away. As if I was waiting for us to look in each other's eyes. Waiting for an apology. He had to be remorseful, right? But nothing, always the same images, made meaningless by their repeated broadcast. The same absent smile, same white, spotted skin, same slumped shoulders, same delicate wrists imprisoned in handcuffs that were too big for him, escorted by two cops from a cheap motel room, in Truth or Consequences, a city that sounded like a cruel joke.

In the trunk of his Chevrolet Cavalier, the police discovered the .32 Smith & Wesson that had killed Ann, as well as a few newspaper articles on me and a woman's outfit. He offered no resistance and quickly admitted his guilt, enabling me to avoid a painful trial. James F. Lovell received the death penalty for two counts of murder.

And that's how I learned the unspeakable news that Ann was two months pregnant. That's what she had been trying to tell me for days, her beautiful face full of optimism, and what she had promised to tell me that very night as we stood in our kitchen, while our friends talked and laughed on the terrace. *I've got something to tell you, but not now. Tonight, when everyone's gone ... It can wait.*

Often, I tried to think about the question as honestly as possible, trying to abstract the feeling of loss, trying not to answer with the broken heart that wanted to say anything just for Ann to still be alive — how would I have reacted, that night, once Dick, Bobby, and Dwayne had left, once we were alone in the kitchen filling the dishwasher with dirty glasses and plates? She would have looked at me, an apron covering the slightly swollen belly I had failed to notice, "I'm pregnant, Romain."

Would I have been joyful? Terrified? Or would I have said something like, "As long as you help me become a model father this time"?

I don't know.

UNSTABLE PRO-LIFE ACTIVIST ARRESTED
IN TRUTH OR CONSEQUENCES
FOR MURDER OF PREGNANT WOMAN

A grotesque headline, almost comical. Enough to make you laugh. Truth or Consequences. Dozens of live news reports covering Ann's murder. And they'd always mention the origin of the idiotic name of the town, a reference to an old game show. Reality wasn't any more real than fiction; the two are always intertwined. The same way you could kill in this country because you felt offended by Chastity, a character that came out of my imagination, out of Ann and me, together.

Ann's family was deeply offended that I hadn't gone to the funeral, her mother especially, but it was simply beyond me. And then there was the email from Judd, Ann's nephew, that had cut me deeply, "Good riddance. We'll never see you again."

Devastated, I left Los Angeles, letting my lawyers take care of everything however they saw fit. I couldn't bear facing off against journalists excited by the smell of fresh blood, "Mr. Carr, does James F. Lovell deserve the death sentence?" The state of California imposed it in gruesome murder cases like this one, but I'd always been against the death penalty and would remain so. Peace through vengeance is an illusion. And the pain I felt wouldn't cease because the murderer's heart wasn't beating.

Despite Dick and Josh's protests, I sold the house on Appian Way and both cars, and gave them total freedom for season 5, which was still being filmed. There were three episodes left to shoot. However, in conjunction with the actors, they decided to cancel them. No one wanted to continue. They would later choose to abandon season 6 entirely.

In Gad We Trust ended without a conclusion, incomplete, just like Ann's short life.

The wind began blowing in gales in Central Park, making snow out of cherry blossoms. I began walking again to warm up, as I'd done often in the early days when I had returned to New York. Walk, that's all I could do then, for long hours, without any purpose — in L.A. you never walk. I rediscovered the freedom of walking, letting my thoughts wander, stirring up the darkest reaches of my mind. Every morning was the same, assaulted by sinister thoughts from the moment I woke, like a bad toothache. My nights were never good, despite the sleeping pills I took. And so I dozed, my eyes opened on emptiness. I avoided television, didn't read. I couldn't deal with all these people who didn't know that their small misfortunes were a kind of happiness.

Len's silence hurt me as well. For weeks, in newspapers, on television, and on the radio, that's all anybody talked about. He couldn't have not heard the news. I hadn't received a letter or even a condolence card that he would've needed only to sign, it wouldn't have been much of an effort. It would have made me happy, though that meant very little to me now. Just a word, just a small gesture to show he wasn't insensitive to my suffering. But no, nothing.

Moïse, Louise, and Ethel (I was only twenty-five minutes on foot from Harperley Hall where she still lived with her husband) were worried about me. "My God!" Moïse said. "You need to snap out of it!" Sometimes, exasperated by my apathy, he would simply hang up on me. It was impossible for him, a nervous guy who burned his anxiety in constant activity, to understand that I'd lost all desire. He had his work at the *New York Times* and his books, novels that he churned out regularly and had a steady market — the last one sold fifty thousand copies. Each time we saw each other he told me to write as well, but I couldn't concentrate on anything, writing most of all. Ann's death had put an end to it.

To avoid going completely mad, I found a job on Amsterdam Avenue — a job that allowed me to stay busy and not get consumed by my thoughts. Moïse was furious, "A slave in a bakery! Good God, you've got to get your dignity back!"

"You're the first one to say I need to get a grip. Well that's what I'm doing. It's what I need right now, okay?"

He stared at me with his steel blue eyes, as if he were looking at an idiot. "And, of course, you're paid. How much? I'm curious."

"Six dollars an hour."

"You're a millionaire!" His fist had smashed against the table. "There's something wrong with you, Romain. You need a psychiatrist."

But what would a psychiatrist tell me? That grief is hard?

My job at Ostrowski's bakery on Amsterdam Avenue was exactly what I was looking for. Some fifteen minutes' walking distance from my place, I was there at five in the morning, putting bread in the oven, then taking it out, in the midst of inhuman heat. I worked until eleven and took half an hour off. Then back in front of the oven until two in the afternoon. I returned home drained, my head and mind on neutral, a sort of welcome fog. It was an exhausting job that knocked me out, getting me into bed early in the evening, like the mine and farm workers in Zola and Steinbeck books.

The owner seemed to be surprised when I entered his shop after seeing the posting through the foggy window. He brought his old Polish immigrant's head near mine, squinting at me through thick glasses. By the end of the interview, however, they agreed to take me on a trial basis.

Stan Ostrowski and his wife Maria were among the few decent people that I have met in my life. Worn down by their modest immigrant existence — she was a short, corpulent woman with swollen legs covered in varicose veins, while he was almost blind as a result of diabetes — they were probably seventy years old, and yet neither ever complained. Every day, they were up at two o'clock in the morning and slaved away until seven at night. Bent over by work, every day they had that thankful look on their faces that people have when they say they've had a lucky life. Short nights, a little bit of vodka, seven days a week without ever, ever, taking a vacation.

After two months, I was forced to quit. Not because I "lacked spirit," as my father would have said, but because I ended up, I don't know how, in the pages of the *Daily News*: FROM TV TO BAKERY,

ROMAN CARR SPOTTED ON AMSTERDAM AVENUE! The Ostrowskis hadn't heard my story because their world was limited to a few Polish newspapers. Stan was so disappointed, so saddened, the poor man, he offered me a small raise on the spot. I felt wretched.

"I told you it would happen!" Moïse said, moralizing. "What did you expect? That no one would notice?"

In fact, I didn't really care. And, unlike Moïse, I found the *Daily News* photomontage actually quite amusing — a picture of the old bakery and its washed-out awning and then a larger picture of me, taken with a long distance lens, so fuzzy it could've been anyone.

In Central Park, I passed a group of noisy Iraq War protestors, students holding signs with shrill slogans, carrying two large papier maché heads of George Bush and Tony Blair. Observing them, I thought of Moïse again, who had appeared at my place full of rage only two hours before. It might have been our worst fight ever. He was holding a copy of the *New Yorker* in his hand, in which I had written an article under my professional name, Roman Carr, author of *In Gad We Trust*. The first time I'd said anything publicly since Ann's death.

I just couldn't be indifferent to what was happening — attacking a country against the will of the Security Council and some ten million people who'd demonstrated in the major capitals of the world to prevent an illegal war. Moïse had railed against the swarming crowds shown on television, "Why the fuck are they meddling in something that's got nothing to do with them, these idiots! It's between Saddam and us!" And when France had refused to participate, "Traitors! How many of *our* soldiers died to kick the Germans out of France? And this is how they thank us?"

Once, over a lunch of pastrami at Zack's, he had warmly thanked the owner for having changed the name french fries to *freedom fries* on his menu.

I said to Moïse, "Freedom fries? That's just ridiculous."

He sniggered, "I don't think so. Freedom fries, liberty fries. It's more New York. Like the Statue of Liberty."

"A gift from the French," I countered, to shut him up.

He didn't reply.

"You agree with what's happening in our country, Moïse? Honest citizens, dissenters, all monitored by your friend Bush? Don't tell me you're okay with that?"

"If there is a threat to national security, the law allows it."

I pushed my plate away, disgusted. "What's wrong with you Moïse? I don't recognize you anymore. Where has my old friend gone? The man who read Thoreau, jealously protected his principles, and was part of something greater than himself?"

"We were kids, goddamn it! With all the naïveté that goes with it! I work, now. I reflect on a dangerous world. Four planes, three thousand dead, that's not enough? What do you think will happen next? You think they'll stop now, if we don't show them that we're stronger? They want to destroy us. Destroy our way of life, as Americans! We can't be dreaming like we used to in the sixties. The world is more dangerous today. But *your* country doesn't realize it. It abandoned us, just like the French."

I stiffened. "*My* country! It's *my* country that welcomed you so you wouldn't get yourself killed in Vietnam! And let me remind you that you are also a citizen of *my* country! But now you're sixty years old and you've got a great job at the *Times*, and you make plenty of money with your books, so you're fine with American kids going to get themselves killed in your place, in a country that did nothing to us."

"Young men who enrolled of their own volition. There's no conscription. No one is forcing them to go."

I was stunned. "For a lot of kids, the army isn't a choice. It's the service or unemployment. You know it very well!"

"Hey, calm down! We won't be there for ten years. We'll be in and out in a few months." He swallowed a mouthful of beer and wiped his mouth with a paper napkin before poking fun at me, "If you're so sure of your truth, why don't you go to Washington and protest with Susan Sarandon?"

Disgusted, I took a taxi back to my apartment, convinced I wouldn't let it go at that. After drinking a double scotch, I sat in front of the computer and began writing a long article that the *New Yorker* would publish a few days later.

"Where are you today?" I asked the generation that fought against the Vietnam War. "Should we understand from your silence that all the rhetoric we gloried in at the time — an illegal, criminal, immoral war — was solely designed to help us avoid the front rather than condemning the indefensible? Were we truly *against the war* or simply *against being sent to war*? ... Today I see a majority of Americans (including former anti-Vietnam activists and rehabilitated draft dodgers) standing behind President George W. Bush. And so I ask myself the question...." Later in the article "Do we really need to once again talk about the Tonkin incident, documented as a lie in the Pentagon Papers? Weren't we scandalized? ... Yesterday it was a Vietnamese torpedo boat invented by the Pentagon's fevered imagination.... Today invisible weapons of mass destruction.... A war without the support of the United Nations is illegal.... France and Canada are on the side of international law...."

I was writing feverishly, a piece conceived in indignation. I should have let it rest for a moment, not sent it off to the magazine so quickly, and yet urgency got the better of me; I felt like I needed to punch a hole in the wall to make myself feel better. I wrote urgently and well, words and phrases running one after the other, my position and arguments clear; I re-read quickly, correcting mistakes, eliminating repetition, tightening a few passages, before sending it to the *New Yorker* after having spoken over the phone with an editor, still on an adrenaline high, but relieved, peaceful, like after an orgasm.

"Oh, Mr. Carr. Yes, of course. We will read it attentively."

Moïse was losing his mind; this country was losing its mind. And I might have been as well.

2

In my car, I replayed every possible scenario, knowing that on this show, the shots came without you seeing them coming. Controversy didn't scare me, certainly not after *In Gad We Trust*; I accepted risk, knowing that a little bit of dissidence might just wake a few people up. But more than anything, I was being given a chance to reply to my critics.

"Impostor," "traitor," "anti-American"… My name in every paper, and with it indignant comments. And Moïse, my friend Moïse, who had slammed the door behind him as he left, mad as hell, and hadn't spoken to me since, "'Rehabilitated draft dodger'! You wanted to go after me, eh? And you did, you did all right, and you did it publicly! Disgusting!"

No one mentioned the name Roman Carr anymore without reminding the reader that I was born Romain Carrier, a French Canadian. I felt like the court of popular opinion had decided to revoke my American citizenship. *Romain Carrier isn't American. He can't be. He's against us.* The award for insanity definitely went to the *New York Post* with its slapstick headline: PARLEZ-VOUS BETRAYAL?

My neighbours avoided me in the building. Especially nasty Ms. Brown, a Democratic donor since Jimmy Carter and an organizer of fundraising activities in New York. Annoyed by her constant haughty air, I called out to her one morning when we bumped into each other in the hall. She stepped back, as if I were about to physically assault her.

"You're for this war, Ms. Brown? Or are you against it but you don't dare say anything for fear of shocking New York's high society?"

Her pinched smile disappeared; livid, she took her awful Pekinese in her arm, "It's a shame we can't use the Patriot Act to expel you from the St. Urban, Mr. Carrier."

My Audi was flying down I-95, northbound. In forty minutes, I'd walk into WXTV in Stamford, Connecticut. I was off to defend my ideas. I was used to cameras and interviewers who believe that a good interview means having your guest on the floor for the count of ten. With people like that, you need to smile more, be more relaxed. I turned the radio on and found the news. The army had captured two presidential palaces in Baghdad, a B-1 combat aircraft dropped four bunker busters on a building thought to hold Saddam Hussein, his sons, and a bunch of officials. A rain of fire, no matter the cost to civilians. The Pentagon invented an ingenious term in the first Gulf War, and everyone used it now, without thinking: surgical strikes. A clean war. Like in video games. You could tell by the tone of their voices that the radio broadcasters were applauding the action — to find Saddam by any means, there was no opposition, everyone united behind a President with eyes containing all the intelligence of a reptile. It was hard to believe I was the only one outraged at this playacting. There were others, of course, so why weren't they speaking out? "Bravo!" Ethel said. "I agree one hundred percent with what you wrote in the *New Yorker*. All my friends do too. They salute your courage." Courage? Had speaking your mind in a democracy become an act of courage?

On the highway, I could practically feel the happy tranquillity of the picturesque small towns I sped through — Larchmont, Mamaroneck, Rye. Communities that were ninety percent white, with average household incomes more than three times higher than in New York. You bet your bottom dollar they couldn't put their finger on Mesopotamia on a map. Why care? George W. Bush was taking care of it for us. Wasn't he the best one to make the right decision?

On the radio, they were bored of Saddam already. A few ads shouted at me, then a quick item on how the Supreme Court had upheld the ban on cross burning in Virginia. "The Ku Klux Klan's case dismissed," the newsreader said before giving the microphone over to a man with a heavy southern accent speaking without irony of a "black day" for freedom of speech. I laughed. These guys set fire to crosses to terrorize Blacks, and preventing them constituted an attack on their freedom of speech? "The First Amendment is not absolute," one of the judges wrote in her opinion. There were still sensible judges in this country. Freedom of speech was proclaimed and defended for all sorts of reasons in the United States, except, of course, when it came time to publicly denounce an illegal war. Enough to make one disgusted, as an American.

I felt feverish at the wheel of my Audi A8. While I was convinced I was right, I knew my positon was fragile. If she were in my place, Dana wouldn't have backed down. If she'd been here, Dana would have told me to confront them. *You know what you're worth, so show them.*

A few polite introductions. I was led in silence to a starkly lit make-up room, where my presence created a certain awkwardness, I could see it in the way people were looking at me, *it's him.*

Over the phone, the show's researcher had informed me that there would be a handful of panelists on set, each with his or her own ideas about the war. He mentioned a Canadian and a Brit. When I asked their names, the researcher became evasive, no confirmations yet, "But," he quickly added, "don't worry, they're all smart people who like to debate and respect differing opinions."

I smiled as I hung up. Bill Sweeney, the host of the *Bill Sweeney Show*, was one of those populist ultraconservative stars who didn't have a reputation for finding middle ground with his guests.

"Mr. Carr, I'm happy to see you!

This was the researcher who had kept the list of other guests vague. He appeared in the make-up room, a conqueror's smile on his lips. Young, confident, perhaps even arrogant, the type of guy who would exploit his proximity to Bill Sweeney to get a table at the best restaurants in New York.

"Feeling good?"

"Always."

"Not too nervous?"

"No, it's fine. But I'm still waiting to hear who else will be on the panel with me."

His smile wavered, and he turned away. "Oh, Bill will explain. Don't you worry. Bill likes giving that sort of information."

"What's your name again?"

"Carter. Carter Lundt."

"Carter, this isn't my first TV interview. I was in a bunch of debates in California, and not once was I given the old 'mystery guest' treatment."

He seemed annoyed, made a face. "All I can tell you is that there will be two people on link-up from outside New York."

"Who?"

"Bill will tell you."

"You're taking me for a ride, here, Carter."

"No. Bill always works this way. He doesn't like it when his guests can anticipate questions...."

"And in studio?"

He looked at his watch. "An evangelical pastor."

"Really? For or against the Iraq War?"

"He was on the front lines of the anti-Vietnam War movement. But he's for this war. He'll be able to answer the questions you asked in the *New Yorker*."

"Do I know him?"

"Uhm ... I don't know...."

"What's his name?"

"Bill will tell you. Come now, we've got to go. Also, wait a second, you need to sign this first."

He held out a document, just a couple of pages.

"What is it?"

"A formality. A statement that asserts your voluntary participation in the show. Every guest has to sign one."

I'd seen this sort of document before, having signed them and seen them at It's All Comedy! Protection for the producer and the network. "Is it necessary? You told me on the phone that these guests you're hiding the identity of are competent people who respect other people's opinions."

"Right. But house rules are house rules."

Carter Lundt led me through a labyrinth of corridors until we reached the empty set. There were three seats — one, off to one side, was the host's, then there were two others, side by side. I was seated in one of them.

"Do you want something to drink?"

"Water."

A technician came near me, put a microphone on my jacket. The researcher came back, glass of water in hand.

"Where's Bill Sweeney?" I asked.

"Don't worry. He's coming."

Bill Sweeney, a man I truly disliked. He'd been in the papers a few years back for sexual harassment. A poor waitress spilled her guts to a newspaper, recounting how he had followed her, woke her up in the middle of night with obscene phone calls, and come to her door naked under a trench coat with a "threatening erection." The exact words she used, which the New York papers re-printed as often as possible. It had been insinuated that Bill Sweeney bought her silence, which she categorically denied, though her complaint had miraculously disappeared. His reputation had been harmed by the episode, though he'd been able to bounce back after September

11, another ultraconservative opportunistically jumping on the post-attack bandwagon. Bill Sweeney, Righteous Billy as some of his followers called him — as if! — rehabilitated as a zealous patriot, parading on stage, attacking those who didn't fight hard enough for the USA. His ratings exploded. A right-wing publication, *The Republican*, even named him Patriot of the Year.

Righteous Billy's set was something else. Sober, clean, constructed like a boxing ring, defined by four red, white, and blue ropes. All around, rows of seats his audience had begun to fill. The atmosphere was good-natured, but that wouldn't last, I knew. Not with Righteous Billy. A boxing fan — though no fan of the legendary Muhammad Ali, whose refusal to serve in Vietnam made him "unpatriotic" — Bill Sweeney appeared in every single one of his ads wearing boxing gloves, ready to get it on with the enemy. Of course, it was all show: you just needed to play his game calmly and with good humour. He was no match for smart, cunning journalists.

He finally appeared. Climbed into the ring to a roar from the crowd. Colgate smile, impeccably styled hair, studied tan. He saluted the crowd, blew kisses out at them. The crowd asked for more, and he smiled, giving them their due. Then he came towards me and offered a firm but distracted hand, telling me in a low voice, all smiles, an eye on the crowd, that I was courageous. Though he said nothing about the other guests.

"Three minutes!" someone shouted. With his hands, Bill Sweeney commanded silence. He held total power over his crowd; they did what he wanted. The lights came on, then the cameras. Nothing was going the way I'd been told. I was beginning to strongly suspect that Bill Sweeney had no interest in discussing the war.

3

Like blurry images of a landscape seen from a train at full speed. Bill Sweeney had started the show, just him and me, alone on the set shaped like a boxing ring, duking it out in front of an overexcited crowd. I was nervous, which was normal; it was always this way when an interview began, so much so that I only heard a few fragments of Righteous Billy's introductions, words catapulted into the audience and bouncing back into the ring. "Roman Carr ... against the invasion of Iraq ... *The New Yorker* ... *In Gad We Trust* ... controversial series ... the anger of Christian conservatives ... abortion ... terrible tragedy ... the murder of his friend by a lunatic...." While he introduced me in his thunderous, almost rage-filled voice, I was surprised to see myself on screen, forehead glistening, despite the powder that had been applied and would be reapplied at every commercial break. Bill Sweeney was getting carried away now, "Trying to moralize with Americans who love their country and seek to protect it from people who would do it harm...." Out of thin air he produced a copy of the *New Yorker* in which I had committed my crime, brandishing it furiously. "When you try to moralize with an entire people — the American people! — in a *liberal* publication," he pronounced that word like some sort of shameful disease, "your own morality better be spick and span."

"Bill! Bill! Bill!" The crowd shouted, supercharged.

"Ladies and gentlemen, welcome to the *Bill Sweeney Show!*"

The pompous theme music sounded through the studio, and the audience started clapping in time. Bill Sweeney smiled, a satisfied smile, almost teasing. A wide shot of the two of us, seated face to face. The third seat had disappeared as if by magic.

"Good afternoon, everyone! We've got a guest today, all right!" He turned towards me. "You mind if I call you Rô ... main Car ... rier? Ah! French names! Unpronounceable!

"Booo!" The crowd shouted.

"Well, what now!" Bill Sweeney exclaimed. "You're not going to insult my guest because he has a French name. Watch out — French-Canadian, it's not the same thing!"

"Canadian socialists," someone shouted out, "can't help us out when we're under siege!"

"People's Republic of Canada!" someone else screamed.

Bill Sweeney chuckled; he was one with his crowd, played with it. Small American flags were being joyously and enthusiastically waved in the room.

"Though having two names might be rather handy," Bill Sweeney went on, ignoring me completely. "Hey, it wasn't me, it was Rô ... main Car ... rier!" Then, adopting an exaggerated French accent, "Who? Roman Carr? Sorry, I don't speak English!" One of the pathetic little numbers he often played. The crowd ate it up. I refused to let myself be rattled.

He was a manipulator, sure, but he knew the limits he couldn't cross if he wanted to make a proper show of it. And so Righteous Billy calmed the crowd down. An unctuous smile, then a falsely contrite air, "A terrible tragedy that befell you...." he began, with calculating effect. "Your friend, the child she was carrying.... What a painful ordeal it must have been." He nodded gravely. "How are you, Rô ... main?"

Where was the bastard going with this? I answered with a simple nod. He went on, "It'll be a relief, won't it, when this James F. Lovell is executed. The man who killed your lover and your baby."

I stiffened. His eyes were burning with malice now, there was no sympathy in them. I answered dryly, "James F. Lovell needs to pay for what he's done. But I'm against the death penalty."

"Booo!" the crowd shouted.

"And yet it's California law," Bill Sweeney solemnly commented. "Don't tell me you feel compassion for the man who killed Ann and the baby?"

Ann and the baby. As if he'd known them. "Of course not!" I said, outraged. "Being against the death sentence isn't about compassion; it's about ethics."

He raised his arms skyward. "Ethics! There we are!" He uncrossed his legs, leaned towards me. "But the law is ethical. The law is just."

"That's right, Bill!" a couple of spectators shouted.

"No," I answered defiantly, despite the nervousness growing in me. "The law isn't always just."

Righteous Billy let loose a small, satisfied cry. As if I had just opened wide the door he was preparing to shoot his way through. He leaned back into his chair, crossed his arms. "You've often gone against the law, if I understand correctly?"

"I'm sorry?"

He got up from his chair, adjusted his expensive, shimmering suit. I felt myself boiling inside. The crowd rumbled with a sour mixture of pleasure and indignation, "Bill! Bill! Bill!" Bill Sweeney turned his playboy's mug towards the camera, and fixed his eyes on it as if on the eyes of a woman he was trying to seduce. "Does Rômain Carrier have something to hide, ladies and gentlemen? Will he tell us the truth? Stay tuned to find out!"

Round 1 was coming up. Cut to commercials.

4

As soon as the cameras were off, Bill Sweeney lost his smile. A woman appeared on the set and began applying powder to our foreheads and noses. I was furious. "What is the meaning of all of this? What are you playing at, Bill?"

He looked at me with bored eyes. "I'm the one asking the questions here. Your role is to answer them as honestly as possible. All the people want is the truth."

The audience was laughing, talking loudly. People looking to be entertained, not to have truth revealed.

"Who do you take me for, good God! And who are the other guests? Look at me, Sweeney! What the hell is your game?"

"Ten seconds!" the director shouted out.

He stared at me and said with barely veiled contempt, "Be honest. That's all you're asked."

Honest? Is that what he said?

Righteous Billy reintroduced me, distributing smiles like playing cards. "Let's now go to Canada, ladies and gentlemen! To Toronto!"

"Noooo!" the crowd shouted.

"Oh yes," he said, laughing. "A courageous man is waiting for us there, you'll see."

On the big screen, a completely bald head, mottled with liver spots. Two moist slits for eyes, under mean, shrivelled eyelids.

Robert Egan? What the hell was he doing *here*? And why *him*?

"Hello, Robert!" Bill Sweeney warmly called out.

I was shocked, stupefied. "Why is this man here?" I called out. "What does he have to do with the Iraq War?"

Once again, Bill Sweeney offered a fake smile. I felt like I was in a bad movie; someone, somewhere, would realize it and put an end to the goddamn thing! Bill Sweeney wasn't one for qualms, that much was clear from what I'd seen of him on television. He would trip up his subjects, have surprise guests on, dramatic witnesses. But this was a new level — an old man shaking with Parkinsons, who, despite Sweeney's friendly welcome, seemed as confused as I was.

"How are you, Robert?"

He nodded once, a collar of flesh around his neck echoing the nod. With a trembling hand, he played with the earpiece he'd been given. The arrogant jock with the iron constitution who terrorized his opponents on the greens and tennis courts of Métis Beach was gone. Without waiting for Righteous Billy's questions, he began talking, mired in a confused monologue, too happy to dig up the hatchet after all these years. He stammered, spat, and mumbled his way through a story in which I raped his poor daughter, dead now, and then ran off to the United States to escape justice.

"That's a lie!" I exclaimed. "Slander, pure and simple!"

Robert Egan bobbed his head, a shifty old man who had come to believe the lie he'd been telling for forty years.

"This ... man raped my daughter!" He continued feverishly. "He ... he destroyed our family!"

"His daughter was never raped!" I protested vehemently. "This man you call courageous disowned his daughter! He refused to see her for more than thirty years. Wasn't even at her bedside when she was dying of cancer, while I, I was there!"

"So you entered the United States in 1962 under false pretenses," Bill Sweeney interrupted. "Like a criminal."

"Robert Egan never laid charges against me! The Canadian authorities never went after me because his story is pure fabrication. I did not rape his daughter!"

"Hmmm." Sweeney groaned, a fake look of regret on his face. "She's no longer here to give her side of the story."

I was mad with rage.

"He got her pregnant and ran!" Robert Egan spat out. "Like a feckless coward!"

I jumped up from my seat. "You and your wife ordered her to get an abortion! Which she refused to do!"

My God, was this the trap? For me to reveal my private life and feel obliged to justify myself in front of Bill Sweeney's indecent cameras?

"In terms of abortion and respect for life, you're not very well positioned to be giving lessons."

I ignored Sweeney's words and went on, "This man made the life of his only daughter miserable. If you looked into it, you'd know. But, clearly, truth matters not one iota to you, Mr. Sweeney."

His smile became fixed, and the crowd immediately came to his defence. "We love you Bill!" "Yes, Bill!" "Bill! Bill! Bill!" Righteous Billy nodded thanks to his faithful, silenced them with a gesture of his hand, and turned towards me. "When you sought asylum in the United States in 1962, you were hoping to get under the radar of Canadian justice, were you not?"

"I won't answer that question."

"Oh! I'm giving you an opportunity to set the record straight, and you're refusing?"

"Truth! We want truth!" the crowd chanted.

"But I didn't commit a crime!"

"And yet you found sanctuary in New York, thinking to escape justice. You're the one who spoke of morality, of ethics, were you not?"

"Nonsense, it's all nonsense. I came here to talk about the Iraq War, not to be the victim of a phony trial!"

"We're giving you a chance to explain yourself, Rômain."

"Explain myself for what, for God's sake!"

"For your life in the United States, entered illegally."

Illegally? "What are you talking about?"

He didn't answer and turned towards the crowd. "Ready for the second round?"

"Yes!" the crowd howled!

"Okay!" Righteous Billy cried out, rubbing his hands together. "Music!"

A booming tune filled the studio. I felt the ground cave under me. On the great screen, Robert Egan's head disappeared. On Bill Sweeney's set, guests were on for only a short amount of time, just enough to reinforce his point, to make him seem smarter. While "God Save the Queen" blared, a bedlam of percussions and brass, I readied myself for the second round.

Should I have gotten up and left? I was far too angry to withdraw in self-defence.

5

Back from the break. The crowd's noise was so loud, it was enough to make me nauseous. I had the feeling of having a rubber band pulled to its limit in my head, about to snap.

"Hello, Mark! Thank you for being here! Great Britain is our most faithful ally in the war against terrorism! My thanks to Tony Blair!"

Mark Feldman. Dana's son. I looked at him, frozen stiff.

The years hadn't been kind. He was thicker, his natural good looks morphed into a sort of Santa Claus maturity, with his long beard and grey hair under a needlepoint kippa. Stone-faced, Mark greeted Bill Sweeney as if addressing a simpleton. Mark certainly wasn't the type to greet anyone warmly, and he treated personal questions with disdain. I almost enjoyed the way he looked down on Bill Sweeney from the large screen, barely repressing a look of disgust, while Righteous Billy enumerated, like an impressionable little boy, his guest's accomplishments — one of the largest fortunes in Great Britain, recipient of the highest honours, a high-profile member of the London Jewish community, "our allies against the Muslims who hate America...." A powerful man, who owned a large chunk of London in the form of hundreds of buildings. As Bill lauded him, Mark seemed bored, even giving an impatient glance at his watch. His time was precious.

Bill Sweeney said, "It was in fact at your mother's home that Rômain found sanctuary in 1962? When he was trying to escape the Canadian justice system?"

I cut in. "Will you cut it out? I wasn't living illegally in the country, as you keep claiming. That's slander, Bill! As soon as I get out of this studio, I'll be giving instructions to my lawyers. There's a limit to how much mud you can throw in people's faces. I won't let you do it with impunity!"

The crowd interrupted my rant, "Bill! Bill! Defend yourself!"

Bill Sweeney smiled slyly and continued, "Robert Egan said that your mother was an accomplice to a young man who raped his daughter. Do you agree?"

An incredible violence filled me. I said, trying to control my rage, "Retract those words, Bill, now. I'm giving you one last chance."

He ignored me completely, all his attention on the screen, "Please, Mark...."

Mark grimaced. In a dull voice, emotionless, he told how I manipulated his mother, an unstable woman — *an unstable woman?* — disturbed by the death of her husband, his father, forcing her to hide me at her place, in New York.

"Now, wait a minute!" Sweeney interrupted. "Your mother was famous at the time. A sort of fury of the feminist cause." The director tossed him a book which he caught and showed the camera. "*The Next War.* A feminist pamphlet your mother published in 1963. An unstable woman, you say?" He flashed a large smile. "Yeah. I think everyone got that one...."

The crowd laughed. Mark didn't. He went on, his voice still devoid of emotion. It was as if the whole episode, his mother and me, had stopped affecting him, no longer made him angry. He was no longer the same man and Bill Sweeney, who seemed disappointed, started peppering him with questions to get him off his game, but Mark persisted with his usual arrogance.

He ended up answering that I "dishonoured his mother" by having an "inappropriate relationship with her" while I was a "minor," and I blackmailed her to "get money off her," forcing her to "write me into her will." "Before killing her."

"That's slander!" I shouted under a hail of indignant cries from the crowd.

"Before killing her?" Righteous Billy asked, back in good spirits.

The crowd was whistling, booing; I thought my head would burst. Mark spoke of the accident on Long Island and how Blema Weinberg and her guests swore they saw me take the wheel in Amagansett. Furious, I defended myself as best I could — the police report was clear on that. The employee at the restaurant who saw us trade places....

"You were drunk?" Sweeney asked.

"No!"

"You were on drugs?"

"At the time, everyone was on drugs."

A voice came from offstage. In the dark, just behind the bright projectors, I couldn't see who it was. A man's voice, as familiar as the smell of urine in a New York subway station.

"Okay!" Bill Sweeney said. "Things are heating up. Stay with us ladies and gentlemen. After the break, Round 3!"

6

He emerged from the shadows, a hazy image at first, in the blind spot of my bad right eye. He extricated himself from the hand of an unseen character helping him up the few steps to the stage. He hated when people noticed his limp. He'd put on some weight over the years; his feminine, Jon Voight face had gotten thick, his hair grey and dull, sparse on top. His eyes, however, were the same — piercing, slightly almond-shaped, separated by two pronounced lines between his brows.

In the same way he got rid of Robert Egan, Bill Sweeney made Mark Feldman disappear, though perhaps with slightly more deference. He ordered a third chair brought up with a dismissive snap of his fingers.

Looking at Ken Lafayette slowly make his way across the ring, wearing a marine blue-striped suit, white shirt and red silk tie (the colours of the American flag?), I realized with surprise that I hadn't thought of him in years. He'd been arrested at my place in San Francisco and imprisoned in San Luis Obispo. From what I remembered, he was released in 1974 because of lack of evidence. A young woman dead, another seriously injured from a bomb on Washington Street. The cops believed he was guilty, but the judge severely criticized their work, their rapidly executed arrest, calling them amateurs. Nolan Tyler of the *San Francisco Chronicle* had been right — the guys who picked him up at my place were kind to me, never believed I was involved. For a while, though, I lived in terror at the thought of Ken denouncing me for having helped his friend Pete enter Canada. Nothing ever came of it. In the end I came to the conclusion that he held his tongue, and I was thankful for it.

But on the *Bill Sweeney Show*?

A bank of commercials — get thinner and better looking, lose weight, forget about heartburn — and back to the studio. "Ladies and Gentlemen, Doctor Ken Lafayette!"

Based on the enthusiasm of the crowd, he wasn't unknown to them. *Doctor Ken Lafayette?* The evangelical pastor Sweeney's researcher mentioned?

"Okay, Ken. Let's see what we have here."

Bill Sweeney briefly looked down at his notes. He lauded Ken. A respected minister in a church in North Carolina. Owner of a not-for-profit Christian radio station. Author of numerous best-selling books, his greatest success (why had I never heard about it? Was Sweeney exaggerating Ken's success?) a memoir about the "judicial error" to which he'd been victim and for which he'd been unjustly imprisoned.

"Ooooh!" the crowd sang. Who was responsible? the crowd seemed to be asking. While Bill Sweeney was telling his story, Ken, next to me, looked triumphant, his back straight, impeccably manicured hands on his thighs. He still had the same habit of crossing his shorter leg over the longer one. He turned his head, gave me a small, strange smile that was hard to interpret. My heart was beating hard and fast. My ears were buzzing.

Two years spent in prison were hard on him, brought him God. His release was a sign from God. God had answered. Since then, he'd been devoting his life to Him.

The crowd applauded. "A great American, ladies and gentlemen!" Bill Sweeney announced. "A patriot!"

Ken Lafayette, a patriot! Was this a joke?

The crowd went wild. Ken Lafayette offered me his condolences for Ann and the baby, a compassionate look on his face, which I was aching to wipe off with my fist. "What a horrible tragedy, Roman. My wife, my children, and I prayed very, very hard for you...." He shook his head theatrically. He then went on with a soft but unyielding voice — not the one from the Berkeley days, with which he used to harangue crowds — about how *In Gad We Trust* had deeply affected him. It was an affront to Christians, to God. Sweeney couldn't even put a word in. Ken Lafayette was up and pacing the ring, like a preacher in his element. He removed his lapel microphone and took a handheld one that Righteous Billy offered reluctantly. Ken Lafayette addressed the crowd directly now, subjugating listeners with his eloquence and his life story — Americans loved nothing more than redemption.

"Wait a minute, now!" Sweeney intervened, his hand extended to take his microphone back. "You can't deny your past! You acted as an Enemy of the Nation during Vietnam! You gravitated around extreme left-wing groups. You had relationships with terrorist bombers!"

The crowd howled, emboldened by Righteous Billy's anger. As if, all of a sudden, Bill Sweeney wanted to even things out in the ring. The crowd, always faithful, followed his lead. "Traitor! Terrorist! Criminal!" A fleeting moment of hope, perhaps I was about to witness the public execution of Ken Lafayette. By the time I finished the thought, the wind had turned, like before a storm. Ken, not at all unnerved, swore that he never had blood on his hands, "God knows it. God is my witness. As for the rest, I've admitted my mistakes a thousand times. I asked for God's forgiveness. I welcomed Him into my heart."

He would have gone to Vietnam to defend the nation had it not been for his disability. While I — in a tone which had become accusatory — I hadn't hesitated a second to help unprincipled young men, *deserters*, to cross through to Canada.

"That's a lie!"

He smiled maliciously. "A lie? Poor old Pete Dobson isn't a figment of my imagination."

What could I answer to that? Ken continued, limping across the stage. The space between the crowd and him seemed to be becoming smaller. I was dizzy. "How many other *deserters* had I helped?" he asked.

"Lies!" I protested, "More lies!" But he continued. He wasn't sure, maybe a dozen, maybe more. Mostly GIs. I had a Westfalia, that was the whole point of the car. Word got around in Berkeley, it wasn't the sort of thing he encouraged, even if he was an antiwar activist and had been in the forefront of the movement, an error he had atoned for since. A litany of lies spoken with conviction, welcomed with outraged grumbling from the audience. Then he spoke of Moïse, and I felt myself weaken. My friend Moïse. Charlie Moses. I had abetted him in his flight to Canada, "So he might flee his patriotic duty!" Charlie Moses, whom I funded during long years of exile in Quebec. Charlie Moses who, from Montreal, flooded American campuses with subversive literature inviting draft dodgers and deserters to gather in Canada. Anti-American every one of them. With that he pulled a pamphlet out of his pocket, God knows where he found it, and brandished it in front of the cameras.

"Charlie Moses, a man you've been able to read in the pages of the *New York Times* for twenty-five years." He paused for effect, turned to the camera. "Romain Carrier, ladies and gentlemen, has been an enemy of the state for forty years, working from within. He loves neither America nor God."

The crowd lost it, raging at me. Bill Sweeney looked triumphant, his face frozen in a radiant smile. He cut to a commercial break with indifference, his work was done. He made his way towards Ken and shook his hand warmly. Two accomplices who had already forgotten they had just executed a man live on air, and not at all worried that they might have to pay a price for it.

I got up from my chair, staggering with rage. A technician ran towards me, fought with the microphone still attached to my vest. The crowd thundered. I called out to Bill Sweeney, promised we'd be seeing each other in court soon. He shrugged insolently, while Ken next to him was shooting me one of his dirty looks, like he used to back in our Berkeley days.

I got out of the ring and sought the exit as if I was about to suffocate. Amidst the boos of my torturers, trying to orient myself in the labyrinthine corridors, closely trailed by Sweeney's researcher. "Mr. Carrier! You forgot this!" My briefcase I had left in the make-up room, which held the document I signed agreeing not to bring my slanderers to court. The briefcase, which held my phone that was ringing, ringing, ringing. Moïse apparently…. Moïse, filled with indignation, who left me a message like a bullet to the heart. "It's over between us. Don't try to contact me."

MÉTIS BEACH

I

John Kinnear said that for all my misfortune, I looked relieved. In truth, I didn't have the slightest idea how I felt, at least for the first few days, except perhaps that I felt *safe*. John, still taking care of the small United church in Métis Beach, wondered how a man like me, who had lived an extraordinary life, one of "luxury and excitement," could find a way to get used to his new existence. The house Dana had given me so many years ago didn't have up-to-date comforts. It needed major renovations; the wiring had to be redone, the insulation as well. The furniture was so old and musty I couldn't have given it away. The bathroom was dilapidated, the bathtub and sink covered in rust. The shingles outside, the ones on the wall most exposed to the sea, were rotting on the frame. The roof was leaking in places. Not to mention the fresh coat of paint that was sorely needed.

So much work to be done. And I promised to do it all myself with help from John's son, Tommy. Exhausting, physical work, like in the days of the Ostrowski bakery in New York.

But I had business to take care of first.

The shock was hard to accept.

It was no longer called Métis Beach. It was Métis-sur-Mer now. The English and the French, both in the same village, with the same Gallicized place name. They shared the same services now, the same borders. Time had flattened differences, washed out the colours. Oh, there were a few ready to protest the change on the Métis Beach side. Small cruelties and old hatreds. Occasionally, the old guard put up a fight, like when Harry Fluke contested the use of the fire truck by what used to be the old French village. "You can't imagine the things he said about francophones!" John said. "You would have thought we were back in the fifties!"

I arrived in Métis by car, a fourteen-hour drive, with three suitcases in the trunk of my Audi. That's all I was bringing with me after forty years of exile. Forty years…. As for the rest, the apartment in the St. Urban was put up for sale. The awful Ms. Brown — and everyone else who wanted my skin — had won. I imagined her triumphant, her horrible dog in her arms. *We got rid of a traitor, an anti-American traitor.* The sale would be completed from Métis. For now, I couldn't imagine returning to New York.

The day following my return, Françoise knocked on my door as if I had never left and our relationship had always been cordial. Not a word about that terrible night at her place in 1995, the last time we'd seen each other, when her brothers went after me bitterly, reproaching me for having abandoned my parents. It was as if she'd forgotten those unpleasant moments, and all the others, a slate wiped clean. Like the time she had denounced Gail and me in the Egan garage. That time crazy Robert Egan tried to crack my skull open with his golf club. I hadn't forgotten about it.

So she knocked on my door, arms filled with food she had prepared for me, looking happy to see me. She was curiously enthusiastic at the idea of taking care of me. At first, it had put me on my guard, though eventually, I came to accept it. It seemed to make her happy, so I indulged her.

And so, every three days, she brought me home-cooked meals, and on Sundays, when she wasn't working at the store, she came by to clean. She refused any form of payment, just like with the winter coat years before. She even had the same look on her face, a mixture of guilt and offence. "No, please! It's my pleasure!" And once again, I accepted her gifts without asking questions about her motivations. I learned to ignore them, just as I ignored her sudden bouts of crying, like a sneeze, a way she had of hiccupping though sudden tears, "Oh, it's nothing ... dust, I think.... Yes, dust makes me cry, and this furniture, and this place...." Confused, I told her she didn't need to come, that I could clean my own house. "No! No! Your mother would never have tolerated it! ..." She was so incoherent I left her alone, telling myself that I could concentrate that much more on my project. A book I had decided to write, still in shock from my take-down at the hands of Bill Sweeney, but convinced I could re-establish the facts. And my reputation.

I had to dissect everything, sequence by sequence, because reality and truth, on Righteous Billy's set, seemed to warp, like through a camera with a split lens. Hours spent on my computer in the living room, where a long time ago the Feldman sisters had enjoyed each other's company as they worked — Dana on her Underwood, Ethel at her easel. In New York, Ethel had been scandalized by the way I'd been treated and implored me to stay, "In New York, people forget. If you leave now, you're saying that they're the ones with the facts, while you're the one who's in the right."

I contacted my lawyers, and they were as outraged as I was. They obtained a tape of the show and sent me a copy. Despite the slanderous rape accusation, the rest wasn't as clear as I claimed on Bill Sweeney's show. It was true that I took asylum in New York for fear of being arrested. It was true that I drove Pete to Canada — Ken Lafayette's insinuations on the number of GIs I "would have helped" were only exaggerations. He had remained vague on the topic, citing rumours; legally, we couldn't do anything about it. As for Dana's death, wasn't it true that I was partially responsible? Not in terms of the law, of course, but for me, was there really a difference? Bill Sweeney had skillfully arranged my lynching; he had a real talent for it. But he abused my trust by lying about the show's topic, my email exchange with his researcher proved it, and that's what my lawyers were particularly interested in — the dishonesty of his staff and of Bill Sweeney first and foremost, as well as some of his allegations. My lawyers studied the voluntary participation agreement I signed and believed they could challenge its validity. But, they told me, "We'll be in a street fight with them, Roman. Are you sure you want to go after them?" Yes, I said. I've got time. And money. They wouldn't get off easy.

In Métis Beach, my days were made up of long walks on the beach and stints working at the computer. The promise of May began to break through the cold April weather and the impetuous wind. Everywhere, patches of snow were melting, the smell of hard earth thawing. Métis Beach seemed dead; it would only come back to life in late June, its houses with their boarded up windows seemed like animals hibernating. The absence of life didn't bother me; to the contrary, it made me feel stronger, as did the wild nature around me, the strong light, the changing waters of the sea, the air that tasted like salt, humid with mist, the rocky beach at the bottom of the cliffs, the sky filled with purple clouds.

One foggy morning, Françoise arrived with her supplies and the mail, which she always picked up for me at my post office box on Main Street. Ads, bills, and, on this rainy day a providential ray of sun — a letter from Len.

We hadn't spoken in five years. He'd sent the letter to It's All Comedy! in Los Angeles, which forwarded it to me. A handwritten letter, I recognized his tight, angular writing. He wasn't saying much. "We weren't fair to you." Was he talking of my detractors? Of himself? Of both? I didn't know. He had left Melody and lost custody of the daughter he had with her. His tone was detached, impersonal. There was no news of Cody and Julia, and no return address. The letter shook me, a surprisingly neutral tone that caused me alarm. I called It's All Comedy!, hoping they knew more, but no dice. There was only this letter, my name on it, and a post office in Toronto from which it had been sent. I looked on the Internet — Len wasn't working for the *Calgary Herald* anymore, or at least his name didn't appear on the site. Perhaps for a Toronto media outfit? I couldn't find his name there either. It was as if he'd disappeared. In a notebook, I'd kept Lynn's phone number in Calgary, but the number was disconnected. She had rebuilt her life, probably, and I felt guilty at never finding out her last name, of never really showing any interest in her life. A ray of hope nonetheless — in his short letter, Len also said, "I understand you might have left for Métis Beach, if I can believe what's written about you. Maybe one day I'll come and visit. If you're okay with it, of course. After all, it's where I'm from, too." I read and re-read his letter, a relief, a moment of peace. I trusted him, trusted that he would come around one day. I asked John Kinnear's thoughts, and he came to the same conclusion. With his soft, kind eyes, he told me, "He wants to spare you, Romain. Not push you too far, too fast. Don't forget he's the one who broke off the relationship. He's also someone who's come out of a difficult place and is trying to find a way back to life. Patience."

I put the letter in a place I knew Françoise wouldn't look. She knew nothing of Len's existence, and it was better that way.

Once Françoise had left, I sat down in front of the computer with a plate of cold ham and potato salad she had made. Light-hearted — my son was thinking of me! — I went through my email with childlike impatience — if Len reached out to me now, why not Moïse? A few clicks of my mouse, still no sign of him. Only messages from slanderers who, I had no idea how, got hold of my email address and didn't hesitate to write. Hateful messages I needed to sort and delete every day. And death threats. I was discovering that the internet, a sort of reverse Big Brother to whom we chose to give all our information, was a perfect tool for slander.

Moïse, please forgive me. I let myself be trapped like an imbecile.

After my appearance on Bill Sweeney's show, an aggressive campaign asking for Moïse's resignation from the *New York Times* began. His past as a draft dodger was revealed, and the pressure on him and his bosses grew. Moïse had been honest with them from the get-go, and the higher-ups knew all about it. But in an era of generalized suspicion, Charlie Moses' shameful past was becoming intolerable for everyone involved.

And so I didn't hear a peep from my friend for a whole month. Our long and deep friendship began suffering after September 11, when he became radicalized and an irrational rage began burning in him. Even physically, he changed. He lost almost all his hair and put on weight. His eyes were filled with a hard light he shone on me as well as Louise, his wife whom he loved so dearly. *You can't understand. You're not Americans. The world has changed, and you can't accept it. While I, I know!*

Was our friendship in danger? Or had it ended completely?

I was devastated.

Louise gave me updates on him; she left their apartment in Brooklyn and had found refuge at her friend Barbara's place on Staten Island. She spoke to him regularly. But he was far too angry to ask her to return. Louise had had enough of New York, of the United States, of George W. Bush, and of Moïse's fits. She wanted to return home to Quebec, but simply couldn't abandon her husband. "You know him Romain. He's always right and everybody else is wrong. Please, call him. Try to convince him.... Please...."

I replied, almost a whisper, my throat tight with sorrow, "I can't, Louise. Not after the message he left me. I destroyed his life. He'll never forgive me."

"Don't say that! You're the one who saved him in 1966! You can't give up on each other! You can't give up on *me*!"

And she cried.

Every day, I went through the websites of major American news outlets trying to find out whether Moïse and the *Times* had succumbed to the pressure. "Can a journalist accomplish honest work in these times of war if he himself illegally fled another war?" the *Washington Post* asked. Everywhere, the general opinion seemed to be, "Scandal! Madness!" The fact that Moïse, like all of the other draft dodgers, received a presidential pardon changed nothing at all. Charlie Moses betrayed his country. Charlie Moses needed to be punished. Then, in early June 2003, the *New York Times* announced his resignation. Buried in an inside page. A short item, as succinct as an erratum you're forced to publish but not to publicize. The *Times* had enough on its plate. Another scandal, this one far more serious — a story of plagiarism and false reporting implicating one of its young journalists. Already in upheaval, *Times* management decided to limit the pain, feeling it no longer had a choice but to send Moïse away.

The past always ends up catching up with us.

The following Tuesday, Françoise came over with shepherd's pie, beef stew, tourtière, and meatloaf. So much food, and all of it fatty. I wasn't used to eating so much, "Françoise, it's too much." But she didn't listen to me and simply pushed me out of the way and began filling my refrigerator. "Françoise...." I followed her, trying to reason with her — her food was delicious, but it was indecent that half of it ended up in the garbage; a single man couldn't eat that much. "Look in the refrigerator, I could feed the whole village!" She opened the door, having to make room on the shelves for what she was bringing over. "No, Françoise. I don't want it. Françoise, listen to me...." I could tell she was about to burst into tears.

"Françoise...."

"The do...." she sobbed.

On the counter, wrapped in wax paper, a turkey sandwich she made that I wouldn't eat. Through the window, the sky and sea, melancholy grey. Françoise was weeping now, her elbows on the counter, her face in her hands

"Françoise, you should see someone. Crying all the time isn't normal."

She fell into a chair and took my hands in hers.

"Forgive me, please ... forgive me...."

"Françoise, I'm calling Jérôme. He'll come and get you."

"It was me...."

"You ... what?"

She lifted her face towards me, and I could see acute distress in her imploring eyes, smeared with mascara, "Locki ... the dog.... It was me...."

2

Through her terrible action, Françoise had determined the course of Gail's life and mine. On the night of August 18, 1962, she went on a mission, trying to find peace. It gave her a feeling of invincibility, that exhilarating feeling you feel when you act, when you seek and obtain justice for yourself. She drank at Mrs. Tees' place — the remainder of a few glasses she and my mother picked up in the garden and brought back in the kitchen. Champagne, whisky, sherry, vodka, swallowed in the disorder of the kitchen, unbeknownst to my mother. She even hid in the bathroom to toast us, Gail and me, laughing nervously. She wasn't drunk, no, but perhaps a little tipsy. From the Tees' kitchen windows, she watched the guests moving about the garden and looked for the Egans, whom she saw near the tall pine trees. They were as drunk as the others, she thought, not about to leave soon. Robert Egan was doing his best swing dance, Mrs. Egan was laughing next to a much younger man, with an impudent hand on his shoulder. Alcohol reduces inhibitions. It transforms people, makes them unrecognizable. She cooked for Mr. and Mrs. Egan. They were rigid employers, rarely complimenting the dishes she painstakingly prepared. And now they looked like dislocated puppets, their manners gone. Watching them, she told herself she had enough time. More than enough.

She didn't really have a plan. She wanted to scare us, but didn't know how. She wrote sentence fragments on pieces of paper and memorized them. Which ones? She couldn't remember. Maybe something like, "My loyalty for your parents forces me to denounce you," or "What you're doing is wrong, and everybody knows it." What was she expecting to do with them? Slip them somewhere? Recite them for us? She hadn't decided.

"Why, Françoise, why?"

"Because I was in love with you, and I knew I couldn't compete with the most beautiful girl in the world. I was fat and ugly, you know that. I was the fat cow. I knew what desire looked like in your eyes, I saw it so often when you looked at Gail when her back was turned. It made me sick with jealousy. I was just the fat cow...."

She managed to leave the Tees' party early, on the pretext of a headache. It wasn't like robust, imposing Françoise to ever be indisposed, and my mother, worried about her, forced her to take a few Aspirins. Françoise pretended to swallow them, before spitting them back in the sink. She left by the back door so that nobody would notice. She left her white apron on the kitchen counter, knowing it would be too easily spotted in the dark. The moon was full. By chance, her dress was black. A straight polyester dress Mrs. Tees had forced her to buy with her own money.

She wasn't drunk. Alcohol gave her courage, courage that might have left her at the crucial moment.

"Why, Françoise, why?"

"Because I hated you, both of you."

She waited until we went up to Gail's room. Through the window, she had seen us laughing in the living room. Drinking alcohol. She thought of surprising us, reciting the words she'd written, but decided against it. She didn't want to be seen. She only wanted to scare us. Make us understand that someone knew.

She hadn't anticipated seeing the great bay doors open, and Gail taking the dog out and tying him outside. From where she was on the veranda, Gail could have seen her, but there was something off about her that night, she seemed strange.

"And that's when you had your idea?"

"Seeing Locki, I thought of Louis, and what he did to animals...."

On the veranda, Locki immediately detected her presence. A smell he recognized. He began wagging his tail. In the Egan kitchen, Françoise often gave him a morsel or two of whatever was left, despite Mrs. Egan's strict orders to the contrary. She would slip food in her hand and give it to him to eat or lick, watching his grateful eyes. But she didn't like Locki. What she liked was to contravene Mrs. Egan's rigid rules.

That night, he looked at her with those same loving eyes. She petted him, before telling him, very softly, to lie down. He turned around a few times, making small scratching sounds with his claws on the wood, then obeyed, unaware of what was about to happen. Françoise knew what she would do now. And that certainty made her lose her nervousness. She took off her shoes, placed them on the veranda. Inside, only the living room was lit, the other rooms basked in the soft silver light of the moon. She walked silently towards the kitchen. The darkness didn't bother her: she knew the place well. The first drawer to the left of the sink. That's where the sharpest knife was, the one she used to cut the Saturday roast. She heard small, joyous slivers of sound coming from upstairs, and was filled with jealousy. Tears of rage slid down her cheeks. She put a hand in her pocket, feeling the small pieces of crumpled paper on which she had written her messages. Perhaps she should slip them under Gail's door, or better yet, throw them in the air like confetti. But, no, she gave up on that idea. *Someone knows we're here. Who? Françoise?* The risk of being caught was too great. She wanted to keep her job as cook; the summer was coming to an end, but there was next year, and the year after that.

She got out of the house, put her shoes back on and petted Locki once more. The dog was rolling on his back, offering up his warm, soft belly. She slit his throat.

"How could you do that? Only maniacs hurt animals!"

"You have a right to hate me, but I ask for your forgiveness...."

She was lucid enough to hide the knife under the veranda. The next day she retrieved it, cleaned it, and put it back in its place, when Mrs. Egan called her in a panic to help her with the suitcases.

Oh, how she wished she could have undone it all the next day, hearing Mrs. Egan on the phone saying how her daughter had been raped by a *French-Canadian bastard*. How she wished she could have said it wasn't true! That nothing wrong had happened. That it was all her fault. But too late. Like a car accident, a broken vase; you can't put shattered things back together.

"Unbearable guilt?"

"Yes, Romain ... my whole life...."

"It didn't stop you from continuing to see my parents, did it? As if nothing had happened. Hypocritically consoling my mother. Taking care of my father, who hated me because he thought it was all my fault. And you accepted that goddamn store he gave you because you, at least, you could be trusted! The daughter he wished he had had, not like me, his scumbag of a son!"

"I beg you, Romain. Forgive me...."

3

"That was then. What happens next depends only on me."

I wrote those lines sitting on the veranda at the very same spot where Moïse and Louise "hosted" me at my own place a long time ago now, the day my mother was buried. I can still hear Moïse, in the tone of a wiser older brother, "Okay, man. Let's be honest. It's time to get you back here." Then, reproachfully, "Amazing! You can't even see what's right in front of your nose!"

I shivered. The wind off the water is still cool in early June, though the sun was out, and radiant. The sea was a deep blue, swaying under frothy peaks, a perfect moment, a postcard. Over the cliffs, I watched an osprey circling, immense and majestic. In a flash, he tumbled towards the waves, aiming to spear a fish only he saw. At the last moment, an unexpected wave forced him to give up and, with amazing power, he climbed back into the sky. I smiled. The bird started off towards the point where the lighthouse stood, his long wings beating like a slow heart. Again, something attracted his attention, and he began circling over the sea. This time when he dove towards the waters he came back up clutching prey between his talons.

Why this fish and not the first?

A tiny modification to initial conditions, an unexpected wave, can change everything.

To punish Gail and me, Françoise killed the dog and thus knocked over the first in a long series of tragic dominoes — the "rape," my escape to New York, Dana and the accident that killed her, my son found, then lost, Ann's murder, the loss of Moïse. What if Françoise hadn't been filled with that macabre desire to satiate her jealousy? *What if she hadn't slit Locki's throat?*

The sensitivity of initial conditions.

In the end, Françoise wasn't very different from Moïse or myself; we all three had something in our pasts that wasn't entirely right, which ended up catching up with us. Was I right to be so mad at her? Hadn't my life been filled with luxury and excitement like John Kinnear said, despite the pain and sadness? A film that I would never tire of watching, despite the innumerable regrets. But we all have regrets.

The osprey was gone. His first prey had perhaps reached deeper waters now, never to know the fatal danger it had barely escaped. I like the idea that a simple wave can change so much.

The sun began its slow descent towards the sea, the blushing sky giving the veranda an unreal colour. The temperature dropped a few degrees, and I felt my fingers numbing with the cold. Yes, I was cold. And I knew exactly why. I got up, taking my note-book with me and the thick wool blanket that kept my legs warm. Inside, I poured myself a scotch for courage. At fifty-eight, I no longer had the rest of my life in front of me to let external forces determine what was to come.

"That was then. What happens next depends only on me."

When it came to Len, there was nothing to do but wait. We hadn't spoken in five years. An eternity. How old was Cody now? Seventeen? And Julia? Fifteen? My God, they were so much older now. Would they remember me? Would they remember Ann? Had Len ever told them what had happened to Ann? No, of course not. It's the sort of thing you'd want to spare your children from. *Grandma Ann was murdered; she was shot twice in the head.* My only hope was this book I was writing, a book that might help Len understand my story. I sometimes think Len got from his mother that tragic inability to be happy, but perhaps I'm wrong. *If one day you read these lines, Len, know that your father is there, waiting for you, in Métis Beach.*

Shaking, I swallowed a mouthful of Johnnie Walker, then another. Anxiety constricted my thoughts, and to calm myself I concentrated on the sequential toppling of dominoes that I needed to stop, the implacable fate that could be turned around if only I could banish fear. My hands shaking, I grabbed the phone, and hesitated only a few more seconds before dialing his number.

"Moïse? It's Romain."

A moment of silence, barely a breath. Then his voice broke. "Hey, man … Ho … How are you?"

"I … I'm sorry, Moïse."

We stayed silent a long time. Both knowing we'd been betrayed by our pasts and, somehow, a little bit by each other as well. Certainly, we could have done things differently, though no one, and especially not that bastard Bill Sweeney, could accuse us of having been truly dishonest. His voice shaky, Moïse mentioned that for the first time in our long friendship, we were each where we were supposed to be. "You in your house in Métis Beach, and me, well, still in New York."

He was injured but not down for the count. He would find a way to get back on his feet, he assured me. Another storm stirred up by the grand inquisitors of the ultraconservative right. "They went after Clinton, and they didn't get him. So how could they get Charlie Moses?" I laughed. How could I not, listening to my friend, his slightly nasal voice, almost cartoonish. I listened to him admiringly. I had no idea whether I would successfully adapt to my new life, now that I had fled his country, Moïse's country, which had offered me freedom, so long ago.

I had a house to rebuild, and a book to write — to establish the truth.

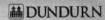